I0655956

THE
VAULTED
SEAS

The Vaulted Seas.
Copyright © 2024 by L. A. Cummings.
All rights reserved.

Book cover design by ebooklaunch.com.

Print ISBN: 979-8-9856153-4-0
ebook ISBN: 979-8-9856153-1-9

THE VAULTED SEAS

a novel

L. A. CUMMINGS

CHAPTER 1
A TRACE

Through the open line in their helmets, even through the faint static and empty air, Brun could sense the councilor's concern. He had felt it stepping out of the shelter craft and back into the storm. She had wanted to say more then. Now, just moments later, standing on his fox, with the winds rumbling through the engines within its broad wings, he awaited her words.

The wind tech in his metal gauntlets and heavy boots and on his back hummed, pulling in wild air and keeping him stable aboard his craft. He looked back, over his right shoulder, passively noting the glowing status feeds in his helmet's panel display. Bethe was twenty yards away, but he could still make out her shape and posture as she stood in the vertical gap of the high-reaching, barely open doorway. The thin light from within cast a faint glow around her, hinting at the life inside the massive, towering shelter.

"Go ahead, Councilor," Brun said plainly.

"It's too dark," said Bethe. She looked up at the sky. A small amount of light reflected off the front of her helmet before she looked back toward him. "The water, that is."

Brun nodded. "You've already made that clear."

"I don't believe I can overstate it, Commander. We've been in these shelter craft for almost a year now. And we are grateful to have survived, but it is far from ideal, even at half capacity. If on top of the rudimentary activities of each day, we have to work harder to filter our water, the people may lose the patience they're clinging to."

"I understand, Councilor. As I said, I'm headed to the North-South now. We will find out what is happening."

"I hope so." She hesitated, and let out a barely-audible sigh. "Who else depends on the great river? How many others?"

"Quite a few villages, and some shelter craft. I'm sure thousands get their water from it."

"And there are other shelters even closer to it than we are."

"Yes, I know. *We* know. That's why-"

"And, they hold more citizens than we do."

"I know, Councilor."

"Well, I would hope so."

Brun's eyes narrowed, and he saw Bethe's posture change. She stood straighter, and shifted a quarter step behind the left side of the doorway.

"Forgive my tone, Commander," she said. "I only speak out of great concern, for myself, and for the citizens in my charge. I would hate for the water to now weaken us, after keeping our lives long for so many generations."

Brun nodded back. "I understand the fear. All of Lwo, and its future, depends on our water. We will report back when we know more. Until then, filter as many times as you need to. We have plenty of supplies for that."

"Yes, Commander."

Brun raised a gloved hand and waved, and motioned for her to step back and close the shelter door. She nodded and obliged. The doors slid back together in front of her. The distant sound of their locks engaging rang through the winds. Suddenly, Brun noticed the looming sound of the shelter's engines. He could see cloudy air rushing out of the vents on the starboard side, causing an almost thunderous roar as it rolled over the ground, keeping the craft safely in place even as it rested on hard soil.

Looking up, he saw the front end of the craft, thirty yards high, wide and curving. There was a haze of light coming from the obstructed cockpit window. Far, far above it, the clouds were their typical shade of gray, with little light floating through from the high sun. Looking back to the ground, to the expanse that was in his charge, he saw a figure in the distance. Another watcher from his division was approaching. As they sped up, and the dark lines of their fox became clearer, he saw the watcher's signal appear in his helmet's display. He opened a line.

"On approach, Commander, Sir," said Lero, his voice heavy through the radio.

"I see you, Private," said Brun.

He looked briefly to his own craft, to the large, black wings

3

on either side of him, and then behind him, to the equipment bar, where the two probes he had brought–both of them heavy and cylindrical, with bottom halves that curved down into sharp anchor points–were still safely mounted. Beyond them, the fox's sharp, jutting tail was steady within the gusting winds.

Looking forward again, he saw Lero's fox slow down as he reached his position. The powerful air streams stabilizing both of their craft collided, and as Lero hovered up next to him, they mixed, giving both craft more stability as the winds continued to whip around and through the tech on their bodies. Lero raised his right fist up in salute, and Brun returned the gesture.

"You're late, Private," he said.

"Sir?" Lero answered.

Brun smirked. "Just a joke."

Lero paused. "Yes, Sir."

"Councilor Bethe is very concerned about the water coming to them from the river. Have you heard any reports today from any other shelters, or villages?"

"No, Sir. None since yesterday. But, her concern is understandable."

"Agreed."

Lero nodded. "Are you ready, Sir?"

"Ready."

Lero saluted once more, and Brun watched as he floated away from him, toward the shelter craft. He stopped five yards in front of it, and turned, facing out and steadying his fox for his time as the shelter's guard. Then, Brun turned.

The wide handle on his fox's waist-high helm was firmly in his grasp. He looked down at the small, glowing display just above it, which was shadowed by the short front shield. The indications of gravity and wind speed matched what was in his helmet display: 32 FT/SS, 125 MPH.

Brun knelt down slightly, putting more of his weight into the deck, widened his stance, steadied his reinforced boot soles, and shifted the handle down. The fox's engines opened wider, and he heard and felt the stronger streams of air rush through them. He knelt down further as he shot forward.

The North-South river was just five miles east. As the winds rushed around and over him, Brun could see a wide stretch of muted green, but little else. This region of the mainland was plain compared to most others. There was only flat, nearly-barren tundra, interwoven with old pathways that were still used to move hauls. To his left, peaks of the Northern Range were ten miles in the distance. He looked for just an instant, to sense the presence of his division at the Spire, and then looked forward again. Seeing no dangerous debris, or breaks in the ground, he took note of his speed. At eighty miles per hour he would reach the river in just minutes.

As he got closer to the river, he whispered a command, and the view through his helmet panel was magnified. Far east, even beyond the river, was the hint of several villages, and somewhere far above them hovered the blinking dot that was the Sky Tower. Far beyond it all, and unseen, was the Eastern Range.

Brun could not help thinking of the entire land, of its hard, heavy, strong ground–his and his watchers' responsibility. It was a daily meditation, whether he was idle or braving the storm at furious speed, as he was now. He took a deep breath of his filtered air, and then exhaled steadily. The warm air was a brief comfort, as the cold air of the winds continued to rush over every part of him. A moment later, the faint sheen of the river's surface appeared as a bright, approaching line in front of him.

He deactivated his magnification and stood up slightly, letting the control handle come up with him, slowing his fox to a suitable approach speed. To his right, the river ran south, through flat plains, flowing to the reservoir dozens of miles away. To his left, it flowed in from the north, from the distant mountains, where it entered the land from the ocean. As he neared the western bank of the river, the sound of rushing water filled his ears. The sense of moisture surrounded his gloved hands. And the array of large tanker trucks entered his view. He stopped the fox a few yards from the flowing water.

There were two tankers to his left, each nearly sixty feet long and holding forty-five foot tanks made of dull, gray metal that peaked at thirty feet off the ground. The long frames of the trucks rested on sets of heavy, stone wheels that were each covered in layers of thick, salvaged rubber. Between the wheels were the vents of the wind tech engines that powered the vehicles. From the rears of the tanks, long, metal pipes extended past the river bank and into the water. Somewhere within the pipes, intricately curved surfaces allowed water to flow up and in, but not out.

The cabs of the tankers were furthest from the water and facing west. The windows within their black frames were narrow, but Brun could make out the shapes of people moving about in the one closest to him. A hand raised toward him, and he opened a line.

"Commander Brun," a man answered. "This is Boss Aarn, in Tanker One. You're right on time, Sir."

"Did you expect anything less?" Brun replied.

Aarn let out a short laugh. "Not at all. We've kept the flow going, as you and Commander Jaan ordered."

"And?"

There was a short pause before Aarn answered. "And, I'm sorry to say, there are, in fact, more contaminants than usual. Our sensors are showing higher concentrations of sediment, man-made microparticles, and some…unrecognizable substances."

Brun thought for a moment, wondering what the sensors, used for decades and regularly updated, might not recognize. "Unrecognizable, eh?"

"Yes, Commander."

"And what's the concentration of MMPs?" he asked.

Aarn paused again before answering. "Right now our tank is at one hundred parts per million. That's up from the usual forty to fifty."

7

Brun let a wave of concern pass through him and shook his head. "What about your test samples? Are the filters picking up the slack?"

"They are, Commander. Our tests show the filtered water as safe. I've tried it myself. Haven't gotten sick. Don't feel any weaker."

"That could be a good sign."

"*Could* be?"

"Yes. What about the others?" Brun looked out over the water. A quarter mile away he could see two more tankers on the eastern bank.

"They're seeing the same thing. We...we have a full tank now. Should we deliver it?"

"Where's it going?"

"To a village five miles south of here."

"Give me fifteen minutes."

"Alright. We'll wait for your call."

"Very well. Brun out."

Brun looked down at his gauntlets and saw the fast streams of wind flowing out from the vents on their outside edges. He also saw the sheen on their metal housings. He had flown over rivers often enough, but hovering over one would be a different endeavor. Watchers' suits and tech were not adept at handling water beyond what fell in a typical rain, and he would have to maintain a steadiness over the river's surface to give himself enough time to position a probe. He took a breath, stood up straighter, and pulled the control handle upward.

The fox began a steady ascent, and as it reached twenty feet, Brun guided it out over the river. Keeping his speed steady at twenty miles per hour, he looked all around as he flew forward. He could feel the faintest droplets, misting the bottom of the craft, doing no harm, but making the water's presence known. The river was louder now, further from the shore. The sounds of rushing water, along with constant winds, pulsed into his helmet with every passing second. He reached a distance of two hundred feet from the shore, then four hundred, then six hundred. As the moisture increased, the fox's engines remained steady. He looked back, and saw the much smaller looking trucks.

As he reached the center of the river, he slowed, pointed the fox north, and idled the engines. The craft stayed in position, but even with the strong exhaust keeping him elevated, Brun could feel the storm's forces all around and below him. He saw the wings almost fluttering as the craft swayed and vibrated.

He turned away from the helm, and stepped, heavily and carefully, toward the equipment bar. He knelt, and set his left hand down on the grated, metal deck as he inched closer. His tech hummed all around him, keeping him steady as he reached forward and detached the rubber strap holding the first probe. He quickly grasped the handle on top of the device and then stood, holding it, and feeling its weight. It was nearly fifty pounds, with most of the weight coming from the bulky, stone vane in its tech engine. Its metal housing was dull, but seemed to shine with the light mist floating up from the river. He turned back toward the helm, carefully stepped up to it, and grasped the control handle once again.

He had prepared both probes hours before, as he had first begun his watch at Bethe's shelter. The devices would dive at high enough speed to push through the storm and the river's wild surface and reach the depths. They would not stop until they were affixed to the river bed, where they would begin measuring. But, they would need fifty feet of elevation to build up the speed to reach the bottom.

Brun looked at the top of the probe, at the flat, dark screen beneath the handle, and the wide knob tightly affixed in the upper right corner. Then, he gently raised the fox's control handle. The winds carried him up further, and at fifty feet, he stopped, and idled the craft again. He knelt down near the starboard wing, and keeping hold of the fox's frame, swung the probe backward, and then swung it forward, tossing it out into the raw air. It dropped quickly, and he stared down as the device's engine shot out streams of whirling exhaust as it spun and flew downward. Its dark screen lit up with green, and it continually shrank as it sped toward the water. The winds pushed it off course for only an instant, just before it disappeared below the surface.

Still kneeling, Brun took the fox back down to twenty feet and watched as the probe's signal, a glow in the shape of the device, appeared in his helmet's display. The icon shook and swayed, and smooth, faint lines cut through it, indicating the forces from the river.

The probe continued to dive, angling and turning as it reached fifty feet, then eighty, then one hundred twenty, and eventually two hundred, where it stopped. A thick line ran through the signal's anchor end, depicting the river bed.

Brun remained steady, holding the fox's handle with his right hand, and keeping his left hand heavy on the deck, near the wing. He breathed steadily, and took time every few seconds to look around, watching for any heavy debris flying through the air. Soon, a glowing, vertical bar appeared in his display, near the probe's signal. It was formed by four white lines, and began to fill as the probe gathered data. With dull chimes, numerical values began to pop up next to the bar: Temp 34 F; Speed 15 MPH; Density 70 LB/FT3. As the bar finally filled, the values Brun had most anticipated appeared. The soils and rock flowing through the river were more concentrated than usual, but he knew that storm surges outside the northern range could be the cause. The man-made microparticles, on the other hand, were over ninety parts per million, slightly lower than what the tankers were seeing, but still twice the normal amount. And there was a measure he did not recognize, highlighted with an empty box, meaning the probe did not recognize the material. Whatever it was, it was at twenty-five parts per million.

A sudden beep sounded, and the signals and values from the probe all turned green as it stopped measuring, leaving Brun's sense of stability–of Lwo's stability–subtly eroding. He checked the time in his display. The probe had only taken a few minutes to prove that something unseen and unknown was in the water. *It could be harmless*, he thought. *Or not.* He looked back at the other probe, still mounted over the fox's tail. He had planned to send it down, but the other had not been damaged, or lost. And it had done its job.

He stood a few inches, and moved to the fox's helm. Through whispered commands, he called for the first probe to ascend. Then, he turned the fox back toward the western bank and guided it downward. The probe shot up from the water just as he neared its entry point. It floated in the winds for a few seconds before he reached out and grabbed its handle. He held it firmly, as he flew the fox clear of the water, back to his original position near the tanker. He hovered for a moment, looking at the probe's screen, knowing that whatever was now in its small tank would need to be measured in a lab at the Spire, to confirm, and hopefully identify, all of the contaminants.

Pointing the fox north, Brun glided toward Aarn's tanker. He avoided the large vehicle's tech engines, as he flew up, stopped near the cab, and opened a line.

"That was fast, Commander," said Aarn. "What do you say?"

Looking up, Brun saw the man looking out through a slim, dark window, and raised his hand toward him. "We have to wait to deliver any more tanks of water, at least from here."

Aarn hesitated. "Are you sure?"

"I'm sure that the unknown is not to be taken lightly. Leave the tanks here at the river if you have to. The people waiting can wait another day. In fact, if their stores are full, they can wait much longer.

Tell the other tankers the same. I will confirm if necessary. And you will hear from us after more samples are analyzed. Understood?"

Aarn nodded through the window, and with a heaviness in his voice replied "Yes, Commander."

Brun nodded back, and then guided the fox away from the tanker. He moved quickly past its front end, avoiding the heavy, cold vortex being pulled through its front engine. Once he was thirty yards out he stopped the fox, turned around, took the probe back to the equipment bar, and carefully re-mounted it next to the other. As he stood and stepped back to the helm, he looked north, where he saw the sky's gray light, and open, plain-looking land, and little else.

CHAPTER 2
GREY LIFE

Rial stared down, though the dense, clear section of floor beneath her seat, watching the ocean surface as its waves crested fifty feet below. The gull's fin, affixed to the metal frame running beneath the center of one clear panel, was steady, meaning the craft was steady, but Rial did not feel as safe as she usually did. As the storm winds were pulled and pushed through the idling gull's engines, and rolled around its outer hull, she held tightly to the control handle in front of her. Her right hand was firmly in place above her left. Her gloves squeaked as she re-stabilized the craft and tightened her grip.

"Would you settle down, Ensign?" Orve called from behind. "You've been rustling since we got here."

Rial took a breath, let go of the handle, and reached for the seat controls on the right armrest. As the pilot's chair turned in place, she looked at her lieutenant, kneeling in the center of the cabin between the bench on the port side wall and the rack of secured equipment on the other. His green helmet and chestplate were alight with the glow from the metal-housed computer tablet in his hands.

"I'm fine, Sir," she replied.

Orve looked up at her, his dark eyes steady behind his helmet panel, with a blinking light from the screen reflecting near them. "You don't appear to be. You've been out here before, haven't you?"

"Yes, of course, Sir. But, not like this. Not to stay."

"Last year you flew to the Isle, didn't you? How long were you there?"

"I meant to stay in position over the water, Sir."

"Ha. I know. You can't answer that question, can you?"

"Not directly."

He shrugged. "It was worth a shot."

Rial thought for a moment about the trip to the Isle the year before, as the flashing on the mainland had begun, and several lead watchers had sought guidance from the Lords. But, she knew little about it beyond her commander meeting with Maia and Brun, and the brief sighting of two civilians. There were only rumors about who the man and the boy had been, and the commanders had not let them take hold in the ranks.

A gust of heavier wind tilted the cabin to the left, and Rial looked to the translucent window of the port side door. Water droplets were beading in every direction, but she saw no imminent danger, nor did the panels behind her indicate any. She looked back at Orve.

"Do you see anything, Sir?" she asked.

Orve shook his head. "No, not yet. But, the probe's only at one hundred feet."

"The commander said it would need to reach at least a few

15

hundred feet to get any real data."

"Right. And these newer probes have never been used in the ocean. I wonder if it can take the pressure that far down."

"So do I. At least one of them worked in the North-South."

"River pressure is much different."

"Yes, Sir."

"Did you see the data from the Spire?"

She nodded. "Yes, I did."

He looked up at her for a moment, with distant concern in his eyes, and then looked back down at the screen. A dot of green light beamed and reflected in his helmet panel. Three quick beeps followed. The pattern repeated, and then repeated again.

"The signal's still strong," he said.

As they waited for the probe to work, Rial looked to the starboard wall, at the equipment they had brought with them. There was another probe, secured near the bottom, and just above it, a yard-wide spool of cable, made of metal and two inches in diameter. Watchers, from any division, rarely used tethering. In their division they only took it when flying far out over the water. She hoped they would not need it today. She looked back over her shoulder, first to the controls, and then out through the windshield. The horizon was distant and gray, defined by the faint light from above the clouds. Somewhere, far beyond her sight, was the storm's edge.

"Five hundred feet," said Orve. "We've got something."

Rial turned back around and saw Orve tap a sequence into the screen. From the lens on the back of the tablet a projection beamed out. Rial watched as the rectangular box of light formed between them, steadying as it reached a height of three feet and a width of four. Within the image she saw faint, wavy white lines indicating the ocean currents. They seemed to move in every direction around the green, three-dimensional signal of the probe. The device's anchoring end was wobbling with every bit of pressure from the water, but it had found something. Above the glowing values of gravity, density, and speed, measures of substances appeared. The highest measure was of salt, followed by man-made microparticles. But, there was something else, something indicated only by a white box, and a measure: 40 PPM.

"It can't identify it," said Orve.

"Same as earlier," said Rial. "At the river."

"I have an idea. Let's take her down, near the surface. We can get a closer look."

Rial felt her brow furrow. "A closer look?"

Orve looked up. "Yes, Ensign."

Rial nodded. "Yes, Sir."

She spun the chair back around and once again took hold of the control handle. She set her right boot onto the wide pedal below, and with a tap on the glowing center panel, enabled propulsion. She felt the winds increase through the engines below, jolting the gull, and felt the increase in pressure from the pedal. Gently, she tilted her boot up, keeping contact, and letting them slowly descend. They reached forty feet, then twenty-five. She could almost feel the waves nipping at their underbelly. They reached fifteen feet.

"There," Orve called, loudly. "Stop."

Rial let out a gentle breath, reached for the engine controls again, and idled the craft.

"Blast your high beams," Orve ordered.

"Yes, Sir," Rial answered.

She reached for the center panel again and activated the gull's lights. They shot out from the front end and down from the roof, creating a circle of nearly-white light on the waves in front of them. She heard Orve stand up behind her, and felt him approach. He squeezed the back of her chair as he stared out through the windshield.

"Point her leftward," he said. "Slowly. I want to look at the probe's entry point."

Rial gently tugged the handle toward her left elbow, and as the gull turned in place, she saw the circle of light move across the waves. Her eyes narrowed as she searched, for something, anything, even the probe bobbing back up to the surface, but there was only the muted green-blue of the wild waves. She could hear them beating against each other, even through the heavy winds, creating a chaotic ambience.

"There!" Orve said, leaning forward, almost touching the windshield as he pointed. "See that?"

Rial looked out at the light on the ocean surface again, but saw nothing. She shook her head. "No, Sir. What is it?"

"Around the edge of the light, the darkness near the surface."

"It all looks the same to me."

"Look closer, Ensign."

She focused on the faint glow that surrounded the light they were casting down. At first, she saw only darker green, and more imposing waves. Then, she saw what appeared to be a shadow, an odd, cloud-like shape. She leaned forward. Her shoulders pressed against the restraining belts.

"What is it?" she asked.

"My guess is it's what we're looking for," said Orve. "We're facing northeast. It's got to be coming from there."

"Was it there when we first arrived?"

"Not sure. I didn't notice anything when I threw the probe out. Maybe the drop, the probe's dive, disrupted it. Whatever it is."

Rial sat back in her seat again, and looked at the control panels. Their sensors showed no indication of danger from the storm or the ocean. "The gull's readings are normal, Sir. No increase in wind speed, and nothing encroaching."

Orve took a breath. "I wonder if we can get a measure from the surface, then. Let's try."

Rial listened as Orve stepped back and began tapping on the tablet's screen. She kept her eyes forward as patterns of beeps and chimes were generated, focusing instead on the circle of light, where the odd, shadowy shape in the water was now unmissable.

"Damn!" Orve snapped.

"Sir?" Rial called, glancing back over her shoulder. "What is it?"

"It's gone."

"Gone?"

"The probe. I tried to bring it back up and lost the signal. It shook, and turned red, and then, then it just disappeared."

Rial thought for a moment, about the pressure below the ocean surface, and the relative strength of the probe's engine and housing. The loss was not a shock. "What about the data?"

"We've still got it. Better save it now."

Rial continued watching the waves as Orve tapped away behind her. Then, a light arose in the windshield. The craft's system activated glowing crosshairs, which began roaming around in front of her, following a shape in the distance. The control panels beeped, and looking down, Rial saw a signal in the center, glowing yellow, and shaped like the large vessel it was coming from, the Ice Maw. Orve walked up behind her.

"Are they in trouble?" he asked.

Rial looked out through the windshield and activated its magnification. She could see the ship, three miles away, moving up and down along with the waves, but it did not appear to be in distress. "Contact," she said. The system chirped in response. "Salvage ship Ice Maw." As the line opened, the sounds of clamoring men poured into the gull's cabin. A few of the men were shouting. "This is Ensign Rial, in Gull One. Are you there, Captain?"

"I'm here, Ensign!" the older-sounding man shouted back.

"You signaled us. What's the problem?"

There was static, and more noise from the ship's crew. The captain ordered them to quiet down and to secure their doors before he responded. "We've been hit!" he yelled.

Rial stomped down on the pedal and pushed the control handle forward, speeding toward the ship's position. She raised the gull to forty feet, keeping a safer distance from the waves. The winds rumbled around and below them, and she spoke again. "Hit by what, Captain?"

"I don't know. We didn't see it."

"Didn't see it?"

"It came from below."

"Understood. We're on approach."

"We've got a haul. The cage is still in good…"

"Captain?"

Rial kept the gull speeding ahead. She felt herself leaning forward in her seat. As they got closer she deactivated the windshield's magnification and looked to the lingering crosshairs. The readout below the circular icon showed that they were just a mile away. Behind her, she felt Orve's looming presence. They got closer and closer to the ship. They were within three hundred feet when he tapped her shoulder.

"Hold here," Orve said. "Look."

Rial pulled back on the handle, eased her pressure on the pedal, and as they came to a stop, idled the engines. Now hovering just a few dozen yards from the ship's front end, she could see the trouble. The waves surrounding the ship were cresting at least ten feet higher than the rest of the water, and the vessel had been tilted up, nearly onto its side. Its port buoy–heavy, black, metal, and over forty yards long–was barely touching the water. The starboard buoy was nearly submerged. The ship's cabin, with its yellow color and trapezoidal forward end, was still fully visible between buoys and connecting decks. But, so were the vents of the tech engines on its underbody.

"We're here, Captain," called Rial. "Can you see us?"

His response was full of static. "...Yes, En-...can't seem-...don't want to leave-..."

"Captain?" she called again.

There was only more static.

"He's worried about the haul," she said aloud.

"Well, they'll have to leave it," said Orve. "Whether he likes it or not. Do you see anyone on the deck?"

Rial looked directly through the crosshairs, which were still hovering over the ship, and said "Scan deck for life." The system chirped back, and a row of code began to tick below the crosshairs. An outline of light surrounded the tilted, shaking ship. Then, the row of code stopped, and displayed the words No Life Signs Present.

"No one, Sir," said Rial. "They must have all reached the cabin in time."

"Good. Tell the captain to detach."

Rial spoke through the open line again. "Captain, are you there?" she called. "You'll have to detach."

After a short pause more static came through, followed by the captain's distorted voice. "...I can't-..I can't leave her out here!"

"Do you want your crew to live?" Rial answered.

"...of course, but-"

"It's an order, Captain. Detach. Right now."

"Yes, En-..."

Rial shifted in her seat, and watched. "I think he'll listen."

A few moments later, red lights began blinking at the corners of the ship's yellow cabin. They beamed brighter as it began to slide out from the ship base. Slowly, its front end got further and further from the deck. Water blasted the underbody, and it stopped for an instant, but it was steady as it finally disengaged, and with winds being pulled through its front vents, flew upward. Nearly-white exhaust shot out below the cabin-craft's aft end, and it turned and flew toward the gull. Light was coming from its short windows, but the few visible members of the crew were only dark silhouettes. The open line was clearer as the captain spoke again.

"Okay, we're free, Ensign," the man said, sounding disappointed. "Barely. She tried to hold onto us. Told you I didn't want to leave the haul. There's a lot there. A lot the land could use."

Rial looked out at the yellow craft as its lights turned green and it slowly moved closer to their port side. "Your lives are more important, Captain," she said. "Now, tell me more about what happened."

"We were moving along as usual and headed back to shore, and we were just…knocked up. Almost came out of the water. The underfins barely kept us from rolling over."

"Did you see anything in your scans?"

"No. We couldn't. We only got a scan of the haul. It happened so fast we didn't have time to boost the range. I just happened to see your signal come up as the crew were rushing back into the cabin. Your trip wasn't on the maneuvers shared before we headed out. What brought the mountain division so far from the coast today?"

Rial paused, and thought carefully before responding. "There was a change, Captain. We just needed to do some observation of the area."

"Right. Well, you know, we could stay out here, hover at a safe distance for a while. The cabin's engines are charging just fine. And maybe the boat'll settle back-"

"No, Captain," Rial interjected. "We don't know enough about what happened yet, and we can't risk you and your crew. Head back to the mainland."

"Alright, Ensign. Understood."

"Rial out."

Rial closed the line, waved out the side of the windshield at the cabin-craft, and watched as it ascended and sped out of sight. She saw its signal on the left panel, blinking away as it flew south. Looking forward again, she saw that the ship base was still floating at an angle. With the absence of the cabin, it was starting to tilt and sway more onto its starboard side.

"Could we bump it?" she asked aloud.

"No, I don't think so," said Orve. "We'd risk being submerged. Maybe we could touch down on the port buoy. Let's move up and get a scan. We'll have to wait and-"

"What was that!?" Rial shouted.

She stared out, her eyes shifting as she looked for something, whatever it had been, which was now gone. She was sure Orve had also seen it, a large shape, with water rolling over it as it came up from the water and hit the ship base's starboard buoy. The base had flown up so high that Rial had seen the firm line of one underfin just before it crashed back into the water.

She had not moved the gull, but the residual force from the crashdown had pushed them back at least ten yards. She pressed down on the pedal, and took them up another twenty feet.

"I think it was alive," said Orve.

Rial shook her head. She looked back and forth between the gull's controls and the ship base. She found the crosshairs in the windshield again and spoke a quiet command to center them near the view of the Ice Maw's base.

"Good idea," said Orve.

The glowing icon hovered over the slowly-leveling base, as it swayed up and down in curves and splashing leaps. She set her eyes toward the water just in front of it, and the crosshairs followed. She spoke the command to scan, but there was no object to find. Beneath the crosshairs a row of code moved furiously, but the resulting output was only an indication of the ocean's status, of its typical surface temperature and the speeds of the winds flowing over and through the waves. Then, the gull's engines suddenly roared.

They were jolted up another twenty feet. The control panels blinked in furious red and sounded a repeating warning signal as they all displayed a large, mysterious shape, which quickly disappeared. Rial squeezed the handle with both hands, set the engines to reverse, and accelerated backwards, taking them another fifty feet away from the ship base. The warnings from the panels eased to orange, and then to yellow, and the tonal signal began to fade.

"That was automated, Sir," said Rial. "It was under us."

"I know," said Orve.

He stepped up, to the right of her seat, set one hand onto the wide console below the windshield, and looked out. Rial watched him, as his head swiveled, left and right, and he searched the ocean surface that was now much further below. Then, she looked down through the clear panels beneath her. Beyond the gull's centered fin she saw nothing but the wild ocean surface.

"Scan," Orve said, and waited.

The light from the crosshairs and control panels blinked and reflected off both their helmets as the system worked. Rial waited, and watched.

Orve shook his head. "Nothing."

"I'm not seeing anything either," said Rial.

"Could have been a fish," said Orve. "Maybe a shark."

Rial heard the doubt in his voice. "Sharks do not grow to that size, Sir. And its body, whatever it was, was almost black under the water pouring over it. Lwo has never had sharks that color."

"Well, it's been a few years since there was a survey."

"Apparently a few too many."

Orve turned and walked away. Rial kept her hands near the controls as she looked back, toward the sound of his heavy boots. He took the tablet up off of the bench, held it, and began tapping as he sat down. As he searched the screen, he tilted his helmet up off of his shoulders. It flipped away from his head and settled top-down, with the curving, metal brace holding it in place near his rear tech engine. Orve's thick, dark hair had a few strands of gray, but there was little else to indicate his decades of service as a watcher.

As he continued working, and searching, Rial turned back to the gull's controls and looked out, down toward the ocean and at the top of the Ice Maw's base. It was floating normally now, no longer at an angle, and despite the height of the waves, it appeared to be in no danger of being submerged. The water surrounding it was now only as wild as it would normally be under the harshness of the constant winds.

"Well, Ensign," Orve started. "It would seem that, at the moment, this is not our domain."

"Agreed, Sir," said Rial.

27

"Let's head back, and report all of this. Then we can formulate a plan to get the Maw's crew back out here."

"Yes, Sir."

Rial gripped the control handle tightly and turned them about, pointing them south, toward the mainland. As she prepared to accelerate, she sensed something above them. There was a glimmer of color in the windshield, and in her helmet. She looked up, toward the gray, unparted clouds, but saw nothing. Checking the panels, there was no indication of anything, alive or otherwise, encroaching. There was nothing anywhere above, or below, or elsewhere. Looking out, she saw that the air ahead of them was clear. She quickly accelerated, as fast as the gull would allow, intent on seeing the mainland's northern coast.

CHAPTER 3
SKY SIGHT

The wide, magnified viewing wall showed an expanse of land leading to the Northern Range. It was full of short, dull, blowing grass. Midday had passed, and the mountains in the distance were a faint, crossing line under the far off gray light. Before the horizon there was a village, and just a few hundred feet to the east, a lone shelter craft, number Twenty-One. The line of steam coming from the large, green craft's sleek roof was visible, but just barely, as the heat was blowing away in the furious winds just as quickly as it was being expelled. Below the shelter, white lines of speeding exhaust revealed how hard its engines were working to keep it stable on the ground.

Maia watched the scene through the glass wall somewhat passively, as in the top right corner of the same wall, there was a live video feed. In it, she could see her sister, Shil, commander of the Watchers of the City. Her short, dark hair was perfectly trimmed just below her ears, and the round, white collar of her suit was sitting high, just below her jawline, showing a readiness to brave the storm, and adding a formalness to her ongoing address. Behind her were the wall, metal door, and wide table of her office in the city's headquarters, which, like most buildings in the city, had not fallen. Next to her image in the feed there was a glowing white box outlining a schematic map of the damaged city from just after the last flash.

The same feed of Shil was running on the other three viewing walls in the Sky Tower's observation level, as Maia had ordered. A regular update of the progress made in repairing and rebuilding the city was as important as any daily flight plan. All eight surveying stations, two before each viewing wall, were occupied by seated airmen, all of whom were adorned in blue, with their mounted helmets resting safely in the grooves of their seats. As they all watched and listened, Maia walked up behind Dilah, who was seated at the station on the right. The young woman's thick, silver, nearly white hair was pulled back into a tight, short bun above her neck.

"Sir?" Dilah asked without turning.

"I just wanted a closer look at the feed," Maia replied. "As you were."

"Yes, Sir."

Maia continued watching as the schematic in the feed faded out, and listened as Shil explained the more recent map that slowly appeared. The city's design was a nearly-perfect circle, and, as everyone in the land knew, the southeast quarter had been hit the hardest. From the park near the city's center, and all the way to the south entry, the rock and concrete foundations beneath the pavement had been broken, if not completely shattered and absorbed by the ground below. As the multi-colored schematic showed, it was worst along a crooked line that ran from the park to the south entry. Red highlighted the line, and arrows identified forces from below that had cut through dozens of buildings, which were shown as red squares and rectangles with angled lines running through them. After a few moments the schematic changed again, and another appeared with many of the damaged buildings removed.

"This is our current state," Shil said, her voice coming through with strength and insistence. "We have been able to clear the wreckage of fifteen buildings, with four more left near the entry. These structures were saved for last to ensure that the watchers and civilian workers here would have a level of protection should the city's shield falter. After months of work, we are now assured that the shield will remain strong. Here is an image of the worksite as it is today."

The schematic faded away, and a photograph, taken from at least ten stories up, showed the broken section of the city. The park, which had been colored with nature and artistically structured, was now a large, sunken patch of dirt. Its elaborate, crafted stage was gone. Its benches, paths, vibrant grass and various flowers were nowhere to be found. Just west of the large space there were several buildings that had not fallen over, but appeared to be leaning. South of the former park there were empty spaces, old imprints of destroyed and removed structures. Further south, and just east, there was an almost clear path, which led to the faint, shimmering shield that was over two miles away. A straight road was still there, cracked, but probably traversable. Heavy, wheeled machines, with some civilian operators visible in and near them, were spread along both sides of the road. On the west side of the road many buildings stood, but the cracks in their dense, reformed plastic windows, and the breaks in their old, stone facades hinted at an underlying instability.

"As you can see, we have made progress," Shil continued. "But, it will take much more time to stabilize the city for a full re-population. As has been the case for many months now, the most skilled, knowledgeable, and able-bodied among us have been in the city, aiding in the repair and rebuild. They have been able to reside, along with the city's watchers, in the city's north end, where the foundations remain as strong as they were before.

"And, slowly, we have been able to examine each building that still stands around the city–inside and out, and above and below. Working with the experts on the structures–many of whom descend from those who built them–we, the watchers, have found that, unfortunately, most of the buildings in the city cannot yet be safely occupied. Though the risk of more flashing has subsided, the forces that a full population would add to the city's foundations could still cause instability, especially beneath the southeast quarter. Therefore, along with the city's councilors, we anticipate two more years before the city can once again be occupied.

"While we know that this is far from ideal, as so many citizens remain in shelters, and many others in villages that they are still becoming accustomed to, we are sure that Lwo can endure this circumstance. In your villages and shelters you have councilors and elders who will be able to provide more information, and hopefully comfort. For now, I will provide a short, anticipated timeline."

Shil paused, and tapped in a sequence somewhere below her camera. "People of Lwo," she continued. "We are strong. And the land is still strong. And, in this trying time, we must remain so. As usual, I will report back to you within one week. And as always, if you must brave the storm, take great care. Shil out."

Shil's image faded, along with the last schematic, and the darkened screen now showed yellow text detailing the timeline for the city's continued rebuild. The remaining buildings set for demolition would be brought down over the next four weeks. At the same time, final examination of the rubble from the buildings already removed would be completed. Any materials that could be salvaged and reused would be. After completion of the salvage operation, detailed lists of any personal belongings found within the wreckage would be sent out to the villages and shelters, so that the most precious items could be returned to their owners. And while all of this was happening, the next stage of examination of the damaged foundations in the southeast quarter would begin.

Though it was not detailed in the timeline, Maia–along with every other watcher, and the councilors from the city, and the skilled civilians in the city–knew that examination of these foundations would include further excavation of the giant hole near the south entry. The commanders had ordered that the depths of damage at the site not be widely shared. Maia had not even heard whispers of the hole from the civilians in their village, and hoped it would remain that way. She had seen the initial crater herself, weeks after the last flash, when she and her supporting squadron had seen firsthand the beginnings of the collapse. What she remembered most was the darkness, and how, hovering in a craft just over the edge, she had felt so many different fears all at once. The hole had reached over one hundred feet in depth not long after the city's evacuation. And, she had heard, it was now closer to three hundred feet.

The click of an opened line sounded behind Maia's right ear, and she quickly pulled her helmet up and firmly down over her head. It snapped into place around her neck, and in the display, she saw her commander's familiar signal, a row of four encircled crosses with a straight line running above them.

"Commander, Sir," she answered. "This is Lieutenant Maia. Go ahead."

"You've watched, I presume," Jaan replied in his heavy voice.

"Yes, Sir. All of us here have."

"Good. I am on my way up to relieve you."

"Yes, Sir. See you shortly."

Maia backed away from the north viewing wall and turned around. She walked toward the walled-in lift in the center of the level. As she neared it, she saw the view to the south, full with gray light coming from the distant horizon. In front of it sat two airmen. Malo was at the station on the left. Gerrin was at the station on the right.

Malo's short, thick, black hair was neatly cut, but his curls were unmissable. She passed by the lift, walked up behind him, and stood. Gerrin glanced back at her, and nodded. His bright eyes were youthful, but intense, and focused. His thick, brown beard made him look slightly older, but he had only been in the ranks for three years, and was barely twenty-five. She nodded back.

"The commander's on his way," she said. "What have you seen thus far today?"

"The south is fairly quiet, Sir," answered Malo.

"Except for shelter Twenty-Three's engines faltering a few minutes ago," Gerrin added.

"Already resolved. There were two foxes headed there within minutes."

"Right."

"And neither of you alerted me," said Maia. "Interesting."

"Sir, it was very quick," said Malo. "We didn't even miss anything from Commander Shil's report."

"Very well. And what did you gather from her report?"

Gerrin shook his head. "Nothing new, except an increased desire to go and help. Two years is a very long time for the displaced to stay out here, in the thick of it. And we're stronger, more capable than probably all of the civilian workers there."

"Understood, Airman. All of us want it to go faster. But, the rest of the land still needs securing as much as the city. We have our place."

"Yes, Sir."

Behind them, Maia heard the door to the lift slide open. She turned and walked up, and raised her right fist up to the side of her helmet to salute Jaan as he stepped out. He returned the gesture. His protective red suit was clean and smooth, and his gauntlets, boots and helmet all had a hint of shine from the light in the room. As his helmet was still down, she kept hers in place, and heard the line click as he approached her. His signal blinked into her display again, but this time it was within a dark box, indicating that it was a secured line. She looked up at him, and through his helmet panel, into his stern, aged eyes.

"It is time, Lieutenant," he said quietly.

"Time, Sir?" she replied.

"Yes."

As she realized what he meant, her heart skipped. "What has happened?"

"As you know, not long after we received the report from Commander Brun on the phenomenon in the North-South, Commander Fits sent two from his division out over the ocean."

"Yes."

"They also detected a mysterious substance in the ocean. It will require more examination. But, while they were there, they had to provide aid to the Ice Maw. Something, something massive, nearly knocked it out of the water. It also nearly hit their gull."

"Excuse me, Sir, but what does that have to do with-"

"Let me finish, Lieutenant."

Maia quieted, and nodded. She stood more firmly, and put her arms behind her back to keep from crossing them in frustration.

"Commander Fits relayed the report from Lieutenant Orve. Ensign Rial was the pilot. After the crew of the Maw was safe, and the threat was no longer present, they prepared to return. But, as they were leaving, the ensign caught a glimpse of something from above. It was apparently colorful, maybe even sparkling. And it disappeared quickly. I'm sure it was them."

Maia breathed deeply, and thought, as she continued to look at her commander. He was quiet. He was being more patient than usual. He had not raised his voice yet, and he had not given a direct order. She stood there, doubtful, and unmoving,

It had been nearly a year since the incident on the Isle, when the two of them had turned against the Lords, if only for a moment, to preserve newly-found life. Two months after, having not heard from them, and having had all calls to the Isle go unanswered, Jaan had devised a plan that he only shared with her. They would seek the Lords' system in the sky, to try to get a message to them that way. But, they had no way to track the system. And they had no idea what it looked like. They only knew that for countless years it had been retrieving Lwoans who had been swept away by the storm, into the clouds and their cold deaths.

They knew the system had to be at least one machine, and that it likely tracked body heat the same way their systems did. In the many months that had passed since Lord Andrew told them of the system, no Lwoan had been lost to the storm, and so there had been no fleeting trail to follow, no jumble of code to trigger any of the tower's discreetly-adjusted sensors. But now, it seemed, there could be something.

"Thoughts, Lieutenant?" Jaan asked.

"Sir, why are you convinced that it is them?" Maia asked.

"I'll admit that I am not fully convinced. Not yet. But, it's something. And it's been too long. We will need the Lords again. We will need their wisdom, their guidance. That I know. But, it was us who failed. It was us who turned. So, it is up to us to keep trying."

Maia was hesitant, but could not hold back. "They failed us, Sir."

Jaan nodded. "Perhaps we all came up short in those moments. But, this is our best chance yet to fix it. Are you ready?"

Maia waited a moment and then nodded. "Yes, Sir."

"And who will you take with you?"

She tilted her head backward. "Airman Malo."

"Well then, this is good timing. And a good sign. Go now."

"Yes, Sir."

As the secure line between them closed, she turned away, and walked up behind Malo again. She patted him on the shoulder. He turned in his seat and looked up. His eyes were steady, and waiting.

"With me, Airman," she said, her voice pushing out through the front of her helmet.

Malo nodded and quickly stood.

Maia turned and headed for the lift. Jaan was now at the west-facing wall, with his helmet up and his back toward them, giving off no hint of anything unusual for the rest of the room to notice. She did not let her eyes linger, and quickly pressed the button next to the lift door. The dense, translucent panel slid open, and she and Malo stepped in. The lift's floor bounced gently as the door closed in front of them. Maia pressed the button to descend to the mezzanine level.

"Helmet on, Airman," she said.

Malo reached back, pulled up his shining blue helmet, and pressed it into place over his head. She felt his eyes on her for a moment, but he quickly faced forward again as the lift stopped and the door slid open.

She stepped out first. Her boots clanked against the metal floor of the mezzanine as she marched toward the stairway. She could hear Malo behind her, and opened a secure line as they moved down the steps to the hangar level. The steady stream of air covering the floor was just barely visible. As she stepped down to the floor, she felt the air pulled through the tech of her boots and felt herself stabilize. She stood there, waiting, as Malo stepped down beside her.

She kept her eyes forward, and with the current task weighing upon her, her mind went back, as it often did, to being caught in a flash, and her bird disintegrating around her, and having to jump out into the raw winds over the forest surrounding the city. She let the thought pass quickly, and spoke quietly through the line. "Do you remember saving my life last year, Airman?"

"I just followed orders, Sir," Malo replied. "All of us were ready, I was just the closest. And, I would add, that I think you would have been fine without us."

"Maybe. Did I thank you?"

"Yes, Sir. That same hour, as we patrolled the city."

"Good. And do you remember what I told you a few months ago, about being ready?"

"Yes, Sir."

"Good. We have a mission."

Multiple birds were idling throughout the hangar. To the left, three of them, blue in color, were spaced out along the wall, hovering a few feet above the floor with their windshields facing out. Turning around, Maia saw two more airmen's birds to the left of the others, in front of the rounded wall of the ground lift. Their tech was expelling air, but having just returned from the outside, they were mounted to clamps below in preparation for inspection. The scarring on their bodies from recent patrolling was minimal, but noticeable. Maia thought for a moment about whether an airman's bird would better entice the Lords' system, if it were to see them. She turned and faced forward again.

Far ahead, winds were being pulled in at the bottom of the wide, west-facing entry. The bottom of the opening was cloudy with forces from the vortex being created by the tower's strong engines. The storm winds continually entered the hangar from every entry, becoming lighter as they flowed throughout. Maia watched a diminishing stream as it approached and was pulled into the idling engines of the two red birds hovering ahead of her. She walked up to the craft on the left and began to examine it.

She held her hand up near the front vent. Its dark, metal lines and dark spaces were clear, and Maia could feel the coolness of the air flowing around them. She looked up at the windshield and saw light from the cabin, and no dirt or debris. She saw Malo moving along the starboard side, and she began walking along the port side. The engine there and the short wing housing it were clear. The craft's body was clean. The slightly-curved roof showed no signs of damage, and the metal bar across its middle was firm and unmoving. She reached the aft end, knelt down slightly, and felt the air flow stronger through her tech as she checked the rear vent. Then she stood, and found the bird's signal in her helmet display, and whispered a command. She listened as the ramp disengaged, and watched as it tilted down, away from the bird's high, wide tail, and down to the floor.

Malo walked up to the other side of the ramp. "All good, Sir," he said.

"Very good," she said. "You're flying."

"Yes, Sir."

Maia followed him up the ramp and watched as he looked around the cabin, at the benches on each side, and the ceiling, and the pilot's chair straight ahead. Though the craft's exterior had been painted red to indicate leadership, the gray interior of an airman's craft

41

had remained. There had been little time, and few resources, to fully outfit the craft after hers was lost.

As she had expected, Malo's eyes lingered on the roll of metal cable mounted on the right, just behind the short windows above the bench. He stopped in place, looking. Maia pressed the button on the wall to close the ramp behind them. As she heard it lock into place, sealing the cabin, Malo turned around to face her.

"Sir?" he started. "What exactly will this mission entail?"

Maia pointed past him to the pilot's chair. "Strap in, Airman," she said. "And take her out. We'll talk on the way."

He nodded back, turned, walked up to the chair, and sat. He pulled the restraining belts onto his shoulders and over his waist, and secured them before reaching for the button below the seat cushion. As he turned in place toward the windshield, he tapped one control panel, and then the other two. Their screens came alight.

Maia moved to the starboard bench, sat down near the mounted cable, and secured a belt over her waist. A message popped up in her helmet's display. It was from Jaan, and only showed coordinates. Their destination was in the north, near where the Maw had met trouble. It was where the search needed to start. She focused on the glowing numbers and whispered a command, transferring them to the bird's system. She saw Malo's focus turn to the blinking panel on the right.

"That's where we're headed," she said through the line.

"Understood, Sir," he replied.

As he took hold of the control handles at his sides, and his right boot met the pedal below, Maia felt the engines growl beneath the floor and behind her seatback. The craft bounced up, and Malo spun them toward the entry. Winds rushed around them as they flew out at high speed. Malo immediately banked right and increased their elevation. Out the short window behind her, Maia caught a glimpse of the blue light emanating from the edges of the Sky Tower. Then she looked past Malo through the windshield, and watched the wide open sky as they flew north. Gusts of wind and breaking debris beat against the bird's body as they sped along.

"Is one of the salvage ships having trouble, Sir?" Malo asked.

Maia closed the line, tilted her helmet up and back, and breathed in the air of the cabin. The faint scent of water from the full clouds floated into her nose, and she breathed out. "No, Airman," she replied. "Not now, at least. The Maw had some trouble earlier in the day, but the crew got back safely."

Malo tilted his helmet toward her as he spoke louder. "And how's the ship?"

"They had to leave the base. It may still be floating out there. The mountain division still has to inspect the area. Apparently there was a large creature, hit the ship from below."

"How large?"

Maia shook her head. "I don't know. It's not important right now. We have something else to focus on. And, what I say from this point on is not to be spoken of. Do you understand?"

He nodded, keeping his eyes forward and the controls steady. "Yes, Sir."

"Again, Airman. Will you speak of this mission?"

"No, Sir."

"Good. We are going over the clouds. Remove the engines' elevation limits, point her up, and push hard."

She watched Malo as he hesitated, fidgeting in his seat as he gripped the control handles tighter. Then he followed her orders. She had already granted him full system access, and the bird complied as he navigated to the engine settings. A small schematic of the craft appeared in the panel on the left, with blinking lights highlighting the engines. As Malo input the command, she felt the winds increase all around them. She held to the seat as he increased their angle, and as they sped upward, leaned to her right and pressed down into her boots to keep herself firmly in place. The control panels blinked orange warnings. They continued to get higher and higher. All around them there was whiteness. Streaks of nearly-frozen water ran along the windows. She looked to one of the panels and saw their elevation: 9000 FT. Then, as they cleared the clouds, she felt the sudden drop in windforce. From the west, a hint of sunlight beamed into the cabin, and she looked out the window across from her as the bird gently floated downward.

She spoke loudly toward Malo. "You'll have to stay in the top of the clouds to keep enough power to the engines."

"Yes, Sir," he said, nodding as he tapped commands into the

center panel.

The bird's warnings gradually diminished, and as they leveled off and settled into the rushing air of the clouds, Maia removed her restraint and stood from the bench. She walked up behind Malo, set her left hand on the chair back, and leaned forward as she checked their status. The map in the center panel was a grid that showed their position, and the location of the coast far behind and below them. They were five miles from the shore and nearly two miles above the ocean. And they were another five miles from their intended destination. Looking out through the windshield again, she could see, just barely, the natural movement of the clouds, and the direction of the constant storm that raged around the land. The bird's front engine roared continually as it inhaled the dense air.

"Just keep her steady," Maia said. "She can handle it."

"Yes, Sir," Malo answered.

As he looked around, his eyes lingering on the distant, lowering, but unobstructed sunlight in the west, Maia went back to the bench and sat.

"I've only heard of flight over the clouds," said Malo. "I never thought I would actually get to do it, or that it would feel…like this. I haven't seen the sun since…"

"Since when?" asked Maia.

"I can't remember. Some months ago, maybe close to a year. It'd be nice if the forecasters could predict when the clouds would part, and for how long."

Maia laughed. "Yes, it would. Now, Airman, to the mission. How do you feel?"

"Ready, Sir."

"Good." She leaned out from the bench and looked toward his seat. "I am only going to tell you what you absolutely need to know. Last year, at the same time of the flashing, the commander and I flew to the Isle to meet with the Lords. While we were there, Lord Andrew informed the commander of a system in the sky, one that tracks those who are lost to the storm. We know that the Lords give proper burials to those this system retrieves, but we do not know how many have been retrieved. Are you following so far?"

"Yes, Sir," he said, sounding calm as he continued to carry them forward.

"Very good. We have not heard from the Lords since that day. They do not respond to our calls. The commander wants to try to get a message to them through this system in the sky. Thus far, we have been unable to find a signal for it, but the mountain watchers who aided the Maw may have encountered it. So, we will attempt to trigger it."

"Sir..." Malo started, hesitant. "Why not simply go to the Isle?"

"They instructed us not to return."

"But, why?"

"That is, unfortunately, classified."

"Well...Do you think the Lords are in danger? After so many

years, do you think they could have finally passed on?"

Maia shook her head. "Not likely. They were…fairly healthy when last we saw them."

"Then, why wouldn't they at least respond to calls from the mainland? From watchers?"

Maia thought carefully before answering. "Our meeting with them that day did not go well. They were very angry when we left."

"And…the reason is also…"

"Classified. Yes."

Malo shifted in his seat and tilted his head back slightly. "Well, they have lived for three centuries. I'd think they have too many years, too much wisdom, to stay angry, especially with us."

Maia leaned back, and looked out through the windshield at the seemingly endless skyscape. "Maybe. But, you don't lose your humanity as you age, Airman. "You'll see in time. I'm inching toward sixty and still feel things as intensely as I did at your age. And for just as long."

Malo seemed eager to say more, but he only nodded. He kept flying forward. The winds continued to rush around the bird as they neared the desired location. Maia stood again, and pulled her helmet up and down over her head. It clicked into place, but she pressed down again, wanting to be sure. With a whisper she brought up a diagram of her wind tech, and saw that each piece–on each leg and forearm, at her back, and on each side of her waist–was functioning normally. She stepped to the center of the cabin, knelt, and lowered her head, thinking, feeling each breath move in and out of her chest. She felt the bird come to a stop, and the winds beneath her, beneath the floor, became slightly quieter as they hovered in place. She opened the secure line once more.

"We're here, Sir," Malo called.

Maia stood back up, and looked out the windshield again. Then, she looked through the narrow windows above each bench. The clouds surrounding them were thick, and their steady motion was more evident. The sky above them had its own thin clouds, and had yet to reveal any stars, or the moon, but she knew that night was close. She stepped backward to the cable on the wall, and grabbed the closed hook from the center of the neatly-wound coil. The rounded metal that formed the hook was an inch thick, and solid. Its spring-loaded base was dark and sturdy, and firmly bolted to the cable. She pried the hook open with both hands, and held it as she pulled her belt out slightly and then let the hook snap closed around it.

"Sir, what are you doing?" Malo called.

Maia looked and saw him nearly standing out of his seat, out of position if a gust, or any large debris, or any hardened precipitate were to knock them out of place. "Back in that seat, Airman!" she ordered.

"Sir, you can't go out there," said Malo, keeping his eyes on her as he sat back down. "The air's thin. And we're up so high. If you lose your position out there-"

"Stop, Airman! Listen. I've already planned for this." She

held a piece of the thick cable up in her gloved hands, tugged at it, and felt its weight. "I'll be fine."

Malo quieted, but spun the pilot's chair around and watched her as she stepped toward the ramp. She kept her eyes on him as she reached for the button to open it.

"You're using your own body to trigger it?" he asked.

Maia nodded. "It's the only way we know of, so we have to try. Don't worry. Just keep the line open. And keep your eyes open. You see anything, you tell me. Understood?"

"Yes, Sir."

Malo raised his right fist in salute, and Maia returned the gesture, then pressed down on the ramp button and held it. As it unlocked and began to lower, she felt the raw winds rush into the cabin. They were not the same as those on or near the mainland. They were not as dense, but they were colder. Even through the protective layers of her suit, she could feel the sharpness of their chill.

She looked at the opening and released the button, leaving the ramp at an angle, with just a few feet of open space. She turned and moved carefully over the ramp, feeling the winds as they were pulled through her tech. She ducked down as she sensed the top of her helmet nearing the bird's high tail. With her left hand she held on to the cable and squeezed, gripping it through her dense glove. With her right hand she reached up and held the cold, curving metal of the bird's frame. Then she ducked slightly, stepped up onto the edge of the ramp, and leapt out.

The cable clanked against the bird's body as the winds were pulled through her tech. With whispered commands and careful movements, she was carried back toward the center of the bird's roof. She found its hard surface with her boots, and knelt down as she slid backward. Her heavy soles rubbed against the hard metal until they hit the crossbar. She still had a firm grip on the cable, but she set her right hand upon the roof and waited a moment. Then she stood, and looked.

The top of the storm was dense, but not so dense that she could not make out anything below. The ocean's dark surface was far, far beneath them. Every few moments, flowing, white clouds of cold, wet air would part just enough for her to get an even better look. She could gauge the full distance to the ocean surface just by sight. She took a deep breath, exhaled, and continued surveying. As she did, she could sense the distant heat of the sun getting weaker. She turned west, and in the distance saw the dimming of yellow-orange light against the gray below and above.

"Sir, are you alright?" Malo called.

Maia turned toward the craft's front end, and looked out at the vastness. She knelt once more, and grasped the crossbar. "I'm fine, Airman," she answered. "Do you see anything?"

"No, Sir. What should we be looking for?"

"Lights. Sparkling. Probably not unlike our own. But, leave yours dark. We'll let dusk hide us as much as possible."

"Yes, Sir."

Maia looked to the display in her helmet panel. Gravity was

constant. Her relative speed was near zero, matching the bird's idleness. She looked around and saw the wild sky, and infinite, clouded distance in every direction, but little else. She hoped that the Lords' system would sense her, that she would get what was needed–a traceable signal and an image of the system, whatever it was.

The sky was getting darker, but it seemed to be coming on too fast. Then, she realized there was a shadow.

"Sir, look out!" Malo yelled through the line.

Maia turned, looked up, and saw a black, metal body. Her heart pounded against her chest, but she kept her voice low. "Quiet, Airman," she said.

It had come up from behind, from the south, without warning, without sound. Maia had not even felt the air shift. The machine hovered there, unmoving, just a few yards above her. Its main body was nearly twenty feet long and flat, with sleek vents running along its bottom. Thin lines of air were flowing out at its tail end and its sides. Its front end, if there was one, held a round, protruding device, not unlike a head. Its red glow illuminated the front of the bird. And attached at its sides were curved extensions that appeared to be legs, with rounded joints connecting them to the main body. The legs suddenly began retracting upward, as if the machine had decided against an action. *It's an unmanned craft*, Maia thought to herself.

The machine pulled away quickly, taking its shadow with it as it passed by the bird's tail end. She could see it from the front now, see that its body was shallow and made up mostly of sleek wind tech engines.

"Wait!" she shouted, holding up her open right hand, still squeezing the cable with the other.

The machine stopped, and the red, round light on its front end doubled in intensity and blinked twice.

"Can you understand me?" she asked.

The red light quickly changed to a softer, but still bright, green.

"Okay? I suppose that will do. I am Lieutenant Maia, of the Watchers of the Sky, honorably promoted by the Lords of Lwo."

An outline of the machine appeared in her helmet's display. With six legs and a simple body, the signal looked almost like an insect as it rotated in place. The word ACKNOWLEDGED appeared below it in white letters, but there was no other information. Where the mass and relative speed of the machine should have been there were plain, white boxes, flickering in and out like static. Maia looked out at the machine again.

"Who are you?" she asked.

I AM THE SYSTEM IN THE SKY.

"Do you have a name? Like the Emissary?"

THAT IS NONE OF YOUR CONCERN, WATCHER.

"Very well then…System. What is your purpose?"

I RETRIEVE THOSE WHO ARE LOST TO THE GREAT STORM, AS YOU ALREADY KNOW.

"And what do you do with those who are lost?"

I TAKE THEM TO OUR LORDS, ON THE ISLE, AS YOU ALSO ALREADY KNOW.

Maia's heart beat faster at the system's level of awareness, and apparent agitation, but she continued. "So, you know what we know. What else do *you* know?"

I AM AWARE OF YOUR SERVICE TO, AND PROTECTION OF, LWO. I AM ALSO AWARE OF YOUR RECENT BETRAYAL OF OUR LORDS. AND NOW, WATCHER, A QUESTION FOR YOU.

"Fine."

WHY DID YOU TRICK ME?

Maia hesitated, and swallowed, fearful of what the large, intelligent, clearly capable machine might do. "We need the Lords," she said. "They do not answer our calls, and we need their guidance. Will you tell them?"

NO. BY OUR LORDS' ORDERS, I WILL NOT. GOODBYE, WATCHER. YOU WILL NOT TRICK ME AGAIN.

"Wait!" she yelled, reaching out with her right hand.

The machine spun around, and, in an instant, was gone, disappearing miles away before Maia could form another thought. She stared into the distance, hoping for something. Then, the bug-like signal disappeared from her display.

She took a deep breath, and suddenly felt the bite from the cold above the clouds. She got to her feet. She stayed low and stepped heavily against the bird's roof. The winds continued to blow around her and move through her tech, as she moved toward the tail end. As the edge of the ramp came into view, she gripped the cable, leapt out, and guided herself back into the cabin. Cold exhaust spun all around her until her boots were safely planted on the floor.

CHAPTER 4
HOME

The electric energy of the shield that roofed the sky watchers' village hummed near Robbins' head. Its hazy light illuminated the view through the front of his helmet and gave him some warmth, some sense of comfort, but he could still hear the howling from the constant storm above. He held tightly to the heavy rope keeping him connected to the metal hook in the top of the stone wall. The rope was still tightly secured to his utility belt, which was hooked to the center pole of the pulley system. The machine felt as stable as it always did, but he was near the top of the five-story wall and still felt a lingering unease. The boss of the village's maintenance crew, Vint, had told him from the beginning that the feeling would always be there. Robbins had spent nearly seven months on the crew. Vint had been right.

"Finished yet?" Vint asked through the open line, his voice kind and even.

"Almost," Robbins answered.

He reached up to his right, grasped the heavy, palm-sized sensor, and pulled it off of the smooth stone of the wall, away from the disc-shaped shield generator. Through his glove he felt a sliver of cold push through the tiny gap between the shield and the stone surface. He kept the soles of his boots firmly planted against the wall and held the sensor up in front of him. The small screen showed normal readings from the generator. He slid the device into the holster on his left side, and then looked left and right at the top of the wall, making sure there were no cracks, holes, or anything else that could compromise the protective barrier. Seeing nothing, he disconnected his rope from the wall, and then reached for the metal cable at his back, tugged, and lifted his boots. He heard the soft shift of components behind him, and then felt himself descending.

A few moments later, his boots hit the ground, first the left, and then the right. He stood up straight, and felt the relief flow through him. Behind him, Vint disconnected his belt from the cable. Now on the ground, and unsupported, his belt felt much heavier, as did the sleeves on his dense, padded coat, and the legs on his heavy pants. He reached up with both hands and took his helmet off, and breathed in the village's air as he backed away from the wall, and the black, metal base of the pulley system.

"Nice work today, Robbins," said Vint.

"Thank you," Robbins replied.

Robbins watched the man, tall and strong, with thick, brown hair that he kept cut short, as he entered commands into the keypad on top of the machine. Far above them, the machine's two flat stabilizers pulled away from the wall, and then began descending along their support rods as the metal cylinders of each support slid smoothly into one another. As they got shorter and neared the base, the center pole began collapsing behind them, simultaneously spooling the cable as it shrank. Robbins was still amazed at the strength of the narrow, metal tubes, but they were also just about the least amazing thing he had seen since arriving on Lwo nearly a year earlier.

"Are you getting used to this yet?" Vint asked, as he watched the system shrinking into itself.

"I think so," said Robbins.

"Well, being from a civilian village, I don't imagine you had a wall or shield quite like ours."

Robbins scratched his head and moved his helmet from his right arm to his left. "No, Sir. But, we did alright."

"Well, we're glad to have you here. Glad the lieutenant found you." He chuckled as he looked at Robbins, and then quickly looked away.

Robbins laughed along. "Yeah, me too."

"I'll finish up here. See you in two days."

Robbins nodded. "Okay. Take great care."

As Vint made a call through the radio affixed to his chest, ordering another crew member to meet him with a transport for the pulley system, Robbins turned to his left, to the west, and began walking. When he had been anchored near the top of the village's wall, looking for weaknesses and trying to avoid shield shock, he had not paid much attention to the sky. But now, looking up through the faint glow, he could see that night was near. The gray of the clouds

57

had faded to near-black.

Looking ahead, the path was clear. On the left were a few homes, which he knew belonged to watchers, and one diner, which had a long, single, darkened window. As he passed by, and looked past the tightly-spaced metal bars and through the window, he could see the bartender standing, cleaning something. But, there was no one else. He nodded, and waved, and the woman looked up. She nodded, and went back to work.

Far ahead, and to the right, was the entry to the path to the sky lift. The arched opening was bright with light. He looked up through the shield again, to the tower hovering in the sky. Its blue lights glowed in the darkness. The sky lift's wide, heavy cable was swaying in the winds beneath it. The lift itself–a wide, round disc–was not affixed to the tower's underbody, which meant it was either on the way up, or had just landed. As Robbins looked ahead again, he saw a group of five airmen, all dressed in blue and with their helmets raised, step through the entry and into the village. He looked away, to the buildings on the left. The turn that would take him home was just past the next wall.

"Robbins, Sir!" a young man called loudly.

Robbins stopped as he reached the open alley and looked one block south. The coolness from the alleyway beckoned, but he turned to face the young man, who he recognized, as he jogged up to meet him.

"Hello, Airman Gerrin," he said.

Gerrin turned back to the other four airmen, as they slowly came up behind him, and stopped two yards back. Then, he faced Robbins again. "Hello," he said. "Has the lieutenant returned yet?"

Robbins shrugged. "I'm not sure. I just finished my shift. Why do you ask?"

"Oh, well…" he hesitated. "Just curious. She left quite a while ago with…"

"With who?"

Gerrin shook his head. "I'm sorry. It was just an assignment. I shouldn't have brought it up, Sir."

"Just call me Robbins. I'm no watcher."

"Well, given your size, I'm sure you could be." He glanced up, at the top of the barrier wall. "And, there is your apparent technical aptitude."

"Ha. Well, you're bigger than I am."

"Not by much."

"And, I've been trained, like every other inspector."

"But, from what I hear, you took to it easily. What village did you say you were from again?"

"Never did."

Silence lingered between them for a moment before Gerrin nodded back.

"Okay," Gerrin said. "Understood. So, how did you come to us? Did you cause some kind of trouble?" He smiled. "Did they run you out?"

Robbins smiled back, and looked into the young man's eyes, wondering what he was reaching for, hoping he would not cause him to involuntarily resort to his non-Lwoan instincts. "Not at all, Airman." he replied.

"They must miss your skills, then."

"Gerrin, come on!" one of the airmen said loudly. She looked as young as he did, and nearly as strong, and had short, straight red hair. "We've been at it all day. So has he."

Gerrin glanced back at her. "Go on without me, then. I can find food on my own."

"Oh, sure you can," she said, and laughed back.

She shook her head, and turned toward the other three airmen. They exchanged looks of agitation, followed by mumbles of curiosity. Robbins wondered if one of them would join in with Gerrin's bothersome inquiry and push him further. Far behind them, another group of airmen entered the village from the arched entry. They were quiet and continued south, passing behind a building and out of sight. Robbins looked back at Gerrin.

"I'm a bit hungry myself," Robbins said. "And you all do look like you've had a long day. How about we continue this another time?"

"I understand," said Gerrin. "It's just that most of us have only seen you a few times since you moved here. Our shifts hardly match up, and it's important that we are familiar with the civilians here. Besides the lieutenant and the commander, hardly anyone knows you or your son."

Robbins tried to keep calm as he felt his eyes narrowing. "Well, Airman, does anyone besides them matter?"

Gerrin stared back. "If we want to survive another century, then we all matter."

Robbins could see the insistence in Gerrin's eyes, along with the subtle aggravation. "I know that, Airman. I meant in terms of our relative places here. Don't you trust your leaders? They trust me."

"Of course."

"And don't you trust that, in an emergency, or a phenomenon, or anything like that, that I know how the village functions, and how to handle myself?"

"Sure, Robbins."

"So, what else is there?"

Gerrin shrugged. "Not much, I suppose. Very well, then. Maybe another time?"

"Maybe." Robbins looked up through the shield again, at the dark sky. "Right now, though, I have to get home to my son. I'm sure his caregiver is waiting."

Gerrin nodded. "Right. Good idea. When I was young, back in the city, I would always be excited when my father got back home. Now he's in a village in the south, and unfortunately, very unsettled."

Robbins thought for a moment, about Shil's earlier report, of which he had only heard a few parts. The whole land was in a predicament. He wished the rest of Lwo knew just how good they had it, but he could not, and would not, tell them himself. "We'll all get through this," he said. "It'll just take time."

"Right. Time. Take great care, Robbins."

"You do the same, Airman."

Gerrin walked on, and the other airmen followed, nodding to Robbins as they passed by. There was only acknowledgement in their eyes. There was no empathy or excess of respect. Robbins preferred it that way. It had been almost the same out at sea, where every human you encountered was just barely surviving and had little energy to think of you, unless they thought you could offer something of value, or might give anything up easily.

As the airmen's voices faded behind him, Robbins turned and headed straight through the alleyway, hoping that his son had not also endured any unwanted questioning from others in the village.

*   *   *   *   *

Robbins was wiping the metal counter next to the sink when he sensed someone off to his right, beyond the small, wooden dining table, outside the front window. The front door unlocked and slid aside, and Maia stepped through. He smiled, but she did not look at him. She turned, closed the door, and locked it. He set the towel down and wiped his hands on his pant legs as he left the kitchen. The display screen on the far wall showed the time: 11:08 PM. Above the time was the storm's status. Winds were steady at one hundred twenty-five miles per hour.

Maia was quiet as she methodically removed her equipment. Her helmet was already up. She reached back and disconnected its support brace from the back of her jacket. Then, she raised the assembly up over her head, and set it on the shelf near the door. Next, she reached into her right gauntlet and detached it, and carefully slid it down her arm and over her gloved hand. It made a light thudding sound as she set it down next to her helmet. Robbins looked right, toward the curving stairway, but heard no movement. He hoped that by now Devon was fast asleep.

He walked up behind Maia just as she set her left gauntlet down, and set his hands on her shoulders, and stood closer as she unzipped the heavy, red jacket, revealing the snug-fitting black shirt underneath. As she slid the jacket off of her arms, she turned and finally looked at him, and smiled. He could see the heaviness in her eyes. He took her jacket and hung it on one of the hooks over the shelf. The boxy, metal tech engine affixed to it shot a dull reflection into his eyes. But, he still saw the small scratches on its housing.

"It still surprises me," he said. "Just how heavy it all is."

Maia knelt down, and began unhooking the latches on the backs of her boots. "Oh, please," she said, almost laughing. "Don't you try to boost my ego."

"I'm not. It's true."

She stepped out of her boots and placed them near the bottom of the shelf, and then stood, unhooked her belt, and laid it in a circle near her helmet and gauntlets. With her back to him again, she reached up, and felt the back of her head, felt the ring of thick, dark braids, checking that it was all still in place, as she so often did. Then, she stretched both arms. Robbins could see that the bruises near her neck from a shift two days prior were starting to fade. He stepped closer, grabbed her by the shoulders, and pulled her back into his chest. She leaned her head back into his neck.

"What happened?" he asked, quietly.

She reached up, pulled his hands down, and set them together over her waist. "Something," she replied.

"Something, huh? Is that why you're so late?"

"Late?" she said, her voice raising. She glanced over at the display screen. "Oh. I hadn't checked in a while. I was very busy. I'm sorry, Love."

"We got along fine without you."

"Ha. I'm sure you did."

She stepped away, gently letting his hands go as she walked toward the sitting area and dropped down onto the cushioned bench across from the display, in front of the grate-covered hearth. Its stones were not glowing as much as they had been hours before, but they were still radiating a decent amount of heat.

Robbins followed her to the bench, sat at the other end, and reached for her legs, pulling them up, and pulling her stocking-covered feet into his slap. She rubbed her heels against his right thigh.

"What is 'something?'" he asked, firmly rubbing her ankles. He slowly moved up to her calves. The fabric of her pants was dense, but he was still able to find the muscles and apply plenty of pressure.

Maia took a deep breath and then sighed out. "Duty. A specific duty. I doubt it's a good idea for me to share it with you."

"Were you ordered not to?"

"Not directly." She looked into his eyes. "But, it was implied. Of course, the commander understands our dynamic. And, he trusts you not to say anything."

Robbins waited, looking back at her. Her eyes were still heavy. "Dynamic?"

"Our marriage. Our *marriage dynamic*."

He smiled. "Glad he understands."

"You know, it was just me for a long time. And, even I'm still getting used to it. So, he is too. Like I told you when you asked, leading watchers don't usually wed."

"I know, I know."

"I know you do." She pulled her legs away from him, and slid closer, and took his right hand into both of hers, rubbing it as she crossed her legs over the cushion. She looked down, and then up at him again. "There's something in the sky."

Robbins peered at her. "Something?"

"The system in the sky."

"Oh. That. Well, we knew that already."

"But today...today I saw it."

Robbins stared back at her, and thoughts of his and Devon's arrival to Lwo, and their time on the Isle, and the changes in his body, and those responsible for them, all rushed through his mind. He had been trying, for months, to ignore them. He had almost gotten to the point of not having a flashback more than once a day. But now, the memories were prominent once again. He felt the warmth of his own body, an energy he had never felt outside the storm, even after the watchers and Kile had brought him back from the brink. He almost winced as he remembered where the excess of rejuvenating cells flowing through him had come from.

"Sometimes I wish I'd never heard of their system," he said.

Maia nodded. "I wish the same. For you, that is. I'm sure it's been hard enough just getting used to this place."

He shook his head. "With you, from the beginning, it's been easy."

She squeezed his hand tighter. "Do you want to know what it looked like?"

"I do. Tell me."

"Like a big, metal insect. Black, with heavy, articulated legs. A body made up almost entirely of wind tech. And, it had intellect."

"Like the Emissary?"

"Yes. Just like it. But, it wasn't the Emissary, as far as I could tell. It's its own system."

"And it saw you, I assume?"

"Yes. Me. My bird. Maybe even the airman that was with me.

It all happened very fast. And, I had to…"

"Had to what?"

"I had to bait it, get it to recognize my heat signature. So, I was outside the bird."

Knowing that the system only dwelled above the clouds, as far as anyone knew, Robbins shook his head. Then, he almost laughed. "You're a bold one, lady. I hardly like leaving this house."

Maia smacked his thigh. "Listen."

"I am."

"Good." She went back to rubbing his hand, softly. "The system…It was almost angry."

"Machines don't have emotions."

"No. But they can be programmed with opposition. And, it knew that I was in no danger, that I had not been lost to the storm. And it knew what happened on the Isle, with us." She paused, and looked deeper into his eyes. "It would barely speak to me, even with my rank and title. They are still angry with us. And, apparently, they've made their systems aware of it."

Robbins thought for a moment, about the centuries-old man, and his two centuries-old daughters, and what he knew had happened after he had been rendered unconscious. "We already knew they were angry," he said. "Didn't we?"

"I suppose so," said Maia. "But, we had hoped for better. Especially after all this time. Now I wonder what else we could do."

There was a rustling above them, and they both looked toward the curved stairwell. They remained quiet, waiting, but Devon did not emerge.

"Did he have a busy day?" Maia asked, looking back at him.

"I think so," said Robbins. "Not just chores or walks. Prynn told me they did a lot of studying too."

"Is he getting used to this? To being here?"

"I think he was at home the day we walked out of the hospital."

Maia laughed. "I think you're right."

"But, I was thinking, with there only being two other children in the village, who are both a bit older than him, it may be time to take another trip."

Maia nodded. "I think you're right. Same village?"

"Sure."

"Okay. I'll make a call."

"Okay. So, Love?"

"Yes?"

"Why do you wonder what else can be done? Why do you need to do anything else?"

She looked away. "I agree with the commander. We will need the Lords' guidance, sooner or later."

"But, not right now?"

"I don't know."

"It's been so long now. Don't you think the commanders can manage without them?"

"They can, yes. They *have*. But…"

"But, what?"

She was hesitant, but as she turned back to him, her eyes strengthened. "But, I have orders to follow. I have a duty. And with the city not yet habitable, and the storm unchanging, dissension is the last thing we need."

Robbins wanted to say more, but seeing her sternness and assuredness, and seeing the hard edge that every watcher, even the few who were as kind as his wife, carried with them beneath the surface, he could not find the words. He simply said "Understood."

Maia sat more upright, and stretched her arms, and then slid closer to him. She turned, and leaned back against him, and stretched her legs out across the bench. As he felt her weight, he leaned back into the armrest. Then, he wrapped his arms around hers, and held her.

As they lay there, quiet, he felt her heart beating, strong and steady. A few minutes later, she drifted off. He stared up at the display screen, thinking, his mind racing from one thing to the next, until it no longer could. The clock read 11:44 PM, as he finally shut his eyes.

CHAPTER 5
UNEARTHED

Shil held firmly to the puller's control handle with both hands, keeping it tilted forward as she flew south through the city's central pathway. The heavy, focused air of the third wind stream, fifteen stories up, was dense around the bottom half of the craft, but it was not as strong as it could have been. She could feel it in the vibrations beneath her seat. She and her division had limited the output of the wind tech engines at all four of the city's entries, knowing that they would need to be preserved as much as possible for the city's eventual repopulation. But, with so few craft navigating the streams, absorbing and pushing the air, the puller's engines were still working efficiently.

An intersection came into view, and Shil saw the wide light of its closest wind mover glowing green. The puller floated over it, and then over the next mover, and she pressed harder upon the pedal as she guided the craft down fifty feet and into the second stream.

It was not quite midday. The gray sky gave light to all of the buildings in the area. As she passed between sectors, she noticed the lines of shade on the stone front of a ten-story building, and the faint shimmer from the glass fronts of two twelve-story buildings. The structures were more than three blocks north of the city's center and had been deemed stable. And the thought of them being empty was a constant bother, but Shil knew that she could not risk shortening the new timeline. The foundation's strong points could still fail, along with the patience of watchers dealing with any increased eagerness from the tens of thousands of displaced. She took the craft downward again and into the first stream.

Even through the air of the stream, Shil could make out the city's main north-south road five stories below. Its pavement was dark, and now, having passed the city's center and the park sector, she could see several orange, wheeled work trucks on both sides of the road. The men and women in protective orange suits, standing outside the vehicles, registered as heat signatures on the map in the puller's bright center control panel. As Shil neared the worksite she looked to her right and saw buildings a block away, no longer obstructed by the ones that had fallen, or been demolished out of necessity. On her left, two buildings were almost leaning and had long cracks running down their fronts. She was hopeful that they could be repaired.

Passing into the next block, she saw high-reaching, more upright buildings on both sides. These buildings, somehow, had little damage. The visual dissonance was no longer shocking; not to her, and not to any of those in her command. Nature had pressed upon the city from below, but not fairly. She continued forward and took the puller down out of the first stream, and felt the engines rumble beneath her as they were forced to work harder. In an instant she was gliding just a yard above the road. She slowed to a stop, and idled the engines. The puller hovered in place.

She waited there, between the fourth sectors of the city's southeast and southwest quarters, and quietly observed. Through the windshield, she could see the road's cracks, but it was still mostly flat, still traversable by foot or by wheels. Directly ahead there were two work trucks on either side of the road. Each of them had a high-reaching, hinged arm extending from rounded connectors in front of the cabins, with the bending joints reaching fifty feet high and the tool ends resting two or three yards above the ground. Their wheels were made of heavy, molded rubber that had an inconsistent, brownish color, and deep, intricate treads. The deep wheel wells allowed for a full range of movement and rotation.

The trucks' cabins were plain, small boxes with clear windows that reflected the flickering lights of the controls within them. A worker hopped out of the truck on the right, which was currently equipped with a shoveling tool, and slid the door closed behind him. The man waved in the direction of the puller. Shil waved back, and watched as he walked toward the drill-equipped truck across the road.

The worksite directly ahead, and over one hundred yards away, was a great hole resting between the seventh sectors. With a quiet command, Shil magnified the view through the windshield and saw a puller hovering at the near side of the wire-formed fence that surrounded the site. The dust-covered craft's lights were radiating yellow, giving a slight luminescence to the immediate area. There were also two unmanned jumpers on either side of it, hovering closer to the east and west edges of the site. She opened a line to her lieutenant and heard the low click. In her helmet panel, Nico's signal blinked, and he began to speak.

"Commander, Sir," he said, his voice slightly less youthful than it had been a year earlier. "This is Lieutenant Nico. Go ahead."

"I'm here to relieve you, Lieutenant," she answered. "How is the day going?"

"We're making progress, Sir. Little by little, as usual. I do have an update for you."

"Alright."

"A few hours ago I counted over a thousand new requests from around the land to return to the city and work."

"Oh? It was less than half that when last I checked."

"I think it might have been your announcement of the new timeline."

"That wouldn't surprise me. "

"Me either. Apparently citizens don't care much for the outside."

"Or, they simply can't handle it as well as others. I doubt most of them have any real idea of how heavy this work really is. But there must be some skilled, maybe highly-skilled, workers and technicians left out there somewhere."

"I recognized a couple of names from the city, and some not

from the city."

"At least they want to contribute."

"Yes, Sir."

"Pick the names you'd like to consider. We can go over them later. In the meantime, head back to headquarters. And get some rest."

"Yes, Sir. Nico out."

Shil watched as Nico's puller elevated slightly and slowly floated away from the fence. As it turned about and flew north, toward her position, she deactivated the magnification in the windshield and guided her craft further south, moving carefully between the buildings and trucks. She waved toward Nico's puller, and saw him behind the windshield as they passed each other. His engines roared as he sped upward and out of sight. She continued forward, slowly approaching the fence. She stopped five yards back, idled the puller again, set its lights to yellow, and looked out.

There was a constant, lingering mist of dust, dirt and debris, and even through the puller's filters Shil could already make out the smells: concrete, topsoil, heavy rock, and minerals that were indistinct, but earthy and bitter. Bright, white lights, set upon tall posts, surrounded the worksite, beaming downward and illuminating the massive hole in a way that the muted daylight could not.

The hole's diameter was close to two hundred feet. Its curving edge, two or so yards beyond the nine-foot fence, was crooked, and at some points sharp. Its plunging walls were visible up to about fifty feet down from where she was sitting, and their uneven surfaces were a speckled mix of blackish, brownish gray. A few, spread out points where there had been utility pipes, or sections of building foundations, were now covered in precisely-cut metal plating, faint sparks within the hole's shadows.

Around the fence, at multiple points, there were closed, secured gates. Inside each gate stood at least one civilian worker, outfitted in orange and with a full tool belt that was attached to the fence by a long cable. Shil could clearly see seven of the workers from her position. Looking down at the center panel she saw that there were twenty of them in place, standing and monitoring the edge of the hole.

Next to half of the edge monitors there were heavy, mechanized spools, each secured by a long, metal plate to a section of road or undamaged pavement far behind the fence. The machines were for use not by the monitors, but by the descenders, those who, when called upon, would don more protective equipment, and bright headlamps, and tether themselves to the surface before getting the deepest possible look within the hole. And when this was called for at least three of those selected had to be watchers. The site bosses had agreed with Shil on this point without argument. On the left panel, she brought up the day's plan and saw the names of the watchers and civilian workers who had been chosen for the descent.

The jumpers hovering off to the sides of the puller belonged to two of the descending patrolmen, Woll and Kine. The other descending watcher, Rienne, had left her jumper idling on the far side, not far from the one still occupied by Duuq. Far behind him, beyond the buildings still standing on the other side of the hole, Shil could just barely see the faint, blue haze of the city's shield. She tapped the right panel, and opened the worksite's regular radio frequency, and immediately heard an ongoing back-and-forth between the watchers and the current site boss, Hehl.

"We're reaching three hundred feet now," said Kine, his voice firm. "Just wait for us to touch."

"I'd like a full scan of that surface, Patrolman," said Hehl, sounding much older than his eighty years. "How are my workers doing down there?"

"They're fine," Woll answered. "It's no different than any other descent. Don't worry."

"Sorry. I don't mean to be impatient, but we're at the bottom now."

"We know, Boss," Rienne chimed in. "We mapped it out, remember?"

"Right, right. Okay. I just want to see what's beneath the foundation, like everyone else."

"We understand," said Kine.

Quieter voices continued through the open line, echoing, along with the distant sounds of climbing, and boots and picks striking rock, and thick, reinforced rope slowly continuing to unroll. Shil looked out the windshield again, and on the far right side of the hole saw the orange truck waiting there. Its long arm was affixed to the ground by the heavy gripping tool. In the right panel she saw Hehl's signal at the truck's position, blinking.

"Commander's on site," Duuq announced through the radio.

A chorus of responses, including the phrase 'Commander, Sir' from her watchers, started and quickly ended. Shil acknowledged them all at once, and then quieted.

"We're here," said Kine.

"Confirmed," said Woll.

"Confirmed," said Rienne. "Boots on the ground. All descenders secure. No injuries. Lamps are up, and we're beginning our survey."

Shil heard more echoes, of boots, both rubber- and metal-soled, tapping and sliding along whatever material was at the bottom of the city's foundation, or had been beneath it. She had prepared her entire division for the day when the foundation materials would be fully excavated, and civilians might encounter what had been hidden. She had told them all, discreetly, and in small groups, of the pillars that had been placed before the city's foundation had been laid, which had been long before any of their parents had even been born. They had all accepted, or at least understood, the first Lords' desire to ensure the stability of the only place most Lwoans would be able to live in relative safety, to keep humanity from going extinct.

"So far it's just more rock," Kine said through the line. "Hard, somewhat porous, but mostly dense and smooth."

"It's not like the rock formed at the flash sites," said Woll. "There's no evidence of an eruption. If there was, it's gone."

"We're checking the walls," said Rienne. "So far, nothing strange."

Finally, Shil spoke up. "How firm is it?" she asked.

"I'm setting a gauge down now, Sir," said Kine. A moment later, he spoke again. "We've got it. The surface hardness is twice that of...wait."

"What is it?" asked Shil.

"There's metal."

"A deposit?"

After another short pause, Kine answered. "Not sure, Sir."

"There's metal over here, too," said Rienne. "Sir, Patrolman Kine is on the west side. I've made my way over to the east. I wouldn't have noticed, but I felt the difference in my boots as soon as I neared the wall."

"Well now," said Hehl, sounding less worried. "This is interesting. Maybe it wasn't a flash from below after all. Just a small quake moving things around."

"We can hope," said Shil. "Patrolman Rienne? Can you take a sample?"

"Yes, Sir," she answered. "We are taking samples now, and-"

"Aaaah!" someone, a civilian, yelled out.

"What is it!?" Shil called.

"What's happened!?" yelled Hehl.

Shil leaned over the controls, wanting to leap up and out. Through the windshield she saw a new plume of dust float up and slowly dissipate in the air. "Watchers!?" she called again.

"We're okay!" Kine answered. "There was shaking, near Patrolman Rienne. She's fine, just took a spill with a couple of others. The ground on the east side may be a bit unstable."

"In what way, Patrolman?"

"Seems like it just shifted, from side to side. But, there are no cracks that I can see. What about you, Patrolman?"

"It was like..." Rienne started. "Like it slid from under us. But we're-"

"There it goes again!" yelled Woll.

There was a short pause, followed by frantic, echoing chatter.

"Everyone out!" Woll yelled.

Shil accessed the site's open line in her helmet, quickly unhooked her restraining belts, and hopped out of the seat. "Monitors, get a hold of those spools!" she ordered. "Start pulling your people up!"

Multiple men and women responded with "Yes, Commander."

"Wait!" Kine called. "Not us. Just the civilians. We're placing sensors."

"Fine, Patrolman," replied Shil. "But, make it quick."

The port door on the puller unlocked and began to slide. Shil jumped out and down to the road before it was fully open. She turned left to see a handful of workers jogging up. Through whispers to the puller's system, she ordered the door closed and secured. Then, she held her open left hand out toward the approaching group.

79

"Don't come any further," she said loudly, projecting her voice from the opening just below her helmet's panel. "We do not yet know how safe it is."

The workers slowed their steps, stopping yards behind the puller. She turned and jogged toward the fence. As she neared the high barrier she sped up, and then leapt and grabbed the top bar. With a boost from the tech in her boots and on her back, she floated over, and landed a few feet from the monitor that was standing there. She stepped quickly toward the man, who was tall, and heavy, but fit. Through the clear panel on his helmet she could see thick, brown eyebrows, and a restrained fear.

"Who's on the end of your line?" she asked.

"Patrolman Kine," he answered.

Shil nodded, and looked down, behind the man's legs, at the large, metal spool. There were still a few yards of the multi-colored, intertwined rope left to give. The base plate and the mounts looked stable. "Okay," she said. "Stay close to it. Keep your hand on that lever."

"Yes, Commander," he said with a nod.

"Hurry!" Hehl yelled through the radio. "Hurry, hurry!"

Shil took a step toward the edge of the hole, and knelt down. Suddenly, she felt the coldness around her. It was not just from the air of the city, which now held so much less heat from humanity. It was the air from below. The massive opening in the ground held no heat, and could not. And its constantly circulating air seemed to pass over every point in the immediate area. She took a deep breath as she made sure the monitor behind her was still at a safe distance. Then she stood, firmed up her stance, held out both arms, and motioned the necessary command with both hands. The jolt of electric energy rushed between her gauntlets and boots and back, and the bright blue haze of the body shield poured over the front of her helmet. She felt the tingle at her neck and chin, the most exposed areas.

"Commander, what are you doing?" Hehl called.

"Don't question me, Boss," she answered. "It's a precaution."

"You think you can just jump down there? There's no winds, no streams."

"Don't you worry about that. Just look after your people."

Shil took a step forward and leaned out over the edge. She looked down, through her haze-covered visor, and ordered her system to scan. All ten heat signatures from below were still active, and strong. She could not see much beyond the rocky walls, and the deep darkness. The light from the beaming lamps around the hole only went so far and were mostly illuminating the floating specks of dust and dirt in the air. Her shield was now keeping her warmer, but it was not easing her beating heart.

"Patrolman Kine," she called. "Give me an update."

"Sensors are placed, Sir," he answered. "Monitors? Pull us up!"

In her right ear Shil heard the shifting of the lever and the hum of the motor as it began turning the spool. She looked back and saw the thick rope winding around it. Near the edge of the hole the mounted, smooth roller was guiding the rope, keeping it aligned as it was retracted. She knelt down and set a hand into the ground right at the edge. There was firmness, but she also knew that the rock there could break if impacted too hard. Looking around the rest of the site, she could see the spools getting thicker and thicker with retracting rope.

Another minute passed and she looked off to the right. A civilian descender, a thin, but strong man, grasped the edge and began to pull himself up. She looked out, across the hole, and briefly magnified her view. A tall woman boosted herself up and out with both hands and landed on her back near the spool. She frantically unhooked herself, waved her monitor away, and stumbled on her way to the nearest gate. The woman's angry, flustered cursing carried through the open line. Looking around the hole, there was still shadowy emptiness, but every few seconds another descender was climbing out. Another plume of dust was blown upward.

Unmoved, Shil called to her watchers again. "How close are you, Patrolmen?" she asked.

"We're nearly there," Rienne answered. "Another sixty feet."

"Hurry."

Shil looked down and heard a boot against the wall directly below her, and watched as Kine's white-gloved hands grabbed the edge, and then, just as fast, fell out of sight. Rock fell where he had been, and she quickly laid flat, looked over the edge, and reached down. She grabbed the inside of his arm just as he grabbed hers. As she pulled him upward he got his footing. Then, he leapt out, and flew by her, almost hitting the fence as he landed.

She got to her feet and looked off to her left. Woll was already there, slowly standing up. Then, she looked across the great hole. Rienne was not up yet, but Duuq was there, off his jumper and inside the fence, at the edge, doing the same thing she had been. The energy of his shield flickered as he reached down.

"Gotcha," Duuq said loudly.

Shil magnified her view and saw him grabbing Rienne's hand, and saw her struggling, but making it up to the edge. The young patrolman sat there for a moment, and then quickly stood and began backing up toward the fence as she disconnected the rope from her belt.

Shil deactivated her shield, and as it faded, felt the coolness of the air again. Then she turned, and looked to Kine. He was hunched over, and breathing heavily. As she approached him, he stood upright and raised his right fist in salute. She returned the gesture, and he took another labored breath.

"Let's regroup," she said, heading toward the gate.

"Yes, Sir," he said, following closely behind.

Shil unlocked the gate, slid it open, and stepped aside. Kine stepped out, followed by the saluting Woll, who had quickly made his way over. She exited behind them.

"Boss Hehl," she called through the open line. "Send whoever

83

is still able to the salvage areas. Let's close and secure the site for the day. Our sensors need time to work."

"No problem, Commander," Hehl replied. "I'll check in with you later."

"Very well. Shil out." She closed the line and then opened a new, secured one to the four patrolmen at the site before speaking again. "All of you, meet at the puller."

Walking back toward her hovering craft, Shil saw that the group of workers were still behind it, lingering. She stopped at the puller's front end and waited. Kine and Woll walked past her, passively blocking the workers, though there was little to see or hear, yet.

"Everyone is safe," Kine said, projecting his voice toward the group. "And as I'm sure some of you heard, the site will be closed for the rest of the day. Report to the salvage areas."

"Understood," one man replied before turning away.

The rest of them, acknowledging the order and following suit, turned and headed north. Shil looked back toward the site and saw Rienne and Duuq, already on their jumpers, flying in a curve around the western edge. The civilian monitors and descenders who were still there were exiting the gates in pairs. The rest were already out of sight.

Rienne and Duuq floated down on their jumpers, settling between the other two jumpers near the gate. The air from their engines poured over the ground, adding pressure to the tech in Shil's boots as it mixed with the light air from the puller. She maintained a firm stance, and the two patrolmen hopped down from their small craft, walked up to her, and saluted.

The five of them stood in a semi-circle, with an eye on each other, and an eye on the workers still headed north. After they were all at least a block away, Shil spoke.

"Are you all well?" she asked.

"Yes, Sir," they answered in unison.

"No injuries? No trouble breathing?"

One by one, they answered "No, Sir."

"Good. Patrolman Kine? You were in charge today. Before the ground became unstable, did anything out of the ordinary happen?"

Kine shook his head. "No, Sir. Not at all. It was a typical descent."

"What about the surface down there? Besides the metal, was there anything unexpected?"

"Not on my side."

"On my side there was," said Rienne.

"What was it?" asked Shil.

"I think it was moisture."

"Moisture?" Shil looked through the young woman's visor, deeper into her eyes. "How much?"

Rienne shook her head. "I can't say, exactly. I'm sure the sensors will pick it up. But, there was just something on the walls. Everything had been so dusty and dry to that point. Then, I felt the rock there, and something slippery." She looked down at her gloves and rubbed her fingers together. "It's gone now. Just dirt, as usual. So, I'd say it was water."

Shil looked around at all of their uniforms. Except for Duuq, they all had dark streaks and spots on their dense, white pants and jackets, typical residue from descending into the hole. She had a passing thought of the happenings outside the city. She had yet to share any of the information widely with her division.

"Well," Shil started. "Our spring is just a few miles away."

"But, Sir," said Duuq. "It's still on the other side of the city. Could the water even reach-"

"No," Shil stopped him, raising one hand. "You're right. The spring is very confined. This is probably…"

"Another aquifer?" asked Rienne.

"Perhaps," said Shil. "Or, something else."

They all quieted, and looked around at each other until finally all of the patrolmen were focused on their commander. Woll looked more intently at her, with hesitance in his eyes.

"What is it, Patrolman?" Shil asked.

"The metal, Sir," said Woll. "I doubt that anyone else noticed, with all the dust and all the commotion, but the shape of it was perfectly round."

Shil stared back at him, thinking. The first Lords, along with the rest of the founders, had never been anything less than brilliant. Finding a way to form perfectly-shaped metal supports, even when

Lwo was raw, and in its infancy, would not have been beyond them. "So, we know they're really there, then," she said. "That's good. Are you sure no one else noticed?"

Woll nodded. "Fairly sure. The civilians were too panicked to get a good look. That little shift in the ground may have saved us from having to explain anything."

"Good eye, Patrolman," said Kine. "I didn't notice."

"Me either," said Rienne. "Of course, I was busy slipping and falling."

Shil tried not to smile as she spoke again. "We'll have to wait for the sensor data before we can determine anything, about the metal, or the moisture, or anything else down there. You all stay here, watch from your craft, from the same points. We'll have to keep the area even more secure now."

They all replied "Yes, Sir."

"To your posts, then," said Shil.

As the four of them saluted and left her, heading back to their hovering jumpers, Shil stepped up into the puller again. The door slowly slid closed behind her, and she sat in the pilot's chair once again, and looked out. The patrolmen reached their posts quickly, with Kine and Woll hovering nearby, and Duuq and Rienne back on the far side of the site.

As they all continued to watch, she tapped the left control panel, and found the signals for the sensors they had left at the bottom of the hole. There were four of them, all symbolized by their flat, round shape, distinguished only by single digits in the short lines of code below them. As the icons blinked with activity, she continued watching, and waiting. Beyond the fence, another plume of dust floated up from below, and dispersed.

CHAPTER 6
CONVERGENCE

The day and night had passed, and Shil was looking out at the city under the morning light, watching through the high windows of the command office. She could see the high-reaching buildings below her and the steep drop-offs that were no longer filled with civilian craft flying through streams of focused winds.

Through her long sleeves she felt a coolness. The office was colder than she wished. With so few people, and so little activity within the city, the building's naturally-regulated temperature was much lower than normal. There was a measure on the panel next to the windows: 62 F. She shook her head, and breathed out, surprised that she could not see her own breath.

She sat down in her high-backed chair, in front of the wide, glowing screen of the computing station. The display was gray and empty, at least for the moment. The two smaller displays on either side, which also served as control panels, showed no incoming information, or impending trouble. She tapped the keyboard below the main screen, and an array of boxes displaying various programs appeared. In the center was the program for primary communication.

She tapped on the box and it expanded, almost filling the screen. She opened her own line and waited.

One by one, the other commanders' signals lit up in separate windows on the screen. Jaan's signal was first. She could see that he was in the Sky Tower, as its trapezoidal symbol hovered over his rank. Brun's signal included the pointed shape of the Spire. Fits's included the asymmetrical lines denoting Lwo's mountains. All three of their signals were radiating, indicating readiness. After a few seconds, Jaan's image faded into view within his window, followed by Fits and Brun below him.

"Thank you, Commanders," Shil began. "For agreeing to this on short notice."

"A day isn't so short," said Jaan.

"I have some time before heading into the field," said Brun.

"Same here," said Fits.

"Good," said Shil. "I will not delay. We have reached the bottom of the great hole here in the city. We are now referring to it as the chasm. And, we have encountered a number of issues, some expected, some unexpected."

"What was expected?" asked Jaan.

"As soon as we cleared the city's foundation, we found two of the pillars."

There was silence, and Shil could see remembrance on the others' faces. She had become accustomed to the worksite. She no longer had constant flashbacks to the shaking and collapsing in the city. And she only occasionally thought of what had led up to it. Now, the work was what mattered most. The others did not have the same luxury.

"So, the Lords have been proven honest," said Jaan. "That is good."

"Perhaps," Shil replied.

"What do the pillars look like?" asked Brun.

"They are a melding of a few different metals, all formed into what appear to be thick discs, and not deep-reaching cylinders. And they are each about fifteen yards in diameter."

"And they begin right where the foundation ends? At three hundred feet?"

"Yes. Roughly."

"And are they holding?" asked Jaan.

"Yes, Sir," said Shil. "They seem undamaged. Whatever flowed up from below during the flashing did not affect them, only the areas around them."

"But, their pressure was still a contributing factor," said Fits. "Was it not?"

"We have no reason to doubt that. Unfortunately, there was also some shaking in the chasm as soon as we found them."

"Shaking, Commander?" Jaan pressed.

Shil saw his eyes widening, and the increased concern from Brun and Fits. "Yes, Sir. We had to clear the site very quickly. But, there were no injuries. We do not yet know what caused it, but there was no increase in temperature, so likely not more flashing. That has been the case this whole time, thankfully."

"That's a relief," said Fits.

"You have no idea," said Shil. "We hope to know more once we are able to get a deeper analysis. Right now we are only getting readings through our sensors."

"Commander, how might this affect the rebuild?" Jaan asked.

"It could delay it," she said. "And it will definitely complicate it, especially given what else we found. There is water in the chasm."

"Water?" said Fits. "How much?"

"Right now it's just moisture on the walls, and some dripping. We have not found the source yet, but I expect we will soon. Also, while we continue our work within the city, I feel a scan of the ground outside the southeast quarter would be in order."

"I'm willing," said Brun. "But I hope you're also looking into your infrastructure."

Shil nodded. "We are. So far we've found that the moisture is not coming from any of our pipes. They're much higher, and seem to be solid at every point. And anything that was known to be broken or cracked has already been repaired or removed."

"If you say so."

"I do."

"And, you'll be using probes for your deeper analysis within the chasm?"

"Yes. At least to start. The ground there is very solid, harder than anything we've ever encountered on the surface. I don't know how the founders were able to carve out space for the pillars."

"The Lords would know," said Fits.

Once again, there was silence, and Shil tried to hide the agitation that was welling up within her. She had not spoken much of the Lords, not after she had learned of what happened on the Isle with her sister, and the man and the boy who were now her family. It had been nearly a year, and devotion had given way to another feeling that filled her heart when she thought of Andrew and his daughters: resentment.

"Someone else might also know," she finally said.

"If you're talking about your old teacher, I'd advise against asking him," said Brun.

"And why is that?"

"Before probing the North-South, I called him for guidance. He was not in the best state of mind. One of his closest friends is approaching death."

Shil's rising anger started to fade, as she thought of her old mentor, who had done so much for their ranks, and the land. "I'm sorry to hear that," she said. "How old is this friend?"

"Barely a century," said Brun. "It's very unexpected. And that whole village is already starting to mourn, and so are some of their neighbors in shelter Eight."

"And how long have they been ill?"

Brun shook his head. "Didn't get that far. We spoke quickly, and duty was calling."

Shil nodded. "I understand."

"This is a very difficult time," said Jaan. "As always. And Doctor Taj may be suffering more than most of us. But, we all have our duties. Let us update Commander Shil on our work outside the city."

"Agreed," said Shil, trying to set aside her sudden concern for her old teacher. "I would like to know the state of our waters."

"Very well, Commander. As planned, after Commander Brun shared his readings from the river, Commander Fits sent two from his division out north over the ocean. They also found an unknown substance in the water, and in higher concentrations. They also found something else. Commander Fits?"

"Lieutenant Orve and Ensign Rial were the watchers on task," said Fits. "After they obtained the data, and unfortunately, lost the probe they'd sent down, they were contacted by the Ice Maw. It had been knocked onto its side. And whatever hit it almost hit their gull as well."

Shil's mind began to race, running through every possibility. "Was it alive?" she asked.

Fits nodded. "Most likely, yes."

She looked up for a moment, out at the quiet city. "What kind of creature could knock a salvage ship out of the water?"

"We don't know yet. Certainly no creature any of us has seen in our lifetimes. It disappeared below the surface before any real scans could be taken. We think it may have taken the probe as well."

"I don't suppose this mysterious creature could be the cause of the contamination?"

Fits hesitated, and looked around his own space before answering. "It's not something we're considering at this time. Whatever the contamination is, it doesn't include any animal-based contents. Scans show it as completely unidentifiable. Blood and mucus, tissue and bone, waste–none of it would fit that category."

"Right," said Shil. "So, now what?"

"We have a plan," said Jaan. "Fits and I will soon be paying a visit to the shop. We will request a more robust device for a deep-ocean survey. It'll likely take some convincing, but I'm sure the special lieutenant can come up with something. If all goes well, we'll know more soon after."

"I suppose that's good enough. For now. What do we do until then?"

"Our duty, Commander."

Shil nodded. "Yes, Sir," she said, and then shifted her focus. "Commander Brun? How soon can you get scans on our southeast side?"

"Well, with everything that's happening…" Brun started. "I'd better get there today. It may be dusk, but I'll get there."

"Thank you."

"Yes, Sir."

"Is there anything else?" asked Jaan. "From anyone?"

"No, Sir," said Shil.

As Fits and Brun said the same, and they all signed off, and the three windows in the screen sequentially closed, a line opened from the worksite. Nico's signal appeared in the center of the screen.

"This is Commander Shil," she answered. "Go ahead, Lieutenant."

"Sir, we're installing the ladders now," said Nico.

"Very good. How long will it take to finish?"

"I expect a few hours. At least."

"And are any of the civilians nearby? Any nosy bosses?"

"No, Sir. I made sure of it."

"Good."

"There's something else, Sir."

"Go ahead."

"More shaking from below."

Shil took a deep breath and looked out at the city again, taking in the quiet expanse. "How much shaking?" she asked.

"Not as much as yesterday. At least not according to Patrolman Kine."

She looked back at the screen. "Is anyone hurt?"

"Not at all, Sir."

"Alright. And what are the sensor readings showing?"

"Increased moisture compared to yesterday. And, more than the usual amount of falling rock."

"And the ground?"

Nico quieted for a moment before answering. "No changes. No increase in temperature. And two very stable surfaces that seem unmoved."

"Good. Do you need me there?"

"No, Sir. Just an update. I will keep you informed."

"Very well, Lieutenant. Thank you."

"Yes, Sir. Nico out."

As the line closed, and her screen emptied again, Shil thought of the many dangers at the chasm, and Nico's likely state of mind. He had been her lieutenant for some years, but he was still fairly young for the position. He was capable, but stubborn. And the past year had been harder on him than any other in the city's division. He and Kine had both been present at the loss of a beloved citizen to the storm. But Nico had felt her slip away, had seen her disappear into the sky. And not long after, the city had endured the collapse. Nico had been more determined since then, but anytime Shil looked into his eyes, she could see something lingering.

She stood from her seat and began pacing, back and forth in the space between the windows and the wide command table. Nico had performed as well as could be expected during the demolitions and excavations. She would have to continue to trust him. And now, there was someone else on her mind. She sat back down and found the contact code for her old teacher.

She tried to settle herself. She opened a secure line to where Taj would likely be–the office, in the library, in his village. The square window in the screen glowed with empty gray. There was a familiar click, followed by a chirp. The sounds repeated for ten seconds, then twenty. She was about to close the line when the window finally filled, first with a simple line of code, and then with an image expanding from the center to the edges. Taj did not look any worse for wear. His gray braids were neat and tight, as they always were. And he was wearing the same old-looking, powder-hued jacket. It had a few more signs of wear, no doubt from his time with the ground watchers in the months that had followed the flashing. The only thing out of place was the stubble on his face.

"Teacher," she greeted him. "Thank you for answering."

"And why wouldn't I, Commander?" he replied. His voice was strong, but also revealed his age, if nothing else did. "You're one of my favorite students, still. And I don't want to risk a reprimand from the land's second-in-command."

She smiled back. "Yes, that would be a good idea. But, you have done plenty for us. And for that reason, and because it is you, Teacher, I called to personally offer my sympathy."

Taj cleared his throat. "Word really travels in this place."

"Yes, it does. How is your friend? Are they just ill, or are they truly dying?"

"He *is* dying, I'm afraid." He hesitated, looking around at nothing before looking back through the screen. "And he's younger than I am. I've known him since before I left the city, before I settled here. He's a good farmer, and he always saved some of the best from

98

his harvest for me. And I always cooked some for him, using old recipes from some of the old texts in this place."

Shil could hear the affection in Taj's voice. "I'm very sorry, Teacher. Do you know the cause yet?"

He shook his head. "No. The doctor here is perplexed. And none of her treatments have helped. I gave her some historical files on similar ailments and possible cures, but she has not found any of it to be useful. A few days ago she told me there was nothing else she could do."

"What are his symptoms?"

"Extreme fatigue. Headaches. Loss of appetite. And now, he's having trouble breathing."

"And what about you, Teacher? What do you think it could be?"

"I've fared no better than the doctor. And all I'd be able to offer anyway is information. I can't get close to him. The doctor doesn't know if he's contagious. He's been in isolation for…for some time now."

"And what is his name?"

"Erul."

Shil breathed deeply. A man younger than Taj suffering from a mysterious illness was one of the rarest things that could occur on Lwo. She could not recall the last such case. "Erul," she said, firmly, acknowledging her fellow Lwoan's presence, and life. "Again, Teacher, I am sorry. Is there anything I can do?"

"No. Not a thing." He cleared his throat again, and tried to look more intently into the screen. "How about you, Commander? How is the city?"

"Well, I can comfortably say that we are making progress. Although, there have been some hiccups in the last couple of days."

"Shaking at the worksite?"

Shil's eyes narrowed as she continued to look into the screen. "How did you-"

"Like I said, Commander. Word really travels."

"So, we have a leak? I suppose the crews need to be re-educated on *every* aspect of the work we're doing."

"I suppose. But, any near-death experiences of civilians should be shared, shouldn't they? With so little humanity, for so many centuries, every bit of knowledge about potential danger is useful for every one of us."

"Certain knowledge is useful. Other knowledge can cause unnecessary panic. There are only a few Lwoans taking risks in the city."

"That's very true."

Shil was hesitant to say anything else about the worksite, but she also knew that there might not be a better time in the near future to gain anything from her old mentor. "There is something else, Teacher," she said.

"Yes?"

"Yesterday, we found two of the pillars. The civilians here do not know, I hope."

He shook his head. "Nothing about that was conveyed to me. Just the shaking."

"Good," she said, still wondering who had shared information from the worksite, but trying not to focus on it.

"So, Commander Jaan was right," said Taj. "No surprise there. What do they look like?"

"We've only seen them from the top. They're made of a mixture of metals, and they are wide and dense. But we don't know much else. I want to start probing around them soon, but measurements and observation show that the ground there is extremely hard, probably the hardest in the land. Do you have any thoughts?"

"Yes. Leave them alone."

"We will. As much as possible. We do not want to shift or alter them in any way. We just need to know-"

"No, Commander. I mean don't go near them. Not at all."

Shil stared back at the screen, and took a moment to compose herself before responding. "That is the second time you have interrupted me," she said firmly.

Taj sighed, and leaned forward, and lowered his head. "I am sorry, Commander."

"Please explain yourself. Doctor."

"I will. The things that the Lords–both ours and the first Lords–did at the founding made this land more stable than any makeshift land should ever be. The turning of the mountain sections to form a protective circle; the placing of earthen and chemical and metal ties between islands that had crashed into each other; determining the most stable places for villages. All of it works to hold Lwo together. The city, of course, is part of that stability."

Shil nodded. "I understand. But last year, the city almost fell. And you were with us through most of the trouble. You know that the Lords have kept much from us."

"Don't you think it was for good reason, Commander?"

"Not in this case. If the land around these two pillars could be shaken as it was, then the land around the others we haven't found might be just as vulnerable. We can hardly reinforce below the whole foundation. But, what is accessible should be made as stable as possible. Don't you agree?"

Taj nodded back. "I do."

"Good. So, the ground in…our chasm here. It is much harder. Why?"

"It's just a harder section of earth."

"It's almost like solid rock."

"But that shallow, it wouldn't be. Not in that section of the land. You would have to go much further down. The Lords knew that."

"So, would a probe work in this instance?"

"Not as well as it would on the surface, but it will work. If you drill a section for it first, a probe should still embed itself, and still project its soundwaves through the ground, no matter how dense. But again, I would advise that you do not disrupt anything. Drilling even a small hole could cause unpredictable reactions."

"If that is the case, Teacher, then we may as well not rebuild where the city collapsed."

Taj stared back. "That may be your best option. It may be *Lwo's* best option."

Shil shook her head. "No. I will not assume that yet. The villages are pressed, almost overpopulated. And the shelter craft are not meant for long-term use. You know all of this. You're living through it."

"Yes, of course. But Lwo can, and should, adapt. Why risk death for comfort, as it seems the Lords did? Who's to say those two pillars didn't directly cause the pressure that caused the crack in that deepest plate, which led to the flashing below?"

"All the more reason to examine the area further."

"I suppose. Commander, there is no perfect answer here. I've given my opinion. There is little else to say."

Shil nodded back. "We do trust your judgment, Teacher. You have been a great help."

"I'm glad. With all that is happening, my years on this Earth may be few."

"Please don't speak that way. You have decades left. At least."

"I hope so. My friend would too, if it weren't for…whatever this is."

Shil nodded. "I'm sure of it."

Taj paused for a moment, looking through the screen with much more concern than he had shown at the start of their conversation. "The Lords, I think, could help you even more."

"I suppose they could. Maybe."

"Are you back in touch with them?"

Shil hesitated, as a realization shot through her heart. "*Back* in touch with them?"

"Oh. Commander, I did not-"

"What do you know?" she stopped him.

"Perhaps, over this line, we shouldn't-"

"You know it's secured. Last year, Doctor, I told you some of what happened on the Isle. We needed a simple record. But, I did *not* tell you that we were no longer in touch with them. What do you know? And whom do you know it from?"

"I'm sorry. I'm tired from all that is happening. It slipped. I should not say another word." He glanced up, past the camera, and then looked back at her. "And I haven't said another word, about what you told me or anything else. Not to anyone."

Shil respected Taj more than any other civilian. But, she could feel the heat in her chest, and her brow furrowing, and her teeth starting to clench. She kept her voice low. "Tell me," she demanded, almost hissing.

Taj shook his head. "I cannot-"

"Right now!"

Taj lifted his hands and rubbed his temples. Then, he spoke quietly. "I know that your commander and his lieutenant actually fought with the Lords on the Isle. I know that Lord Andrew was injured in the confrontation. I know that a man and his son were the cause of the conflict, and that that man has been given what I understand to be an extension of life. I know that the watchers are no longer-"

"That's enough!" she snapped, stopping him. She looked around, and sensing no one outside the closed door to the office, looked back at the screen. She tried to keep her voice low. "You know entirely too much."

"I've told no one else. I assure you."

"Who? Who told you all of this?"

"I can say that it was not a watcher. None trust me as much as you do. And it was not a child."

"Him." Shil looked up from the screen, and beyond it again, at the wide, calm cityscape. Her mind started to go numb with frustration as she stared out. She looked back down at the live image of her old mentor. "Take care, Doctor Taj," she started. "That you do not slip again, in your old age."

Taj pinched his lips together, holding something back. "I promise that I will endeavor to-"

Shil closed the line, cutting him off. As the wide screen emptied again, her thoughts went immediately to Robbins, and then to his family. Her family.

CHAPTER 7
THE BUILDER

Terre looked up from the wide display of her computer. She leaned out to her left, nearly tipping the seat as she looked toward the end of the shop's center walk. One of the wide doors above the end of the walk, at the top of the wide, metal stairs, had rolled up, revealing a red-hued bird from the sky division. Looking back at her screen, she suddenly noticed the signals of the two commanders she had been expecting. She quickly got up from her seat and descended the short set of steps out of the operations room.

She moved swiftly through the shop floor, feeling the warm air on her dense sleeves. The assembly cell was almost behind her now, but she glanced back at the lone metal fox frame that was sitting there, waiting to be outfitted. Ahead of it, on her left, was the crowded component cell. There were already watchers there, each outfitted in one of the same gray work suits that she was wearing, with their helmets retracted and their gauntlets raised slightly to allow more hand movement. They were busy arranging the re-formed plastic boxes of various tech housings and stone vanes that had been accumulated.

She continued through the walk, her steps echoing in the high-reaching, airy space, as she passed the milling and pressing cells on the right. They were empty, and the machines were idle, but that would only be the case for a short time. The watchers assigned to the cells would soon return from their scheduled break.

On her left, the raw materials cage was empty. The shop had not received a delivery in days. Supplies had been less abundant in the past year, due mostly to the flashes, and the collapse in the city. But, she had heard there had also been trouble with the salvage from the Ice Maw two days before. She had yet to find the time to gather more details. There was already enough work to do.

Cool, rushing air from the outside blew downward, surrounding Terre and lightly passing through the tech on her arms and legs as she stopped at the stairway and looked up. Dull daylight was beaming in. She was almost ready to pull her helmet on when she saw Jaan moving down the steps, followed closely by Fits. She stood more firmly. Behind the two men, the door rolled back down, cutting off the storm winds.

"Commander, Sir," said Terre, raising her right fist and saluting Jaan. He tilted his helmet up and back, revealing short, gray hair, and thick stubble. She turned to Fits. "Commander, Sir," she said again, still saluting. Fits's hair and beard were as red as ever, despite his decades at the mountains facing down the brunt of the storm. "Welcome back. It has been some time."

"Thank you, Special Lieutenant," said Jaan. "Now, at ease."

"Yes, Sir," she said, lowering her arm.

"We'll need to speak in private."

"Yes, Sir. Follow me."

Terre turned and headed back through the walk. The small control panel on one of the tall presses on the left was blinking, ready for activity. As they neared the component cell, the watchers there stopped working to salute the commanders. Terre looked leftward again, through the wide window at the back of the milling cell and into the operations room, and saw that no others had entered since she had left. They reached the short stairway to the open room, and she stepped aside, deferring to the commanders, who moved quickly up the steps. She followed behind them, and then stepped back behind her workstation.

Checking the wide display, Terre saw no changes, and nothing else that needed her immediate attention. As Fits stood near the window to the milling cell and Jaan stood at the adjacent back wall, near the shelves of flat panels and ready-to-program circuit boards, Terre stepped around her seat and checked the door in the back corner. It was still closed and locked, but as she leaned up to it, she could hear the sounds of her watchers' voices diminishing. They would soon leave the rest area and return to the shop floor.

She turned and glanced at Fits before stepping closer to Jaan. "Sir," she started. "Whatever it is, I'll need a month."

Jaan crossed his arms and looked back at her. "What happened to the deference and agreeableness you greeted us with,

Lieutenant?"

"I'm just being up front. We don't have many raw materials, and as you know, there's a constant flow of work from every division."

Fits turned away from the viewing window, and stepped closer to them. "Are you saying you're under a lot of stress, Lieutenant?" he asked, smiling. "That would explain those two new streaks of gray on the side there."

Terre reached up, and patted the right side of her pulled-back hair. "Very funny, Sir," she said. "This is not stress. This is ninety years on Lwo. You'll find out soon enough, just like our commander here has."

Jaan shook his head. "Okay, that's enough banter. We do not have a month, Lieutenant. We have, maybe, one week."

Terre looked into Jaan's eyes. They were not as intense as usual. He had softened, somehow, but he was still insistent. "A week, Sir?" she asked.

"Yes."

"And why so little time?"

"It's our water."

At first, Terre felt confusion. Then, she felt a distant fear. The storm was still unrelenting, and the flashing nearly a year earlier had been terrifying for most, but a problem with the land's water would be much worse. "And what is happening with our water?"

"We don't know yet. Two days ago, after multiple reports of

darkness in the North-South, we finally conducted a survey. Commander Brun found the presence of an unknown substance. The tanker trucks have, seemingly, been able to filter it out, and the affected villages and shelters have been filtering their water even more. But, as a precaution, we have temporarily halted deliveries of water from the North-South. And we'll be checking the other rivers."

"I saw the survey data right after the commander," Fits started. "And I sent two of my watchers out north, over the ocean. They also found an unknown substance, and in higher concentrations."

Terre shook her head. "If it's not one thing, it's another."

Fits smiled at her. "Well, after all these years, I'm sure you're used to it."

She bit her tongue. "Right. So, what can I do to help?"

"We need a craft that can dive into the ocean," said Fits. "One that can take the pressure. We have to get some sustained readings. And..." He hesitated, glancing at the walk before continuing. "We also need to see what creatures may be lurking that we have not encountered before."

"Creatures?" said Terre, her heart beating faster. "What could be there besides sharks and the schools they feed on?"

"Well..." Fits started. "While my watchers were over the ocean, they had to assist the Ice Maw. Something knocked the ship onto its side and nearly hit their gull after. We think it was alive."

Terre crossed her arms. "Great. Well, a craft can't handle an ocean dive. Not a gull, or a bird, or any other. The salvagers that come here tell us plenty about their treks. At a certain point, anything with a cabin would just get crushed, not just by the pressure, but by the currents."

"So, what *could* handle it?" asked Jaan.

"Something unmanned, maybe. The salvage ships' underfins and nets endure because of their cutting shapes and the density and malleability of the steel. But there's not much of that steel left."

"How much is 'not much?'"

"About a quarter of a ton."

"Sounds like plenty to me."

"Me too," Fits agreed.

Terre smirked back. "Okay. For something this pressing, I can probably make it work. But, a week-"

"You can do it," said Jaan, interrupting her doubt.

"*We*," said Terre. "And, Sir, I can't keep something like this secret in here. I have fifteen skilled watchers, and we all see what we all do."

"That's fine, Lieutenant. Your watchers may not traverse the land as much as we do, but they are still watchers. You can tell them as much as you feel you need to."

"I'll tell them everything I know."

Jaan nodded. "Very well."

"There's something else, Sir."

"Go ahead."

"I'd like whatever data you have from the surveys of the water. The river and the ocean."

Jaan peered back at her. "Do you really need that?"

"Sir, it could help with programming this new…machine. Whatever it turns out to be."

Fits looked at Jaan, and then reached behind his back and pulled a small, black, rectangular data drive from one of the compartments on his belt. "It's all here," he said. He stepped closer to her, and held out the drive.

Terre took the drive, held it up in one hand, and stared at it, wondering. "Now," she continued. "How does one go about obtaining this data?"

"How do you think, Lieutenant?" Jaan replied.

She looked back at him. "You used one of my probes, didn't you?"

"*Your* probes?"

"The probes that this shop built…for the divisions, Sir."

"Yes, we used two of them."

"And how did they fare? I gather not so well, given your request."

"The one sent into the river did its job perfectly."

"Mine did too," said Fits. "To a point."

"What point?" asked Terre.

"We lost it in the ocean. But, it did make it to five hundred feet before that. We were still able to get a decent amount of data, just no samples."

"Sir, those probes are based on the ones the old teacher has, only strengthened a bit. I could have told you the ocean forces would probably be too much."

"We hardly had time to ask," said Jaan.

"And we're not sure it was just the water," added Fits. "It may have been the creature."

Terre looked back at him. "If there *was* a creature."

"Data from the gull's reactions shows that it's likely. It's not much, but it is on that drive."

"Good." She turned to Jaan again. "One week?"

"One week," he answered.

"We'll do our best."

As Jaan stepped away from the wall, the sound of bustling filled the shop. Terre listened to the sounds of watchers returning to the floor. Tall men and women in matching gray suits began walking by the open side of the operations room. All of their helmets were retracted, and some of their faces were still grimy from the beginning of the shift. One by one, as they looked into the room, they stopped, turned, and saluted. Jaan and Fits maintained saluting postures until ten of them had passed by. Then one more, yards behind the rest of the group, walked up the steps.

Beed looked neither young, nor old. His light-colored hair was cut short, and his face was clean shaven, though it was also dusty from a half-day's work. He was holding a computer tablet in his left hand. As he reached the workstation, he saluted the room with his right.

"Commanders," said Beed, nodding to Jaan and Fits.

"At ease, Crafter," said Terre. She walked up, meeting him in front of her computer. "What's this?" she asked, looking at his tablet as he set it down onto the desk. There was a glowing schematic of a fox with the underbody highlighted.

"Sir, I was looking at these plans for the fox here," he said, nodding backward. "With the ground division's new specifications, we'll need to change the reinforcement brace in the center of the undercarriage. It has to have a higher arch than this. See?"

As Beed pointed, Terre ran a finger over the lines on the screen, and saw the slight difference in the curve of the newly-designed brace. "Good catch, Crafter Beed," she said. "Tell the crafters on the presses to set aside those puller brackets for the time being. The city can afford to wait. Get this piece done fast, and test it before outfitting the frame. We have another project right on our tails."

"Yes, Sir," said Beed.

The watcher turned and moved quickly, down the steps, along the walk, and out of sight. The sounds of the now busy shop floor began to rise. Through the viewing window across from her, Terre could see the pistons on the presses in the distance, moving up and down in sequences as they began to warm up. Before them, the mills were already grinding, sending sparks over and around their operators as they shaped pieces of metal.

Voices began to carry, across the walk, and through the heights of the space. Two watchers jogged up to the door of the assembly cell. Terre moved toward the steps and looked across the walk. One of the watchers stepped into the open, metal fox frame and stood in the middle. The other got down on his back, slid beneath the frame, took out a long wrench, and began working. Beed approached the cell a moment later, looking at his tablet as he entered. Jaan walked up and stood two yards to her right. Fits was right behind him.

"Is this every day?" Jaan asked.

"Yes, Sir," said Terre. "Actually, this is a slow day."

"We require quite a bit, I suppose."

"Yes. But, it is all necessary. We keep the people living, and Mother wants us to live long, as the Lords would say." She breathed in deeply, and quietly. "We can do it in five days, Sir."

Jaan nodded back. "Very well. I will see you then."

Terre descended the steps ahead of the two commanders and led them as they all walked through the shop, observing the workers as they did. As they reached the steps at the end of the walk, the commanders each reached back, pulled their helmets up, and brought them down over their heads. She heard Jaan's muffled voice as he spoke a command. The left door at the top of the wide steps rolled upward. The light and blowing coolness from the outside floated down again. Terre thought about the deadline she had just given herself. Then she thought about what Lwo would become if its water

115

were to become undrinkable.

Fits and Jaan moved up the steps quickly. As they reached the top, they turned and waved down at her. She waved back, and watched as they walked out of sight, to the rear of the waiting bird. She listened as the craft's engines roared and watched it float upward, as the heavy door rolled back down and locked.

The shop was secure, and the image of a possible design arose in Terre's mind. She walked to the right, away from the high stairway, passing the now less-noisy pressing cell. She turned left and saw the wide, solid door of the shop's secured storage room. The light above the door activated as she approached, revealing its plain green color, and illuminating the access panel. She was intent, as she input her code, on pulling three ingots of the old steel onto the floor, where she could spend the rest of her day prepping them for formation.

CHAPTER 8
THE VISIT

Idha's village was in an ideal location for Maia to visit with her family–in the mainland's southeast, halfway between the mountain ranges and the land's center. It was not far from the Sky Tower, but not so close that she would feel the constant pull of duty. And it was hardly exposed to the winds. The village's barrier wall was five stories high, and it was roofed by an electromagnetic shield, which made it safer than many other villages, and more comfortable for the boy who was now Maia's son.

The village also had more children than any other in the region. Its textile mills, which housed machines that produced little to no exhaust, were some of the least dangerous places to work outside of the city. Because of this, over the years, the villagers who had children had often chosen not to relocate. Shil estimated, based on the group sitting on the wide patch of grass behind her, and their age ranges, that there were likely close to twenty children currently living in the village.

She looked over her left shoulder at the youths. All of them wore heavy clothing. Their pants and coats were much heavier than what children in the city would be wearing, if they were there. The group was relatively quiet now, after they had loudly run by her on the way to their outdoor class. Only a small girl, who was perhaps five years old, had hesitated as she passed by, and looked up into the dark brown hood over Shil's head. There had been curiosity in her bright, young eyes, and pondering, but not full recognition. The girl had run off with a friend a moment later. Now she was at the front of the group, fully enthralled. The children in the back row–too young to be left on their own, but not yet strong enough to work in the mills–were not quite as focused on the lesson being given by the village's leader.

Idha was a tall and stout woman, with bright gray hair that shined almost like metal. She was wearing a long, purple dress with streaks of blue running through it. A thick, matching belt was wrapped around it, and beneath it, gray cotton covered her arms and neck. Shil glanced back and forth between Idha and the children, as the woman used her hands to emphasize the most important points.

"We have to remember that the land is under constant threat," she said, somehow keeping any foreboding out of her tone. "But, Mother Earth wants to keep us strong for when she is done healing."

"From the collapse?" one of the younger boys asked.

"That's right."

"But how can she keep us strong?" a girl asked.

"As scary as it may be, the storm protects Lwo," Idha answered. "And our watchers protect us. And the Lords are wise, and guide the watchers in their duty to protect the people."

Shil averted her eyes as Idha glanced toward her. Then she turned and stepped away from the wall of the large, three-story mill. She walked along a narrow, paved path toward a smaller, sand-colored mill. It was the sorting mill, closest to the village's main entry and responsible for handling and cleaning raw materials, whether they came from salvagers or other villages. Shil could smell the fibers being treated in the building. There was new cotton, and recycled fabric that smelled of mild chemicals. And there were broken-down plastics, which smelled mainly of heat.

She stopped at the nearest corner of the mill, her hood still fully raised, and looked to the wide main entry area. On either side of it, just outside the high barrier wall and within protective metal cages, high-reaching, vertical windmills spun at high speeds, generating the village's power. Shil could see the tops of the heavy vanes as they turned, appearing to touch the sky.

Between and below the high, spinning vanes, the entry area was shadowy, even in the gray light of day. She could just barely make out the front of the civilian craft she had flown to the village. It was sleek, but its black paint was dull, reflecting little light. Beneath it, between strips of short, faintly green grass, the clamps of the paved landing pad held it in place. The rest of the entry area was empty.

A thin beam of light suddenly appeared next to the dark craft, and Shil knew that the village's main doors had parted. She stepped away from the sorting mill, glanced back at Idha and her class, and then moved carefully toward the entry. Twenty yards to her right, from

119

the other side of the mill, a man in a protective, brown suit appeared. He was one of the bosses, Chon, and one of the few people in the village whom Idha had told of Shil's presence.

Chon was wearing heavy boots and had a belt with multiple holsters and tools clamped tightly around his waist. He looked to be near sixty years of age, though it was hard to be sure. His dark beard was thick, and his face was speckled with powder and fibers, nearly as much as the multi-pocketed front of his jacket. He nodded to Shil, and she nodded back before moving closer to the heavy, locked access door near the base of the windmill. She could hear the rhythmic whirring of the machine, even through the shield, as the winds above whipped through the heavy vane. As she leaned against the cold stone of the barrier wall, she felt the machine's vibrations.

The sound of wind tech engines, powerful but restrained, bellowed into the space, and then slowly weakened, as the entering craft decreased its power. Shil could not see the craft, but she knew its sound, and its familiar-looking lights briefly beamed onto the wall of the sorting mill. She heard the metal doors of the main entry close and lock. Then, as the tech engines became nearly silent, she heard the ramp of the craft unlock and begin to lower. From somewhere below, the sound of clamps grasping the craft's underbody echoed. Chon took a few steps forward.

"Welcome, Lieutenant," the boss said, smiling. "And to your family, welcome back. Elder Idha has already started with the children over there." He pointed past Shil.

120

She tugged her hood forward another inch.

"Thank you, Boss Chon," Maia replied.

As Maia approached Chon, Shil saw her from behind. She saw her retracted helmet, and her dense, red suit, and her idle tech, and her intricate braids, woven into inch-wide rows and flowing from the front of her head to the back, where they were wound into a tight ring. Robbins walked up behind her, wearing a deep blue jacket that fell almost to the knees of his heavy, gray pants. He was not wearing a helmet, and his dark, curly hair looked even thicker than it had when Shil had last seen him, nearly two months before.

"Thank you for having us," Robbins said.

"Oh, you're more than welcome," Chon replied. "Idha's always happy to accommodate when she can. It's one of the reasons we get along so well with the shelter."

"And how are things there?" asked Maia, the concern evident in her tone. "How are things really?"

"Well, they seem alright. Or, as alright as they could be. It's crowded, but it's crowded here too. Can't tell now, of course, with everyone working. But adding a hundred people to a village isn't easy. We're, uh…we're making it work."

"That's good to hear."

"Can Devon…" Robbins started. "Can he go ahead?"

"Sure, sure," answered Chon. He nodded down and pointed again toward Idha's class. "Go on, young man."

Devon stepped toward Chon, said "Thank you," and turned

away. He was walking eagerly, and then, sensing Shil's presence, stopped and turned toward her. Looking up slightly, he whispered "Hi, Auntie."

Shil approached the boy, knelt down, and tried not to smile too wide as he came closer. "And who told you you could call me that?" she asked.

She set her hands down onto his shoulders. He was dressed in blue, like his father, in the same kind of heavy fabric, and wearing similar boots. And he looked to be at least an inch taller than he had been just weeks before. The boy did not attempt to hug her, and looking into his young eyes, she knew exactly why. He had been quick to adapt to civilian-watcher dynamics, quicker even than some Lwoan-born children. He simply stood there, and smiled back at her.

"Sorry," he said. "Commander, Sir."

"Well, don't call me that either," said Shil.

"What are you doing out here with us? Is there trouble?"

She shook her head. "No, no trouble. I wanted to talk to your parents."

"But, don't you have a lot to do in the city?"

"Always. But, family is still important."

"Yeah, it is. Okay."

Shil nodded, smiled, and gently nudged Devon toward Idha's class. She watched as he walked briskly toward the group. As he reached the back row, he was greeted by one of the older children, a girl who looked to be about fourteen. She stood and walked him to the middle row. Then he sat, quietly, next to another boy who was also about eight years old. Shil could faintly hear the other children greeting Devon before Idha went on with her teaching.

"This does seem a bit strange," said Robbins. "You could have called."

Shil let the words linger there for a moment. She felt Robbins and Maia approaching, and as she stood, saw them stop a yard in front of her. Chon was far behind them, already heading back to the sorting mill. Shil looked into Robbins' eyes.

"So, you feel the same as your son?" she asked. "I should just be at work in the city?"

She walked up and patted him on the shoulder, hoping that it would make anyone who happened to look their way see her as just another civilian. She turned to her sister, and nodded, and took a step back.

"That was nice," Robbins said, smirking. "And please, don't take it the wrong way. I'm just surprised to see you. And I know my wife. She wouldn't have asked you to meet us all the way out here for a visit like this."

"You're right," said Shil. "And she didn't."

"Commander, Sir," Maia said, quietly. "Why have you come? We passed by the shelter just a few minutes ago. All looks well there. And I've kept my line open. There was no immediate trouble in the area."

"I wanted to speak to you in person. I wanted to see my

family. And, I needed a respite from the city."

"So, you tracked Maia's flight plan?" Robbins asked.

Maia set a hand on his shoulder. "They're visible to all commanders, Love. It's okay."

He looked at Maia, and then back at Shil. "But why look at ours?"

"I told you," said Shil. "I wanted to see my family. You're not questioning my intentions, are you, Robbins?"

"I'm not your subordinate, Commander. Remember? I can ask. And, it is *my* family first."

"*Easy*," said Maia. "Both of you. Please. Let's talk in private."

Maia turned and walked, and Robbins followed her back toward the entry. Shil followed closely behind. They passed the civilian craft and then passed the front of Maia's bird. They turned at its port side and moved into the shadows of the entry area. Robbins stayed near the front corner of the wall, keeping an eye on the class in the distance. Shil stood near the bird's front end. The light air passing through the craft's idling engines flowed around the bottom of her cloak. She turned to Maia, who had stopped near the short port wing.

"It is good to see you, Sister," Maia said. "How are things in the city?"

Shil glanced back at Robbins, whose attention was still divided. "It is good to see you too, Sister. The city is in decent shape, all things considered. But, there are issues in the chasm, things we could not have expected."

"You mean the shaking, and the…pillars?"

"Yes. But, there's more. It turns out the pillars have shifted in recent years. At least that's what multiple sets of scans have shown."

"How much have they shifted?"

"Not much, but enough for us to be even more cautious."

"And are there any signs of impending flashing?"

Shil shook her head. "No. We've found some hardened earth from the one that caused the initial collapse, but no more signs of molten heat."

"That's good. What else?"

"I assume you also know about the moisture that was found?"

"Yes."

"Well, the source is a stream, deep, hundreds of feet underground. It took Brun some time to ascertain what exactly the probes were showing, but that was his conclusion. Mine too. And it extends far south, possibly all the way to the coast."

"An underground stream?" Maia shook her head. "And so long? What else does Mother have in store for us?"

"Knowing her, I would imagine quite a bit more."

Maia smiled and nodded. "I would agree."

"We think the moisture from this stream may be what caused the pillars to shift. It's spreading around the bottom of the chasm walls, like the stream hit a fork somewhere and split."

Maia paused, and looked away for a moment, her eyes pondering. "Doctor Taj can help with all of this, can't he?" she asked.

"Help clarify things before you move forward?"

Shil glanced at Robbins again. "Yes, he could. But, for the time being, he is not available. He has a friend who has fallen ill, unexpectedly."

"I'm sorry to hear that. How old are they?"

"The man must be one hundred five, one hundred ten."

"A bit young for illness to set in."

"Agreed."

"Does the commander know? About all of this?"

Shil nodded. "I gave him a full report, but only a few hours ago. And I asked Brun not to share anything widely. Not yet."

Maia's eyes narrowed. "But, why?"

"The issues in the chasm could further impact the timetable for re-populating the city. We need to know more about the size and strength of the stream. We have to examine or reexamine every surface. And we have to be sure that the pillars will not shift again, not significantly anyway."

Maia nodded. "I understand. I will say nothing until my commanders do."

"I know. You've never been one to step out of line, or even speak out of turn. You are an excellent watcher, Lieutenant."

"Thank you."

"And what of your husband?" She turned toward Robbins. "I trust he can hold his tongue?"

Maia stepped closer to him and set a hand on his shoulder.

"Sure he can."

Robbins looked at her and nodded, and then looked back toward Idha's class.

"And how is marriage?" asked Shil. "It's been some months now."

Maia smiled. "It's wonderful. Thank you for asking."

"And Devon seems to be adapting well to everything."

"He is," said Robbins. He turned toward them. "He's done better than I would have expected. Better than I have."

"Well, he's young," said Shil. "He's fortunate not to know as much as we do."

"He knows more than you think." He paused, and looked at Shil. "I'm sorry, Commander, to hear about the city. I wanted us to live there when we first..." He paused again, and looked around, and lowered his voice. "When we first got here."

Maia let her hand slide down from his shoulder and onto his elbow. "And now?"

He smiled at her. "Now, we go wherever you go."

"Good," Maia said, smiling back.

Shil managed to not roll her eyes. Robbins looked out toward the class again, and happy, childlike sounds began to carry through the space. Shil stepped out from the bird's front end and saw two children, Devon and a young girl, jogging toward them. As they got closer, she tugged her hood forward again, and leaned back into the bird's cold, metal body. Maia stepped out in front of her, as did Robbins.

"Lieutenant, Sir!" said the young girl, her voice high and joyous. She was as tall as Devon was. Her long, brown hair was tied into a braided tail behind her. And her eyes were deep black. She looked up at Maia and firmed up her stance, as if awaiting orders.

Maia knelt down. "Hello, fellow Lwoan," she said. "And what is your name?"

"I'm Marlin, Sir."

"And how old are you, Marlin?"

"I'm seven years old. My father is in maintenance. My mother is a seamstress."

"Oh, that's wonderful! And what does your mother make?"

The girl pointed downward. "She makes watchers' pants like yours, except they're blue."

Maia looked down at her uniform, and then back at the young girl. "Well then, you'll have to thank her for me. Watchers feel very safe in these pants."

"Um, Marlin..." Devon started. "Don't you want to-"

"Oh, yeah!" the girl blurted. "Sir, can Devon come and play with us?"

Maia looked back at Robbins, who silently nodded. Then she turned back to the girl. "Well, where are you going to play?" she asked.

"In the park close to my house," the girl said, pointing. "In the middle of the village."

Maia glanced up at the sky, and then looked back at the girl. "I think someone will have to go with you."

"The older children will watch us."

"And what about Elder Idha?"

"She had to go to the welting mill. That's why we finished early."

Shil leaned out from the bird and looked. The class had fully dispersed, with a few children lingering in a group near the edge of the sorting mill. Idha was out sight, and Shil wondered if the elder had come to trust the walls and the shield a bit too much.

"Alright," said Maia. "Then one of us will go." She stood and looked at Shil, and then Robbins. "Why don't you go with them, Love? Keep watch?"

Shil looked down at her nephew. "Devon, will you and your friend wait with the other children? I'd like to speak to the lieutenant and her husband."

"Okay," he answered.

Devon and Marlin turned and jogged away. The youthful chatter increased as they reached the other group of children.

Shil turned to her sister. "I'd like to speak with Robbins alone, Lieutenant. If you don't mind."

Maia looked back at her, seemingly perplexed, but hesitant to respond. "What about?"

"It would be good to further ascertain how well he's adapted after nearly a year. And, we don't know each other all that well. Not yet."

Maia's eyes were still questioning. "He's adapted just fine. I've made sure of it."

"Then, I'm asking as your sister. You know I have no ill intentions. But, Lieutenant, also consider our positions."

Maia nodded. "Very well, Sir. But, you do know he'll tell me if-"

"I know," said Shil, raising a gentle hand. "I promise not to press too hard."

Maia nodded back, and touched Robbins' arm. He patted her hand and winked, and she turned away and jogged toward the lingering children. All of them, small and not-so-small, turned toward her and stood firmly, even Devon. She greeted them and pointed toward a path between two mills, the same one Shil had stood in as she awaited her family's arrival. The children turned and ran down the path and out of sight, with Maia following closely behind.

"My sister is too good for you," Shil said, turning and looking at Robbins.

He turned and walked, deeper into the entry area, and stood across from the bird's port wing. "How so, Commander?" he asked.

Shil approached him, careful to keep some distance between them. "She's kind, and considerate," she said. "And strong on top of it. And she's dedicated, to the people and to the land. You, I'm not so sure about."

"Maia is nearly sixty years old. Do you doubt her judgment?"

"No. I doubt yours."

"And why is that?" He slowly crossed his arms.

"You broke your agreement with the commander."

His eyes narrowed back at her, and his jaw tightened, as he struggled to speak. "And…what exactly do you-"

"Do not feign ignorance with me. Doctor Taj may not be available for any serious work, but I was still able to speak with him recently. It seems that as he's aging, his tongue is loosening. I know you talked to him about what happened on the Isle."

Robbins took a step back, leaned into the wall, and looked down. "Does anyone else know?"

"Not yet."

"Thank you."

"Oh, don't thank me yet. Explain yourself."

He sighed, and kept his eyes on the ground. "I just needed someone else to talk to. Someone besides Maia. Besides Jaan, or any other commander. Besides Doctor Kile. Taj was the only civilian I suspected could keep it all to himself. He's the only one who knows nearly as much as you all do."

"And what was there to talk about?"

He looked up at her. "Are you *serious*? Everything. My body is changing, I suppose for the better, but it doesn't feel natural. My mind goes back, over and over again, to my son being at the mercy of…of those lords you all love so much. What would they have done had I not awoken when I did. And, we are in the last bastion of life on…on the *entire* planet." He looked deeper into her eyes. "How is it that *you* bear it all?"

"We have borne it all from birth," said Shil. "Not what you have, but what Lwo is. Everything that it is, and every vital soul that it holds, including those of the Lords. But the burdens that come with trying to live another century so that humanity might thrive again are not reasons for disloyalty. Your sharing what you did with Taj, however you did it, is not safe. If all of Lwo found out everything that happened on the Isle, or even just where you and your son came from, it would disrupt the small amount of balance we are able to hold on to from year to year."

Robbins shook his head. "No. Everything is in order here. Trust me. And Lwoans are wise, and understanding. And they do not cross watchers."

"You did."

He looked out into the village. "Didn't you all cross me first? You offered us shelter, then you took us to the Isle, and your lords violated my basic right to choose how to live, how long to live." He looked back at her, his eyes tense. "What if I outlive my own son?"

"That is no excuse. You agreed not to speak of what happened to anyone else. And, don't forget, you married the one who took you to the Isle, took you to the Lords in the first place."

"She didn't know I would meet them, or what they would do."

"Neither did the rest of us."

"I'm not so sure."

Shil stepped closer, and looked into his eyes. They were just inches apart now, but he did not look away. She kept her voice low. "What are you saying?"

"Jaan has been extended," he whispered back. "Remember? Long before I was, he was. And he ordered that we be taken to the Isle, maybe for safety, as the flashing started. But Brun had already planned to contact your lords, if he deemed it necessary, in agreement with Jaan. So, why wouldn't I seek solace and guidance from outside your ranks?"

Shil took a single step back. She looked at Robbins' broad shoulders, and his smooth skin, and his strong facial features. She could see the strength in his tensing hands as he kept his arms crossed. And his overall muscle was evident. He was much stronger than when she had first seen him, much stronger than he would have been without the extension, even if Kile had nursed him for another six months. The evidence of the procedure was undeniable, even if only to those who knew it had happened.

"Will you tell anyone else?" he asked, his voice still low. "Your sister? Your commander?"

Shil took two more steps back, and leaned back against the bird. "Commanders hate, detest, secrets amongst ourselves. Protecting the hearts and minds of the people is one thing, but we have to share knowledge to protect our watchers and each other, so that we *can* protect the people. But still, sometimes, secrets are necessary. I care for you, Robbins. More importantly, I care for your family. I will keep this to myself. For now."

"Thank you."

"Do not thank me. I just don't want to cause any more disruption than necessary. We are all being tested enough as it is."

"I agree. We are." He cleared his throat. "I wonder, is there anything more I can do to help? Maybe even in the city?"

"Don't make any more offers you can't follow through on, Robbins. You have work in a village, and a family to look after. That's enough."

He nodded. "Alright."

"I have to get back to the city. I'd recommend you stay here, not wander off, until my sister and your son return. But, like you said, you're not under my command."

"But, I do agree with you."

She nodded. "Good." She stepped away from the bird, turned, and walked around the front end of the craft. "Tell them goodbye for me," she said. "And that duty called me away."

"I will," he answered.

Shil walked up to the port door of her black craft, found the hidden button, and pressed firmly. The door unlocked and slid backward, and she stepped up and in. As she made her way to the pilot's chair, and the door closed behind her, she tossed her hood back and breathed deeply.

She reached for the wide, glowing control panel, opened a line, and called to the ground watcher stationed outside the village to open the entry. She opened the engines, grasped the two short handles in front of her, and found the pedal below. As the clamps released the craft's underbody, and light and wind entered from the outside, she felt the storm's forces enter the engines beneath her. Looking out, she saw Robbins moving to the front of the bird, shielding himself from the winds gusting inward. He watched her as she eased the craft out of the village and slowly floated upward. He turned away as the wide, metal doors slowly shut between them.

CHAPTER 9
THE DIVE

The operations space in the north station had one flat, stone wall, and three walls of carved mountain, all formed by Lwoans three generations past. The room had held up for centuries. Only its outfittings had changed. The computing stations were less than a decade old. The mounted desks upon which they sat were now metal instead of wood. The lighting fixtures were no longer connected by visible wiring, but self-contained. They provided just enough light to see the earthen color of the walls, and to see where you were walking, and who was nearby. It was all that was needed. Fits saw no reason to use any more energy.

He stared at the screen of the computer station in front of him. It showed the view to the south, inside the mainland, and the wide, roaring North-South river below the station. A lone gull was hovering close to the mountainside, low, near the river's western bank. Its lights radiated green, a constant signal for the expected craft that they were cleared for approach. Fits increased the camera's magnification until he could see a mile south. Everything looked relatively calm. Then he pointed the camera slightly west, and saw the dark gray craft approaching.

The hauler was the simplest looking craft that any watchers used. It was wide at the front, sloping from all sides into a narrow edge beneath the windshield that helped it cut through the winds. Its underbody wind tech engines were flat, but broad enough to bring in plenty of air for high propulsion. There were short wings on either side, which each held engines for both acceleration and maneuvering. And the roof sloped up and back. From the front, if one did not look closely, it was like a plain rectangle. Fits shrank the camera view on his screen and opened a line to the craft. There was a chirp, followed by a click as they answered.

"This is Special Lieutenant Terre. Go ahead."

"This is Commander Fits," he replied. "Your pilot can land on the east side of the deck. If your hauler can fit, that is."

"You know that it will, Commander, Sir. See you shortly."

The line closed, and Fits backed away from the computer. He reached back and pulled his helmet up and down over his head, and pressed it down as it secured itself. Then he walked up to the arched doorway and looked at the ensign stationed on the right.

"Monitor landing and delivery," he ordered.

She looked up from her station, nodded, and said "Yes, Sir."

He tapped a button next to the entry, and as the metal door slid aside, he felt the obstructed, but still strong storm winds begin flowing through all of his tech. He hopped out onto the solid, metal platform and turned to see the door slide shut behind him. The winds steadied through the engines on his arms and legs and back and waist. He checked his footing and took a look around the space.

The station's dark ceiling, composed of more carved mountain, and holding an array of lights that constantly beamed down, was fifty feet up. To his left, a gate twenty-five feet high blocked the harshest of the winds coming in from the north. Above it, raw winds sped inward. To his right the platform extended another fifty feet, where it ended at the craggy mountain wall, right before the dropoff to the river and into the mainland. The sound of rushing, crashing water below was nearly as loud as the winds rushing in.

Just below his boots, between him and the other platform forty feet across from him, was the grated, metal deck. Tiny gaps in its construction allowed a partial view of the ocean water that was rushing in far below. A lone gull was hovering ten feet away, near the suspended, metal rack above the center of the deck. On the other side of the rack another gull was waiting.

Fits turned and walked toward the inland entry. As he neared the wide view to the land, the hauler approached. Its massive, dark shape cast a soft shadow within the station. He hopped down onto the deck. The metal in his boots hummed with the landing. Pushing through the cold, blowing air, he walked behind the nearby gull, toward the other side.

The hauler descended just behind the other gull. As the roar of its engines decreased, and it settled and idled, Fits approached its wide, port side ramp. The long, gray door tilted out, and began lowering. Fits stopped and waited. As the edge of the ramp touched the deck near his boots, he looked up into the cabin. There, within the hauler's simple, pale interior, and mounted on a short, metal bracket, he saw the ray.

Terre had already sent him the schematics of the unmanned craft, but the drawings had not conveyed just how striking it was. Its center was nearly eight feet long, oval-shaped, and made of a shining, black metal. At its front end, extending a few inches from the ovoid along a heavy bar, was a disc that held a camera, two small sensors, and a glowing light at the center. A short fin ran along the top of the main body and extended forward, ending in a sharp point just above the disc. From the sides of the body, two long, pointed fins sloped out and slanted back, towards its aft end. Below them, another, shorter fin, similar in shape to the fins on every gull's underbody, but more sleek and aggressive, extended down.

As light from the station briefly reflected off of the ray, Fits finally noticed the wide, shining vents on its underbody. Then, from the forward end of the hauler's cabin, Terre stepped into view.

"Not what you expected, Sir?" she called through a newly-opened line.

She saluted him as she stepped down along the ramp. The exhaust from her tech sent cloudy streaks of white flowing behind her. Her eyes were lively behind her helmet's tinted panel.

Fits saluted back, and then crossed his arms. "I think it will do," he said. "Good work, Lieutenant."

"Thank you. I will relay it to the others at the shop. Are you ready?"

He raised a halting hand and added Jaan to their open line. "Ready, Sir?" he called.

"Yes," Jaan answered. "On my way out."

Fits nodded and looked up at the ray again, and then back to Terre. "Is it activated?"

She reached toward the side of her helmet, and Fits heard her whisper. Then, looking up the ramp, he saw a burst of white air as the ray's engines opened. Wind exhaust enveloped its underbody, and most of the cabin filled with the focused air. Terre reached for Fits's left arm, and guided him back, as the ray disconnected from the bracket and floated sideways out into the station. They continued backing away as it reached the deck. The hauler's door tilted back upward, slowly closing, giving them more room. Then the ray floated back toward the large craft, and Terre took her hand away from Fits and walked, almost proudly, toward her creation.

Having exited the observation space, Jaan approached them from the front of the hauler. Terre saluted him. He returned the gesture, stopped, and gazed upon the ray. "That old metal couldn't have been this polished," he said.

"If it's going to cut through ocean water, it needs to be as smooth as possible," Terre replied. "This was the best we could do."

"It's quite impressive, Lieutenant. Fits, are you ready to pilot it?"

140

Fits nodded. "Yes, Sir. I've already gone over the programming and instructions that the lieutenant sent along with schematics."

"Very well," said Terre. "Transferring controls."

Fits could only make out some of the words in Terre's whispers–'access', 'transfer', 'on-board'–before the display in his helmet was filled with the glowing shape of the ray. He whispered his own commands to shrink the icon and place it in the bottom right corner of his view. After he was sure he had control, he whispered "Fly. Follow. Gull One." A short beep was followed by the ray's signal blinking green, confirming its flight instructions. He, Terre, and Jaan all watched as the sharp, shining craft rose three feet, glided over and around the front of the hauler, stopped behind the gull, and hovered.

Fits turned to Terre. "We have enough to operate it. Is there anything else, Lieutenant?"

Terre nodded. "Yes, Sir. I copied our basic database to its drive. Its sensors will be able to identify anything that our divisions already have. It's also programmed with the data from both drops of the probes. It knows the forces of the currents and undertows, and will anticipate and manage any dangers from the ocean that your probe previously encountered, alive or not."

"And we don't need to tether it? It can *really* handle the storm?"

"Of course," she answered, smirking behind her helmet panel.

141

"You saw the schematics. The main engine's vents are wide, and its vanes are much more durable than those in the probes. And all of the fins are strong and will help it cut through the winds and the water. It's no manned craft, but it can handle itself. We tested it and made sure."

"I'm sure it will fly well," said Jaan. "Let's go."

"Yes, Sir," said Fits. "Lieutenant, you are welcome to wait here for us."

Terre shook her head. "Not today, Sir. We have plenty of work back at the shop."

"Very well, then. Thank you, and take great care."

"Take great care, Sir."

Terre stepped aside, and Jaan walked by Fits, toward the gull near the operations space. Fits walked toward the gull in front of the hauler. He moved quickly past the ray, feeling the force of its exhaust with each step. He reached the gull's open port door and hopped one yard up to step into the cabin. The craft's body swayed gently with his weight. As the door slid closed behind him, he moved over to the starboard bench, picked up the resting, metal computer tablet, and sat. He tilted his helmet up and back, breathed in the calm, filtered cabin air, and looked toward the pilot's chair.

Rial's helmet was retracted and resting in the groove of the headrest. Her short, straight, dark hair looked duller than usual, and Fits could see the sheen of sweat on the side of her face. But, if she was nervous, she was working through it. Her fingers were busy on two of the three control panels in front of her.

"Are you ready, Ensign?" he asked.

She turned slightly toward him, and nodded. "Yes, Sir. I've already got the ray's signal pulled up. It's mirroring our position and flight plan, and I'm tracking it."

"Good. You know where we're going. Take us out."

"Yes, Sir."

Fits sat back, looked down at the tablet, and added the ray's signal and program controls to the device. The gull leapt up, and the winds pushing in over the station's high fence rushed through the engines below him. He looked past Rial, through the windshield. Gray light from outside the mountains flowed into the cabin. He saw Rial's hands and feet shift, and the gull shot forward, over the fence, under carved mountain, and out from the station.

Rial piloted the craft smoothly, taking them up higher and higher each moment and at an angle slightly less than the fifty degrees Fits would have preferred. He looked out, through the translucence of the port side door. The other gull was there, five yards away and just a few feet behind them. Ensign Murg was its pilot. He was a decade older than Rial and less likely to have any disagreements with Jaan, as rare as they were.

The gull rattled as they entered the lowest level of clouds and started to level off. Fits looked down at the tablet's screen and saw the ray's flight pattern. As expected, it was matching theirs exactly. He activated its main camera. After a moment, a wide window appeared, and a clear view of their aft end came into focus. Though the green of the gull's body was not bright, it stood out in the misty dullness of the sky.

As they continued to fly, he watched the ray's path. With each tilt, and every slight rise or brief descent that Fits felt, the camera's view shifted. He looked back and forth, between the tablet and the outside, between the sky ahead and the other gull off to their side. After some time, feeling assured that the ray's tech would endure, he found the readouts from its sensors. The data currently matched the composition of elements from thin air at high elevation.

"We're just a few minutes out, Sir," said Rial.

Fits looked up. "Already? I barely noticed how fast we were going."

"That's understandable. You seemed busy."

He nodded. "Are you alright, Ensign? I know you were a bit shaken up after the situation with the Maw."

She stretched her fingers, and then re-gripped the control handle. "I'm fine, Sir."

"Good. I brought you because of your experience flying north, and flying with me. You've never let us down."

"Thank you, Sir. I'm beginning our descent. We're right on target."

Fits leaned to his right to get a better look at the gull's center control panel. There was a blue circle, blinking around a spot two miles ahead with the coordinates in glowing text just above it. It was where Orve and Rial had encountered the unknown, unidentifiable force that had toppled a salvage ship and threatened their own. It was where lights–lights that were no longer mysterious–had passed over them. And, perhaps most importantly, it was where they had found high concentrations of the unknown substance compromising the mainland's water supply.

"We have contact from the others," Rial said. "This is Ensign Rial in Gull One. Go ahead."

Jaan's voice came through the line. "This is Commander Jaan in Gull Two."

"Yes, Sir."

"Look's like we're close. I suggest we send the ray down once we reach five hundred feet. Let's make sure it can punch through."

Fits stood, and walked up behind Rial. He leaned over her to get a closer look at the center panel and their relative position over the ocean's surface. "This is Commander Fits," he said. "I agree, Sir. Are you tracking the ray's signal?"

"We are."

"Very well. I estimate one minute."

"Same here. Keep all lines open."

"Yes, Sir."

"One thousand feet," Rial announced.

Fits went back to the bench and sat. On the tablet he found the ray's signal, next to its camera feed. "Helmets on, Ensign," he ordered, and reached back to grab his own. He watched as Rial pulled hers back up, and down over her head.

145

In his helmet's display, he found the ray's blinking icon, but kept it small, and kept his focus on the tablet's screen. He whispered a command to the unmanned craft to disengage from the gull's vector. As it confirmed, he whispered another command and saw the camera's view shift. Their aft end floated out of sight, and the view changed again as the camera was aimed downward, at the wild, cresting ocean surface.

"Five hundred feet," said Rial.

"Fly," Fits whispered. "Dive."

He watched the feed as the ray raced toward the ocean. After a few furious seconds of high speed, water splashed by the camera on all sides. What followed was clear, but dark, and enveloped the entire view. There was no visible debris, and there were no creatures, but the shaking of the camera was still evident. The ray's shaking signal in Fits's helmet confirmed it. He would have been concerned, but the ray quickly adjusted, increasing its speed and straightening its downward vector. The view steadied. He felt the gull settling, and glanced up at Rial.

"What do you see, Ensign?" he called.

"We're at one hundred feet," she said. "And the ocean surface is clear. Everything looks normal. Should we go lower?"

"No, not yet. Stay right here."

He looked down at the tablet again. The ray had already reached a depth of six hundred feet. The target depth was one thousand, where the water would be much calmer, and any kind of debris would be more concentrated and easier to avoid. The ray's speed began to slow, and as it reached nine hundred feet, Fits whispered another command. A few moments passed, and its signal blinked in confirmation. Its speed slowed more, and at one thousand feet, it stopped. Its signal blinked green once and was then surrounded with a steady glow, as it awaited further instruction.

Fits expanded the window of the ray's feed until it filled most of the tablet's screen, and then began to study. This section of ocean was a dark void. There was only faint, indistinguishable sound coming through the feed, but from the slight sways and tilts in the view he could almost feel the rush of the deep currents. They surrounded the ray and were being constantly pulled through its tech. After several minutes of inactivity, Jaan's voice entered the cabin again.

"Anything, Commander?" he called.

Fits looked up. "No, Sir," he answered. "Not yet. But, I was just about to do a visual comparison."

"Let me know what you see."

Fits tapped an icon in the corner of the tablet to bring up a file, one he had chosen the day before. In the file was a set of images, ancient, but clear, of the ocean depths before Lwo had been fully established, and before the storm had reached its full strength. He tapped on one image, and it expanded, and he saw water that was dark but had a distinct blue-green color. In the distance there was a school of large-looking fish. In another image, dated a few years later, the water had lost much of its color, and there were only a few dots in the shadowy distance that might have been creatures. Next to the current feed from the ray, however, the images were like daylight.

"No surprise, Sir," said Fits. "It's much murkier now than at the founding. I'm going to begin surveying."

"Very well," Jaan answered.

Fits whispered another command, and waited. He looked around the cabin, and out through the windows, and continued waiting. Jaan checked in twice more. A full five minutes passed before a row of fluctuating values lined the bottom of the feed. They settled at expected measurements: Temp 30 F; Speed 7 MPH; Density 85 LB/FT3. He looked up from the screen and spoke again.

"So far the readings are normal," he said aloud.

"Keep looking," said Jaan.

Fits kept his eyes on the screen as the ray began sending data on the contents surrounding it. He sat up in his seat, and nearly gasped, as he saw the values. "MMP's here are at two hundred parts per million," he said. "And there's a...much higher concentration of this unknown substance."

"How much higher?" asked Jaan.

Fits shook his head. "It's doubled. Eighty parts per million."

After a short silence, Jaan spoke again. "That is not good."

"Double?" Rial whispered.

"Ensign, do you see anything out there?" Fits asked, looking toward her.

"No, Sir. Just..."

"What is it?"

She quickly took the gull up twenty feet, and looked out. "Sir, it's the same cloudiness that we saw before," she said. "But, it's wider."

"How much wider?"

"Look, Sir," she said, pointing. "I couldn't see it before, because it goes on and on."

Fits stood from the bench, and kept the tablet with him as he walked up behind her. Looking out at the ocean, he saw it, a wide, dark shape on the surface, steady even as the currents and crests were beating through it. He set his free hand down near one of the panels and leaned forward, trying to prove it to himself.

"So it does," he said. "Commander, do you see what we see?"

Faint chatter floated through the line before Jaan answered. "We do. What else are you getting from the ray?"

Fits backed into the center of the cabin, and began pacing as he looked at the tablet again. "Nothing yet. How long should we…"

"What is it?"

"The speeds around the ray just jumped, up from seven miles per hour to twenty." He looked at the live image more closely and saw a spot much darker than the ray's surroundings, concentrated in the distance. Then, the ray's signal blinked a fiery shade of red. The camera jumped upward and then pointed down. A dark shape flew by. "I think it's our underwater friend."

"Or, one of *his* friends," Rial added.

"What's it doing?" asked Jaan.

Fits stepped to the port door, and looked down through the hazy view for any surface activity. Then he turned and went to the gull's aft end. The small, high window there was crystal clear, but he saw nothing more than the ocean, shadowy as it was, surrounding them. "I'm not sure, Sir," he answered. "It's not headed for us."

"Probably because it can't see us," said Rial. "Yet."

"That's likely. Worried, Ensign?"

"No, Sir. Just observing."

"Good. Commander, do you see anything from your position?"

"No, not on the surface," answered Jaan. "What's in your feed?"

Fits looked down at the tablet again. The image was turning, as the ray rotated in place along its center axis. It had entered into a defensive mode, revealed by its still-red signal projecting short, curving waves. But, it was also awaiting direction. He whispered a command, and the signal changed back to green and rotated. The camera turned and faced south, where the large creature had swam to.

"Things seem to have calmed down," Fits replied. "I'm resuming the survey."

"While you're doing that, point her downward, and go to two thousand feet."

He hesitated, and felt a glance from Rial before answering. "Yes, Sir."

As Fits whispered more commands to the ray, his mind went to what Jaan now wanted to look for. The only mountain watchers he had told were Rial and Murg, and only the little that they might need to know, that the commander suspected ancient structures were somewhere close to the bottom of the ocean. But he suspected that Rial, who had been closer than any others in his command to the events of the previous year, knew much more than she was letting on.

He looked down at the tablet screen, and watched as the ray settled at the lower depth. In the distance of the feed, much deeper than two thousand feet, there was something. He whispered another command, and the ray's scanning function activated. Another three minutes passed before an image was returned. Whatever it was, it appeared to be idle, and man-made. He went back to the starboard bench and sat.

"Ensign, turn around," he said, looking toward his pilot. "I want you to see this."

As Rial's seat turned, he sent the image out through a projection from the tablet, placing the box of light into the center of the cabin floor. The rendering was bright, but patchy. There was a slanted surface in one spot, with straight, upright objects just beneath it. A round, pointed piece was not far from it. Below the shapes, near the bottom of the projection, there was what appeared to be a wall.

"What do you see, Ensign?" Fits asked.

Rial leaned forward slightly, her eyes searching from behind her helmet panel. "Looks like it could be an old church," she said.

"That's what I was thinking."

"The scan's refreshing."

The projection flickered, and the arrangement of objects became clearer. If it was an old church, it had a surrounding wall that was more fit for an ancient castle.

"Whatever it is…" said Fits. "It can't be just one thing."

"We never learned about buildings like this sinking near Lwo," said Rial.

"Neither did we."

"Commander, send us the image," Jaan called through the open line.

"Yes, Sir. Sending it now." Fits navigated through the tablet's programs, found the other gull's system, and sent all of the data the ray had gathered so far through a secured channel. "Sent, along with everything else."

"We have it."

"What do you think it is?"

Jaan quietly exhaled. "Something else we'll need to learn about."

"Why have they kept so much from us?" Rial asked aloud.

Fits looked at her, and saw confusion, and agitation. "The Lords know things from centuries ago that we could never know, and maybe should never know."

"So then, you don't know?"

Fits had a good idea of the reasons for some of the Lords'

secrets, from discussions with Jaan, and from all he had learned about what had happened on the Isle with the new man and his son, but he just nodded back. "Right."

"It's not our main concern, Ensign," Jaan called, his voice stern. "They have given us what we need to do our duty."

"Yes, Sir," she answered, and continued staring at the projection. "So, do we have enough data?"

Fits looked up and out. "Sir?"

"Just a few more minutes," said Jaan.

Fits nodded, and as he was about to respond, glanced down at the feed from the ray, and saw the view shoot upward again. This time, the dark shape had gotten closer. He could just barely make out a large swaying fin. The ray continued to move, keeping its camera on the threat. The creature turned upward, and two faint, almost glowing eyes briefly entered the view.

"I don't think we have a few minutes," said Fits.

The gull's panels suddenly radiated orange, and a low, monotone caution bell sounded. Fits deactivated the projection, jumped up from the bench, and took two big strides toward Rial, who was already facing the controls and grasping the handle. Looking out at the ocean, he saw nothing in front of them. Then he looked down, through the clear section in the floor. Beyond their fin, and far below, a creature surfaced. It was a dark, wet shade of gray, with small, bright spots spread across its body. It dove back down as quickly as it had shown itself.

"Did you see it, Sir!?" Fits called loudly.

"We did," said Jaan. "Much bigger than I expected."

"Agreed."

"And the ray?"

Fits held the tablet up in front of him and found the camera feed again. The ray was moving, but slowly, trying to evade the creature's encroachments as it was rocked back and forth. "I think the forces coming from the creature are affecting the engines," said Fits. "But it's still close to two thousand feet. Sir, if we just saw one here, there must be two of them."

"Maybe more," said Jaan. "Can the ray make it up?"

"Not sure." He navigated to the ray's signal in the tablet and enlarged it on the screen. It became a diagram, glowing red, still relaying its distress. He found the engines on the underbody, and tapped. They were functioning, but the lines flowing through them indicated nearly-overwhelming currents coming from every direction. "Fly," he whispered. "Ascend."

He went back to the feed and watched as the camera spun away from the creature, or creatures, and pointed upward. He could only see the ocean's darkness. The diagram showed the ray's side fins folding downward as it opened its engines more and began to rise. It reached eighteen hundred feet, then fifteen hundred. The shadowy, massive body of a creature flew by above it as it reached one thousand feet.

The ocean's darkness gradually brightened as the ray

154

continued toward the surface. It reached five hundred feet, then three hundred. The camera view swayed as forces from somewhere below increased. It reached one hundred feet, and passed by a creature's massive, gliding body. Then, finally, it surfaced, leaping from the water. Light from the sky above filled the feed.

"Got her!" Fits said aloud.

"Is it intact?" asked Jaan.

"Checking now." Fits shrank the feed and enlarged the ray's signal into a diagram once again. The light surrounding it was green, and no parts were flashing red. "Fly," he whispered. "Face. Gull One."

He looked out through the windshield. The ray ascended, settled fifteen feet in front of them, and turned in place. The last mists of water from the ocean vanished into the winds. Fits looked at the ray's body and saw no obvious damage. Its fins were shaking lightly, but did not appear to be unstable. And the front end–with its camera, sensors, and glowing light–was steady and unscathed.

"Looks to be in good condition," said Fits.

"Good," said Jaan. "Did it get samples?"

Fits looked back at the diagram and found the ray's enclosed canister. It was filled to ninety percent of its capacity. "Yes, Sir. Nearly four liters."

"And the creatures? Was there time for it to get any scans?"

Fits navigated away from the diagram and found the ray's data files. There were files for temperature, speed, and density, and a large file for substances. There was a single video file. There were two files for scans. Opening the first, Fits saw the partial imaging for the mysterious structure they had found. Opening the second, he saw a scan of one of the creatures, taken from above. He tried not to smile so wide that Rial might turn and notice.

"Sir," he started. "The special lieutenant did her job well. We have a scan of one of them, from the second encounter."

"Very good," said Jaan. "Then, I would suggest we head back. I'm not sure how many there are, but it seems that we are in *their* territory. And who knows what they think of us."

"Agreed, Sir. We will follow you."

"Very well."

Fits took a few steps back and whispered "Fly. Follow. Gull One."

He watched as Rial worked the controls, deactivating the warnings and cautions as she turned the craft about. The ray hovered in place as it left their view. As they faced the rear of the other gull, Fits turned and walked to their aft end, looked out through the window, and saw the ray there, waiting behind them. As they sped up, it sped up, keeping a short distance between them. He turned back around, went back to the bench, and sat. The engines roared beneath them as they ascended toward the clouds.

"What were they, Sir?" asked Rial.

Fits looked at the tablet again, found the scan of the creature, and enlarged it. "Some kind of whale species. I think."

"Sir, if that's the case, then that means they've migrated here."

"I know."

CHAPTER 10
OLD LIFE

As the ongoing changes in the bottom of the chasm had continued to send hazards into its air, Shil had ordered that all watchers in the city carry filtering scarves. They had been easier to acquire than modified helmets, and were just as easy to wrap twice around the neck and still ensure tight coverage around the bottom of a helmet's visor. Standing at the northern edge of the chasm, Nico looked down at the scarf over his mouth. With its multicolored pattern and light chemical treatment, it sparkled in the light illuminating the worksite. He looked back up, and saw his steady oxygen level blinking in the right side of his visor's display.

"Ready, Sir?" asked Woll.

Nico turned his head toward the patrolman behind him, and then looked across the dark expanse in front of him. The other three watchers had already descended minutes before. He could almost see the tautness in the securing ropes next to the ladders at each of their drop points. "Ready," he answered.

He leapt out three yards. Light air from the city's street level pushed through the tech on his arms and legs and back, keeping him steady as he turned in place and floated downward. The rope secured to his belt still had a fair amount of slack. As he dropped further he looked up and briefly saw Woll, kneeling near the motorized spool before disappearing behind the curving, craggy edge of the chasm. Nico grabbed the rope with his right hand, and felt it tighten. He swung forward, extended his legs, and stomped into the chasm wall.

He was less than ten yards down. He gripped the rope with both hands and continued moving, one step at a time, along the rocky surface. Two feet to his right was the ladder, but using it would take too long. It was a failsafe, mostly for any civilian workers that might return. Watchers had not been using them.

"How's the rope, Sir?" Woll asked through their open line.

"It's fine," Nico replied. "Just keep it steady." He looked up at the shrinking opening, and past it, at the dark night sky in the unreachable distance. "How far have I gone?"

"About eighty feet."

Nico turned to look down as he continued to descend. There were lights at the bottom, but it was still relatively dark all around. He turned back toward the wall and continued his careful steps. He could see the various textures in the surface, the dense sediment littered with black and gray rock, and even some bright specks. He could also smell the earth. His oxygen level was still normal, and he was breathing with ease through the scarf, but even after dozens of descents over the past several months, he had not grown accustomed to the scent. There was an organic layer within the inorganic rock that reminded him of fields in farming villages. There was also an elemental smell, something that he could not make out, but reminded him of the plant-based oils used in some craft and tech.

"Two hundred forty feet, Sir," said Woll.

"Copy that," Nico answered.

He turned in place, and looked down again. The light from the lamps below hit his white sleeves and pant legs. The three patrolmen who had preceded him were spread around the space. He could clearly see Rienne off to his left. Her rope was loosely resting on the ground behind her as she checked her boots and gauntlets. He turned to his right, and in the distance saw Kine just as he landed, with dust floating around him. Duuq was only a presence, far away, near the wall on the south side.

Nico faced his wall again, let his knees bend to get closer, and then pushed out. The rope loosened as he glided ten feet out and floated down another fifteen. He felt the soft hum of his tech as it continued to work with minimal air. He swung back in, stomped into the wall again, and repeated his downward jump. Chips of rock and soil fell from the wall, their tiny sounds echoing as they hit the chasm floor thirty feet below. His boots hit again, and he leapt out once more, and finally straightened his body and pointed his boots toward the ground as he swung back inward. He landed firmly and reached out with his left hand to balance along the wall. Immediately, he felt the slippery wetness against his glove.

"Nice landing, Sir," Rienne called.

"Agreed," said Kine. "Not bad."

"Thank you," said Nico. "Now focus."

He turned around and got a good look at the bottom of the chasm. There were eight strong lamps, spread at equal distances along the walls that formed the mostly circular space. They illuminated the floor and the walls, where swaths of moisture reflected the light, creating an inconsistent sheen. As his rope continued to float down behind him, he walked toward the center of the floor.

The air in the space was cold, though not as cold as the city above. The ground beneath him was full of dust and scattered pebbles, and its firm, compacted soil felt harder than rock. There were a few long streaks running through it, which were not dry, but also not muddy. Nico still avoided them as he reached one of the eight sensors that were now placed around the chasm bottom. He quickly found its signal in his visor, and with a whispered command, enlarged it in his display. Then he knelt, and tapped the pad on top of the foot-wide, metallic disc.

The sensor's flat, semicircular display illuminated in green. After a few seconds, rows of data began to appear. The density of the chasm floor in the immediate area was unchanged, as was its temperature. The oxygen level, unsurprisingly, was lower than it was on the surface, but not dangerous. Nico looked again at his own level blinking in his helmet's display. It had dropped slightly.

"I don't see any new readings," he called through the line. "Do any of you?"

Sixty feet to his left, and closer to the centerline of the floor, Kine walked up to another sensor, knelt, and began working. Far across from him, Rienne was doing the same. Further away, about eighty feet to the south, Duuq was moving away from one sensor and heading for another.

"Nothing new here, Sir," said Kine.

"Same here," said Rienne.

"Same on this side," said Duuq.

Nico stood and continued moving forward, and felt the anticipated difference in the grip of his boot soles. He had crossed onto a pillar. The metal surface was almost the same color as everything around it, as if it had taken on the characteristics of the rock and soil that had encased it for centuries. But the thin, curving line it formed through the floor was unmissable in the light. It extended from somewhere near Rienne and almost reached back to where he had touched down. Nico continued to look upon the pillar as he neared the center of the floor. As he stepped off the top of the metal he felt the increased coarseness below. He stopped as he reached the humming probe.

"All eight sensors show no changes, Sir," said Kine.

Nico turned to his left and saw Kine about thirty feet away, kneeling and waiting. In his display he shrank the signal for the sensor he had just examined, and then found the signals for the other seven. One by one, the icons of the glowing discs appeared with lines of data beneath them before disappearing, until all of them had cycled through. He nodded toward Kine.

"Very good, Patrolman," he said. "We check the probe next, and then examine the walls. For now, you three stay where you are."

As all three of the patrolmen answered in the affirmative, Nico knelt down in front of the probe. The device looked stable. Nico had been the one to place it, tossing it down from a puller hovering in the second stream three days before. Before that, they had spent a day just drilling and softening a landing hole for the device to locate and then embed itself. And Taj's advice had worked. The probe was firmly set, with the end of its sharp anchor nearly two feet down. There was only a small gap between its round housing and the hard surface, where the impact had resulted in short cracks, but left no points of instability. Nico brought the probe's signal up in his display.

The icon was idle. Beneath it, extending from the pointed anchor, was an array of stacked, glowing lines, which were pulsing every few seconds, indicating the rhythmic waves being sent down into the earth. The data beneath the lines showed the wave depth, which was currently five hundred feet beyond the chasm floor, along with the temperature and hardness. The values indicated no changes since the day before. The earth below was still stable, despite the constant evidence of past shifting in the pillars. But not all of the data returned in recent days had been reassuring.

Nico had seen the deep scar. One hundred feet below the chasm there was a cut through the earth, from an unrealized eruption, a contained flash that had not broken through the city's ground. There had been too much density, it seemed, for the molten heat to find a place to escape. The compaction beneath the city, occurring over centuries of occupation, had been effective in protecting against the viscous fire, but not all of the resulting forces. The city had been shaken, only in the southeast quarter, but shaken nonetheless. Nico would have felt relief, but he knew that the pillars had contributed to the pressure that had cracked a plate deep below. And the pillars had been created to support the city, which was where most Lwoans had lived after the land's founding. His thoughts started to wander toward the Lords' many secrets. Then the probe's icon blinked red.

The rotating symbol changed back to green quickly, but the red warning had been undeniable. Nico looked around. The patrolmen were still in their places. He leaned over, and pressed his right palm into the ground around the probe, feeling. There was no shaking, no sense of anything beyond the device's steady, subdued vibrations. Then, to his left, there was a sound, something familiar, but something that he could not place. He looked, and saw Kine stand to face the wall.

"I think we have a problem, Sir," Kine called through the line.

Nico stood, and looked. "What is it?"

Kine turned, and walked. Then he stopped and turned toward the wall again. "There's some kind of pressure here," he said, pointing insistently. "Right here."

Nico jogged toward Kine's position, and as he did, heard echoes of cracking. "Everyone, stay where you are," he ordered.

164

As he neared Kine, a fist-sized rock shot past the patrolman, barely missing his helmet as he dodged. It landed somewhere near Rienne. Nico sped up. Two much larger pieces of the wall flew over his head. He quickly jumped and tackled Kine to the ground. The two of them stayed down, with their hands over their helmets, as rocks cracked against the floor behind them. After a few moments, Nico sensed a change in the air. It was the smell, a freshness accompanied by a swift drop in temperature. He felt the cold in his gloves and on his back. His tech began to hum faster from increased air movement. He got to one knee, and Kine rose with him, but they were both knocked backward by a blast of bright, chilling water.

Nico hit the ground hard, landing on his back engine. He held his arms over his helmet as the water hit his legs and pushed him further. He hit the probe, and felt the heavy, sharp blow from the metal on the top of his helmet. If the device had moved, it was only slightly. He got to his feet, and next to him, Kine did the same. They were both dripping with water, and the sound of its rushing in filled the chasm. There was already over an inch covering the entire floor, It quickly rose past their boot soles.

Nico spun around, looking. Rienne and Duuq were both rushing toward them, kicking up water with long, powerful strides. Behind them their ropes were still connected, flailing with their movements. Nico reached for the rope on his own waist. It was still tightly secured.

"Keep those ropes loose!" he ordered through the line.

The patrolmen far above them all answered in the affirmative.

"What's happening!?" Woll called back.

"The underground stream is no stream," said Nico. "It's a river. And it's just revealed itself."

"It's freezing!" said Rienne.

Nico looked down. The water was passing his ankles. The sound of it rushing in was getting louder. "Don't move!" he ordered.

Kine shot him a look. "Sir, our tech isn't built for this."

"I know that. But, I think we have a few minutes."

"To do what?"

"To examine the source. Deactivate your shields. We don't want any unexpected shocks."

Nico whispered a command and saw a diagram of a body arise, with all of his tech highlighted. He whispered again and saw an outline blink in white around the diagram, and then disappear. Then the image faded, and he looked out to see a rushing, white wave in front of them. More broken rock shot out, flying over their heads, landing in the distance in barely-audible splashes.

"It's into my leg engines, Sir," said Duuq.

"Mine too," said Rienne.

"I know," Nico answered.

He turned, and looked at all three of the patrolmen, as they looked back and forth, between him, and the growing hole in the wall, and the rising water below. Danger from water was something they rarely faced in the city. All watchers across the land had been trained to manage it, but only in minimal amounts unless they were in the ranks of the mountain division.

With the coldness and pressure of the water rising around them, the risk was increasing by the moment. And suddenly, Nico had a flashback. It was as if Loren's screaming stare pierced his eyes, and he felt her snatched away by the storm all over again.

"You three go," he said. "I'll stay."

"Sir, we can't do that," Kine said, turning to him.

Nico shook his head. "You can and you will. I can survey on my own." He looked around at the water, now nearing his knees. "I think we've got a few minutes until it reaches waist level. You can still walk. Turn your boot engines off. That'll make it easier."

"Sir we can help," said Kine. "It's too dangerous. Please, let us stay."

"I'm with Kine," said Duuq.

"Same here," said Rienne.

Nico looked around at all of them. He could see their stubborn concern even as they stood in place. "No. Go. All of you. You can watch from the ladders if you want, but I don't want to look back and see any of you even close to this water. Understood?"

The three of them quietly nodded, and then began to move, steadily trudging toward their drop points. As Kine passed by in front of him, Nico moved toward the water's source. As expected, the flow into the tech on his boots was much faster than the flow out. The water was too dense for the vanes to move freely. He deactivated the two engines, and a moment later felt the water begin to pass through the vents with more ease. But, his steps were still labored. In the distant splashes all around him he could hear that it was the same for his patrolmen. He looked around, and saw that the three of them were getting closer to their ladders. He was getting closer to the powerful water's source, and felt more of it splash into his chestplate. Looking down, he saw that it had risen well above his knees.

"Lieutenant, Sir," Woll called through the line. "Are you all safe? We can hear the rushing all the way up here."

"We're fine, Patrolman," Nico answered. "Just keep the slack in our ropes. I'm going to examine the break from the river."

"And the others?"

Nico looked around again. Kine, Duuq and Rienne were each within steps of their ladders. "They'll watch from afar."

"How close are you, Sir?"

Nico looked up, and saw the flowing water, and continued struggling forward. "Fifteen feet. Stand by."

The water was approaching his waist, and Nico deactivated the two small engines there. A chill surged through his legs, and a rush of air from the large opening blew around him. He breathed deeper. The engines in his gauntlets, and the one on his back, were still humming. He reached the wide flow of water, and stopped. It was just over his head, and large droplets were raining down onto his suit. The river's rush was no longer so furious, but the pouring wall of water was dense, and it was blocking the chasm wall. He looked up at the hole that had been created, now more than three yards wide, expecting only darkness. Instead, there was mysterious light.

Nico's entire suit was wet, as if he had just swum through the river, but most of the water was not penetrating. He felt the most moisture in his filtering scarf, but he was still breathing easily, and the cleansed air still smelled safe enough. He took another breath, exhaled, and with slow, trudging steps, moved to the left side of the heavy water flow. He was sure he could reach the opening. He set both his gloved hands into the wall, and leaned, raised his left knee out of the water, and set his boot sole against the wall. Then, in a single motion, he leapt off of the wall, toward the hole.

The tech on his arms and back worked hard to pull in as much air as it could, boosting him up as he reached for the rocky, wet edge. He nearly slipped back down, but was able to get just enough of a grip to hang on. He set both his knees into the wall and pushed, lifting himself up into the opening, and landing on his side within the heavy flow of water.

He rolled quickly onto his backside and scooted back into the wall behind him. There was still a cold flow passing over his legs. Looking up, he saw a craggy, sparkling ceiling. Pressing down with his hands, he felt the soft surface beneath him. The soil there felt like plain mud, at first. Then he began to notice the grain of the sand, and the countless pebbles within it. He grabbed a handful and lifted it out of the water. The wet soil sparkled within his palm. He looked left, deeper into the river's cave. Then, he looked up.

"Sir, what do you see?" called Kine.

Nico brushed his gloves clean, shook the water off of his helmet, and got up to one knee. The flow remained just above his ankles. "Crystals?" he answered. "Gems maybe. I'm not sure."

"Sir?"

"Above the water, from here to deep into this cave, there are shining forms hanging down." He continued to look around the cave, and then looked back over his shoulder to the opening. The chasm was fully visible, and still slowly filling. He turned to look into the cave again. "They're reflecting the light from our lamps."

"Those are probably stalactites," said Rienne.

"Sounds like it," said Duuq.

Nico looked up again, and nodded. "Of course they are."

"Just minerals then," said Kine. "Maybe you've been in the city too long, Sir."

Nico shook his head. "Careful, Patrolman."

After a short pause, Kine replied. "Yes, Sir. Just glad you're safe."

"I'm fine. I'm heading in."

"You've got another thirty yards of rope, Sir," said Woll.

"Understood," Nico answered.

Nico got to his feet, but stayed low. The ceiling was no more than a yard above his head, and even lower at the pointed ends of the sparkling formations. He took a few steps, keeping his eyes wide, looking all around at every surface. The water was still heavy around his boots, but it was flowing with less and less force and was easy to move through. The air was cold, colder than he would have expected, even for a deep cave. And it smelled of earth, and faintly of salt. He moved in another three yards, whispered a command, and watched as the light atop his helmet beamed out. He whispered again, and the scanning function appeared in his visor. He looked up at some of the formations and waited for his system to analyze. The data was returned quickly.

"The formations here are the same as those in a few of the caves under the mountain ranges," he said. "I just haven't seen any in a while."

"Neither have I," said Rienne. "Not since training."

"Then, how long has that river been there?" asked Duuq.

"This far down?" Nico replied. "From the founding, I'm sure. Maybe earlier."

Nico looked back again. He was nearly twenty yards from the opening. The river's speed was decreasing more and more, and the amount of water in the chasm actually looked unchanged, though he knew it was still rising. He thought about how long he could swim with all of his equipment on, and wondered if he would have to.

He turned and looked ahead twenty feet, and aimed his light downward. It pierced through the water's surface, revealing more soil and colorful specks beneath the flowing ripples. A new scan showed the sediment to be almost the same as what would be at the bottom of any river in the mainland above. But there was also rock, composed of the same elements they had found in the chasm.

"Ten yards left, Sir," Woll called.

Nico ignored the slight static in the line and answered. "Understood."

As he continued forward, he noticed the ceiling getting higher and the walls getting wider. He reached up with his right hand and brushed by the bottom of one of the larger stalactites. He touched another, thinner one and then grasped it. Its surface was hard, but he pushed and tugged, and was able to break off a small piece. Chips fell around him as he held the piece in his hand and stared down. A scan revealed the same information as the last analysis. He slid the sample into any empty compartment on the back of his belt, took another step forward, and immediately felt his foot drop.

He slipped, and landed hard in the water, his hips and elbows slamming into the heavy sediment. His left foot was still stable, but barely. His right foot was hanging over a dropoff, swaying well below the surface of the water. He quickly pushed himself up and leapt backward. He widened his stance, extended both arms, and looked around. For the first time since he had descended he noticed the display of his heart rate in his panel, blinking in yellow to indicate the sudden, slight increase. "Stable," he whispered. The alert slowly faded.

He still felt the pounding in his chest as he looked to where he had fallen. There, beneath the water's surface, and beyond the brown sediment, there was darkness. His scans indicated the presence of multiple life signs, which appeared as red dots on the right side of his visor. Whatever they were, they were small. They had to be for so many to fit into the relatively narrow breadth of the river. As he continued looking down, a pair of brilliant eyes neared the surface, and within the light from his helmet, the creature's colorful body and lively fins were revealed.

The fish was barely the size of his hand, and was covered in blue and yellow spots. It was staying in place, easily steadying within the flow of water. Another fish came up right behind it, but quickly turned and swam away. The one that stayed looked up at him, or his light, long enough for his system to complete another scan. Then it turned and barreled off fearfully behind its friend.

"Any updates, Sir?" called Kine.

Nico looked further ahead. There was much more cave and much more water. The darkness in the river seemed to get deeper and deeper beneath the surface. The sound of the flow was constant, and continued into the distance. "I'm fine," he answered. "I'm coming back. Patrolman Woll? Start reeling me in."

"Yes, Sir," Woll answered.

"Did you find anything else, Sir?" asked Rienne.

"Life," said Nico. He kept his eyes forward as he started backing away, pushing purposefully through the water with each step. "Sea life."

"What kind?"

He checked his display. The species had not been identified

173

yet. "Just fish. Not sure what kind, but they're small, and appear to be harmless."

"As do many creatures."

"Good point."

He stopped, turned, and looked back at the opening to the chasm. It was another fifty feet away. He turned back around, keeping an eye out for any other signs of life from the darkness. His helmet lamp continued to beam out into the distance. He felt his rope rising behind him and reached back to grab it as he continued backing away, toward the chasm.

He had felt more assured when he entered the cave, when he had pushed through his fears as if it was just another impromptu assignment. Now he felt uneasy. The land had revealed a powerful water source, one flowing from an unknown place, one that could make the city even more unstable. He looked back over his shoulder and saw that he was less than fifteen feet from the opening.

As he neared the edge, he reactivated the tech on his waist and boots. Then, he turned, took two long, splashing steps, and jumped out through the opening, up into the wide chasm. He looked down, preparing to land, and saw how much more the water had risen. He entered feet-first and felt the crash of the chilling, reflecting water as it surrounded him and obstructed his view.

Beneath his boot soles he felt the ground. As he rose up, and the water around him settled, he saw that it was just past his shoulders. He turned in place and looked. Kine, Duuq and Rienne were far from him, and still waiting on their ladders. He deactivated all of his tech, took a deep breath, held it, jumped forward, and dove down.

The water pushed through his scarf, covering his face up to his cheeks. He swam slowly, but strongly, holding his hands together and kicking for fifty feet before finally swinging his arms out and back. The water continued to rise within his helmet, nearing his eyes. His lamp was still beaming out, illuminating his path as he continued to hold his breath and swim, looking up only once to gauge his position. After a minute, his ladder was nearly within arms reach.

He pulled through his last stroke as strongly as he could, and finally touched the wall. As he stood, and felt the water surrounding his neck, he looked up to see his rope rising above him. He reached out to his right, grabbed the ladder, found the bottom rung with his boot, and climbed.

"He's out," Kine said through the line. "We're on our way."

"Copy," answered Woll.

After getting a few yards between his boots and the water, Nico stopped climbing. He held on to the ladder as he shook himself, sending water out and down off of his body. With one hand he pulled down his soaked scarf, and squeezed some of the water out of it before continuing upward. With quiet commands he reactivated all of his tech, and deactivated his lamp. Looking up, past the ladder, and the few buildings around the chasm, he saw that the night sky had not changed. But, their situation had.

"Are you alright, Sir?" called Duuq.

"I'm good," Nico answered. He shook more water off of his face and moved up a few more rungs. The status of his tech appeared in his visor. "Looks like I'll have to dry out for a while. Keep that rope secure up there."

"Heard, Sir," answered Woll.

"What do you think our next steps will be?" asked Duuq.

Nico coughed once, and shook his head, and breathed deeply. "I think we'll need to put the special lieutenant's new creation back to work."

He stopped climbing again, and held tightly to the ladder as he turned to look back down. The water was distant, but full of reflections from their sensors and lamps, which had all been displaced, and were all fully submerged. The probe, in all likelihood, had not been moved. Nico shook off more water, from what felt like everywhere, creating a mist all around him. As he turned back around, and continued moving up, he opened a secured line to Shil's home.

CHAPTER 11
CONTACT

Through the viewing wall Jaan could tell that the sun was still high. The southern sky was full of clouded light, making clear the expanse of land below and the line of the horizon in the distance. The time on the left panel at the workstation read 1:43 PM. The lines of data in the center of the wide display showed the Sky Tower's status. Their elevation was steady at one thousand feet. The winds whipping around and pressing into the tower's walls were fluctuating normally, staying around their typical speed of one hundred twenty-five miles per hour. And the tower's engines were unwavering, pulling air in and forcing it down, perfectly countering gravity. Feeling reassured, Jaan looked to the right panel, hoping, and waiting for a signal.

The observation level was fully occupied. Jaan had relieved both airmen that had been stationed at the south-facing wall, but they were still nearby, beyond the lift, standing near the two airmen sitting at the west-facing wall. No one, however, was close enough to get a full view of his screens. He looked to his right, where both screens at the empty station had defaulted to a constant display of status feeds. He looked behind the station and saw that the airmen at the east-facing wall were at a safe distance. Over his left shoulder he sensed Gerrin standing, and quickly turning his attention away.

Turning back to the screens in front of him, Jaan finally saw what he had been anticipating–a simple, blinking depiction of mountains. He reached back, pulled his helmet up, and set it down over his head. Then he tapped the signal from the station at the Southern Range and opened a line into his helmet.

"Commander, Sir," said Fits.

"I see that you're back on land, Commander," Jaan answered. "Do you have an update?"

"Yes, Sir. We made it back safely enough. The trek itself, however, was not without trouble."

"As expected."

"Yes, Sir. We were able to send the ray down off the southern coast without any issue. The special lieutenant's recommended maintenance was helpful. It dove faster and swam stronger. And, it found the opening in the earth, the one that Commander Shil and Commander Brun thought would be there. It's a little over three hundred feet down, as they said it would be."

"And, what did it look like?"

"It's fairly small, about nine feet high and less than a yard wide. The water flowing into it is strong. I'm sure the ocean currents have been pushing through for centuries, maybe since before our land masses were even situated, or had even floated north. That's why the river is so extensive. It's had lifetimes to form."

Jaan nodded. "Alright. What else?"

"The opening was dark, but as the ray got closer and aimed its light, there were visible reflections from deep inside. From scans we were able to see that the cave that's formed expands, and there are indeed many mineral deposits, much like those found beneath the city. And there is life; not a lot, but life nonetheless."

"The same species spotted by Lieutenant Nico?"

"Yes, Sir. And a few more. All small, all colorful, and all moving in the same direction"

"Away from something?"

There was a short pause before Fits answered. "Yes. More whales. The same kind, maybe the same two creatures, though I doubt it."

"So do I. Have your people been able to identify their species yet?"

"No, Sir. We've gone through every record. I'm fairly certain that it's something new."

Jaan nodded again. "I've been studying as well. I would agree."

"We'll have to name it. The ray was able to get even better images this time out. They were more concerned with eating than they were with us. With their fin positions, and large eye spots, and their rounded shapes, I was thinking something like the *giant spotted orca.*"

Jaan paused to consider the suggestion, recalling the old images of sea creatures he had recently retrieved. "Sounds fitting. The better question is, where did they come from?"

"Right. Since there weren't any whales here at the founding, at least not according to records, they must have come…"

Jaan was hesitant, but spoke the words anyway. "From the outside?"

"Yes, Sir. From the outside."

"More evidence that the storm is not as protective as we once thought."

"Maybe it's dying down on the edges, allowing things to push through."

"Maybe. Alright. What else, Commander?"

"Well, the largest sea creatures here that were noted at the founding were sharks. The thing is, Sir, we haven't seen any sharks; not in this outing, or the last."

Jaan paused, thinking. "I wonder if they've gone extinct."

"Possibly. But given their initial numbers and typical lifespans at the time, I think it's more likely that they were all eaten by these whales."

Jaan shook his head. "What a terrible way to go."

"Wild animals accept nature's ferocity, even better than watchers do."

"Indeed they do. But my concern now is what these changes in ocean life mean for the ecosystem, and whether or not they're related to our water issues."

"The new water samples from the ray haven't been fully

analyzed yet, but I can tell you that they're clearer than the ones we got from the first outing."

"That could be a good sign."

"Hopefully. Have you been able to identify the substance yet?"

"No. Not yet."

"Same here," said Fits. "There's no element or composition like it in any texts, any old files. Nothing. And with our new friends arriving, we need more expertise."

"Like Doctor Taj?"

"Yes, Sir. I think so. Or, a recommendation from him."

"And we'd need it soon."

"Agreed, Sir."

"We'll have to meet, discuss this as a group. I will make plans. In the meantime, contact the other commanders. At least you can let them know what you've found."

"Yes, Sir. We'll look forward to your call. Fits out."

As the line closed, Jaan looked down at the screens, and then out through the viewing wall again. The landscape looked normal, but he could sense something, a pressure, from beneath the land and around it. He wondered how much longer they would, or could, go without using the water flowing in from the ocean. He wondered if the ancient, underground river now flowing into the city was the only one. He wondered just how many of the new, massive creatures lurked in the depths, and if they posed any threat beyond disrupting ocean salvages.

He focused on his breathing, keeping it steady, and looked around the room. The airmen were all still focused on their own tasks. Gerrin and the other standing watcher had moved further away, to the wall facing north. He turned back to the workstation, and seeing no alerts, opened a small, square window in the right panel.

The window was dark and empty. He kept it on the left side of the screen, out of easy view if someone were to approach. He entered his access code, and five of his personal files came into view. From there, he navigated to a folder he had simply labeled 'S' and tapped to open it. It prompted him for another code, and he entered the one he had created a day earlier, which was twelve characters longer than the previous code. The dark window blinked once, and a bright, blue circle gradually appeared. He could see its small reflection in his helmet panel. He looked up and out through the wall. No one was in his peripheral vision.

The blue circle of light began to pulsate, growing from a dot to a wide circle that filled the square every three seconds. Layered beneath the circle was a simple map of Lwo that included both the mainland and the Isle, which was near the top of the window. At the bottom of the window, a row of eight ticking symbols indicated the scanning frequencies from the tower's auxiliary communication array. Upon entering the level thirty minutes earlier, Jaan had discreetly locked the rest of the division, excluding his lieutenant, out of the array for a period of three hours. It was enough time for the obscure signal of the system in the sky to appear, he hoped.

Maia and Malo had been able to identify the mysterious system's unique signal patterns after their encounter. The bird's system had passively scanned the unmanned craft as Maia had communicated with it, and it had saved as much of the data as it could before the craft had disappeared. Later, Maia and Malo had deciphered some of the coded information, and identified the patterns, and passed their findings on to him. But, he had not told either of them when he might use what they had found. Now, with all that was pressing upon the land, and upon him, he had no choice. The Lords–the most aged Lwoans, and those most familiar with the land's ecology–could offer sound guidance, if they would forgive him, and if they would listen. He patched the audio feed from the auxiliary array into his helmet and began listening for anomalies. The sound was steady in his left ear–soft, electric, and pulsing with the same beat of the blue circle.

Long lines denoting signal frequencies began to appear in the square window, but they were all too familiar. One was from the Spire, the land's second-strongest antenna after the tower. Two more came from birds that were en route back to the tower. Another, not far from the mountains in the southeast, was from shelter Thirty-two. The bright circle continued to pulse, from the center to the edge of the map-filled window, completing its cycle over and over again.

"Sir?" an airman called.

Jaan looked over his right shoulder and saw Gerrin standing there, three yards back with his arms firmly at his side. Jaan shrank the window without looking, raised his helmet, and spun his chair around to face the young watcher. "Go ahead, Airman."

"Sir, we've picked up a signal," Gerrin said. "It's from the Isle."

Jaan stood, slowly, and approached him. "Are you sure?"

"Yes, Sir. It's been a while since we've seen the Isle's signal, but we're fairly sure."

Gerrin stepped aside and extended an arm toward the north-facing wall. Jaan walked past him. As he moved between the lift and the west-facing wall, he could feel the attention of the entire room. He approached the north-facing wall and walked up behind Dilah, who was seated at the workstation on the right. As he stopped, and looked down at her left screen, he saw the familiar symbol–a diamond surrounding a slim, triangular peak–flickering in golden lines. He stepped closer, and Dilah quickly stood and moved aside. Jaan did not sit, but tapped the symbol, and began searching in the window that opened. There was no indication of an attempted call, or a message. There was just the symbol, and then, below it, the symbol of the Sky Tower appeared, making it clear that the signal had only been sent to them. With a few inputs he rerouted the signal to his station and then closed the window.

"I will respond to our Lords," he said aloud. Then he turned and walked. "Back to your duties, Airmen."

Boots thumped and seats shifted as the other watchers obeyed his order, and Jaan returned to his seat at the south-facing wall and spun around to the station. He pulled his helmet back on, and again heard the steady pulsing from the auxiliary array. He opened the small, square window again and saw no changes in the repeating scan. He opened a slightly larger, rectangular window and found the signal from the Isle. As he stared down, the golden lines continued to flicker, almost in a pattern, as if a message was in fact being sent. Then a small, blinking cursor appeared below the symbol. At the same time, there was a blip in his right ear. He looked at the smaller window again, but saw no changes within the pulsing blue circle. Looking back at the flickering symbol, he saw text, slowly appearing behind the shifting cursor.

COMMANDER, JAAN. DID YOUR LIEUTENANT FAIL TO WARN YOU?

Jaan almost spoke in response, but caught himself. He shifted the two windows up within the screen and brought up an on-screen keyboard below them. Then, below the unprompted text, he typed a response. *Warn me of what?*

OF THE USELESSNESS IN TRYING TO TRICK ME AGAIN.

So, System in the Sky, I presume?

OF COURSE, COMMANDER. YOU WERE SCANNING FOR MY PRESENCE, WEREN'T YOU? WHAT IS IT YOU SEEK?

Jaan glanced at the square window. There were still no changes. He continued typing. *So, you are there, then?*

ALWAYS.

And, where are you exactly?

THAT IS NONE OF YOUR CONCERN, WATCHER. OUR LORDS WERE NOT PLEASED WITH YOUR LIEUTENANT'S ACTIONS; ACTIONS, NO DOUBT, ORDERED BY YOU. I WILL ONLY FOLLOW PROTOCOL.

Have they programmed you to avoid us?

UNLESS FOUND, YES. AND, ONE OF MY CRAFT WAS JUST INCHES FROM ENTERING YOUR SCANNING FIELD. LOOK NOW.

Once again, Jaan looked at the small square. A row of digits from a new signal had arisen, north of the mainland. It matched the pattern he had been searching for. He typed again. *I see.*

SINCE YOU WERE CLOSE TO FINDING ME AGAIN, PROTOCOL WAS THAT I SEND THE SIGNAL OF THE ISLE. NOW YOUR WATCHERS WILL KNOW THAT THEIR LORDS ARE ALIVE AND WELL, AS ALWAYS, DESPITE MANY MONTHS OF SILENCE. AND, YOU CAN REST ASSURED THAT YOU WILL NOT YET HAVE TO TELL THEM WHAT YOU DID TO OSTRACIZE YOURSELVES.

Jaan shook his head, and started typing again. *We had no-*

STOP, COMMANDER. ANSWER MY QUESTION. WHAT IS IT YOU SEEK?

Jaan typed quickly. *The same thing that my lieutenant sought. Guidance from our Lords.*

AS EXPECTED. HOWEVER, THEY OFFER NO

GUIDANCE. GOODBYE, COM-

Stop! Our water is contaminated!

There was a pause, and the pulsing from the auxiliary array was the only sound Jaan could focus on, until a pattern of blips arose, followed by another text response.

IT IS NOT. OUR LORDS ARE MADE CONSTANTLY AWARE OF THE WATER'S STATUS.

But, how?

THROUGH SAMPLES FROM THE OCEAN, NOT THAT IT IS ANY OF YOUR CONCERN.

Then, they have not sampled from where we have. An unknown substance is flowing in from the north.

There was another pause, and Jaan patiently waited. He looked up, and then calmly looked around the room. All of the airmen were still focused on their own duties. Looking back to the screen, he saw more words appearing from the Lords' system.

THERE HAVE BEEN NO REPORTED DEATHS SINCE LAST YEAR.

Jaan's eyes narrowed in confusion. The system's reasoning was imperfect, or, at least, its programming was. *And? No death does not mean that there is no danger.*

VERY WELL, WATCHER. THIS, I WILL REPORT TO OUR LORDS.

What will you report?

YOUR CLAIM OF CONTAMINATED WATER FROM THE

NORTH.

Thank you, System. And what of the new, large creatures in the ocean? The whales?

OUR LORDS ARE AWARE, AND HAVE BEEN. THEY POSE NO THREAT.

One of them attacked a salvage ship.

WRONG. IT PROTECTED ITS HABITAT.

It could have caused death.

BUT, IT DID NOT. AND, IT WOULD NOT HAVE. I WAS THERE.

We know.

I KNOW. GOODBYE, COM-

Jaan typed furiously. *What of the great structure in the depths of the north?*

OUR LORDS ARE AWARE. IT IS ALSO NONE OF YOUR CONCERN. NOW, LEAD WATCHER OF LWO, DO YOUR DUTY. IT IS OUR LORDS' ONLY COMMAND FOR YOU. GOODBYE.

Jaan started to type again, but all of the text in the window suddenly disappeared, along with the symbol of the Isle. He looked back to the square window and saw that the signal from the unmanned craft had disappeared.

He stared at the wide screen, and then deactivated the keyboard and closed both windows. He looked left, to the other screen, and saw that the tower's status had not changed. Raising his helmet, he quietly, carefully breathed, in and out. He listened to the low chatter of the airmen behind him, and then stood from his seat, and walked past the station, toward the viewing wall. Looking out at the horizon in the south, he was sure that there was little else he could do on his own.

CHAPTER 12
FOCUS

Brun was not comfortable, not just sitting and waiting. Looking out from the Spire's second observation level, nearly three hundred feet above ground, he felt an agitation. Jaan had called for a meeting of commanders. And based on what Fits had told him just hours before, there was more than enough cause for it. But evening was approaching, and Brun preferred to be on the ground as light faded, to see to it that shift changes among his watchers went smoothly, and to get a good look at the night sky.

He looked around the room. The high-backed seats at the other three workstations, with one facing north, and the other two facing east and west, were all empty. Behind him, the snow at the base of the nearby mountain sparkled, even in the dim light of dusk. He turned back around, and jostled in his chair. His gauntlets and back engine always seemed to crowd the seat. Every generation of ground watchers had been slightly larger than the last, and his was no exception. He tried to settle himself, and looked past the wide, glowing screen just below his shoulders, out through the heavy, curved glass wall facing south. The thin lines of the narrow doorway to the surrounding platform were almost invisible.

In the village below, smoke and steam steadily billowed out from nearly every roof, only to be whisked away in the winds as soon as they were expelled. Beyond the rows of flat-roofed, tightly-spaced homes that were on either side of the main road, he could see the lights of two foxes, both stationed near the village's unmarked edge. The two privates on board the foxes would be watching the land, especially the space around two shelter craft that had settled just a mile away.

The shelters, numbers Seventeen and Eighteen, had arrived, and permanently idled, in the days following the last flash. In the months that followed, those at the Spire had become accustomed to their presence, and the presence of the citizens that inhabited them. At least once a week a small group from each shelter had embarked on a carefully guided trip to the village, to become more accustomed to the environment, to prepare for a future less certain than one that would be spent in the city.

To their credit, Brun's fellow villagers had adapted well. The displaced Lwoans had been welcomed into many homes, and some had even stayed a night in one of the few unoccupied buildings. But, the village at the Spire was unlike any other in the entire land. There was no barrier wall, and no electromagnetic protection from above. One night of howling, pressing winds, winds that were only ambience to Brun and his people, was all that even the bravest of the visitors had been able to take.

The wide, glowing screen blinked with white light and then settled to a gray background, as three windows opened. In the top window was the signal of the Sky Tower, and in the adjacent windows below it were the signals of the city and mountain divisions. Jaan's live image appeared first, and the concern in his eyes–a distant worry that their leader rarely showed–was immediately evident. Brun straightened up in his seat, as Shil and Fits appeared in their windows.

"Greetings, Commanders," Jaan said through the feed. "I apologize for the short notice, but I believe it is the best time, given our circumstances."

Brun disregarded Jaan's uncharacteristic apology as he answered. "It is not a problem, Commander, Sir."

"Thank you, Commander. I thought it necessary for us to go over everything. With the knowledge that Commander Fits has shared with you by now, I believe we are nearing the limits of our burdens, and that at least one issue must be resolved, and quickly."

"Agreed, Commander, Sir," said Shil.

"Agreed, Commander, Sir," said Fits.

"Agreed," said Brun.

"Very well then," said Jaan. "Let us first understand what it is that is happening in the ocean. Commander Fits?"

"Yes, Sir," Fits answered. "As all of you are now aware, a new species has emerged. I have shared with each of you the images retrieved by the ray, and a proposed name until we have something more official. For now, I will simply refer to them as whales. Based on the two outings with the ray, and looking at the distance between the three encounters, and the historical movements of similar creatures, we have estimated that there are between sixty and seventy of them in our oceans, between the land and the edge of the storm."

"Quite a few, then?" asked Brun.

"Yes. At the moment, they seem to pose no further threat to us. I will share the data we've gathered on the creatures with the salvage ship captains, if you agree, Sir."

"I do," said Jaan.

"And those of us at the mountains will also have to be more cautious when going out. The whales at the southern coast seem to be chasing their prey into the underground river, which, of course, now flows into the city."

"We were able to analyze the scans of the small fish," said Shil. "They also pose no threat, beyond drawing whales closer that is."

"We did the same," said Fits. "And came to the same conclusion. What's surprising is that they have lasted this long. In the past, such fish did not dwell so deep. It's likely that the changes in their shallower habitats forced them down."

"That is no surprise," said Brun. "As the Lords would say, nature has more wisdom than humanity."

"Yes," said Jaan. "As they would say. Go on, Commander."

"Outside of these issues, there is the matter of the water," said Fits. "We are still working, but have yet to identify the mysterious substance. I have sent a message, discreetly, to Doctor Taj, requesting his assistance. In the meantime, we are still testing filtered water samples. So far, we've found no traces of the substance after treatment here at the mountains. So, should we consider allowing it to be consumed again?"

Jaan shook his head. "Not yet. Not until we know *exactly* what it is."

Brun nodded. "Agreed. The villages and shelters still have some weeks worth in their stores."

"Understood," said Fits.

"Thank you, Commander Fits," said Jaan. "Commander Shil? What is your status in the city?"

"Yes, Sir," said Shil. "The influx of water into the chasm has ceased, stopping at a depth of seventy-two feet. It has been a day, and it seems that this may be its natural stopping point. Based on data from the lone probe that is still at the bottom, the status of things deep below our foundation is unchanged. Above ground, we have halted demolition of the last few structures until we determine if adjustments need to be made.

"With the sensitivity of the issue and the potential dangers from the chasm, the civilian workers in the city have been kept away from the worksite for the time being. I am sure, as confined as the city is, and as few of us dwell within, that most of them know about the influx of water. However, they are all focused on completing the salvage operation. That being said, I will temporarily suspend bringing in any more workers. We have received more than enough requests to come to the city since my last address. My lieutenant and I have selected several dozen qualified, capable Lwoans, but they will not yet be contacted."

"Very well, Commander," said Jaan. "Thank you."

"Commander Shil?" Brun said, turning his eyes to her feed. "How long do you think it will be before you can continue with demolition and begin reconstruction?"

"Reconstruction..." Shil started. "Is a distant thought. And I do not know when demolition will continue. We will work as quickly as possible to assess the stability around the worksite."

"As I'm sure you know, the dangers in the Middle Lands remain the same. The storm rumbles over every expanse, as always. And the sheltered citizens have not grown any more courageous."

Shil peered back through the screen. "What do you mean?"

"The fear that they brought with them last year has barely subsided. I receive reports of worry and panic almost daily, and I have seen it myself. They are approaching their limits, just as we are, especially given your announced delay for returning to the city. The timeline you provided is-"

"Is the best case scenario," she stopped him.

"But, it is far from ideal."

"I know that. We all know that."

"Yes," Jaan interjected. "We all know. And we are all frustrated, but let us not lose ourselves to this. All troubles are still temporary, as long as we press through them. Now, this is a good time for a proper report from the ground. Go ahead, Commander Brun."

"Yes, Sir," said Brun. He took a breath, and glanced out at the village. "The weather on the ground is unchanged. It threatens, but is relatively stable. Our sensors at the various flash sites have detected no sudden spikes in temperature, nor have they detected any increased temperature at all."

"That is good news," said Jaan.

"Yes, Sir. However, the land at the sites remains hardened, and infertile."

Jaan nodded. "Understood. Go on."

"As I was saying, the strain in the shelters and in the villages is increasing. The people have been able to adapt at a basic level, but it is clear that there is no real sense of stability. Stress from increased occupation in villages, and those villages' lack of shelters as failsafes, is tangible. The people as a whole remain relatively cordial, but I believe the recent concerns over the water could make things worse in the villages that depend on rivers. Until we have a real solution to at least one of these issues, the comfort and hospitality in every village and shelter will be tested."

"Have a little more faith, Commander," said Jaan. "We are Lwoans. We are strong. The people are strong."

"Many are, Sir. But citizens, those born and raised there, have not been able to adapt as easily as those who were already here, in nature. That is why the timeline for the city is much less than desirable."

"We can't risk lives for comfort," said Shil. "And, if necessary, I will speak to this issue. In fact, I may soon have to."

"And why is that?" asked Brun.

Shil hesitated, looking to some unknown place in the city before looking back through the screen and answering. "There is another problem. I fear the city will no longer hold the number it once did."

Brun pinched his lips together, and then quietly, almost whispering, responded. "I figured as much, Sir. I just wanted you to say it."

"Well, I have," said Shil. "It's out of our hands. The influx of water has changed everything. It's not feasible, at least not currently, to rebuild where so much has poured in. As old and compacted as the deep soil of the chasm is, moisture is still destabilizing. Our data from the probe indicates decreasing hardness in the parts of the floor that do not contain metal. It's likely that the walls have been affected in the same way. And with the number of buildings already lost, and those yet to be demolished, I estimate that ten percent of the city's previous occupants will have to remain outside the city."

Quiet swept through all of their feeds. Brun contemplated the number. Ten percent was roughly ten thousand people. He looked up, and out, beyond his village, and beyond the nearby shelters, to the expanse of the land. Night was getting closer and closer. "That's equivalent to nine shelters," he said, looking back at the screen.

"I know," said Shil. "I wish it were not the case."

"We all do," Fits added. "But, it makes sense. You're right about the water. You'll only be able to stabilize so much of the area around the chasm now."

"I agree," said Jaan.

"Then, we need another city," said Brun.

Jaan shook his head. "Stay focused, Commander. We all know that we no longer have the resources. And even if we did, it would take a generation, at least. We have to adapt."

Brun could still see the minor strain in Jaan's eyes from an invisible stressor. Even with the confident words of guidance he had spoken, it had not decreased. He ignored it again. "I am on the ground every day, Sir. I doubt that ten thousand people will adapt for the long term."

"They will," said Jaan. "They will have to. All of the people have always known that our numbers might eventually require more homes. And they have always known that the city has limits. We will adapt, and so will they. And we will find the ones that are most able."

Brun nodded. "I'm sure we will have to."

"I understand your position, Commander. And so does Commander Shil. And she knows her people. She can best address their concerns, when the time is right."

"The time is now," said Shil. "The sooner they know, the better."

"I agree," said Jaan.

"And what about a plan?" asked Brun. "A plan for fewer

people in the city. A plan that does not rely on shelter craft. They weren't built for long-term use. They could falter."

"If I may," said Fits. "We *do* still have some quarries near the mountains. They're not currently active, but there are some resources left."

"So, more villages?" asked Brun.

"Yes," said Jaan, nodding. "Perhaps one, with basic accommodations. It might be built in a year."

"But where?"

"Wherever you say, Commander."

Brun quieted, and thought. He thought of the farthest points of the mainland, of the places near mountains, where the fewest villages had been placed. He thought of the most fertile areas that were still unoccupied. He thought of the old machines he had found with Taj's help the previous year, and where they had been placed after being repaired, and how much effort it would take to move them again to help prepare any suitable build site. Then, he breathed out, and spoke. "I can find a place. We could build something, something that may hold up to two thousand. Maybe."

"That's a start," said Jaan. "Perhaps you should address the land as well. What do you think, Commander Shil?"

Shil nodded. "I have no problem with that, Sir."

"Very good. Then, we are all in agreement."

Brun nodded, as did Fits and Shil. But, he had one more question. "What of the sky, Sir?"

Jaan hesitated, and then calmly spoke. "A reasonable question, Commander. The sky is unchanged. Now, let us coordinate discreetly before the land is addressed. Jaan out."

As they all saluted, Fits and Jaan's windows both closed, but Shil remained visible. Her window expanded until it nearly filled the screen. Her dark eyes were intense. Her face was still, but Brun could see her readiness. She was always ready. He tried to choose his words carefully. "Sir," he said. "I know that it is not your fault."

She nodded back. "Well, so do I. And…I know that you are right about my citizens."

"I suspect they have more strength than they have shown, somewhere. Their ancestors are our ancestors."

"I would agree."

"So, when do you think we should address the people?"

"The day after tomorrow. Early."

Brun nodded. "Very well, Sir. I will see you in the city."

"Very well. Shil out."

As her window closed, and the screen went blank again, Brun stood from the chair. He stepped away from the station, looked around the empty space again, and then walked up to the narrow door facing south. He reached back with his left hand and pulled his helmet up and then down over his head. The door slid open, and the high winds filled all of his tech. He angled his body to move through and carefully stepped out onto the platform. His heavy soles felt stable on the metal surface. The sudden chill was slightly comforting. The exhaust from the vents on his arms and legs shot out and back at an upward angle, keeping him pressed down.

The sky was still darkening. The horizon was less and less visible. But the lights from the shelters remained. They blinked steadily in the distance. In front of them, the lights of two foxes were getting closer to the Spire. Their pilots were, no doubt, ready to return home, to turn their duties over to two fellow watchers of the ground. Brun whispered a command, and the day's duty schedule appeared in his helmet's display.

CHAPTER 13
THE IN BETWEEN

The heart of shelter Eight, like every other shelter craft spread across the land, was like a great hall. The space was longer than a row of ten houses at the Spire, and the height from the floor to the ceiling was over forty feet. From where he stood, near the sealed doors at the aft end, where the muted sounds of the winds continually rumbled through, Lero could see movement on all four levels.

The first level was wide, with the open floor stretching fifty feet across and extending to the front end nearly two hundred feet away. The people currently on the level, citizens who had been displaced for nearly a year, were moving hastily, going in and out of the large kitchens on the left side, and the large lavatories on the right as they prepared for the day. There were a few dozen children, more than Lero was used to seeing. But most children from the city had settled in shelters, and not the more exposed villages. It was early, and both the children and adults were noisy, and through the noise Lero could hear their anticipation.

Looking up, he could see more people moving along the grated walkways on all four sides of the second and third levels. The empty space between the walkways was narrow compared to the first level, but still allowed an airiness within the crowded shelter. The many doorways to the many private rooms on the levels were opening and closing constantly. There were close to three hundred private quarters, arranged in symmetrical patterns along the shelter's high walls. Lero had examined some of them. They were fairly small, but warm.

The shelters had been designed well, and with great foresight, long before the storm had reached its current strength. Once settled on land, a shelter craft would trap any heat from below, pulling it in through the long anchors attached to its frame. With the additional heat they absorbed from available daylight, shelters were warmer than most villages. But the people in Eight, ever wary, as all Lwoans were, still dressed in heavy fabrics, and even wore boots as they moved about.

The shelter's top level held only a few living spaces, and they were mostly occupied by the chosen elders, and in some shelters, though not in Eight, a councilor. From the ground level Lero could see the narrower space at the top, and some of the natural light coming in from the observation spaces. But he could not see any activity near the front end, where the bridge and the operations center were situated. The shelter's operator was there, along with Elder Fogg. He had spoken to both of them upon entering a half hour before, when they had welcomed him, expressing hope that his presence would limit any negative reactions from the scheduled address. After he had settled in, they had gone up, taking the stairway at the forward end, to facilitate the reception of signals and feeds that would be incoming.

The shelter's shared screens were spread around the first level, thirty feet apart, and mounted just below the second level's walkways. With his helmet retracted, Lero checked the time on the screen closest to him. It was 8:14 AM. The text on the screen read 'Upcoming: Important Update on Stability in the City.' Shil, along with Brun, was to appear and address the entire land in just moments. Lero knew from the lieutenant that it was not good news, that, among other things, the city's capacity had been significantly diminished. All of the details had not been conveyed, but the orders for the day had included maintaining peace in all of the shelters. It was the only reason that Lero was inside, instead of watching the land and listening to the address from his fox.

As the time on the screen reached 8:15 AM, the image changed. A chime rang out, the text faded away, and a live feed of Shil appeared. The image quickly expanded, revealing Brun standing behind her, his helmet retracted, his strong, full beard almost hiding his intense demeanor. Lero stepped away from the aft doors and began walking. As he moved, people began to gather around the screens. On the second level the people stood near the railing, looking down. On the third level the people looked out at two large, flat projections that had materialized from lenses near the ceiling. Their hazy images cast more light down into the space. Lero reached the center of the first level and turned toward a screen. The people seemed to be avoiding him, even as the crowds around the screen grew. They all watched, and waited.

"People of Lwo," Shil started, her strong, raspy voice echoing through the shelter. "I am Commander Shil, of the Watchers of the City, and Second Lead Watcher of Lwo. I am joined by Commander Brun, of the Watchers of the Ground. As you have already been informed, we must share important information about the stability of the city. To begin, we must go back to what happened after the collapse in the city last year.

"Though it has not been widely shared, the collapse, which ran from the southeast quarter all the way up to the city's park, created a deep crater. The crater grew deeper and deeper each day, for weeks. Those of us working in the city now refer to it as the chasm. It no longer grows, but it is nearly two hundred feet wide and three hundred feet deep. It lies between the seventh sectors in the city's south."

Lero heard the rise of low chatter from the people around him, and looked. They were still listening and watching, but he could hear their surprise at the first revelation. Some of them exchanged glances, while others whispered lower and lower. Shil continued.

"We thought that we would be able to fill it in," she said. "That the rubble left from the buildings lost might be repurposed. The ground at the bottom of the chasm remains strong. However..."

As Shil hesitated, Lero saw something fleeting in her eyes. She looked into the camera as if it were planned, for effect. But, Lero knew her well enough. Whatever the emotion was, it had not slipped by him. She quickly continued.

"However, as is often the case…" she continued. "And as we have all experienced, Mother Earth has forced us to alter our plans. Water, water from a deep, underground river has broken through the wall of the chasm, and now fills much of it. It has stopped at a depth of seventy-two feet, but it is dense and not completely calm. It is the ocean that has broken through, into the land beneath the city. And it has even brought with it some precious sea life. But it has also weakened the compacted soil. And so, we will not be able to rebuild where the chasm lies, nor in the immediate area. What this means for you, the people, is that some from the city will be asked not to return."

Shil paused again, and the chatter in the shelter picked up. A number of people, some close to Lero, and some further away, became visibly agitated.

"What!?" yelped a young woman, as she picked up her small child.

"Not me!" said an older man.

Up above, it was the same, as people were almost leaning over the railings, as if they had misheard what Shil had said. The entire shelter was chattering nervously. Shil spoke again.

"I know that this is difficult to take," she said, her voice still carrying. "But here, you will see the gravity of the situation."

An image appeared next to Shil in a brightly-outlined window. It was a live video feed of the worksite in the city, being taken from a height of about five stories. As her and Brun's image slid aside, and the image of the site expanded, the darkness of the chasm, and its breadth, and the damage to the nearby structures, became clear. There were audible gasps in the shelter, as the image of broken, nearly-fallen building faces surrounding a seemingly endless pit filled the screens and projections. The people's chatter continued, but there was less anger in their voices.

"I can only imagine what is running through your minds," Shil continued, leaving the image of the site fully expanded. "To be completely forthcoming, the number that must remain outside the city is not small. It is ten thousand. But, only those of you who can manage outside the city will be asked to take on this burden. No children will be asked. None with compromised physical ability due to age will be asked."

"That's still most of us!" a woman said loudly.

Lero took a deep breath, and finally spoke, looking up and projecting his voice. "Please, keep quiet," he said. "Let the commander finish."

The voices in the shelter lowered, as Shil went on, with her and Brun reappearing.

"It will take weeks of planning and consulting with your elders and councilors to determine who will be asked to take this on. Also, please know that the ground watchers have agreed to begin plans for a new village, a village that can safely house many who are asked to remain outside the city.

"So, we ask that you do not worry. Your shelters remain safe.

207

We, the Lwoan people, are no weaker. We are strong. And if we maintain our strength, the strength of generations who have all endured in the midst of constant calamity, we will only become stronger, and more ready for when Mother forgives us and restores herself.

"Speak to your leaders. Listen to the watchers. And as always, if you must brave the storm, take great care. Shil out."

A hush fell over the shelter as the screens went dark. Only the current time was left displayed, glowing, like the heat of emotion left from Shil's words. Lero looked around and observed the people. Most of them were still looking toward the screens. Then, after a few quiet moments, they began to disperse. Some of them commented loudly as they departed.

"Next time it'll be another year added!" one young man joked.

"Bet you a kitchen shift it won't!" another man replied.

"What will it be instead then?"

"My guess? A faulty shield."

"Ha! That's a bet!"

"You two stop that!" an older woman shouted down from the second level. "You saw that hole, or chasm. There's constant danger, and they're doing all they can. Everyone just settle down."

A man a few feet from Lero quietly said "We have to laugh sometimes, to keep ourselves from crying."

Lero stepped closer to the man, set a hand on his shoulder, and gently squeezed. The man nodded back, and walked off toward the front of the shelter.

The people continued to spread out, going back to their morning rituals and daily routines, disappearing into kitchens and narrow lifts, and going up stairwells at the forward and aft ends. But they were moving slower than before, and they were not as noisy as they had been before the address. Each resident of the shelter had, it seemed, accepted the announcement, accepted the evidence of yet another trouble. Lero knew that Shil's careful wording had helped.

In his right ear, Lero heard a familiar beep. He reached back, and pulled his helmet up and down over his head. The call was from Jore, who was stationed at the village just south of the shelter. "This is Private Lero," he answered. "Go ahead."

"This is Private Jore. How is the shelter?"

"Doing well enough, surprisingly. How's the village?"

"Not so good. They're very upset by all of this, understandably. And they're not interested in listening to reason, at least not from me. There's a crowd gathering around me near the entrance. They're asking questions that I cannot answer."

"Understood. Don't act just yet. I'm on my way. Lero out."

Lero turned and marched toward the shelter's front entry, drawing looks from all around as his boots clanged against the floor. He ignored the attention and picked up his pace. As he neared the forward end he looked up, toward the bridge. He slowed down as he saw Fogg leaning over the highest railing, waving down through his bulky, dark sleeves, with his white hair reflecting light from a window somewhere near the roof. Lero waved back, and kept moving forward as he opened a line. He watched as the old man turned and walked. A moment later his voice came through the line.

"Yes, Private Lero," said Fogg, sounding strong despite his many years. "How may I help you?"

"I must depart to the village," said Lero. "How do you feel about your status here?"

"I think…I think we are well, Private. Better than I anticipated. If we need help, we will call. We thank you for your presence."

"No need. It's our duty. Lero out."

The line closed, and Lero approached the right side of the high archway that covered the entry. There, he saw the glowing keypad. He entered his code, and the large button above the keypad turned green. He looked back, and seeing that no one was within twenty feet, he hit the button. The echo of heavy, disengaging locks filled the immediate area, and Lero looked back again. People were stepping even further away, as they were no doubt accustomed to doing.

The pair of heavy doors slid apart slowly, and Lero stepped up to the windy gap. His tech engines dispersed most of the wind, and as the opening widened to three feet, he quickly turned his body, stepped out, and jumped to the covered keypad on the right side. He hit the glowing button, and the doors stopped. The mechanism clanged as it reversed itself, and the doors slowly began to close. Lero stood there until he saw the doors touch and heard the locks engage. Then, he jumped down the short ramp to the hard ground.

His fox was still anchored by its pointed tail, with its wings angled up at seventy-five degrees. The heavy winds flowed through all of his tech as he took long, swift strides for ten yards and then lowered his shoulder and leapt up into the fox's floorboard. As its tail was pulled free, he kept his knees on the board and reached up with his left hand, grasping the control handle. With his right hand he held on near the starboard wing until the fox leveled off. Once he was steady, with the fox fifteen feet up and gliding, he set his boots down firmly into the squared sections on each side. Then he turned south, knelt, and pulled the handle down. He took one last look at shelter Eight as he sped by its starboard side.

The village was only a few miles south, and already visible in the distance. Lero would reach it in moments. He wondered what exactly he would find. As he got closer, the construction of its high barrier wall was more evident. He could see the lines of the methodically-stacked arrangement of natural and manufactured stone. Above the east and west sides of the wall he could see the whirling tops of the vertical windmills. As he neared the heavy entry doors, he saw the shadow being cast by the boxy metal frame that surrounded them. Within the shadows, the access pad to the right of the doors glowed.

Jore's fox was anchored off to the left, with its status lights intermittently blinking yellow, indicating a normal level of caution. Lero guided his fox to the opposite side and decreased his speed. He turned slightly west, stood more upright, and then stepped back heavily with his right leg. As the fox pointed upward, he reversed its engines, and after hovering for an instant, it dropped tail-first into the ground, firmly planting itself. He quickly let go of the handle, pushed off, and whispered the commands needed for his tech to adjust and guide his landing. As his boots hit the ground he turned away from his fox, and then jogged up to the village entry. Stepping into the dark entryway, he input his code, and listened as the doors unlocked.

The farming village had no covering shield, but as the doors opened a great amount of light was revealed, more than usual, more than what was coming from the clouded sun. Lero stepped through the narrow, bright opening and immediately saw why. Jore's lights were beaming from five points: his helmet, his shoulders, and his arms, which he was extending toward a crowd of at least forty people. Though he and Jore were a head taller than most of them, none of them were small, and only a handful of them looked to be over seventy years old. Lero heard the doors lock back behind him, walked up near Jore's left side, and gently placed his hand on his shoulder. The line between them opened once again.

"I see you," Jore said, tilting his head back slightly.

"They're fairly quiet," Lero answered.

"Only because the beams are so bright."

Jore gradually lowered his lights, but kept his arms extended toward the crowd. The people were keeping their voices low, but without their squinting, Lero could better see the emotion in their eyes. He looked around and saw two large, metal-housed screens, mounted into the stone wall just above eye level, ten yards away from either side of the entry. They were not only displaying the current time, as those in the shelter had after the address. The current temperature and the storm's wind speed were also being shown.

Turning and looking beyond the crowd, he saw the dozens of patches of crops and the dozens of machines tending to them. But there were no people working any of the land. He looked beyond the fields to the buildings in the distance. The main path, in the center, was busy with people walking about. Some of them were coming toward the entry.

"What have they been asking up to now?" asked Lero.

"Who will have to stay behind," said Jore. "And why aren't the watchers working faster? And what about all the undamaged buildings and spaces in the city?"

"I've never seen farmers this upset. How many people from the city are here now?"

"Not many. Maybe twenty. No roof shield made it harder to place many here."

"Right. I remember. So, it's not just the displaced causing this much disruption."

"No. But, some of them are here, right in front of us."

Lero looked at the crowd again, and noticed two men near

213

fifty years of age, and a woman a few years older. They were all dressed in slightly more colorful, less distressed clothing. Their eyes, along with everyone else's, revealed an intense agitation. Lero moved a step past Jore. He lifted his hands up, keeping them open, trying to encourage calm. Then, he tilted his helmet up and back. It settled in place near his right shoulder. He heard Jore's helmet do the same.

"People," Lero started. "Fellow Lwoans. We understand your frustration. The entire land is facing the same challenges. We do not want to cause anyone discomfort. We are still, and will always be, grateful for the village's open arms and the willingness of citizens to settle here."

"Why aren't you working faster!?" a woman in front, the one clearly from the city, shouted. "There's death lurking out here!"

Lero looked around again. He looked up. The winds were loud, but passing over, as the high walls had been designed to let them. He looked down and saw the woman's boots, boots heavier than what was needed in the city, but no heavier than those he had seen in the shelter. He looked at the boots on those standing around her and saw the same. And he saw that everyone, despite the breezes flowing through their lapels, and around and through some of their hair, was stable on the compacted ground beneath them.

"There is no more danger here than usual."

"That's not what I meant! It's-"

"Quiet, citizen!" an older man shouted from the back of the crowd.

The people turned toward him and began stepping aside, making a path. There were two people following closely behind Taj: a woman over seventy years in a long, heavy white coat, and a man clearly near one hundred years, dressed in light shades of brown. Taj was well over a century, but still strong. His skin was firm. His thick braids were gray, but full, and tightly wound. His bluish, powder-hued jacket was visibly worn, though evidently not too much for him. Looking at the trio, Lero saw that all of their eyes were heavy. Taj set a gentle hand on the quieted citizen's shoulder as he passed by. The woman nodded, and seemed to settle some, but her eyes remained tense.

"Doctor Taj," Lero greeted him, lowering his arms. "Thank you for your presence. Perhaps you can help settle your people down."

Taj looked up at him. "Perhaps, Private…"

"Lero."

Taj nodded. "Lero. As you and Private Jore both know, the people here have been through a lot. It is a village with less protection, but we still work hard. We've learned to sleep through the howling storm, just as you do at the Spire. The farmers diligently till the land, so that many may eat, and eat well. And even those here from the city have been patient as they have adapted. But, we all have limits. And Commander Shil's address was too much. At least today it was."

"And why was it too much today?"

"We've just lost someone here."

Lero squinted back at him. "Lost?"

215

"A man. No, a friend, who fell ill some weeks ago. He died this morning, very early. His name was Erul."

Lero took a breath. He looked to Jore, who shook his head, making it clear that he had not been made aware. Then, he faced the crowd again. "Erul," he said with a nod. "We are sorry for your loss. The land will mourn."

"Thank you," said Taj. "We know that all things will proceed, as is customary. But, this was not a normal death from an illness. Erul was old, but strong, as all of us here are. The doctor here..." He nodded toward the woman in white. "For a long time, she was unable to find a cause. But last night I had a hunch, and I followed it. I tested the water we still had left from the inlet to the south. It had already been filtered and treated. No water is perfect, but there was a trace amount of something left in this sample, something not documented in our databases. It's likely the same thing that other villages and shelters dependent on the rivers have also noticed, so it was not a complete shock."

"You're supposed to be using your stores of water," said Lero.

"We are, Private. Now."

"Good. So, what did you do after this test?"

"I expanded it. The doctor allowed me to check a sample of Erul's blood using the same methods. And the same substance, unknown, but with the same characteristics, was there. That is what killed our friend."

Lero shook his head. "It killed your friend, but hurt no one else? How?"

Taj peered back at him. "Erul had a rather strict diet. He was stubborn, and some things he just wouldn't eat, like potatoes, and kale. Over the years, we noticed that he would get ill more often, and we warned him to bolster his diet, but he would just take some herbs and recover fairly quickly. But this time, when he fell ill, it was different. We didn't think much of it at first, but there was no good reason for the symptoms he experienced, the kinds of pain he felt, and for the length of time that he did. We watched, from a safe distance, as he slowly suffered, and got lighter and weaker each day.

"Now, that water from the inlet was mostly used for irrigation. We generally do not drink it. But sometimes, if a farmer gets thirsty, and their canteen is empty, they'll go to the basin instead of all the way back to their home, or the bar, or the store. Erul was one such farmer. And he's the only one over seventy that anyone's seen go to the basin for weeks. And no one else has fallen ill. I'm sure it was this unknown substance that killed him."

Lero felt disbelief, and a growing fear. "If that is the case, Doctor, then I have to report it as such. And you won't be able to bury him right away. Someone from command will have to confirm what I report."

Taj nodded. "We understand. And since your leaders must be informed anyway, then I will wait to share the test results with them."

"Oh? And why is that?"

"After all I've done, they would advise you not to ask me that.

Don't you agree?"

Lero hesitantly nodded. "Fine. I am sorry it came to this, Doctor."

"All of us are."

"There's nothing more we can do at the moment. Will your people be able to manage now?"

"Manage!?" someone yelled from a few yards away.

Lero looked out, and lifted his hands toward the crowd again. "Fellow Lwoans," he started. "We are all suffering. And we recognize that you are suffering, perhaps a great deal more. But life demands that we continue on. We cannot wallow and sulk in adversity."

"We only need answers," someone else replied. "Not pity."

"The commander shared what she did, the same thing that was shared with the entire land. I have no more answers for you at this time."

"Why not!?" a man yelled.

"We have experts and doctors for a reason."

"But every watcher's an expert!" the man snapped back.

"But not in every field. We all have different strengths. Every watcher is where they belong. Every commander is guiding them toward answers. Now, can you all endure?"

"Someone has to tell the Lords!" another man yelled out. "About all of this!"

Lero aimed one open hand toward the man and raised his voice more. "I am sure that the commanders will. However, all of this takes time."

"Big surprise!"

Lero raised both his hands higher, almost touching Taj as he lifted them over his head and spoke again. "People, I will ask again. Can you endure?"

A quietness spread over the crowd. All of them were looking back and forth, between themselves and up at him and Jore. From behind, Lero heard the shriek from Jore's gauntlets and felt the heat from the electromagnetic energy that had surrounded them. He reacted in kind. He quickly pulled his helmet back on, and with a precise motion of his fingers, activated his own gauntlet shields. As the bright blue energy surrounded his forearms, he shifted his right foot back and widened his stance. He sensed Jore move back and off to the right, properly spacing for possible action. He spread his arms further apart, and watched the people. They were all, suddenly, backing away, but slowly.

"We do not wish to enforce in this way," Lero said loudly, his voice slightly distorted by his helmet and the lingering energy. "But, we will if we have to."

"Wait!" yelled Taj.

Lero watched as the old teacher turned and motioned for the people to go, urging them to return to their work. The fear and anger in their eyes remained, but they listened. They backed away faster, keeping their eyes on him and Jore. Then, one by one, they turned away, and began to disperse. Most of them made their way back to patches of crops. A few of them walked further, into the blocks of buildings. After a few minutes, only Taj remained. He turned to face Lero again.

"Private, that was not-"

"Yes, it was," Lero stopped him. "You are wise, Doctor. You know that humanity is small. We can hardly afford uprisings, especially now. The storm is strong, but Mother still cares for us, and we have to be ready–unwarring and united–when she is ready to show us mercy."

Taj nodded calmly. "I know, Private." Carefully, he raised one hand. "Please. Will you lower your weapons?"

Lero obliged, motioning commands with both hands, and watching as the energy from his gauntlets was pulled back. Behind him, he heard Jore's gauntlets as they also weakened. He kept his helmet on as he looked back at Taj. "Will your people endure, Doctor?" he asked. "Or, do you all need more supervision?"

Taj shook his head. "We are in pain, but we will be fine. When will you tell Commander Brun about this? About Erul's death and what I have to share?"

"Right away. And, I'm sure he will come quickly."

"And, when do you think…that the Lords will be told?"

Lero peered back at him. "You know that that is not up to me."

"Yes." He nodded. "I do."

CHAPTER 14
ENGAGEMENT

The streets in the village were quiet. Midday had come and gone, but not without some commotion. Every watcher of the sky that Robbins had seen, or passed by, had been talking about Shil's address. He had overheard one conversation in the morning, right after it ended. And after his shift at the south end of the barrier wall, he had heard even more. At home, Prynn had only mentioned it briefly before leaving for the day, expressing her concerns for friends in other villages. Devon had been fairly quiet. But now, leaving the village hospital after their monthly visit with Kile, his son seemed anxious to talk. Most of the blue-clad airmen in the hospital had been unusually liberal with their words.

"Dad, are you scared?" Devon asked.

"Ha," Robbins scoffed, as they stepped out onto the street. The usual, lingering presence of light air floated around their boots. "We've seen much worse than this, son."

"I know, I know. But, I've never heard the watchers talk so much about anything."

"Well, this is probably something they haven't dealt with

before. At least, not in this generation."

"Yeah, but the first watchers had it way worse, Dad. There were only a few places to live, and sometimes they had to sleep outside in much weaker shelters than we have now."

"Sounds like you've learned a lot."

"I have."

"And in your lessons, has where we came from come up?"

Devon hesitated. "The outside has, yes. Nothing about us, though."

"That's good."

"Prynn isn't nosy. And I think the kids in Idha's village are afraid to ask me much because of Maia."

Robbins chuckled. "Maybe."

As they walked on, and their two-story home came into view, Robbins looked up. The hazy energy of the shield was barely noticeable, and the gray of the clouds loomed, as always. The sounds of the howling winds were muffled, but constant. When he looked back to the street, he saw a familiar group of airmen approaching. They were fronted, once again, by Gerrin. He tried not to focus on them and moved left, toward the side of the street their home was on, guiding Devon in the same direction. The boy kicked a pebble. It bounced once before a waft of air carried it off course.

"Hello, Robbins," Gerrin called.

They were only a few yards from their door, but Robbins stopped, and pulled Devon back a step, as the young watcher

222

approached. The other four watchers kept walking. All of their helmets were retracted, and they nodded at Robbins as they passed by. Fatigue was in all of their faces, and one of them had visible bruising on his neck, but did not appear to be in pain. As they moved along, toward the hospital, Robbins looked back at Gerrin, who was standing two yards in front of him. He looked less tired than his friends.

"Hey," Devon said, looking up.

Robbins looked down at his son, almost surprised at his forwardness and lack of formality. "Devon, that's not how we greet a watcher," he said.

"Right," Devon answered. "Hello, Airman."

"Hello, young Lwoan," Gerrin replied, nodding down at him. "How is your day going?"

"Fine. How about yours?"

"Not as fine as I'd like. There were some rough outings through the clouds today. And there was Commander Shil's address. Did you see it?"

Robbins interjected. "We did. Quite a predicament we're in."

"I'd say so," Gerrin said. "Mother Earth continually tests us. But..." he rubbed at his neck. "We continue to press on. Wouldn't you say, Robbins?"

He nodded. "I would."

Gerrin nodded back, and Robbins nudged his son, and took a short step toward their home, but Gerrin spoke again.

"Are you afraid?"

Robbins shook his head. "No. Are you, Airman?"

Gerrin's eyes remained steady, but he replied hesitantly. "A little."

Surprised by the response, Robbins pressed him. "Why? You've been trained for this. And trained well."

"Yes. We all have. But this time, this circumstance, it seems different."

"How so?"

"For one thing, the people haven't been stretched this thin since the founding. We hear reports from the ground. Our village is strong, because of us, because there aren't many civilians. But many other villages are struggling. There was already a long timeline for the city, and then came the issues with the river water, and now this."

"Right. But I'm sure the commanders can handle it."

"I'm not so sure. The people outnumber us. Even the ground watchers couldn't stand up to everyone."

Robbins looked down at his son, who was looking up at the young watcher, mostly with admiration. Devon was still somewhat in awe of watchers, not just because of their general size, but because of their impressive uniforms and unique equipment. Whenever the boy saw Maia working on her tech, he would sit down and watch, smiling. He looked back up at Gerrin, surprised at what the watcher was saying so freely, but also wondering if the words were sincere.

"The ground watchers are strong," said Robbins. "And so are the other divisions. And the people respect all of you a great deal.

They are only being human."

"And how about where you come from?" said Gerrin. "Just how *human* did you see people behave?"

Robbins stared back at him. "As human as you, or me."

"And did you ever see a watcher have trouble with a civilian?"

He shook his head. "Never."

"Good for you. But, it does happen. And I suspect that our leaders may fear it."

"Airman, this doesn't seem like something you should discuss with-"

"You're the perfect person to discuss it with, Robbins."

"How do you figure?"

"For a Lwoan man over fifty, you seem uncomfortable. It's subtle, but it's there. And I've noticed it more since you married the lieutenant."

"Ha. I didn't even know you before that."

"But, we saw you. Our village is not nearly as big as most, and you were new, so you and your son stood out."

"So what?"

"So, you were comfortable, at first. You got your job. You worked. You took care of your son. Then you married. After that, you became more apprehensive. I think, since being wed to a leading watcher, that you've learned more about how they think, how they operate, and it changed your perspective."

Robbins suddenly realized just how observant Gerrin, and likely many others in the village, had been from a distance. When first settling in the village, he had, in fact, been more comfortable. Having learned so much about the lords, and what had happened on the Isle when he was unconscious, and having been strengthened by the lords' extension procedure, he had felt confident. He had knowledge, and the upper hand. Then, he fell in love with Maia, and they married, and soon after he wanted safety more than anything, for him and his family. And he became less willing to hold anything over Jaan's head, to risk stability for influence.

"I'm right," said Gerrin. "Aren't I?"

"You wish," Robbins answered. "The lieutenant doesn't reveal much to me."

"Maybe. Maybe she does, and you just don't notice."

Robbins looked down at Devon, and squeezed his shoulder. "Son, you can go home now. I'll be in after a while."

Devon turned and looked up at him, confused. "But, I don't wanna leave you here to-"

"Go on, Devon," he stopped him. "Do you need help with the door?"

The boy shook his head and sighed in exasperation. Then, he turned and walked on, passing Gerrin. He made the short walk, approached their door, and input the access code. As the door slid open, he grabbed it, and used most of his young strength to push it aside. Then he entered, and slowly pulled the door shut. From the short distance, Robbins heard the lock engage. Then, he turned back to Gerrin.

"You're pressing up against the line of protocol, Airman," he said. "Discussing these things with a civilian, and in front of a child? What exactly are you getting at?"

"Protocol, huh?" Gerrin answered with a smirk. "I think you know plenty, Robbins. But, I apologize for-"

"You're not sorry. Just get to it."

"You're right." He took a step closer, stopping within arm's reach. "I'm not sorry, so I will. Our leaders are hiding things. I can feel it. So can others."

"You're young, still. Young in the ranks. How would you know?"

"I may be young, but I'm experienced. I've been in the ranks long enough. I was here last year. There was a day when we were ordered out of observation for a meeting of three leaders. That is not so strange. But, not long after, the flashing started. A couple of days later, we were ordered out of observation again, this time for the commander to meet with an airman, a woman I haven't seen since. Then, right after, there was the collapse in the city. We managed to get through it, and the people endured, and things seemed relatively normal for a while.

"But now, all of a sudden, we have Shil's announcements of the city's troubles, and the water issues, all happening at once. And at the same time, the lieutenant takes an unexpected trek with Airman

Malo, who suddenly doesn't care to share mission details. And two days ago the commander ordered two of us away from our stations in observation so that he could work alone. And he lives for instruction, so he never shifts more than one of us at a time.

"All of it adds up to things being kept from the rest of us. I suspect your wife, being so close to command, and taking secret trips, knows why."

Robbins tried not to show his concern over the young watcher's words. Gerrin had begun to notice unusual occurrences around the same time that he and Devon had arrived from the outside. Those days had been tumultuous, but, for the most part, he and his son had not been aware of the commanders' actions. He knew what they had done for the two of them, and that they had been very discreet. For that, he was thankful. Now, it was another challenging time, and the leading watchers were, apparently, being so discreet as to cause doubt within their divisions.

"So, this is why you're so interested in me?" Robbins asked, smiling. "You think I can share some supposed secrets?"

"That, and I could use a strong ally."

"Ally? For what?"

"For confronting them."

Robbins shook his head. "You're a bold one, watcher."

"So are you. Coming to our village for work and then wedding the lieutenant. Even being able to court the lieutenant so quickly shows something. She wouldn't choose anyone weak."

"Are you jealous?"

Gerrin smiled. "No, Robbins. Just impressed. You know, very few civilians, skilled or not, get escorts from our leaders. Even fewer get to see command centers. That all happened for you almost as soon as you arrived."

Robbins thought back to his and Devon's early trips with Maia, after they had first recovered and after the incidents on the Isle. He peered back at Gerrin. "So what?"

"So, I know you have some kind of leverage. And you had it before the lieutenant fell for you."

"Leverage? Listen, Airman. I'm just a skilled man, who happened to meet and connect with a woman who happens to be one of your leaders. You're reaching."

Gerrin shook his head. "I don't think so. You know things. I'm sure of it."

"Oh? Things like what?"

"I don't know, but things I know are important. And I suspect you don't have quite as much admiration for our leaders as most civilians."

"Get to it already."

"Fine. Will you help? Will you help me confront them?"

Robbins held up one hand, and then crossed his arms. "Even if I knew anything, you think I would betray my wife's trust, just because you're nervous? Just because you have suspicions? You don't realize just how young you really are."

Gerrin shook his head. "You don't seem to realize the predicament we're really in. Think about our history. The flashing last year? That was once in a generation. The city's weakening? That's unprecedented. And our leaders hide things, and aren't exactly quick to find solutions. If we can confront them, get them to share more, then we'll all be better equipped to help. The people will be safer. Humanity will be safer."

Robbins sighed, almost shocked at what he had become engaged in. "I'm sure the leaders have their reasons. And, like I said, the lieutenant doesn't share much with me. But even if she did, it wouldn't be my place to tell you. Why don't you ask them yourself?"

Gerrin looked off, into the distance, and Robbins saw the doubt in his eyes. He also saw the fear. The young man had revealed much to be fearful of.

"Awfully quiet, aren't we?" said Robbins. "Are we finished?"

Gerrin glanced back at him, and then looked past him and quickly straightened up. Robbins turned to look in the same direction, and saw Maia approaching. Her helmet was back, and though she had been on duty since the early morning hours, she looked as if the day had just begun. Her steps were strong and steady.

"Finished with what?" she asked, stopping at Robbins' side.

Robbins smiled at her, but was careful not to embrace her. "Hello," he said plainly.

She nodded back. "Hello. And hello to you, Airman Gerrin."

Gerrin raised his right fist in salute. "Lieutenant, Sir."

Maia motioned for him to lower his hand. "At ease."

"Yes, Sir. We were just chatting. I'll be on my way."

As Gerrin took a step, Maia reached out and set her right hand on his arm. Their gauntlets inadvertently touched, and a low, metallic clang rang out.

"Hold it," said Maia. Then, she turned to Robbins. "Finished with what? What did he say to upset you?"

Robbins looked back at her and answered in a whisper. "I'll tell you later."

"You sure it shouldn't be dealt with now?"

Robbins nodded. "Yes, I'm sure. Let's go home."

Maia's eyes were full of concern. She shook her head, turned back to Gerrin, and squeezed his arm. "Talk, Airman."

"Sir," Gerrin started. "I was just sharing with Robbins my concerns about the happenings in the land, and how we are dealing with them."

"Oh, is that so?"

"Yes, Sir."

She turned to Robbins again. "I have to deal with this. I'll see you shortly."

Robbins nodded, and said "Alright."

He walked away, and quickly reached the door to their home. As he input the access code, he looked back and saw Maia step in front of Gerrin and stare hard into his eyes. She was speaking too quietly for him to discern anything, but he could see her intensity.

Gerrin was only standing firm and nodding. Robbins turned away, slid the door aside, and stepped inside. Devon was sitting on the cushioned bench, and looked up at him, and crossed his arms in aggravation.

"Don't start," said Robbins.

A few minutes passed. The house was quiet, and outside the window, so was the street. Robbins was sitting at the dining table, with one eye on Devon, thinking. Gerrin had been too observant for too long. Not only did he have the common, largely manufactured knowledge about him and his son's arrival to the village, he knew of their movements. And, no doubt, so did many others. Two airmen had helped him and Devon board Maia's bird on their first trip out after recovering. And airmen had been all around when Maia had escorted them up to the Sky Tower for the first time. He felt his heart begin to beat against his chest.

The front door unlocked and slid aside, and Maia stepped in. Robbins slowly stood from the table.

"Hey!" Devon greeted her, jumping up from the bench. He jogged up to her, and threw his arms around her waist.

"Hey, Devon," she said, smiling, and leaning over to embrace him.

"You got back early." He stepped back and looked up at her. "What happened?"

"Not much. Commander Jaan just wanted to give me a short day, so I went to visit a friend."

"Oh. I thought maybe it was because of the address."

She shook her head. "No, I don't think so."

"Okay. Was it Prynn? Did you go and visit with Prynn?"

She nodded and smiled. "You don't miss much. But I do have other friends, you know."

"I know. She cooked right? What did she make? The same thing she makes for me?"

"She made some heavy, sweet bread. And, we had fruit pudding with some almonds and cashews. Has she made that for you before?"

Devon shook his head, looking disappointed. "No. She always makes me vegetable soup, or some kind of...uh...porridge. And she only makes me plain bread."

Maia patted him on the shoulder. "Well, you need that kind of food if you want to grow up big and strong like me and your father."

"Sweeter bread wouldn't hurt, though."

She laughed. "No, it wouldn't. Why don't you go upstairs and get washed up, and I'll see what I can find for you."

"Okay."

"Get really clean, now. Okay?"

"Okay."

Devon turned away and moved quickly, lunging up two steps at a time as he ascended the curving stairwell. He passed the ceiling, leaving their sight. Robbins walked up to Maia, and embraced her. Her equipment felt cold, as it often did, but she was warm. She rubbed his back, and then leaned away and reached back to disconnect her helmet mount. She lifted the assembly up and off of her heavy jacket and set it down on the shelf near the door. Then she disconnected her gauntlets, slid them off, and set them down next to the assembly before facing him again.

"How was your appointment with the doctor?" she asked.

"It was fine," he answered.

"That's good."

She touched his face gently with her palm, and smiled, and then headed into the kitchen. She rinsed and dried her hands quickly, and then opened the door of the short cooler, reached in, and pulled out a covered plate. Lifting the cover, she looked down and saw what was left of the sweet bread they had shared the night before, after Devon had gone to bed. There were still three large pieces.

"I guess we can give him a treat," she said. She turned and looked at him. "Is that okay with you? It's not too late, and this is much lighter than Prynn's."

"Sure," Robbins said, and sat back down at the table.

She turned back, replaced the cover, and set the plate down on the counter top. Then she set her hands down. They were clearly tense. "Did Kile notice anything out of the ordinary?" she asked.

Robbins shook his head. "No. She said my cells are…still regenerative. No surprises."

"Is the process slowing down?"

"Yes."

"So, you won't live forever, then?"

Robbins laughed quietly. "No, Love."

"But, you'll probably outlive me." She turned around and leaned back into the counter, and smirked.

"Doubtful." He looked out through the thin curtain, to the street, wondering if another watcher might be lurking, even listening. "You've been here your whole life," he continued. "You've absorbed all the land's nutrients over all that time. Your parents lived for well over a century. You'll live longer than them."

"I suppose." She crossed her arms, and glanced toward the stairwell. "So. Airman Gerrin was out of line, I gather?"

Robbins hesitated. "What do you mean? What did he tell you?"

"Not much. Pretty much the answer you heard him give me. But, I heard your tone, Love. You were upset."

"Yes, I was. He, uh, suspects that you all–the commanders and lieutenants–are hiding something. He wanted my help confronting you about it."

Maia's eyes remained steady, and her posture did not change. "Just me?"

"No. You. Jaan. Every leader, I suppose."

"We can't have that."

"I know. He knows quite a bit, though. About us."

"You mean you and Devon?"

Robbins nodded. "He knows a little more than anyone else has ever let on."

"But, not how you got here, right?"

"No, I don't think so. But he does suspect that I know a lot, and that it's given me leverage over leadership. He thinks I knew something before we even started courting."

Maia let out a chuckle, and then covered her mouth. "Sorry. That's just a funny phrase."

Robbins shook his head. "Well, I'm glad you can laugh at a moment like this."

"Couldn't help it. But..." She settled herself. "This is serious. I will speak with the commander about it."

"And what will happen to Gerrin?"

Her eyes strengthened as she answered. "That is not your concern, my love. And I'd hate to give you even more for someone to try to coerce you."

"Right. Good idea."

"You do know a lot. You've experienced more in a year here than most civilians do in a century."

"I know."

She moved away from the counter, walked to the table, and sat down next to him, with her back toward the stairwell. She set her arms down in front of her. "I probably shouldn't have told you about my trip over the clouds," she said. "Or, about the Lords' system. But..."

"I haven't told anyone," he said. "I wouldn't."

"I know."

Robbins reached out with both hands and grasped hers. She squeezed back. "But, I do have to tell you something."

She nodded. "Okay. Go ahead."

"After everything on the Isle, and after we married, I had a moment. It was a moment of great doubt. I was confused, afraid for some reason, about everything. And I talked to someone. I talked to Taj."

Maia's eyes softened, even as she pinched her lips together. "I suspected as much."

"You did?"

"Intimacy, I've been told, can increase intuition over time. And the systems here track just about everything. I knew from the logs that you'd talked to someone outside the village, about something. I'm just glad it was him."

"I'm sorry, Maia."

She shook her head, and squeezed his hands tighter. "Don't be. Taj knows so much, and we've depended on him so much, that he may as well be one of us. And, if you ask me, I think even the Lords trust him to a point."

"But, I'm sorry, because…I told him everything. About us. About the Isle. Everything."

Maia slowly released his hands, and leaned back in her seat. She took a deep, long breath, and exhaled. The smell of sweetness was still on her breath as she spoke again.

"He won't tell," she said.

"Your sister knows. The old teacher let something slip."

Maia nodded. "Okay. Even better. So, that was what she wanted to talk to you about?"

"Yes."

"Okay."

"Are you angry?"

"Yes."

"I'm sorry."

She leaned forward, and reached, and set her hands down on his. "I know it was a lot to take in: landing here, the Isle, the extension, the fighting, trying to protect Devon." She looked back at the empty stairwell, and then back at him. "And, it's not my place to tell you how to handle all of it. And the commander didn't exactly give you an order of silence. But, you did make a promise. And he got you work, work that you're good at. And it helps us. And it helps the village."

He sighed. "I know, I know."

Devon's steps thumped above them as he moved toward the stairs again. They both glanced up at the ceiling, and then looked back into each other's eyes.

"I knew you'd never go too far," she said. "Even after you basically threatened the commander. But, I wish you had talked to me first. We took vows. I trust you. And you can trust me."

"I know, Love. I'm sorry."

She squeezed his hands, and sat there, quiet, for what seemed like minutes. Then, as Devon hopped down the last step and onto the floor, she leaned in, kissed him on the cheek, and whispered "I forgive you, Love."

CHAPTER 15
UNSHAKEN

The observation side of the north station was noisy. The gated lookout that faced the ocean left it more exposed to the storm, allowing the rushing and whipping sounds of the outside to push through. And the narrow corridor that led to the lookout carried sounds from within, where a handful of mountain watchers were currently stationed, working and observing from relative safety.

The corridor was shadowy and dark. The glow from the rugged display screen to the right of the gate was minimal. The light from the outside, gray as it was, was what truly illuminated Jaan's vision. He looked out from a yard behind the heavy, narrow, firmly-embedded arrangement of metal bars, watching the crashing of waves and the blowing of broken rock and icy air. The barely-obstructed winds blew around him unevenly. All of his tech hummed as it absorbed the air and kept him stable.

Looking to the display, he saw the signal. A bright, green circle expanded from the center of the rectangular screen to its outer edges, moving over a simple map of the northern coastline. After thirty seconds it repeated, and then repeated again. So far, the scan had indicated no danger beyond the storm itself. The wind speed was displayed in the corner, along with the time: 10:09 AM / 125 MPH. The circle would only change color if a sizable rock flew nearby, or the wind suddenly gusted, or an unexpected, large object approached. None of this had occurred in the hours since Jaan had arrived. He stepped closer to the gate and crossed his arms as he stared out.

Most of the data in his helmet display was steady. His heartbeat was normal. His tech was functioning. His relative speed and gravity were as expected, given his position. But another line of data, one indicating a signal that only his system had been programmed to track, was fluctuating. He had discreetly patched into one of the station's antennas, and through it, his system was scanning for the unique code of the system in the sky. Limited by his personal equipment, it would not be as strong as a scan from the tower, but he was also over one hundred miles closer to the Isle. He hoped the shortened distance would make up the difference. He could not remember the last time he had felt such desperation. The Lords had not contacted him, or anyone else as far as he knew, since his previous encounter with their mysterious, lurking, seemingly ill-tempered system.

As the data from his scan continued to fluctuate, he heard a low beep. He looked back at the display screen and saw three blinking, red dots, indicating life signs. They were ten miles out. He knew right away who they were: a trio of the giant whales that had so recently revealed themselves. And if the station's scans were picking

241

them up so far out, they had to be surfacing. He looked out through the gate again, and into the distance.

"Magnify," he whispered. "Maximum."

A rectangle filled most of his helmet's front panel, and an accelerating view appeared within it. He stepped closer to the gate, almost touching it. His tech hummed faster as it adjusted. With his helmet's cameras less obstructed by the gate's bars, he had a clearer image of the ocean. The water's muted, greenish hue was more evident, as were the heights of the cresting and crashing waves. But the magnification was still less than two miles. All he could see was water and cold sky.

The display screen behind him beeped again, and he turned to see that the life signs had gotten a mile closer. The whales were not just frolicking or coming up for air. They were swimming toward the mainland. He backed away from the gate, reset the view through his helmet, and waited, and thought. A line clicked open behind his right ear, and the symbol of the mountain division blinked into view.

"This is Commander Jaan," he answered. "Go ahead."

"Sir, this is Ensign Gill," the young woman replied. "We have life signs coming in directly from the north. Do you see them?"

"I do, Ensign. I gather they're some of our new, large friends."

"We gathered the same, Sir. We've already alerted Commander Fits at the west station. We're waiting to hear back. Do you have an order?"

Jaan looked back over his shoulder, and in the distance, in the room at the end of the corridor, saw Gill looking at him. She raised a hand toward him, and he returned the gesture. "Let them come," he answered. "Let's see what they do."

"Yes, Sir. Gill out."

The line closed, and Jaan looked back out at the ocean. He magnified his view once again, hoping, but the creatures were not yet within range. He did not know what to expect, other than more data on how they moved, and how fast they were, and perhaps how heavy and strong they were. He was about to reset his view again, but the rectangle shrank on its own. A blinking light drew his attention to the lines of data coming from his system, and he saw that the coded scanning signal had steadied. A line of text in white letters appeared near the bottom of his helmet's display.

I SEE, COMMANDER, THAT YOU HAVE FAILED TO LEARN YOUR LESSON.

Jaan made sure the line was secure on his end and glanced back down the corridor before speaking in response. "It has been days," he said, quietly. "We still have not heard from our Lords. And now, as I'm sure you can see, the new, and massive life is coming closer to us."

THEY ARE MERELY HUNTING AND BREATHING. THEY POSE NO THREAT TO ANY LWOANS.

"I suppose I can accept that. What else can you tell me?"

OUR LORDS HAVE BEGUN TO ANALYZE SAMPLES OF THE WATER. HOW THEY RESPOND AFTER THEY HAVE

FINISHED IS, OF COURSE, UP TO THEM. YOU WOULD HAVE HEARD FROM ME WHEN THEY WERE READY TO COMMUNICATE.

"Are they still angry? With us? With me?"

THEY ARE CAUTIOUS. I DO NOT KNOW IF THEY REMAIN ANGRY.

"Very well, System. Thank you."

TURN OFF YOUR SCANS, COMMANDER.

Jaan almost obeyed. His lips parted as he prepared to whisper, but then, suddenly, something else occurred to him. "Can you not hide your signal better?" he asked.

There was no response.

"Finally at a loss for words, are we?"

Still no response.

Jaan stepped closer to the gate, and looked up. He brought up an image of his ongoing scan. The radiating circle that appeared in his helmet's display was light blue, and a black dot within it showed that the system in the sky was ten miles north of the station, in the same spot, the exact same spot, where the whales had first revealed themselves.

"I guess you were constructed too long ago to make that kind of change," he said. "Or, maybe-"

PLEASE COMPOSE YOURSELF, COMMANDER. THERE IS NO NEED FOR INSULTS. OF COURSE I CAN HIDE MY SIGNAL.

"But you haven't? Why?"

Another absence of text.

"Maybe our Lords wanted us to find you."

I DO NOT KNOW THE REASONS FOR THEIR PROGRAMMING.

"So, it is a matter of your programming, then?"

I WILL BE DEPARTING NOW, COM-

"You sent the whales this way. Didn't you?"

Once again, the system did not reply. And Jann suddenly suspected why. The sunken structure that they had found days before, when they had first sent the ray into the ocean, was only a short distance from where the whales had just appeared. He tried not to smile as he considered what might have happened.

"You didn't want them near that sunken structure," he said. "Or, the Lords didn't. Why?"

NONE OF YOUR CONCERN, COMMANDER. I WOULD SUGGEST YOU-

"If they will not speak to us, then we will find the answers ourselves. We will not be left in the dark. Humanity depends on it."

HUMANITY DEPENDS ON THE WATCHERS DOING THEIR DUTY, AND OBEYING. I WOULD SUGGEST THAT YOU ABANDON THIS LINE OF THINKING, COMMANDER.

"Only suggest?"

I AM FOLLOWING MY PROGRAMMING.

"I'm sure that you are, System. Goodbye."

Jaan quickly closed his line, and deactivated the scan. The blue circle and its corresponding row of code faded out of his view. What the system in the sky could, or would do was not concerning. He suspected now that it would only communicate with the Lords and try to guide any others it encountered, human or otherwise, based on its programming. The Lords had wanted the whales to stay away from the mysterious underwater structure, and Jaan felt assured of his previous suspicion that it was, in fact, their burial site. It was where the bodies drained of their origin cells had been placed. It was the place where, according to Lord Andrew, the lost Lwoans had been properly and honorably entombed. Standing at the gate, Jaan continued watching the ocean, as he recalled all that had happened on the Isle nearly a year before.

It was as clear now as it had been then. In the Lords' home, their safe haven, he had turned on them to defend Robbins' life, and freedom. Under his threat, Lord Andrew had revealed that, over the years, Lwoans lost to the storm and found by their previously-unseen system in the sky were retrieved and taken to the Isle. Their lifeless bodies were then drained of their origin cells before being buried. These origin cells had been used to extend the lives of others, including Jaan's own, and Robbins'.

Jaan recalled the searing, sad anger he had felt, at the Lords' selfishness, and their secrets. He recalled Andrew, for the first time, revealing his own intense anger before using his surprising physical strength. The Emissary had been turned upon him and Maia, and its flying weapons had attacked. Maia had defended well against them. He had done the same against Andrew, only to see that the aged man was no longer fully human. One of his arms, having been hit with a gauntlet blast, had broken too easily, and revealed contents–sparking, fuming contents–that was more than bone and blood. Jaan knew then that the Lords' impressive lifetimes were due to more than just extension.

A click in his helmet pulled him out of his memory. "Go ahead, Ensign," he answered.

"Sir, the whales have stopped less than a mile from the shore," said Gill. "Can you see them yet?"

Jaan looked out again, and again magnified his view. He saw the waves and the cold, blowing wind. There was the constant grayness. He thought he saw a distant splash, an upward spray from something other than the water's regular movements, but it quickly disappeared. He deactivated the magnification, turned, and looked at the display screen. The whales' life signs were there, as Gill had said. The creatures were moving, but they were not coming any closer. He shook his head.

"No, Ensign," he answered. "They must be hiding. But, they are here."

"Do you think they pose any threat, Sir?"

"Doubtful. They're just trying to survive, like us. If we stay away from them, I suspect they will stay away from us."

"Yes, Sir. Commander Fits has already told us that we may

have to adjust our surveys because of them."

"I know. I think he's right. When is he due to report here?"

"This afternoon, Sir. About five hours from now."

Jaan nodded, knowing and dreading that he would have to alter Fits's plans, as well as those of the other commanders. "Very well. Thank you, Ensign."

*   *   *   *   *

It was nearly dusk. Most of the light drifting through the curved, glass walls of the Spire's second observation level was coming from the snow-capped mountains that continued to sparkle in the diminishing light. The rest was from the sky, and from the gull and the puller that were hovering on the other side of the glass, just above the surrounding platform.

Jaan was standing in the center of the level, with the mountains behind him. The other commanders were equally spaced around him. Fits was to his right. Brun was to his left. And Shil was in front of him, with her arms crossed and her gaze strong. Jaan mirrored her, and began.

"Here we are again," he started. "Thank you all for agreeing to meet here. Based on the day's duty schedules, I knew this would be the most convenient place."

"I'd say you traveled the furthest, Sir," said Fits.

"I won't argue that."

"But for what purpose?" asked Shil. "I left the city for something you said was too sensitive to reveal over a secured line."

"We will get to that, Commander," said Jaan. "First, how about you tell us what is happening in the city?"

"Very well. We are, very slowly, continuing the work that has to be done. But, there has been some disruption. Not long after our broadcast yesterday, some of the civilian workers, including one of the bosses, became a bit unruly. After Commander Brun had departed, I went to the worksite, where I was soon surrounded by a group that had come to the site without approval. They said they had friends, family outside the city that are still struggling to adjust. I guess the thought of any of them having to stay outside was too much. I had to subdue two men before patrolmen arrived to deal with the rest."

"Which men?" asked Brun.

Shil shook her head. "Not important right now. They're safe in the holding cells at headquarters, and we'll deal with them soon enough. What is important is the rest of the land. I've heard citizens are not the only angry civilians."

Brun nodded. "You're right. Something similar happened in a village." He turned to Jaan. "Unfortunately, Sir, the old teacher had to intervene after the address drew anger from the people in his village. Had he not done so, two of my watchers would have been forced to physically subdue multiple people. They were distraught, and after Erul's death, some may be terrified."

"Erul," said Jaan, acknowledging the deceased Lwoan. "What

did your examination determine? Is Doctor Taj correct?"

"We are still examining him, Sir. His body hasn't been here long. Samples of his blood are being analyzed. But most of the scans are complete, if you care to see for yourself."

"Perhaps after. But, at least we are managing. And until things get back to normal, we will continue to do just that."

"But, Sir, are we not years away from anything being anywhere near normal?"

"Maybe. Maybe not."

Shil's eyes became more focused as she stared at Jaan and spoke. "We can't work any faster. It'll be weeks before we can be sure that the ground surrounding the chasm is stable. Then it will be months before we can fully stabilize the salvageable buildings in the quarter. And it will take more time to-"

"I understand all of that," Jaan stopped her. "But, we cannot be discouraged."

"I am not discouraged. I'm only being realistic, as we all should be."

"Lwo was not established on being realistic. We were founded on achieving the extraordinary, and achieving it in extraordinary times."

"That sounds good, but-"

"No, Commander. It is not a matter of how it sounds. It is what happened and what will continue to happen, as long as we heed our calling. All of us. Do you all agree?"

"Our calling is unchanged," said Shil. "And I will continue to heed it."

Brun and Fits both nodded and agreed, and as Jaan looked around at each of them, they straightened up their stances more.

"Good," Jaan continued. "Commander Fits? Is there anything new from the mountains?"

Fits shook his head. "Nothing since what you and I learned earlier today."

Jaan nodded back. "Very well."

"Care to inform us?" asked Shil. "Sir?"

"Yes. I went to the north station today, to watch the ocean and to learn as much as I could from closer observation. And while I was there, some of the whales came nearer to the coast."

"So, now they're on every side of us," said Shil. "What should we do about that?"

"Nothing. They pose no threat, as long as we respect their habitat."

"Are we sure of that?"

"Fairly sure," said Fits. "The Maw was only hit when it got too close to one. The Hammer and the Roamer have had no problems. And my lieutenant has already advised all three ships of the patterns the creatures have been swimming in. Analyzing our regular scans, we've found that they're predictable. Salvaging will continue with some altered movements."

"I would hope so," said Shil. "We still need supplies if we're going to fix anything, in the city or anyplace else."

"We'll be fine," said Jaan. "The whales can't digest old plastic and metal, and it seems they're smart enough to know that. They've been swimming through the old discard to chase fish to the shoreline, after all."

"Did you get a good look at them?" asked Shil. "Any of them?"

Jaan shook his head. "A splash or two in the distance. That's all."

"Too bad. So..." Shil hesitated, and took a breath. "Why did you really want us to meet here, Sir? We could have learned all of this from a call and from our reports."

"I felt it was necessary to speak to you all in person. To be clear, the ocean was not all I hoped to observe today. There was also the sky. And, I was hoping to see something. Something specific."

"Which was?"

"The Lords' system in the sky."

Shil, Brun and Fits all stared at him, silent.

"Why?" Shil asked, her eyes glaring.

Jaan raised a gentle hand. "Settle yourself, Commander. It was an attempt to make contact with the Lords. And I have been able to, in a way."

Brun's gauntlets rubbed against each other as he nervously shifted his arms and stance. "What do you mean by 'in a way'?" he asked.

"We were all already aware that the Lords have a system in the sky," said Jaan. "I have made contact with it. *We* have. Lieutenant Maia was the first to communicate with it."

Shil looked away, to the east, toward the far off city, as she spoke. "How did she manage that, Sir?"

"She, along with an airman, took a bird over the clouds, and triggered the system."

Shil shook her head, and turned back to Jaan. "I won't ask how. So, now an airman knows of their wretched system? Anyone else?"

"Not that I'm aware of."

"So, probably."

"No, Commander."

"Sir," said Fits. "Since you called all of us here, you must have learned something important. What was it?"

"The system did not reveal much. But, with what it did reveal, I was able to make a determination. The sunken structure, the one we found far north of these mountains, is the Lords' burial site."

Shil scoffed.

"Commander!" Jaan snapped back. "I've been extremely patient up to this point. Watch yourself. Speak with dignity, or do not speak."

Shil nodded. "I apologize, Sir. But I'm sure you understand, after all they did, after all we've learned, that I care very little about any of this. What will bodies tell us? How will they help us? We have

253

a broken city. We have contaminated water. We…Wait…"

Jaan watched and waited, and saw the other commanders' attention shift to her.

"Sir," she continued. "Do you think their cemetery is what's contaminating the water?"

Jaan was impressed, but unwilling to show it. "I had not considered that, Commander. But, after all this time, I doubt anything from coffins would cause this kind, and this amount of contamination."

"But we don't know what the coffins are made of, or how many there are, *if* they are in fact there."

"They are, Commander. But all of this is something that our next trek will help us to determine."

"Then, Sir, respectfully, what were you hoping to learn from a sunken burial site?"

"Anything we don't already know, Commander. The more we know, from them, from their ocean secrets, the better equipped we are to deal with our own troubles. And, if the bodies have been honored, then the Lords still have honor."

"You care so much for them," Shil said, quietly. "Why? We've heard nothing–most of us anyway–from the Isle in nearly a year. We struggle and struggle, and they do not help. And, as you said yourself, we are managing. We'll survive, somehow. Do we really need them anymore?"

"We will not live forever, Commander," Jaan answered. He

looked around at each of them. "None of us will. And none of us possess their knowledge, or wisdom, or anything close to their years on this Earth. If we, if the people are to not only survive, but thrive, then we need them. We need their knowledge. And the burial site might reveal something, something that they have not."

"But, Sir, they also will not live forever. Not that they aren't trying. If they care, and if they have honor as you say, won't they share whatever it is we need?"

"They are still human. I imagine they feel wronged and betrayed, in a way that we cannot understand. It's why I reached out, the only other way I could think to, after so much came upon us in these past weeks. And there are signs that they will reach back. The system told me that they are now inspecting the water. And it told me that the whales are not a threat. I imagine that soon they will tell us more, and hopefully tell us themselves."

"So, Sir?" Brun started. "Why not wait for them?"

"Do you think we can afford to wait, if we can learn something now?"

Brun nodded. "Good point. So, what's your plan?"

"We make another trek over the water. We take the ray, and let it do its work. And we learn everything we can about the burial site."

"And then what?" asked Shil.

"Then, we use whatever we learn."

"And, if it's nothing?"

"It won't be."

"If it's nothing besides entombed bodies?"

"Then, we leave them to rest. And we continue on, as we have been."

"And will *that* be enough for you?"

Jaan hesitated, and breathed out. "I will not correct you again, Commander."

Shil nodded back, and stood silently, trying to subdue the anger in her eyes. Jaan watched her for another moment, allowing her emotions and all of the other emotions moving around the room to settle.

"Good," said Jaan. "Return to the city, Commander. Commander Fits? Prepare the ray, and whatever else you need. We leave tomorrow."

"Yes, Sir," said Fits.

"I will stay behind with Commander Brun. I want to see the results of Erul's examination. We will share them as soon as it is reasonable."

The four of them exchanged salutes, and Jaan watched as Shil and Fits departed. Each of them exited the narrow opening that faced south, and then entered their respective craft. After a few moments, the gull and the puller each bounced off of the platform and flew out of sight. He followed Brun to a computing station, and watched as he navigated the Spire's systems, and found the logs of interest from the ground watchers' hospital.

CHAPTER 16
REVELATION

Maia had already told Malo everything she could. She had been stern, as they had prepped the bird. She had told him that the commander needed an airman for a mission outside the mainland, as she would have to stay behind to oversee the division. She had told him that she had recommended him for the mission because he was a good pilot, but more so because of what he already knew, and because she knew that he could be trusted with whatever he would come to know.

She had told him of the sunken structure, near where they had encountered the Lords' system in the sky. She had told him that the commander wanted to investigate further. She had told him more about the device that Terre and her crafters had constructed, which he had heard about, but not yet seen. Then, after Jaan had arrived, ready to board the bird, she had stopped explaining, and wished him well.

As Malo had continued prepping the craft for flight, he had heard Maia and Jaan speaking quietly at the base of the ramp. But he had not been able to decipher much, besides the clear trepidation in her voice.

"How much did the lieutenant tell you, Airman?" asked Jaan.

Malo continued holding firmly to the control handles at his sides and kept his eyes forward as he tilted his head back and answered. "About what, Sir?"

"About all of it."

"Whatever she could in the few minutes we had before you arrived."

"So, just the basics, then?"

"I suppose."

"You already knew about the system in the sky. Your work on deciphering its signal was commendable."

"Thank you, SIr."

"The lieutenant trusts you, I think more than any other airman. Do you trust her?"

"Yes, Sir."

"Do you trust me?"

"Of course, Sir."

"You should know that what we're doing would be frowned upon by past generations of watchers, but I've determined it to be the only course of action. They didn't have the kinds of challenges that we do. And our Lords have left us little choice."

Malo hesitated before responding. "What exactly are we doing, Sir?"

"I've been able to make contact with their system since you and the lieutenant did. It has stopped short of bringing us back into direct communication with the Lords. But, it did let slip that they do not want us near the sunken structure we're headed to. I'm going against their wishes to find out more about it."

"What do you think it is?"

"I *know* that it's a burial site."

"Like ours?"

"Maybe. But, there is more to it. It's where they've buried the lost Lwoans retrieved from the storm. There could be centuries' worth of deceased there."

"Then, maybe they just don't want us to disturb it."

"I suspect more. But, don't worry. We will not disturb the dead."

Malo nodded, and continued to keep the bird steady, flying closely behind the ray, which was mirroring the movements of the gull in front of it. At first, when they had departed from the north station, he had been in awe of the device. It was sleek, and fast, and it seemed durable despite the evidence of being battered from its recent use. And it flew as if it understood its purpose. But now he was concerned that Rial's movements might cause it to malfunction.

Flying low and without radio contact made sense. The commander wanted to avoid triggering the system in the sky. And Rial had warned them that her vector would not only be close to the ocean's surface, but purposely unpredictable. But Malo had never flown so close to any water for so long. It had been slashing and beading off the sides of the bird's windshield for miles. And the gull's path had seemed more dangerous than unpredictable.

Malo looked out, past the ray, to the underbody of the gull. Mists of water were kicking up from below its aft end. Its underfin was keeping it steady as it skidded left and right, through the tops of the crashing waves. But birds did not have fins. Malo was relying on the draft from the gull and the ray to help him stay on track. Through his boot soles, through the floorboard, he could feel the water beating against their underbody. The bird was the commander's, one he was not used to piloting. Thus far, its engines had done more than he suspected they were accustomed to. But, they had not taken in too much moisture, they sounded steady, and their roars were strong. Malo still gripped the handles tightly as they flew for another five miles.

The bird's line clicked open, and low static pushed through the cabin before Rial spoke.

"Gull One to Bird One," she called.

Malo found the gray, encoded signal on the right panel, and tapped it. "This is Airman Malo in Bird One," he answered. "Go ahead."

"Airman, this is Commander Fits in Gull One. We are two miles out. Commander, Sir? Are you ready?"

Malo heard Jaan stand, and felt him walk up behind him.

"This is Commander Jaan in Bird One," he answered. "We're ready, Commander. Proceed."

"Yes, Sir. Fits out."

The line closed, and Malo checked the panel to make sure the signal was gone. A few seconds later, the gull began to ascend and was followed by the ray. Malo followed suit, pulling the handles back gently to meet their vector. The gull's line steadied, and it quickly reached sixty feet before slowing to a stop and hovering in place. They were high enough to avoid the most dangerous waves, and low enough that the Lord's system might not notice them in the chaos of the ocean. Malo leveled the bird off near the gull, and the ray continued upward. He leaned forward in his seat, watching as the device moved closer and closer to the clouded, gray light of day. The wet mists around its body dissipated in the storm's dry, beating winds. It stopped at five hundred feet, a dark shape awaiting orders. They could only let it stay so high for a few moments.

The gull spun around and faced their bird. Being just thirty feet away, Malo could see through the gull's slightly-tinted windshield and see its two occupants. Familiar white blurs of winds rolled through the gull's engines, surrounding it as it hovered. As he sensed the bird's engines creating the same powerful, steadying exhaust, Malo felt slightly reassured in the midst of their unprecedented mission.

Taps and beeps sounded behind Malo's seat. Jaan was working on the tablet connected to the ray. Malo looked up again, and watched as the dark, shining device turned in place and faced east. It pointed its nose down, toward the water. Then, it dove. In a blur it shot by the bird's windshield and out of sight. Malo nearly stood up, trying

261

to get a better look as it moved.

"Turn around, Airman," said Jaan. "You'll get a better view."

Malo reached down for the chair controls. As the mechanism turned him in place, the light from the tablet's projection reflected in his helmet. He reached back and tilted his helmet up and off. As it settled behind him, he sat further back into the seat. Jaan was sitting on the starboard bench, with his helmet also retracted, resting his elbows on his knees as he worked, simultaneously focused on the tablet and the empty, glowing, cubic projection.

"We'll get an image soon," said Jaan. "Here's what she's seeing."

He tapped a command into the tablet, and a dark box appeared in the top right corner of the cube. It was quickly filled by the video feed from the ray, and Malo saw the dark color of the water. Specks of ocean debris were flying by the camera. Small, ticking lines of data at the bottom of the feed revealed the ray's depth and speed, along with the water's temperature, pressure and gravity.

"How far down is it?" Malo asked.

"The target is three thousand five hundred feet. You can see right now she's only at one thousand."

"She's fast, then."

"Very."

"How long did it take the special lieutenant to build it?"

"A few days. She knew how important it was."

"So, she also knows about the burial site?"

"Not yet." Jaan looked up. "And until I say otherwise, do not speak of it with anyone else. *Anyone*. Understood?"

Malo nodded. "Yes, Sir. I think I see something."

There was movement in the video feed, and Malo could see that the ray was making turns as it continued diving deeper and deeper. As it reached a depth of two thousand feet, the readings indicated an increase in the forces below it.

"It's just the currents," said Jaan. "They're strong here. She's navigating fairly well. At least it's not our new friends. They've moved further in, but I still don't think they'd want us exploring more of their territory."

"So I've heard," said Malo.

Malo continued to watch the feed, and listened as Jaan whispered focused commands telling the ray to halt, and then to focus, and scan, and pan. The feed showed that the ray was turning in place, searching. As it pointed northeast, the entire projection refreshed, and Malo saw the outline of a structure. It was distant, and appeared to be surrounded by shadows. Jaan whispered another command, and the ray moved toward it.

Malo looked over his shoulder, to the gull, and saw that there was more light in their cabin, light clearly coming from their own projection. He held up one thumb, and saw Rial do the same. Then he turned back to the cube of light in front of him. A few, quiet moments passed. The projection refreshed again, and more details were revealed. An encircling structure depicted in white lines of light appeared to be a wall made of old stone. Within it, slanted surfaces atop tall, narrow sections appeared to be roofs. There were arched openings, each shown as an absence of light below the roofs. There were at least twelve such sections, equally-spaced, and forming multiple rows.

Malo looked at the feed again. Jaan ordered the ray to move further in, and activated its front light. As it floated closer, and its light beamed out, it became clear that the narrow structures were light in color. But, there was still plenty of darkness, from the surrounding waters, and from below the deep construction.

"It's still not showing enough," Jaan said aloud. "It's almost too dark here."

"There are some stones near the base," said Malo, noticing the hints of pale color within the darkness. "I can see green, and red. They look like they used to be polished. And there's what looks like…"

"Like what, Airman?"

"Old coral, on top of the surrounding wall. It's dead."

Jaan nodded. "I see it."

"It's too deep and dark here. It shouldn't even be there."

"Unless it was recently carried down by something."

The ray moved closer, floated over the surrounding wall, dipped downward, and swam ahead. As it moved about, between the narrow, slant-roofed towers, Malo noticed a reflection in the feed. It was quick, and had come from far below the ray's camera, but it had been there. He leaned forward in his seat. There was silt, and small rocks and debris floated about, but he could not make out much else. Then, the projection refreshed again, and showed an object near the base of one of the towers. It was rectangular, and upright. The data in the projection indicated that it was metal. At Jaan's command the ray stopped, and aimed its camera at the object. As it did, the bird suddenly shook around them.

They were tilted toward their port side, and the bird jumped in reverse. Proximity warnings blared into Malo's ears as he quickly turned his chair back around. The control panels were all blinking red. He gripped the left handle firmly and leveled them off as he began navigating through the panels. Looking out, he could see that the gull had also moved further away. There were now more than thirty yards between them. He looked down, below the bird's front end, but saw nothing from below. He looked to the port and starboard sides, but nothing was approaching. Then he looked up, and saw a dark, familiar shape. It was hovering above the space between them and the gull. Behind his seat, he heard Jaan stand.

"System," Jaan said, his voice now distorted by his helmet. "We've done nothing wrong. You refused to share more. Or, our Lords did. They have not helped us. So, we have to help ourselves." He paused. "I told you what we would do." Another pause. "They gave us no choice, and now we know why."

Malo shook his head, trying to rid himself of the fear and confusion rising up within him. He deactivated the bird's warnings and tried to open a secured line to the gull. They declined. In the distance, he thought he saw Rial shake her head, but he was not sure. His mind raced. He had no idea what was being communicated from the Lords' system, nor did he know how grave or chastising it might be. He glanced up at the dark, looming unmanned craft again. Its front light was glaring red. Powerful, billowing air flowed in and out of its engines, keeping it steady. He looked back, over his shoulder, and saw that the projection and feed from the ray were still active, beaming out from the tablet that Jaan had left on the bench. The ray was still lingering within the sunken structure. The projection showed that the metal box was settled into the ground between two roofed sections, with angular pieces attached, apparently to support it.

Malo kept his hands close to the controls, and his seat forward, but turned more within the seat. The ray's feed made it clear. The object was a casket. A small window near the top was covered in specks of sticking dirt. There was darkness within. Beneath the window there appeared to be text etched into the metal, but he could not decipher the rows of words. He looked up, beyond the feed and the projection, and saw Jaan moving toward the rear of the cabin. He was near the mounted tethering cable, and Malo wondered if his commander would jump out to confront the Lords' system, as the lieutenant had. But, he stopped near the sealed ramp. He raised his left hand to grip the bird's frame as he held his helmet with his right.

"Then, I have something else to tell them," said Jaan, continuing his back and forth with the ominous presence. "The most recent death on Lwo, of the civilian Erul, was not due to his many years, but due to the contaminated water flowing in from the ocean, from this very direction." He paused, listening. "It seems that his body could not handle whatever is in the water here." Another pause. "Ask our Lords if they are willing to let all of us die, and if they have the resources to bury the rest of humanity."

Malo turned back around, and again looked out through the windshield. The dark craft's red light flickered in an unrecognizable pattern. Behind him, Jaan walked up, and then leaned past the right side of the chair. He looked out and up, and waited. The unmanned craft quickly ascended, and then bolted away. Malo heard its steady engines as it departed, and watched as its distant shape shrank into a dot, high above and further north, before disappearing. A call from the gull clicked into the cabin, and Malo tapped the icon on the right panel to answer.

"This is Commander Fits. Do you have an update, Sir?"

Jaan pushed his helmet up and off, and backed away from the controls as he answered. "This is Commander Jaan," he said. "I've told the Lords' system of our recent loss, and that it was a result of the contaminated water. If they do not help us now, then there is no doubt that we are on our own."

"Agreed, Sir," said Fits. "Shall we continue?"

"Yes. While the ray continues scanning, I'll make sure it's sampling the water in the area. And we may as well keep our lines open, since they already know, or will soon know, that we're here."

"Yes, Sir."

Malo guided the bird forward. Rial did the same with the gull, and they both idled in their previous positions. He wanted to turn the chair around again, but the sense of anticipation in his body would not subside. *At any moment*, he thought, *it could return. We may have to evade. We may have to flee.* His lingering confusion was suddenly met with doubts about what they were doing. He wondered if Rial was having the same doubts. He had encountered the Lords' unmanned craft before. So had she, he had come to learn. But, she had not seen it. And she had not just heard the contentious back and forth between the system and the commander.

Looking out at the gull, Malo raised a thumb once again, and clearly saw Rial do the same. Then, she spun her chair around. She seemed to be more at ease, for some reason. He wondered if Fits had told her something that Jaan had not told him.

"It won't hurt us, Airman," said Jaan.

Malo glanced up at the sky. "I would hope not, Sir," he said.

"The Lords do not wish to harm us, and thus far, their system has only spoken to us."

"What, are you worried, Airman?" Fits asked through the line, with a hint of levity in his voice as it pushed through faint static.

Malo shook his head. "No, Sir," he answered. "I...I was. It's not like we see this kind of thing every week, or every month, or *ever.*"

"I know. Actually, I'm quite uncomfortable myself."

"Really, Sir?"

"No."

He heard Rial quietly chuckle. Fortunately for her, Fits was a leader who often allowed his subordinates to be at ease. So was his lieutenant. But Jaan was no such leader. Malo shook his head again, and turned the chair away from the controls.

Jaan was sitting again, holding the tablet as he worked. The projection had not filled anymore, and it did not need to. Glowing lines outlined the entirety of the sunken site. The encircling wall was close to thirty yards in diameter. The spaces near the inside of the wall were filled with dark sediment, which was floating upwards as the ray moved over it, but little else. The tall structures appeared to be carefully arranged within the circle. The casket was at the center. *There are no others here*, Malo thought. *Just one buried.*

"Who do you think it is, Sir?" Malo asked.

"I wondered the same," called Rial.

Jaan glanced up, briefly looking out the short, port side window, and then went back to work on the tablet, silent.

The feed showed a pair of fish, both gray, and both spotted. They swam toward the ray, and then quickly turned and fled into the darkness. The ray drifted away from the casket, glided toward the surrounding wall, and descended toward the floor. Through the cloudiness, Malo could now see specks of white in the sediment, as well as rocks of various sizes and colors. Brief reflections littered the feed, indicating the presence of gems. It was what he expected an ocean floor to be. As the ray swam along the wall, precisely following the curve, he could see more coral, their various colors all faded, falling away from the stone.

"There's no contamination here," Jaan said aloud. "None at all. But, when the ray first dove in, I saw the dark clouds. The deep currents must be protecting this site."

"I'm sure they chose it on purpose," said Fits. "Lord Andrew said they took great care with the burials. But, there's only one here, Sir."

"It's probably more protected than any of our sites," Jaan said, ignoring Fits's last comment.

There were a few uncomfortable moments of silence before Fits responded. "Probably so. Our sites off the southern coast are old, and not so deep. And we haven't gotten an actual view of them in generations."

"We've hardly needed to," said Jaan. "We have few burials, and no lost, floating coffins."

"Maybe that should be the ray's next mission."

"Maybe."

The time slowly passed. Malo spent it looking back and forth to the sky, checking the ray's feed, and avoiding the temptation to find a way to communicate only with Rial. The cabins of the bird and the gull were too small to do it easily. Even speaking quietly just through their helmets would draw their commanders' attention. But, he was sure that she was just as suspicious as he was. There was no reason, not that he could think of, for the Lords to have hidden a practice of retrieving Lwoans already lost to the storm. But if they had, and it was as the commander had said, there should have been more caskets. He turned and looked out the windshield again, wondering if the Lords' system was nearby, hovering, waiting for them to make some kind of misstep. Checking the time, he saw that an hour had passed.

"I think that's enough," said Jaan, breaking minutes of silence.

Malo turned back to his commander, mildly concerned. "Sir?" he asked.

"We have enough information," he said. "There's no contamination. The casket, whomever it holds, seems to honor them. The currents are no stronger than could be expected. And, there is no more danger than expected. We're back to where we were."

"I agree, Sir," Fits said through the line. "We'll have to focus on analyzing the samples, and finding a better way to filter what's coming into the mainland."

Jaan took a deep breath, and slowly exhaled. "Agreed, Commander. Airman, take us down a bit."

"Yes, Sir," said Malo.

He turned the chair back around, took hold of the control handles, and looked to the panels to confirm the bird's status. He looked out the windshield, at the gull, and then at the sky above, where a dark shape appeared. In what seemed like an instant, the Lords' unmanned craft dropped down and settled right between their two craft. Its front end faced the bird, and its glowing, red light seemed to be looking right at Malo. He reached back, raised his helmet, and lowered it back down over his head. He gripped the control handles firmly, but he did not descend as he had been ordered. *Too risky*, he thought.

"Returned, have you?" Jaan said, his voice distorted again. He paused. "Would you care to repeat that?"

Malo listened intently, but Jaan had stopped speaking. The system in the sky lingered, still eyeing them, and apparently still communicating, but something had silenced the commander. He could feel the discomfort. His eyes raced–to the sky, and the gull, and down to the water. He tried not to look directly at the glowing red eye aimed at him. After a few more tense moments, it turned green. He looked back at his commander, just as he was walking up. The projection was gone, and he was carrying the tablet in his hand.

"We've reached them," Jaan said, looking out through the windshield. "The Lords have called us to the Isle."

"Understood, Sir," Fits said through the line. "How long before the ray is up?"

"Just a few minutes now. However, we've been ordered to leave it behind."

Fits hesitated before responding. "I suppose she'll be okay, for a while."

"Don't worry, Commander."

"Yes, Sir. But, I would advise entering a command to flee if anything else, or *anyone* else, approaches."

"Done."

Malo looked out and saw the Lords' unmanned craft slowly rise. This time it did not move so quickly. It drifted northward, just yards above them, as if waiting for them. He looked ahead and saw the gull pull back, ascend, and then turn northward. He looked to Jaan and saw him working on the tablet. A series of beeps preceded a flicker of green light from the screen before he turned away and went back to the bench.

"Orders, Sir?" Malo asked.

"When you see the ray emerge and reach our height, follow the Lords' system."

"Yes, Sir."

Malo looked out, waiting. His heart was pounding. He could see his heartrate in his helmet's display, and took a few deep, slow breaths to settle himself. Another five minutes passed, and the ray floated up into view. The winds carried water away from its shining body and fins, and it turned toward the bird before floating off to the right, clearing the way for their new vector. He took the bird up, steadying his right foot on the pedal, as the Lords' craft departed. He flew behind it. The gull trailed them closely. They all ascended into the clouds, and settled there, speeding toward the Isle with the sun's light beaming down.

CHAPTER 17
FROM THE DEAD

The cavern was cool, as always. Gem never failed to notice the difference when she exited her more insulated bedroom, passed through the east hall, and entered the common space, where the carved stone walls of the old cave always bore the cold of the constant storm and the freezing ocean. As she sat on the soft bench, across from their three chairs, she sipped her warm tea. The old cup, one she had seen even her mother use centuries before, was dense, but still radiated warmth from its contents. She held it near her lips and let the steam float into her nose as she took another sip. The bitter-sweet flavor was almost soothing.

She looked past the chairs, and above them, at the display screen mounted on the east wall. The storm's speed was unchanged. The outside temperature hovered near fifty degrees. The digital clock read 11:05 AM. She took another sip, breathed in, and exhaled slowly.

She leaned over and set the cup down just below her knees, on the wide, oval table. As she sat back into the bench, she rubbed at her forearms. The gauntlets beneath her thick, gray sleeves were heavy. She had not worn them in nearly a year. It had been that long since two of the land's protectors had forced her and her sister, and their father, to take defensive measures. She shook her head, trying to evade the intensity of the memory. *It would serve no purpose today*, she thought. She folded her hands in her lap and looked up at the display again.

Coral entered from the east hall, and as the door closed behind her, turned and entered the kitchen. Her dress was dark green, with vibrant streaks of a brighter green running through it. The necklace she had chosen for the day was made of copper links, and held a blue stone that hung near her chest. Her always-brilliant red hair, even with its streaks of gray, was tied in a tight bun at the back of her head, just above her neck.

She reached down beneath the counter, pulled open a cabinet, and brought up a short, purple cup. Behind her, the water that Gem had heated for her own tea was still steaming on the cooktop. Coral turned, opened the tin canister on the counter, scooped a small amount of the powder and leaves into the cup, and carefully poured the water in over it. Then, she turned back around, set the cup down, picked up a spoon, and stirred as she looked across the room at the closed door to the bunker.

"Are they close?" she asked.

Gem retrieved her tea from the table and took another sip before answering. "It's been almost an hour," she said. "They should be here any moment."

"Emissary?" Coral called.

"Yes, my Lord," the system answered, its voice both artificial and full of personality, both close and spread out.

"Can you track the watchers coming to the Isle yet?"

"Yes, my Lord. Craft Three of the System in the Sky is just five miles south, on a vector heading directly to the Isle. The signals of one bird and one gull are directly behind it."

"Thank you."

"Of course, my Lord."

"Anxious?" Gem asked, looking at her sister.

Coral finished a sip of tea, and then set the cup down on the counter. "I do not want to see them. I do not want to see *him*."

"It's not what father-"

"Do not mention him, Sister. Please."

"Fine. But, you know it's true."

"I know. We have a duty. I am not angry."

"Aren't you?"

"No. But, I will stay behind. You can engage them without me."

Gem nodded, stood, and walked slowly to the high counter that enclosed the kitchen. She stopped in front of her sister and held out one hand. Coral reached back, looked up into her eyes, and gently squeezed. "That is a good idea," said Gem. "The less they see of us, the better."

Coral nodded back. "Agreed." She moved her thumb along Gem's wrist, and then up slightly, to the metal surrounding her arm. "I thought you weren't worried."

Gem gently pulled her hand back, clenched her fist, and felt the gauntlet twitch, waiting for hand commands. "I'm not. It's a precaution." She looked closer at Coral's long, heavy sleeves. "Aren't you wearing yours?"

Coral took another sip of tea. "Yes. Less conspicuously, though. They can rest a little higher, you know."

"Of course I know. But my arms are much thinner than yours."

"So, eat more."

"Think it'll make a difference? Now?"

Coral smiled. "No. Not at all."

As Gem turned, ready to return to the bench and continue waiting, the Emissary's familiar alert chime rang out.

"Watchers approach, my Lords," the system said. "Craft Three has returned to the sky, and the bird and the gull are now entering the south cave."

Gem looked upward. "I will greet them, Emissary. Do not allow them access until I say so. Open the door to the cavern."

"Yes, my Lord."

Gem listened as the heavy, stone door disengaged from the floor. As it began sliding up, Coral leaned away from the counter, took up her tea, and walked toward the closed door between the kitchen and the open dining space.

"Will you be alright?" Gem asked.

"Yes," Coral answered, and waved back without looking.

Gem watched her sister pass through the narrow doorway, step downward, and disappear as the door closed behind her. The chamber was comfortable, and out of sight, and secured. Should the meeting with the watchers go awry, again, Coral would have a safe place to think before acting. Gem turned away from the counter and looked out through the high, wide opening.

She walked behind their three chairs, making a smooth, curved line as she approached the doorway, then passed through it, and took the three steps down into the bunker. As her boot soles hit the flat, stone floor, she ordered the Emissary to seal the cavern. As the system obeyed, and the door behind her began to lower, she continued walking.

The rows of beds on either side of the bunker were still neatly made, as they had been when they checked the day before. The cabinets between the beds were still closed. The chairs near them were still in the same positions. Glancing back over her right shoulder, she saw that the bunker's computing station looked untouched. She turned and walked on, looking ahead, to the high, metal doors to the south cave.

"Have they exited their craft?" she asked aloud.

"Yes, my Lord," the Emissary answered. "Commander Jaan and Commander Fits both wait, humbly, on the other side of the entry. Each of their pilots has remained in their respective craft. There are no other Lwoans with them."

"Can you see the pilots? Who are they?"

"I have not run a full scan. If you give me a moment, I can-"

"No, it's fine. Leave them be. The commanders will be enough to worry about. Have they requested entry?"

"Yes, my Lord. Commanders Jaan and Fits have each entered their codes."

"Very well. Open the doors. Fully."

Gem stayed back three yards, and the metal doors echoed as they disengaged. Slowly, they began to slide apart. Blinking, yellow lights from the watchers' two craft immediately entered her vision. The gull on the left and the bird on the right were each facing the cave opening, with their aft ends angled back and nearly touching, forming a makeshift shield from the elements drifting in. The winds coming into the cave were not heavy near the doors, but they were constant and steady. Their cold, blowing dampness hit Gem's face and hands, but she felt more refreshed than concerned. A small amount of exhaust from her gauntlets breezed through her sleeves. She took three steps forward, stopped, looked down at Jaan and Fits, and crossed her arms.

The two commanders were each down on one knee, with their left hands on the ground and their right fists pressed into their chestplates. Their helmets were still securely in place, and low concentrations of air from the cave floor moved through and around the tech on their legs and arms. Gem took another step forward, keeping some distance, but making sure that her boots were within their lines of sight. Neither of them flinched. Then, in unison, they greeted her with the words "My Lord."

Gem nodded, to herself. "Welcome back, Commanders."

"Thank you, my Lord," said Jaan. "Thank you for allowing us to return."

Gem waited, breathing in the air from the cave and smelling the ocean and rock and soil. She looked at both of the idling craft again. Their constant, heavy whirring, along with their dense exhaust, revealed the impressive power of their engines, even as they were expending minimal effort to rest in the cave. "And, who have you brought with you?" she asked.

"Our pilots, my Lord," Jaan replied. "Airman Malo, and Ensign Rial."

"No lieutenants?"

"No, my Lord."

"Good." She paused, letting her response linger. "And, what have you told your pilots?"

"To remain where they are unless called, my Lord."

"And what do they know about why you are here?"

"Everything, my Lord."

"And what do they know about the last time you were here, Commander Jaan?"

"Very little, my Lord."

Gem pressed her lips together as another memory came and went. Her father had not wailed, nor had he expressed much beyond acceptance and forgiveness after he had been hit with a blast from the lead watcher's gauntlet. She breathed steadily. The two commanders still had not moved. "Very well, Commanders," she said. "You may stand, and enter the bunker."

She stepped aside as the two men stood, and watched them carefully as they nodded to her and walked in. She glanced back at their craft, making sure their cabin doors were closed, and that their pilots were not visible, before turning and following the commanders. As they all entered the bunker, both of the men reached up, raised their helmets, and quietly breathed in. Gem looked upward, and ordered the Emissary to close and secure the doors.

Now standing in the space between the two closest beds to the cave entry, Jaan and Fits turned around to face her. There was humility in their eyes as they looked past her and watched the doors to the cave meet and lock in place. Then, the two of them stood more firmly and held their arms behind their backs, as if awaiting orders.

"At ease, Commanders," said Gem. She stepped toward the bed on the right.

Jaan and Fits both eased their demeanors, but only slightly, looking to each other for confirmation as they did. Fits's hair was more red and striking than Coral's, and he was an inch or two taller than his commander. Jaan's face was still strong and stoic, and his short, graying hair had what appeared to be new streaks of white on the sides. He was shorter than Gem, but only just. She crossed her arms, and felt the gauntlets rub beneath her sleeves as she looked at them.

"Thank you," said Jaan. "What…Will you help us, my Lord?"

Gem stared back at him. "*We* will help the people."

"Thank you. And, will Lord Andrew and Lord Coral be joining us?"

She shook her head. "No. Not today. They do not wish to commune with you. I can tell you what we have found, and what we propose."

Jaan nodded back. "Very well."

Gem took a step back and sat on the end of the bed. She motioned for the two men to do the same, and they followed suit. Jaan sat on the end of the bed directly across from her, several yards away. Fits retrieved a chair, set it down near Jaan, and sat. Gem crossed her legs and set her folded hands on her knee. Then, she began.

"Before the world collapsed, before Mother truly unleashed her wrath, mankind created much waste. We all know this, not just from historical records, but from what the salvagers still pull from the ocean. It has been three centuries now since Lwo's founding, and discard still surrounds us. But, some of this ancient waste is more dangerous than the rest. Old, ancient men had to find ways to dispose of the more dangerous materials in a way that kept them from contaminating water, soil, and sources of food.

"Days ago, Commander, after our System in the Sky reported what you said about the water, we began our own analysis. We started near the site of the Maw's encounter with one of the whales. Our system examined the area and tracked the darkness in the water. It also took samples of the water and brought them to us here, where we studied them. What we have found is quite disturbing."

After an exchanged glance with Fits, Jaan spoke up. "And what have you found?" he asked.

"The darkness in the water is from a substance far outside the land, miles outside the edge of the storm. And it has come to us from deep underwater, near the bottom of the old ocean."

Jaan stared back at her. "The system went outside the storm?"

"No, Commander. Of course not. It went close, but not beyond the edge. But we have many records here, some of which are not duplicated in any files on the mainland. Some of these records were retrieved long before the founding, and some were brought here at the founding. Many of them–too many of them–contain logs of purposely sunken waste. That is what has seeped into our ocean."

"*Purposely* sunken?" Fits asked, squinting.

"Yes, Commander. Before the collapse, even at the beginning of the collapse, mankind created much of his waste from generating energy. Some was carbon-based. Some was oil-based. And some was from a process called fusion. I know it's been decades for each of you, but I'm sure if you try you'll remember learning about these things, even if the lessons were brief. I personally remember the teachers from your time as youths."

"I vaguely remember," said Jaan.

"Same here," said Fits.

"Good enough," Gem said with a nod. She gently rubbed her

hands together, trying to warm them in the slightly cooler air of the bunker, and trying to settle her unease with the entire circumstance. "One of the massive containers that these men of old used to store an oil-based waste near the bottom of the ocean has burst. Or, perhaps just cracked. At least that is what we believe has happened. Its contents are the source of our contamination."

"Oil-based," Fits repeated. "What is in it, exactly?"

"Fossil fuels, and derivatives. It is clear that much of it was burned in some way before being disposed of. It must have been too dense, or too much, to burn off completely. And, it must have been unusable for the same reasons."

"We've suffered a loss because of this," said Jaan. "But only one. Is there a chance it is not from fossil fuels? That it is from another source?"

Gem shook her head. "No. Our tests were conclusive. We've only had one loss because your filtering process is so effective. Erul–may he rest peacefully–was aging, and also likely had a genetic condition that allowed a small toxin that got through the filtration system to weaken him."

Jaan looked back at her strangely. "You know his name?" he asked.

"I reported it, Sir," said Fits. "As is the norm. I just sent the message out this morning, and I included the post-mortem data. But, I did not expect a response."

"Well, you have one," said Gem. "And we mourn him as well.

I trust that you will bury him off the southern coast soon?"

Fits nodded. "Yes."

"Good."

"And..." Jaan started, hesitating. "My Lord, what of your burials?"

Gem stared back at him, waiting to see if he would look away, or perhaps lower his eyes, but he was stubborn. "Given all that you've done to get our attention, Commander, I am pleasantly surprised that it took you this long to ask. But, that is a topic for another time. We *may* be willing to address your curiosity, but only after we have addressed the water, and the safety of the people."

"Understood," he said with a nod. "Then, may I ask, what can we do about this contamination?"

Gem sighed, releasing some of the tension that was pulsing through her, and stood. She turned and walked toward the cabinet between her bed and the one a few feet away. She moved the chair aside, and then grabbed the handle on the cabinet and slid it upward, disengaging the doors. The sound of old metal echoed in the open space, and she looked upward.

"Emissary," she called. "A drone aid, please."

The system chimed in affirmation, and a distant hum came from above the door to their cavern. She reached into the cabinet, and retrieved the cylindrical canister that she had stored there. The silvery alloy felt cold in her hands. And being wide, and as long as her forearms, the canister was cumbersome. She grasped the black, composite cap that widened at the bottom end, and looked through the thick, glass viewing window of the metal cap on the top. The dense, blue liquid within it created glowing streaks as it moved about, indicating it had not degraded in the hours since she had stored it. She closed the cabinet and turned around with the container. Jaan and Fits were now standing, and looking upward.

Gem tried not to show any emotion as she approached them, and followed their gaze to the round, hovering machine that was lowering toward her. The drone's familiar, green glow was constant on its underbody, surrounding the small vents of the engines that were keeping it elevated. Looking at the two watchers, she noticed that their arms were at their sides, their stances were wide, and that they had added another yard of distance between them.

"You are in no danger," Gem said, almost relaxing at the thought of the watchers' concern. It meant that they still had a fear–even if it was minimal–of them, and of the Isle. "Please, settle yourselves."

The drone, now hovering just a few feet to her right, turned its glowing eye toward the two watchers, and then back to her. Jaan and Fits both looked at her, nodded in response, and remained standing as she passed by the drone and held out the canister.

"This should help," she said.

Jaan walked toward her, glanced at the drone, and then looked at the canister and took it into his gloved hands. His arms gave slightly under its weight. "What is it, my Lord?" he asked.

"A relatively simple compound," she answered. "In water, or oil, it will expand into a sponge-like substance. Over time, it will absorb–and hopefully neutralize–the toxins in the seepage from the outside."

Fits walked up behind Jaan. He looked down at the canister and into its window. "It's active," he said. "My Lord, how did you-"

"We still have some resources here," she stopped him. "Our systems help us. We are able to retrieve things–from the ocean, from the natural deposits on the Isle, even from the gasses in the sky. But, that is not your concern. You have to get this compound to the source of the contamination."

Holding the canister closer to him, and with a surer grip, Jaan looked up at her. "You want us to take it outside the storm?"

"It is unprecedented, Commander. But, yes. You must. You must find a way."

Fits took a step back, and glanced up at the drone, and then at the ceiling, before looking back at her. "My Lord, we've never, not in any generation, gone back to the outside. Not for anything. And now, only the salvagers even get to within ten miles of the edge, and that's only when they can convince us that there's value, and we actually believe them enough to escort them. And even then, we keep our distance."

"Commander Fits," she said. "You sound afraid."

"Yes, my Lord, I am. The outside is dead, and dying. We know from history. And there is the more recent confirmation, from

Robbins, and his son."

Gem felt her face twitch at the thought of the man who had come to them the year before. She quickly dismissed the memory of his arm closing around her neck. "Well," she said. "Perhaps they can help you."

Jaan looked at her with doubtful eyes. "Even if they could…" he started. "They can only *tell* us about the outside. How do we deliver this compound? What does the old container even look like?"

"I have never heard such doubt from the lead watcher. Perhaps it is time for you to be supplanted."

Jaan shook his head. "Please, my Lord. It's just that we have never, and would never think to-"

"You've done plenty in the past few weeks that you never would have before. And that was for yourself. But, this is for the people. You said you want no more death? Neither do we. This is the way. Unless, of course, you have a better idea."

Jaan looked to Fits, and then back to her. "No, my Lord. We do not." He nodded. "This is wise. We will find a way. We will do it."

"Good," she replied. "Then, there is something else. Emissary? Display the final design of the orb."

The lingering drone's front lens blinked, and they all watched. After a distant beep the lens blinked again, and then projected downward. Gem took a step back as the round glow hit the floor between the three of them. Slowly, a cylinder of light, four feet in diameter, arose. The luminescence was strong, but not unbearable.

The projection remained empty for a moment, and then the image began to emerge. The outlines of the globe-like shape came first, followed by the round duct passing through its center from top to bottom. Then, a flat plane rolled directly through the middle, from left to right, and the top and bottom halves parted slightly. In both halves, the boxy shapes of the tech engines appeared, followed by vents extending from the engines to the outer edge. The on-board computing system appeared last, an enclosed array of circuits and switches near the top of the orb.

"That canister in your hands will fit into the central duct," Gem said, pointing. "The engines will carry it through water. The computer will process any type of signals you send it, and the program will follow your direction. The rest is up to you."

Jaan handed the canister to Fits and stepped closer to the projection. "It's quite impressive, my Lord."

"I know," she said. "Can you build it?"

He looked through the light, and their eyes met. "I was hoping that you already had."

"No. The plans were just finished last night. It would take another week, maybe longer, for us to build something like this. I don't know how much time we have, but I imagine you can build it much faster on the mainland."

Jaan nodded back. "We can."

"Then, you must."

"We will."

"Very well." She looked upward. "That is enough, Emissary."

The projection slowly faded, and the drone drifted backward, but remained hovering just over Gem's right shoulder. She reached into the right pocket of her heavy pants, and grasped the small data drive. She took a few steps toward Jaan. Fits stepped closer to them. Behind her, the drone quietly clicked. It was following its programming, watching, waiting to act if needed.

"Open your hand," she ordered.

Jaan obliged, and held his right hand out palm up. She had not touched any watcher since the year before, when they had given her no choice. And she could not bring herself to offer even a light grasping of hands, as her father likely would have. Instead, she reached out, held the drive over his hand, and gently let go.

"That is everything we can offer," she said. "The design of the orb, the formula for the neutralizing compound, the likely location of the leaking container, and historical files of what was sunken in the north before the collapse. Do not lose any of it."

"We will not," said Jaan. He reached back, opened a small compartment on his belt, and slid the small drive in before closing it.

Gem held her arm out, motioning toward the door to the cave. "Very well. Now, go. Do your duty."

Jaan and Fits each saluted her, bringing their right fists up to their chests and lowering their heads. Then, they turned and walked. The Emissary had heard her, and the two heavy, metal doors disengaged and began to slide apart. Jaan was a step ahead of Fits, who was holding firmly to the canister as they headed toward the coldness. The obstructed winds of the storm drifted in from the cave. Gem felt her gauntlets softly humming again.

The doors stopped three yards apart, and as they did, Jaan stopped walking. He motioned for Fits to go on, and then turned back to Gem. She watched Fits, as he pulled his helmet back up and down over his head, and then jogged toward the waiting gull. Then, she turned to Jaan, already expecting more questions. She approached him, slowly, and he looked at her, silent but searching, as he secured his own helmet over his head.

"You have disrupted our balance, Commander," she said.

"I know, my Lord," he replied. "I felt I had no choice."

"The only good thing to come of it is that we were able to identify the threat from the outside. The *only* good thing."

He nodded. "We thank you."

She stepped closer to him, crossed her arms, and lowered her voice. "Do what you will with this knowledge, Commander. That the burial site you found, with your new device's help, was not the one we use for those we retrieve from the sky. That, you will never find."

The bewilderment in Jaan's face was visible even through his tinted front panel. Gem cautiously continued.

"What you did find was my father's final resting place. His last request was that he be buried near the people, so we found a place. It is sacred. Do not forget that." She looked upward, and stepped back. "Emissary? Seal the bunker."

Jaan stared back at her for another moment, and then quickly backed away and jumped out into the cave. He continued to face her through the shrinking opening. She stared back at him. Then, he turned and moved slowly toward the waiting bird. The doors shut behind him. The clang echoed throughout the bunker as they locked back into place.

CHAPTER 18
DUTY

"I don't suppose you could tell me why you have to leave so late?" asked Robbins.

"It's not that late," Maia replied.

She sat down in front of the hearth, where warmed stones were radiating heat throughout the first floor. She pulled her braids back over her shoulders and reached down for her boots. She slid her feet in, pressed them down into the soles, and secured the sides of the boots around her calves. Then, she reached back behind her neck, and with a dense, red band in hand, began looping and tying her braids together.

"Well, you weren't ready," said Robbins. "And you barely have time to make decent rings. Let me help."

She felt him walk up behind her, and waved him off. "No. This is fine for now. And I *was* ready. The commander's message was clear that it would be within three hours. I just wanted to rest a little more. I wanted all of us to."

She stood from the bench and finished placing the last few braids. She did not want to check them in the mirror. She patted around them and felt that they were decently bound. She needed to hurry. She did not want more of her husband's attention. There would be time enough for it later, she hoped. She took her jacket up from the bench and checked the tech engine affixed to the back. It looked clear. She slid her arms in and secured the jacket at the front, around her waist and at her chest. Then she looked to the shelf, where her helmet assembly and gauntlets were still sitting.

She glanced at Robbins, standing behind the bench with his arms crossed, and then went to her equipment. She put her gloves on first. Then she took up the left gauntlet, and slid her arm in, and felt it tighten near her elbow. She did the same with the right gauntlet. She grabbed her helmet near its base and lifted it up high, giving room to the metal support brace before carefully bringing it down near the tech on her back. Then, she felt a tug.

"It's heavy," Robbins said, as he grasped the brace and pressed it into place at the connecting points. "All of it is."

"Always has been," said Maia. "But you get used to it."

She turned around and looked into his eyes. He moved closer to her and held his arms out. She gently grasped his forearms and held them, keeping some space between them. He felt as strong as ever. She was sure that he was much stronger than her now. The cells of the lost Lwoans that ran through him were doing their job. She might have felt envious, were it not for the admiration that had been there for so long.

"Can you at least tell me what it's about?" he asked, stepping back and letting their arms part.

Maia reached back and pressed around her helmet brace, checking its stability. She tugged at her belt, and then at her gauntlets, making sure everything was secure. "I can and will," she said. "We've found the source of contamination in the ocean. Or, rather, the Lords have found it."

Robbins peered at her. "How did they...How..."

"The commander, along with a few others, was called to the Isle earlier today. And Lord Gem, apparently, explained it all. And now, we have to act."

Robbins nodded. "Okay."

"Okay? *Are* you okay?"

"I'm fine. At least we're...working together again, to improve the...the things out there."

She saw the wandering in his eyes and immediately knew that he was recalling the outside, and his life there. "You don't have to pretend," she said. "Not with me."

"Really, I'm fine. I'm better than fine. Out there, people only looked out for each other. People expected death at any moment, any day. They only lived for the day, as dark as each one was. Here– Lwoans–we live for possibility."

She swung her right arm up, quickly. He reflexively raised his left arm just as she tapped him on the shoulder. She laughed. "Now you're getting it. You're really one of us."

"Ha. I have been for a while now."

"Yeah, okay."

"You're starting to sound like our son."

"I guess you're both rubbing off on me. Some of that old, outside world must be good."

He shook his head. "Not much. But sometime, somewhere in the future, I hope so."

Maia heard a beep, followed by the click of her line opening. She quickly reached back, and pulled her helmet up and then down over her head. Robbins backed away. Looking into her display, she saw Jaan's signal and answered. "Commander, Sir. This is Lieutenant Maia. Go ahead."

"Lieutenant, we are almost ready," said Jaan. "How close are you?"

"I'm on my way out the door, Sir."

"Don't leave just yet. I want you to bring Robbins with you."

She paused, thinking, confused. "Sir?"

"Have him wait on the mezzanine once you get here. What we will discuss may require his input."

"Sir, how could it?"

"If you'll think, Lieutenant, and not be his wife for a moment, I'm sure you'll know. But I can explain all of that later. This is an order. For the both of you. Move quickly. Jaan out."

The line closed, and Maia tried to hide her frustration as she raised her helmet, and looked at her husband. Their eyes met. "The commander wants you to come with me," she said.

"To your meeting?" said Robbins. "A *watcher's* meeting? Why?"

She paused. "You–you and Devon–spent a lot of time in the ocean before you came to us. The source of contamination is there." She paused again, thinking. "It may even be outside the storm."

Robbins breathed in, and exhaled slowly. "Alright."

"You get ready. I'll call Prynn."

After Robbins had gone upstairs, and Maia had made her call, several minutes passed. She sat at the dining table, tapping her right boot over and over and listening to the bustling above as her husband continued to prepare. She could hear his and Devon's muffled voices. The boy's tone was far from happy, but he was still listening to his father.

As the sound of Robbins' steps moved away from the dining area and toward the curved stairwell, there was a knock at the front door. Maia stood from the table, moved quickly to the door, unlocked it, and slid it aside. She smiled as she saw her friend.

Prynn was not small, not for a civilian, but her eyes only came up to Maia's chin. Her ear-length hair was thick and full, and gray, as was the case with many Lwoans who had surpassed a century of life. Her eyes were bright, and calm. She was wearing a familiar dress, one with a long, sand-colored bottom and patterns of purple and blue flower shapes looping up, from around the tops of her dark boots to just above her waist. Her tan sleeves were long. Her purple scarf was heavy, and wrapped loosely around her shoulders. Maia hugged her, and whispered "Thank you" into her ear before letting her go.

"Hello to you too," said Prynn, in her high, hopeful voice. "And you already thanked me. You know I'd do just about anything for a watcher, especially you."

"I know," said Maia. She stepped aside and held her arm out for Prynn to enter.

"Devon, why are you making that face?" Prynn said as she walked in.

Maia stayed near the door, but turned around to see Robbins and Devon leaving the stairwell and heading toward Prynn. The boy looked calm, and his face was not the most sour it had ever been, but he was clearly upset.

"Something's wrong," said Devon. "I know it. This hasn't happened before–you having to come over so fast, and Dad having to leave with Maia."

Prynn walked to him, leaned over, held his shoulders, and looked into his eyes. "Well, watchers never really have a day off, do they? If something is wrong, and Maia has been called, then she can help. And your father…" She paused, and looked up at Robbins. "He's big and strong enough to be a watcher. Maybe they need his help too. That wouldn't be so bad, would it? Wouldn't you want him to help if the watchers needed him?"

"Yeah, I guess," said Devon.

"What's that?"

"I mean, yes, I would. But, they've never needed him before."

"By now, Devon, you're old enough to know that the land is unpredictable. Things happen that force the watchers to take action, and sometimes civilians as well. For three centuries now, every generation of watchers has done well to protect the people. We can trust them. And if they trust your father, then that's even better for you. Understand?"

"Yes, I do."

"Good."

"But…something's still wrong." He turned, and looked up at his father. "What is it, Dad?"

"I don't know yet, son," said Robbins. "But, we're going to fix it. Understand?"

"Not as much as I'd like to."

"Well, same here. But, I will soon. And everything's going to be fine."

"You've said that before."

"I know."

The boy managed a nod, and quieted. Prynn stood upright, nodded to Robbins, and stepped aside. He quickly thanked her and then walked up to Maia. He was covered in gray. The heavy pants, and the jacket, and the boots were the very same that he had been given the year before, just after he and Devon had been found, and after they had recovered from their time lost at sea. His helmet was firmly in his grasp, under his left arm. As he stepped past Maia and out the door, she looked into his eyes. She could feel his trepidation, though he was trying his best not to show it. He stepped into the street, and stopped. Maia looked back into their home.

"We'll be in touch as soon as we can," she said to Prynn. "Devon? I know you'll behave."

"Yes, I will," the boy said.

"I know," she said with a smile. "You always do."

With a nod to Prynn, Maia stepped out, slid the door shut, and listened as it locked back into place. She turned around to see Robbins already headed west, and jogged up to meet him. She moved to his right side and stayed close, but carefully avoided contact, maintaining her presence as the lieutenant of the division. From this point forward, until they were back in their home together, she was a watcher, and he was a civilian who might be able to aid the watchers.

"There was lots of darkness in the water," he said, keeping his voice low.

Maia kept her eyes forward. "I know. You've told me before."

They neared the high, heavy doors of the village's west entry, and then turned right, rounding a corner. The entry to the covered walkway was in the distance, straight ahead.

"I never really knew what it was," he went on. "Not exactly. No one did. We knew it smelled. We knew deadly, massive creatures lurked. And sometimes the waters were rough, but most times even the waves didn't reflect much light."

"But, you could see the sun," said Maia. "Right?"

"Sometimes. Far away. Most of the time it was just like it is here. It was covered in clouds. But the clouds out there, they're darker. They're…polluted. When it rained, it smelled worse. And you never got used to it."

Maia surveyed the street, and seeing no one in sight, replied. "All of that…it's why you're so strong now. Remember how durable your body was, just from exposure, and survival? And Devon's? You've survived, and endured, for decades. And now with your…" She hesitated, and looked around again. "With your extension, you're even stronger."

"You're saying it worked?" he asked.

"Yes."

"So, am I *more* Lwoan, as they intended? More than I would have been without it?"

She shook her head. "No."

She sensed his discomfort, but she kept herself from reaching for him, from touching a hand or a shoulder, and looked ahead as they passed by the last building on the right. Looking down the road that ran east, she saw a group of airmen lingering and conversing a block away. They did not look back, and she turned and continued walking with Robbins. They passed through the arched entryway and entered the covered, brightly-lit pathway to the tower's lift.

The sounds of the winds outside the pathway's clear, re-formed plastic covering immediately hit her ears. Maia was accustomed to walking the path, more so than Robbins. He looked up for a moment, with mild concern in his eyes, as the sounds of bouncing rocks and surges of air pushed through. Far, far above them, the Sky Tower hovered. Its equally-spaced corner lights blinked in plain white, forming a trapezoidal constellation in the darkness. The wide cable that ran from its underbody down to the ground reflected the light, creating a slim, gleaming line that faded as it moved downward. There was a flicker, and Maia saw the round shape of the ground lift as it began another thousand-foot descent.

Together, she and Robbins stopped at the wide double doors to the lift, and waited. She stepped off to the right, and he followed suit, and stood a few feet behind her. She looked back and saw him donning his helmet. And though it was not yet necessary, she did the same. Her helmet display indicated that all of her tech was idle, but fully functional. Her heartbeat and body temperature were normal. Gravity was normal. As a chime rang out, and the door to the lift unlocked and parted, she looked ahead.

A group of airmen–twelve in total, and all with their helmets retracted–filled the entry. Their boots clanged against the lift floor as they departed, and each of them saluted her as they passed by. Maia held her right fist up at the side of her head, silently acknowledging each of them until they had all passed. Then, she stepped in. She felt Robbins following closely behind.

She walked around the lift's center ring of seats, making sure that no other watchers remained. Then, she sat down in a seat facing the doorway. Robbins sat across from her and to the right, in a seat on the outer ring, and strapped in. As the lift chimed again, and the doors shut in front of her, she could not help grinning.

"What?" Robbins asked, his muffled voice carrying through the open space. "I'm still not used to this thing. You know that."

"You know…" she started. "If something did happen, if the cable gave way, or the lift disengaged for some reason, we'd be better off closer together."

"That cable rang my bell the last time. I hate that feeling."

"It's just vibrations."

"Too many vibrations."

Maia strapped herself in. A moment later the lift bounced up, drifted down, and then shot upward. The forces pushed through from below her seat, and she heard and felt the cable jittering through the wall behind her as the lift ascended at high speed. Less than one minute later, it slowed, and they hovered just before steadily sliding upward. Maia felt the lift lock into place above and behind her, and then heard the chime, and looked ahead as the doors parted.

The partially-diminished winds flowing through the hangar level drifted into the lift, and she unstrapped herself and stood. The tech along her legs and arms, and at her back, went to work, sending rapid, humming energy through her entire body. As she walked forward, Robbins stood up from his seat, grasped the lift wall, and checked his footing before following her out.

To their left, along the south wall, five blue birds, all in a row, were idling two yards above the floor. The light the hangar reflected off of their curves and edges. Two airmen nearby saluted.

Maia saluted back and kept moving. Ahead, and slightly right, her red bird was idling in the same place she had left it hours before. Far behind it, to the west, the wide entry revealed the evening sky and the cloudy haze of the storm winds being pulled through the tower's support engines.

As Maia neared the front of her bird, she turned, grabbed the hand railing, and moved up the grated metal steps. Looking back, she saw that Robbins was still close behind. As they reached the mezzanine level, she saw another squad of airmen. There were eight of them, all helmeted, conversing near the railing on the left side. They gradually quieted and straightened up as they saw her. As she saluted, they all did the same. Walking toward them, she could see Dilah on the end, closest to the tower's center lift. She disregarded the airmens' attention on her husband as she approached Dilah.

"At ease, Airman," she said. "Why are you all here?"

Dilah nodded back. "Lieutenant, Sir. The commander ordered us out of observation after the other commanders had all arrived. Do you know what is happening?"

"I do. It seems we've found the source of the contamination in the ocean. And, as usual, observation is the best place to convene."

"Understood, Sir. What about him?" she asked, looking past her, at Robbins.

Maia looked back, and then faced Dilah again. "This civilian's knowledge may be of use as we determine how to address the contamination."

"Civilian? Sir, is that not your husband?"

"It is. And where he comes from, in the south, he learned much about the ocean."

"Very well, Sir."

"But, he is not needed yet. I want you to look after him until he is either called up, or I return for him. Understood?"

Dilah nodded back. "Yes, Sir."

"Good."

Maia looked to Robbins again. He raised an open hand to bid her away, and then backed up several yards to the other side of the mezzanine. She turned toward the lift, walked up, and tapped the call button. The translucent door slid aside, and she stepped in, turned around, and tapped the button to ascend. The door closed, the lift pushed up from below, and she felt her heart sink. She could not remember the last time the motion had caused her any unease.

The lift stopped at observation, and the door slid open. The viewing wall that faced south showed only the land, and its darkness, and the shadowy hint of clouds above. Maia stepped out into the level and down the short step, and moved right, passing the two stations at the south-facing wall. She turned and saw that the west-facing wall's view was nearly identical to the south's. Then she heard familiar voices. She pushed her helmet up, and felt it settle behind her as she walked up to the group of leading watchers gathered at the north-facing wall. She was the last to arrive. She saluted as they all turned toward her.

"Lieutenant," Jaan said with a nod.

"Sir," she replied.

"It's good to see you, Lieutenant," said Terre.

Maia looked at the woman standing to her left and offered a subdued smile. "Likewise," she said. "Special Lieutenant."

It had been months since she had even heard from Terre, though she knew that the shop had been busy. She noticed a streak of gray in her dark hair that had not been as prominent before. She was standing just behind the workstation on the left. Brun was standing next to her, obstructing the view between the two stations. Fits was next to him, and was flanked by Orve. Jaan was close to the station on the right, holding a computer tablet in one arm. Shil was next to him. Maia walked up, stopping a yard from her sister. She stood firmly, and waited.

"Is he here?" asked Jaan.

Maia nodded back. "Yes, Sir. On the mezzanine, as ordered. Airman Dilah is with him."

"Very good."

With a few taps on the tablet, Jaan activated a projection, and aimed it at the floor between all of them. A wide square of light gradually arose, forming a box nearly three yards high. Within it, a multi-dimensional map appeared. Lwo's mainland was to the south and was only an inch or so wide. Most of the map showed a greenish-blue, oscillating surface, depicting the ocean. At its north end, near Jaan, a hazy, gray curve depicted the edge of the storm. Jaan tapped again, and a dot of white light emerged just north of the mainland, and then extended into a line, and continued extending, past a location marker for the Isle, all the way out to the storm's edge. Then, it went just beyond the edge, to a thin, dark area on the map, where it stopped at another point. The finished line was not quite straight. It had made slight turns and curves along its entire route.

"This is the approximate location of our source of contamination," said Jaan, pointing at the spot outside the storm. He handed the tablet to Shil, and she kept the image steady as he walked closer to it. "This is also the approximate path the contaminants took through the ocean to reach the mainland. The Lords have revealed to us that a broken container of some kind, likely sitting at this point outside the storm, is leaking its contents. We have to get there in order to stop it. They have also provided something to help us. Fits?"

Fits turned, reached back to the chair at the workstation, and pulled up a large, metal, cylindrical container. A hint of blue light was visible at the top. "We did a brief analysis on the way back from the Isle," he said. "The compound in this canister contains plant cells, soil particles, a foaming agent, and multiple natural and synthetic binders among other things. In the water it will expand, and then absorb and very likely neutralize the oil-based contents from the container. We just have to…"

"Get it down to the container?" asked Brun.

"Yes," said Jaan.

"And, how do we do that?"

"Lieutenant Terre? By now you've seen the plans for the orb, correct?"

"Only just," said Terre.

"And what do you say?"

Terre walked up to the projection, almost touching it as she stopped. The light beamed around her face, revealing a strain in her eyes. "Sir, will you bring up the plans here?"

Jaan stepped closer to Shil, and after a few words were exchanged, she began tapping. Maia watched her sister's fingers as they moved through the tablet's files and found one labeled 'Orb Final.' She tapped the icon, and the projection of the map slowly lowered. Above it, another shape emerged. The design of the device was almost a perfect globe, with an array of wind tech engines and a simple computer. Maia moved one step closer, and watched as the schematic rotated.

"I can build it," said Terre. "It will take two days."

"We hardly have that much time," said Jaan.

Terre shook her head. "If we rush, it could malfunction in the water. These tech engines will have to endure pressure at unknown depths. So will the body, and so will the center duct that will hold that compound. It will have to be reinforced from the center out. Not to mention, we will have to be extremely precise. There is much less of the metal that we used for the ray."

"Alright," said Jaan. "Then, we have two days to get ready. Does…Does everyone agree?"

The attention in the room shifted heavily toward Jaan. Maia could not help noticing. Being the closest to their commander, she had sensed some doubt from him before. To the others, the slight change in his voice had likely been unexpected.

"We agree," said Fits, in a tone that almost conveyed a defense of the commander. "But, we'll need something else from the shop."

Terre backed away from the projection, and then looked through it at Fits. "Something else?" she said.

"Yes. Our craft are not built to traverse dense water. Gull engines can take in more than others, but not much more. But out there, we already know that the winds, if any, are much weaker. The rotation of forces that forms the edge of the storm creates a vortex that could not be sustained were it not for much weaker forces on the outside."

A sense of realization floated through the room. Deep within every watcher's mind, and the minds of most Lwoans of adequate age, was the basic knowledge of how the vortex around the land, which was protective in addition to being deadly, sustained itself. Maia stared downward, at the glowing map below the glowing orb, at the cloudy edge on its north side.

Terre nodded, and gently set her hands on her hips, submitting to the circumstance. "How many gulls will need to be modified?"

"First, Lieutenant, how would you do it?" asked Jaan.

"We can remove the standard vent covers and replace them

with wide-gapped covers. But, on the way out and back, you'll have to fly low to avoid the debris at higher elevations."

"That will slow us down."

Terre nodded. "Yes, but it would be the safest way. A trek to the edge at high altitude would take at least six hours. Another hour to avoid catastrophe would be worth it."

Fits nodded. "I agree. And, I would recommend that we take five gulls—one to carry the orb and the neutralizing compound, and four others to flank it and provide support if needed."

"Beyond the low winds…" Terre continued. "And the forces at the edge, what else do we know about what might be out there?"

"Not much," said Brun. He looked around, at everyone. "Right?"

"Right," said Fits.

"Right," said Shil.

"But, we can learn," said Jaan. He lifted his eyes toward Maia. "Lieutenant Maia? What would the civilian Robbins have to say?"

The room quieted, and Maia felt everyone's attention on her. Her heart pounded beneath her crossed arms as she looked around at them and thought. Every commander and lieutenant in all four divisions had been made aware of Robbins and Devon's origins, around the same time, if not before, that they had all been made aware of what had happened on the Isle. But, they rarely spoke of any of it. It was a habit not worth the risk of starting.

"Sir..." Maia started. "He would certainly say that there is death, and foulness, and pollution. And there is a lack of sunlight, as there is here."

"And what else?"

She shook her head. "I'm not sure."

"Then, we need him up here. Now. Call him."

"Sir, I..."

"Now, Lieutenant."

Maia nodded, stepped back, and turned around. She reached back for her helmet, and pulled it up and then down over her head. She opened a line to Robbins, and then added Dilah. He answered first.

"Yes," he said plainly.

"We will need your knowledge now, Robbins," she said. "Airman Dilah, please escort our civilian guest up to observation."

"Yes, Sir," said Dilah.

"Thank you. Maia out."

The lines closed, and Maia tilted her helmet back up and marched toward the lift. She passed by the empty workstations, turned, and stopped directly in front of the lift. She stood there and watched as lines arose behind the translucent door, and two figures appeared. The lift stopped, the door slid aside, and Robbins stepped out into the level. Maia looked through his helmet's tinted panel and into his eyes. She motioned for him to remove the helmet, and he obliged. Behind him, Dilah saluted, as the lift door closed in front of her. Maia watched and listened as the lift descended, and then guided Robbins toward the group.

"Welcome, Robbins," Jaan said as they approached.

Maia stopped in the same spot, next to Shil, and Robbins stood to her left. She watched him as he looked around the room at each of the leaders and finally settled on Jaan.

"Thank you, Commander," he replied. "I'm afraid I do not know everyone here."

"Yes, I know," said Jaan. "Those you have yet to meet are Special Lieutenant Terre, our head technician, and Lieutenant Orve of the mountain division. Watchers?"

"Greetings Robbins," said Orve.

"Greetings," said Terre.

Robbins nodded to both of them, and then looked around again, acknowledging Brun, and then Fits, and finally Shil. "Greetings, all."

Jaan continued. "Everyone here, Robbins, knows where you come from. You, and your son."

"I suppose that will make this a little easier," said Robbins. "There's nothing to hide."

"I hope so."

"I have to say, you seem quite strong," said Terre. "It's surprising, considering what's likely out there, and what you and your son likely endured."

"We were well cared for after we were found," said Robbins.

"The food and water here are much more beneficial than anything on the outside."

"True," Terre said with a nod.

Maia saw the sudden suspicion in Terre's eyes, and spoke up. "And he was extended, by our Lords. And against his will. And we all know this."

"I know," said Terre. "I just wanted to hear it out loud."

"Why?"

Terre hesitated, and sighed, shaking her head. "Because we hardly know this man."

"I do. Commander Shil does. So does Commander Jaan. And they trust him."

"That's good, but still, the Lords were not able to finish with him. Right?"

"Finish?" Robbins said, staring back at Terre.

"That's right. Are you really one of us? Isn't that what they intended? Did they strengthen your mind along with your body? Or, do you still harbor anger, from everything that happened?"

Robbins crossed his arms. "I have been here nearly a year now. I have given to the land, done my part. And I care for Lwo, because Lwo has cared for me and my son. But nothing–no procedure, no treatment–could erase my memory or my experience."

"And that is why you are here," said Jaan. "Special Lieutenant? Robbins has proven himself a true Lwoan. If you have more doubts, I will be happy to address them after we have finalized our plans. Understood?"

"Yes, Sir," Terre said with a nod.

"Good. Robbins?" he called, and motioned toward the images still glowing between all of them. "Please observe the projection. We have recently learned much from the Lords. This line running from near the mainland and out past the storm's edge shows the path of the contaminants in the water. You can see that it originated just beyond the edge. We will have to travel outside the storm to neutralize it. So, we ask, what can you tell us about the outside?"

Robbins stepped closer to the projection and ran a hand slowly along the edge, disrupting the light. He looked at the map, and at the round design hovering above it, and then back at the map. He reached into the projection, placed his finger near the white line, and began to walk and trace, from the spot near the mainland out to the point beyond the storm's edge, until he was standing near the dark space depicting the outside. He was right in front of Jaan, and stood there, quiet. Maia could see that he was remembering.

"Why do you have to go there?" Robbins asked. "If you have a way to neutralize the contamination, why can't you do it from here?"

"The Lords provided us much information beyond what you see here," said Jaan. "The ancient container, from which the contaminants emerged, has likely only leaked a small amount of what it holds. If we do not stop it there, we may never be able to, and we'll be forced to constantly, continually treat the inflowing water much more than we already do. It would not be sustainable."

"Neither would a trip to the outside. Not for long."

"The decision has been made, Rob-"

"I've already told you," Robbins stopped him. "I've told you before how awful our lives were out there. We barely lived. I was sure when we left the last ship–left behind my battered, dead wife–that my son and I would die. But, compared to what we were enduring, it would not have been a terrible fate."

"Robbins," Jaan continued, keeping his voice calm. "From the little you've told me, I have only gotten a sense of how bad it was. We need details. We are going. You can help, or you can not help and hope that we don't fail and die ourselves."

Robbins backed away from Jaan, passing through a corner of the projection, and turned around, and looked at Shil, and then Maia. She could see the fear in his eyes, a fear like she had not seen before. She stepped toward him, but he raised a hand, stopping her, and turned to face Jaan again.

"My wife stays," he said.

"What?" Jaan said, almost smiling.

"I'll help, if my wife stays."

"Civilian!" Maia called, loudly, before Jaan could respond more harshly. She moved closer to him and lowered her voice. "What are you doing?"

He kept an eye on Jaan as he answered her. "I want my son–our son–to be safe here. Your staying here will ensure that, and ensure that he always has a place, even if I do not."

"It is not your place to ask."

"The lieutenant is right," said Jaan. "We will decide who goes and who does not. But, my civilian friend, procedure already dictates that at least one leader from each division stay behind in a situation like this."

Robbins turned to face him again. "You've broken the procedure before," he said. "You did it when you came to get me and my son from the Isle last year. For that, I am still thankful. But, I want a promise. And believe me, there's plenty more I could tell you. It may hurt me to remember it all, but if you don't know it, you'll be hurt a lot more."

"Alright, Robbins. Agreed."

"Commander!" Terre said, her voice firm, but low. "You can't let-"

Jaan raised both his hands, stopping her, and urging the entire group to remain calm. "It is not much to ask," he said. "Robbins, you have my word. Lieutenant Maia will stay. I would not have sent her in my place anyway. And, you will be able to confirm it yourself. You will come with us."

"What!?" Maia snapped, unable to contain her emotion. "Commander, I-"

"Quiet, Lieutenant!" Jaan said sternly. "Your husband made a request. And I think it is a fair one. Now, he can live up to his stated concern for the people. If he goes, we have a much better chance of succeeding."

"You're right, Commander," said Robbins. He nodded to him. "I will come."

Maia moved up closer to her husband, almost touching him before she stopped herself and whispered into his ear. "Why? Why would you agree to go? You don't have to. You're the only one here who wouldn't have to. With all you've said, all you've told me, how could you even consider it?"

Robbins turned and faced her. "He's right. If I go, there's a higher chance of success, and survival. If you were to go and not make it back, Devon and I would have few allies here. And secrets, I gather, are not as well kept on this land as we'd all like to think."

"He's right," said Shil.

Maia turned to her sister, and looked into her eyes. She saw calmness and focus, and she could feel her strength. She tried to gather herself. She wiped at her face, but there were no tears on her cheeks, just heat. She stepped back to where she had been, and faced the rest of the group. No one was especially focused on her. They were paying more attention to Robbins. He walked by her, and then stood next to her again.

"We'll take care of him, Lieutenant," Fits said, pushing his voice through the projection. "Don't worry."

Maia nodded, and they all quieted and waited for Jaan. He directed Shil to deactivate the projection. As the image compressed and faded away, he opened the floor to Robbins.

CHAPTER 19
ENDANGERED

"I hope that this will be enough," he started. "I was young when I left the East Coast. At the time I couldn't prove it, but I was sure I had seen all of the land sinking. Years later, it was confirmed. I had traveled around the globe, who knows how many times. We used the instruments that worked on the ships, and when they stopped working, we used the stars. But after a while, you stopped counting. At least, I did. I was over thirty when I saw the alignments that matched up with where I had been born and raised. And all that remained, poking up through the dark, smelling water, was a small mound with some ragged-looking vegetation.

"In that moment, I tried to reminisce. I really tried to remember my parents. But their faces had faded, replaced by years of darkness and strangers. And my phone and the pictures in it had been long gone. So many memories were gone. Had the ship stayed a bit longer, some of them might have come back, but we saw the large hump of a creature and turned away, even leaving the possibility of food behind.

"The creature's body had been bright in color, but it had

disappeared so quickly that none of us on the old ship had been able to see any real detail. We knew it was massive. We were on an old freighter, and it was probably as big as that, if not bigger. We were–all of us–just happy to have avoided it, to have lived another day. A week later we found another mound, and there was no creature to stop us from moving toward it. I was with the group that went down, harvested a few bushels, and were quickly brought back up. I got to the railing on the ship's starboard bow. I got a hold of it. Then, a woman took the bushel from my arm and shoved me.

"'More for my children,' was what she whispered, to herself I suppose, because she turned away quickly. I dropped a few yards, yelling for what seemed like forever before the rope around my waist was tugged and I stopped. Two other harvesters above me were being pulled over the railing, but no one was pulling me. I set my feet into the side of the ship and started climbing back up. I heard a commotion as I got closer to the deck. It was Tamra, Devon's mother, who had intervened.

"She was young then–very young, barely an adult–but she was fiery. She kept some others–who had determined that I was some kind of threat–at bay until I could get myself over the railing. I let the mother who had pushed me go. She did, in fact, have small children who were already sickly. But there were two men in her group, much older than me, who were boasting about how they had come up with the plan. No one intervened when I pushed Tamra aside, grabbed the bigger man by his collar, and dragged him toward the railing. No one stopped me as I held him over the edge. Then, as I looked past him, down at the water, I saw another creature. It must have been only its top, but this time its size was much more evident. And it lingered, as if it were waiting to be fed. I pulled the old man back, threw him to his people, gave a warning to the others standing around, and went off to my room below deck.

"On that ship, for another year, no one ever mentioned to me what had happened. And no one ever asked me to descend again for fishing or harvesting. The old man was eventually thrown overboard by someone else. I didn't see it, but I heard he was able to tread water for a little while.

"A few months later, on a very cold day, the ship became moored. It was something below the surface, in a part of the world we called the Old South Pacific. After a few weeks, barely surviving, we were able to board another ship that floated close by. The woman and her children, who had all managed to get a bit healthier, were on a crowded dinghy in front of mine. One of the children, a young girl, fell out halfway between the ships. Had it not been for the undertow, she might have survived. The rest of us managed to make it onto the new ship, and spent the rest of the night trying to block out the woman's constant wails.

"It was only a few weeks later that Tamra even spoke to me. She came to me in a corner of one of the big, open rooms. She was ill and bordering on frail, but she was walking. She wouldn't say a word until I handed her a handful of old, dry greens I had in a bucket. Then she sat, and ate quietly, and told me her name.

"It was another year before she was anywhere near healthy, and I finally realized how she had managed to survive without another man getting a hold to her. She had, somehow, been hiding the lovely things about her face. And she had regularly worn clothing that was old and dirty, even for us survivors. And when the rain didn't sting, she would stay covered up, instead of taking the chance to get a good bath like the rest of us. And when she did have a cough, I think she made it last for weeks instead of days. But, she was brave, and determined to survive. And, she said, she saw the same in me.

"We had been bound to each other, in more ways than one, for just over two years when I saw a flash for the first time. We were somewhere far north of the equator. We came upon what we thought was just another mound. But as the ship inched closer, and some of us went to look, we saw smoke, billowing up into a darkening sky. Then, we felt a heat in the air, and a bright, orange light erupted. Some were in awe. Some ran back inside. Tamra went back into our cabin. But I stayed out and watched, and realized that whatever it was, it would not reach us. It died down after a few minutes of lighting up the sky.

"Most of us who had watched began heading back inside. Someone else, though–a man much younger than me–had gotten too excited and was leaning over the railing just a bit too far. He was staring up at the fading light, smiling, when something bumped the ship's front end from below. I held tightly to that railing, as tight as I ever had on any ship, and looked down. I saw something disturbing

321

the water, then I heard the man scream loudly, and then stop screaming as he crashed into the water. A few minutes later a group came out with a rope. They were about to toss it over when I ran up to stop them. I had seen the creature, whatever it was, for just an instant. Then, I heard splashing, and some kind of groans or grumbling where the man had entered the water. It was dark, but when I looked down again, I saw the red splotches on the ocean surface. The only good thing about any of it was that the boy had left no one behind. We changed course right away."

He sighed and looked up for a moment before continuing. "This was life, out there. Every year was the same–darkness, bad air, sour fish when we were lucky, and death. Unpredictable death, from nature or from mankind, even with so few of us. In my life before Lwo I encountered, maybe, a few hundred people. All of them were like me–terrified, and unsure, and desperate. Very few had any hope, or any character, left in them. Tamra conceiving was the only thing that kept me from becoming any worse, and her too. Devon being born renewed us both, somehow, even though he was another burden. For her, it was more physical. The pregnancy had helped her overcome her reoccurring illness, and her desire to disguise herself. She wanted our son to see the love in her eyes. And that…that was what led to her death. After that, my son and I left, heading blindly north, hoping for something, but expecting nothing."

Robbins stopped, and the group remained silent, taking in all that he had just shared. After a few minutes, Terre turned to him.

"Can you describe the smells more?" she asked.

Robbins nodded back. "Rotten. Like dying vegetation, or a dying creature. Sometimes like human waste, though that was usually in the air inside the ships."

"What about off the ships? Where did the smells come from?"

"Everywhere. The water. The mounds where we managed to find food. They weren't constant out there, though. We had a few hours sometimes, usually early in the day, when all we smelled was salt and rain."

"And what about the rain? How often were you stung by it?"

"All the time."

"But, it didn't damage your skin?"

Robbins reached down, and began tugging his left sleeve. The heavy fabric was resistant, but he got it past his elbow and revealed the faded scar curving from the outside to the inside of his upper forearm. "It did," he said. "This is from a downpour we hit in the Old South Atlantic, not long after I left the East Coast. I have more on my legs and ankles. They took days to stop burning, and weeks to heal."

Terre moved toward him, stopping two yards away to get a better look at the discolored skin. "Was there any bleeding?" she asked.

Robbins shook his head. "No. Redness, and dryness. Throbbing, but no bleeding. Probably because we learned to always rinse anything that was exposed in a toxic storm with clean water, and right away."

Terre nodded. "And, how is it you didn't get out of those storms in time?"

"They were random, unpredictable. And if they were predictable, we didn't have any useful instruments to do it."

"And did the storms damage the ships you were on?"

"Over time? Always. It's one of the reasons they didn't last long. The metal hulls, as heavy as they were, would slowly disintegrate."

"Okay," said Terre, backing away. "Thank you."

"Special Lieutenant, why did you ask these things?" asked Jaan.

"Sir, it is important to know what elements the craft we send out may be exposed to," she said. "Without any samples from the outside, I can only guess. So, we'll have to add another layer of repellent coating to every gull that's going, just as a precaution."

"Alright. Very good." Jaan looked around the room. "Any other questions?"

"The creatures you encountered," Brun started. "How big were they again?"

Robbins looked over at Brun. "The biggest ship I was ever on was a hundred yards from end to end. I once saw the top of a creature–just the top–that was as long, if not longer."

"Did they ever sink a ship?"

"I saw the ends of many sunken ships, near many sunken coasts. They may have been sunk by sea beasts. They may have just worn out. I don't know."

"So…" said Orve, hesitating. "These creatures were much more dangerous than, say, our new whale species?"

Robbins looked at Orve, and then at everyone else. "I've never said it out loud, or to Lieutenant Maia, but I don't think these whales are looking for food. I don't even think they're running from the pollution. I think they're running from predators."

"You don't think that's your lifetime of fear talking?" asked Jaan.

"Yes, fear," said Robbins. "And experience. If the whales are as big as the salvage ships, they're still much smaller than the things I saw. And, nature is nature."

"He's probably right," said Shil. She turned to Terre. "Special Lieutenant? Is there anything you can do to the gulls to help? Can you give them any kind of defense?"

Terre crossed her arms and looked up at the high, metal ceiling. A gust of wind howled somewhere above as she looked back down. "We can add shield generators," she said. "We could, possibly, put arrays on the roofs. There, they would avoid too much exposure to water. But we haven't tried to shield any craft in centuries, not since the founders feared a threat might still come from the outside."

"Then, make sure you test them," said Jaan. "If they don't work, so be it. Elevation and speed control will be much more important for this mission."

Terre nodded. "Yes, Sir."

"Then, we may as well make sure they can shoot," said Fits. "Since the tech will already be there."

"We don't want to hurt the creatures," said Shil.

"You can't," said Robbins. The rest of the group stared back at him, but he continued. "You may be able to stun one. Maybe."

"Very well," said Jaan. "Lieutenant Terre?"

"We can do it, Sir," said Terre. "We need to get started right away. The orb will be enough work just for me, without having to oversee the rest."

"Very well. You are dismissed. Commander Fits will maintain communication with you."

"Yes, Sir. Good luck, to everyone. May Mother protect us."

Terre saluted, and everyone except for Robbins, who only nodded, saluted back. She headed for the lift, and after she had gone, the rest of the group gradually moved in closer, with Jaan near the center.

"I don't have to tell you all how critical this mission is," Jaan said. "If the water coming in remains contaminated, we're not going to last very long. Probably not even a generation."

Shil looked around before speaking. "Sir?" she started. "Who will lead?"

"I will. And Commander Fits will. You have enough to do in the city, and if for some reason we do not return, the people will need you."

"Yes, Sir," she answered, nodding.

"And Commander Brun? You will need to maintain order on the ground. Manage our water, and make sure the people are kept informed, as much as they need to be."

"Yes, Sir," said Brun.

"Lieutenant Maia," Jaan said, turning toward her. "I will leave the division in your charge. You'll have to make arrangements for your son to be looked after."

Maia nodded, and replied "Yes, Sir."

"Robbins?"

Robbins looked at Jaan, and tilted his chin upward, and waited.

"You need to be trained."

"Trained?" Robbins replied.

"To use a watcher's suit. You'll need protection out there. You don't have time to learn everything, but you can learn enough to help you survive."

"Respectfully, Commander, I survived without one of your suits my whole life."

"But mostly outside the storm, and then only until you couldn't take anymore, and you drifted to us. And it's been some time since then. You will be exposed to Lwo's elements in new ways. Lieutenant Maia can find a suit for you from our supplies. And she can train you. Understood?"

Robbins nodded. "Understood."

"Good. Everyone, keep your lines open. And be ready. Our

team will leave in two days. Dismissed."

*   *   *   *   *

The gym in the village, where watchers of the sky trained daily, was in the southeast quarter, two blocks south of the hospital. It was built along the barrier wall's edge, with dark, floor-to-ceiling vents that allowed the storm's natural winds to flow in. The winds pushing through the room were filtered, and controlled, like the low winds that floated throughout the village, but with fewer safeguards in place.

Behind the sand-colored north wall of the gym there was an entry area, where watchers could prepare for training, and observe others from the lone viewing window twenty feet up. The opposite side held the majority of the looming vents, which constantly howled, whether the training winds were kept high, or low.

The ceiling was three stories high, with flat lights that could, apparently, simulate any time of day. At the moment they were fairly bright, like the typical gray of day. The floor was an eighty-foot-wide circle, with a minimal fabric padding covering most of its paved surface, but not all of it. Most of the room was neutral in color, but the fabric was deep red, as a warning for any trainee who might be on their way to crashing.

Several two-yard-high blocks–all made of wood and metal, painted various colors, and resting on wide, wheeled supports–were

328

spread along the east wall, where Maia was standing and watching. She had said the obstacles would not be needed, but Robbins had been watching her during their short breaks. She had examined each one, running her gloved hands along their surfaces, pressing them to test for stability, or weakness, or something else. Now, sitting on the floor on the west side of the room, he wondered if she had changed her mind, and would force him to dodge while falling or jumping. He was already exhausted from just a few hours of those simple movements.

He stood from his sitting position, and stretched his arms, and leaned back and forth on each leg. The fabric of the blue suit was comfortable. The inside of the pants and jacket were soft, but tacky enough to remain in place on his skin and the snug undergarments. The gloves felt the same. The boots were heavy, especially with the affixed engines that his usual boots could never hold. But, he could move his legs well enough. The main issue was the tightness. The securing straps near his ankles and calves felt a bit too secure, but it was how Maia had instructed him to wear them. He could have gotten used to all of it, he felt, were it not for the heavy wind tech.

Each tech engine weighed at least eight pounds. Handling Maia's on occasion, the gauntlets had never felt as heavy as they did now, resting on his forearms. The engine mounted to the back of his jacket felt even heavier. And he could feel its constant humming, along with the humming from the other pieces spread around his body, especially the small, flat engines on his waist. There was a constant tingle around his midsection. That had not been the case outside the gym. As he had carefully donned it all, following Maia's direction, he had felt the weight. Now, he felt the weight of each engine and every force being pulled through them. But, in the critical moments since they had entered the gym–moments when it seemed the winds coming in would overpower him–the weight had felt like nothing.

"Helmet on!" Maia yelled from across the room.

Robbins reached back, pulled the helmet up, and felt the tension along the flexible, metal mounting arm as he pulled it down over his head. He pressed his open hands into both sides, and pulled it down further, and listened to the subtle snap as it was secured in place around his neck. He breathed in deeply. The air in the helmet was stale and artificial, as the filters blocked even some safe natural gasses along with any invisible debris. He looked into the clear display and saw green at every point of tech along the body diagram. The line in the helmet clicked open, and Maia's signal blinked into view.

"Ready, trainee?" she called.

"Ready," he answered.

Off to his right he heard the vent mechanisms shifting, echoing from within the walls. The wind forces quickly increased. He spread his stance, bent his knees, and closed his fists as the forces increased more and pressed upon his body as they moved around him. The humming of his tech intensified, and he saw their concentrated streams of exhaust flowing out to his left.

"Your readiness is good," said Maia. "Now, leap off the wall."

Robbins took a moment to feel the stability in his boots, then leapt backward, and tilted his body forward. He was carried left, but quickly got his boot soles into the wall and pushed off. The momentum took him up, and further left, toward the viewing window. He whispered "stabilize," and felt the engines on his left arm and left leg increase their power as those on his right began to weaken. Gradually, the wind stopped carrying him, and he remained hovering in place. He looked down at the floor, now twenty feet below him.

"Very good," said Maia. "Now, a drop."

Robbins felt the slight decrease in the winds and knew what was coming. He prepared himself, tensing both legs. His tech quieted as he moved toward the ground. As his boots touched, he widened his stance and let his knees bend. Then he stood firm, feeling the forces flowing around him, and looked over at Maia. She was behind one of the obstacles, resting one arm on its edge. She only nudged the large block, but it shot out, powered by the tech in its wheeled base as it sped at him. As it got closer, the winds picked up again.

He did not hesitate. He did what he had been taught. He jogged toward the threatening object. His tech reacted to his movements without commands, and as he leapt, and floated up, the engines kept his vector stable. He kicked off the top of the speeding block and flew up another three yards. The winds decreased, and he drifted downward, and onto another moving block, landing with one knee down. The winds picked up again, and he leapt off the obstacle. This time it felt as if he had lost some control. His display indicated the new wind speed: 110 MPH. He adjusted his arms and legs, angled himself downward, and began to drop. As he landed on the floor, he knelt again.

The heavy, directed winds flowed all around him and through his tech, and he looked up and saw two more obstacles. One was on the left side of the high-reaching vents. The other was on the right. Their base engines were keeping them in place, but being closer to the vents, they were still noticeably tilting back and forth. He looked back, over his left shoulder, at Maia, but she was only watching, motionless as cloudy exhaust flowed around her. When he looked forward again both obstacles were racing at him.

He stood quickly and adjusted his stance, getting a feeling for the forces moving around him before acting. He took one giant step forward, and then another, and then another. He got to a steady jogging pace and leapt forward. The obstacle on the right grazed his shoulder. The one on the left bumped his knee as it sped by him. He landed, and looked back to see them crash into each other before rolling off in different directions.

"Good," Maia said. "Now, come to me."

The winds coming at Robbins were still strong, pressing on him from all sides as he tried to keep a wide, strong stance. His display indicated no decrease in speed. "How?" he asked.

"Go through the winds," she answered. "Go to the source."

A sudden gust pushed Robbins back a yard, and he adjusted his stance again. He took one step forward, and then another, gradually getting faster with each movement. He felt the heat on his back, as his largest piece of tech worked even harder. His arms and legs burned, more and more with each step. His chest felt almost numb, but he kept advancing. He got to within five yards of the vents before he was forced to change direction. He turned left, and felt the nudge from behind. Then, he leapt again and let the winds carry him.

He whispered "float," and felt his tech adjust. Each engine remained open just enough to let the winds move around his body without pushing him too hard. Cool, white exhaust flowed outward and upward, from every piece of tech. As he neared Maia's position, she stepped out, away from the wall. He adjusted his arms and legs, moving them carefully through all of the surrounding forces until he touched the wall where she had been. The winds from the high vents began to decrease, and he kept one hand on the wall as he slid down to the floor, where he took a deep breath. The heat of his body seemed to flow through the suit.

"Not bad," said Maia.

Robbins took another breath, looked up at her, stood, and pushed his helmet up and back. The light winds that remained flowing around them cooled his face. He stretched his shoulders as the helmet settled just above his rear engine. "Not bad?" he replied. "That's all?"

"Didn't you see me standing in place with no trouble?"

He nodded. "Yes. I did. I could have too."

"Really? With no trouble at all?"

"Maybe."

She managed a smirk. "Still, not bad for a brand new

watcher."

"I'm not a watcher."

"For the sake of this mission, you are. Understood?"

He saw the intensity and focus in her eyes. "Alright. Understood."

She reached out and set her hand gently on his left arm. "With your strength, and some more discipline, you'd do well as one of us."

He wiped a bead of sweat off of his forehead. "Can we talk about that after we're all back home safe?"

"Very well then. Could you use a break?"

"What time is it?"

Maia tilted her helmet up and back. "Always note your status, and your environment's status, before removing your helmet. Understand?"

He nodded.

"It's six forty-two."

"Then, I could use some food. We've been here for hours."

"Your pack," she said pointing. "On the back of your waist."

He shook his head. "Real food...Sir."

"Our ready bars *are* real food. They're made from real vegetables, real grains, real fruit."

"Is that all we'll have tomorrow? For the whole day?"

"I don't know what the commander's plans are. But, you'll definitely have plenty of bars. Every watcher craft is always stocked with them."

"Because you never know where duty will take you, or for how long. Right?"

She smiled. "Right."

He nodded back, and breathed deeply again, and wiped his brow.

Maia's posture eased, and she looked around the room and up at the bright ceiling. "Actually, we should go," she said, looking back at him. "And you should definitely eat. I can't really teach you anymore, not in the time we have left. You're leaving early tomorrow."

"I know."

A quietness settled between them, but did not linger, as Maia quickly turned, and motioned for him to follow her. He marched in step behind her, and as they approached the high double doors that led out to the entry area, he looked up at the viewing window. He caught a glimpse of Prynn's short, silvery hair, but he could not see Devon.

The doors unlocked and slowly parted, revealing two blue-clad airmen waiting on the other side, and behind them, the expansive entry area, filled with dark walls, benches, and a handful of open equipment cabinets. Both airmen had their helmets on. They saluted Maia, and she saluted back. Robbins only nodded at each of them. Even with their tinted helmet panels covering their faces, he knew that he had seen their eyes before, but he did not know their names. The two of them jogged into the training space, and Robbins followed Maia out, and turned to see the doors close and lock again.

Then, to his right, he heard two sets of steps moving down the metal staircase. He looked up to see Prynn, in one of her long, flowing skirts. Devon was close behind her.

"Not bad for just a day of practice," Prynn said, stepping down onto the floor. She looked up at Robbins and smiled. "I suppose you think you're ready now."

"I suppose so," said Robbins.

Devon stepped past Prynn and looked up at him. "Are you really ready, Dad?" he asked.

Robbins reached under his right gauntlet, tugged at his glove, and carefully removed it before setting his hand on top of the boy's head. His dark, curly hair was still soft. "I am, son," he answered.

Devon leaned away. "Your hands are sweaty."

"Oh." He lifted his hand up, and noticed the sheen. "Sorry about that."

"Maia's never are."

"Not that you see," said Maia.

She pointed Robbins toward the benches and motioned for Prynn and Devon to follow her out. Robbins watched the three of them depart through the shorter set of double doors, out into the brighter village streets. Then, he moved over to the wide bench where he had prepared hours earlier, and sat down. He breathed deeply again. His heart was steadying, but still beating hard, a sign of the lingering stress and strain on his body.

He removed his other glove, and then carefully, and slowly,

removed both gauntlets. He set them down next to him, then reached back, and disconnected the helmet assembly. He set it down next to the gauntlets, then removed the jacket. The coolness of the room hit his arms, and he felt his heart rate slowing down more. His civilian clothes were still safely stored in the open cabinet in front of him. He stood, took his dark blue jacket off one of the hooks, and swung it around as he slid both arms in. He took his gray pants off of their hook and laid them over his left arm. Then, he turned and took up the blue airman's jacket, and then the gauntlets and helmet assembly, and set them all on top of the gray pants before grabbing his civilian boots from the floor.

He moved carefully away from the bench, holding tightly to everything in his arms as he slowly approached the doors to the outside. As he reached the doors, they slowly parted, and he stepped out onto the street. Maia, Prynn and Devon were standing off to the left, chatting amongst themselves as a group of five airmen approached the gym. Robbins moved aside, and to his surprise, saw salutes from two of them. Again, he only nodded back, and then moved toward his family, wondering who the saluters had been. It was more evidence that the plans for the mission were, or were becoming, widely known.

"There's a new appreciation for you," said Maia.

Robbins handed his son his civilian boots to hold, and then handed him the helmet assembly. The boy struggled with the items at first, but quickly became more comfortable as he admired the helmet and its complex brace. Robbins looked back at his wife. "Because of what I've agreed to do?" he asked.

She looked down at Devon, and the wobbling helmet assembly, and then looked back at him and nodded. "Exactly," she said. "Because you're willing to share your…expertise."

"And they should appreciate you," said Prynn.

Robbins turned to the woman, and saw Maia's eyes shift as well.

"Being wed to a leading watcher," Prynn continued. "You could relax, but you haven't. You give and give. I've still got an ear to the ground in this village. Some didn't really care for you until yesterday, and they were late for no good reason."

"Thank you, Prynn," said Robbins.

"Is anyone else hungry?" Devon asked, looking up at them, no longer impressed with the equipment he was holding. "I am. And, you have to leave soon. Can we go home?"

"Sure, son," Robbins replied.

He reached down, and as Devon held up the helmet assembly, took it up into his left arm. But, as Devon held up the boots, Robbins shook his head. The boy did the same. Then they all followed Maia as she turned and walked north, toward their street.

CHAPTER 20
THE LINE

The squadron was still fifteen miles from the storm's misting, cloudy edge, but even through their gull's walls, Fits could already hear the difference. The winds were stronger than any that whirled around and into the mainland, and the smoother sounds coming from the craft's engines indicated a decrease in air density. The external readings on the glowing center panel in front of Rial confirmed it. He looked out, past her and past the controls, through the constant droplets flying off the windshield, and beyond the gull flying ten yards ahead of them.

They were almost as far as Fits had ever been from the mainland. The waters, just a few yards below, were much wilder near the storm's edge. The waves crested higher and flung water into their underbody more aggressively. Thus far, Rial had piloted as well as he had ever seen her. There was calmness in her shoulders and hands. As a high wave shot up from their starboard side, she gently squeezed the control handle and tilted it left. He pressed his hand into the ceiling as they leaned and shook, and then relaxed as they settled back into a stable vector.

"They're getting more frequent," said Rial. "And they're much less predictable out here."

"I know," said Fits.

"We're at six and a half hours now. The power cells are down to sixty percent, but they shouldn't lose much more before we get there."

"Very good."

"We're just five minutes out. Decreasing speed."

"Understood."

Fits turned around and stepped into the space between the benches, where the orb was mounted. The globe-shaped device was just over a yard in diameter. Its metal was highly polished, as it needed to be to cut faster through the water. The equally-spaced array of vents on its bottom half, all slightly more curved than those in the Lords' original design, were letting out intermittent blasts of the air circulating in the cabin. The orb's computer, beneath the dense, glass access panel near the top, glowed in a constant shade of blue. Fits stepped closer and took a look at the small screen. It showed the orb's inner and outer temperatures, and the currently-negligible amount of pressure on its outer hull. Next to the readings was an outline of the canister that had already been placed inside. It was still full. The word 'STABLE' was displayed within the cylindrical icon.

"Perhaps we should consider a promotion for the Special Lieutenant," said Fits. "What do you think, Sir?"

"We will certainly tell the Lords of her contribution," said

Jaan. He looked up at Fits from his seat on the port side bench. "Although, I don't believe they're happy about her creation of the ray."

"It helped get us to this point. And, they wouldn't be angry with *her*."

"Right. It was our request."

"Wasn't it *your* request, Sir?"

Jaan eyed him, hiding a subdued scowl. "Well, you were right next to me. When we make it back, you can come with me to give them a full report, and your recommendation."

"How long has it been?" asked Robbins. "Since she attained her current rank?"

Fits looked at Robbins, sitting on the bench across from Jaan. He had been quiet for over an hour, slowly munching on his second or third ready bar. Seeing him in an airman's suit was something Fits was still getting used to. He took another bite of the bar as he looked over at Jaan.

"Special Lieutenant Terre attained her designation over ten years ago," Jaan answered. "Before that, she spent two decades as a lieutenant under her predecessor."

"How does it work again?" Robbins asked.

"We notify the Lords of our recommendation, and the circumstances that have led to it. If they accept, a ceremony takes place on the Isle, and at least two commanders accompany the watcher being promoted to the ceremony."

"How old are you, Robbins?" Rial called from the front of the gull.

Fits looked back over his shoulder, and saw that they were even closer to the edge. Their speed was still steadily decreasing, as was the speed of the gull in front of them.

"Fifty-one," Robbins answered.

"A bit young to have forgotten basic watcher practices, aren't you?" Rial asked.

Robbins chuckled. "Yes, I suppose so."

Fits turned, walked up to Rial's right side, and leaned over the back of her seat as he looked out through the windshield again. She gently pulled the handle back and held it, and slowly, they came to a stop. Their engines quieted, and the sounds from the wild, churning wall of precipitate–heavy, howling, and crashing–enveloped them. Fits turned to see Jaan walk up and stand on the other side of Rial's seat.

"Gull Two to squadron," Murg called through the open line. "Confirming arrival at the storm's edge. Current distance is twenty yards ahead."

"Acknowledged, Gull Two," said Fits. "Squadron, hold position and wait for further instruction."

Murg and the other three pilots–Hino, Laik and Yarl–all sequentially replied "Yes, Sir" through the line.

Fits looked back at Robbins, who looked up. "Check on the ray, please, Robbins."

Robbins nodded back, stood from his seat, and stepped into

the aft end of the cabin. From where he stood, Fits could only see the glare of the ray's front light, swaying as it beamed out in plain white.

"Still there," said Robbins. "And still in position, four yards back and in front of Gull Five."

"Good," said Fits. "Commander, Sir?"

Jaan held up the control tablet and tapped on the screen. "Readings are stable," he said. "She's handled the changes out here well. I'd say we're ready."

"Agreed," said Fits. He turned back toward the controls. "All craft. Begin scans and report back."

The other four pilots all replied "Acknowledged."

"Starting scans, Sir," said Rial.

Rial began tapping away on the control panels, accessing multiple programs. The system's glowing crosshairs appeared in the windshield, and she whispered out simple commands. As she worked, Fits got down to one knee. The growls from the storm's wall were constant and looming. They were at an elevation of twenty feet, and the waves continued to beat hard against their underbody. He looked down, through the clear panels beneath the pilot's seat, and saw the ocean's fierceness, and the steady streaks of white coming from their front engine. The exhaust could only deflect some of the forces.

Looking upward through the windshield, he saw no end to the wall. The sky was not visible, nor was the source of its distant light. The wall itself was more pale than the typical clouds of midday. It had appeared as a mist just minutes before, but was now revealed to be a dense, blowing mix of water, wind, ice, and seemingly all possible combinations of the three. A sudden, heavy bellow pushed out, and in front of them, Gull Two was nudged backward.

"Recommend increased idling force," Murg called.

"Acknowledged," Rial answered. She quickly made the engine adjustments before continuing her scans.

"The sounds out here..." Robbins said aloud. "They're so different."

"Indeed," said Jaan.

"It's overbearing."

Fits kept his eyes on the control panels, waiting for data to come back, as the roaring from the wall, which now seemed to be getting closer, continued to push into the cabin. The sounds from the outside were undeniably more furious than anything on the mainland, even at the coasts. And with their engines only working to keep them in position, there was hardly any other sound to consider.

"How long has it been since you've been out here, Robbins?" asked Rial.

"Almost..." Robbins started, sounding hesitant. "Almost a year now. Of course, the Hammer never got quite this close."

"Right. The sounds still reached you though, didn't they?"

"Yes, they did, I suppose. I was really just trying to survive."

"Understandable. It was brave enough of you to go out with a salvage crew."

"How are those scans coming along, Ensign?" Fits asked,

trying to shift the conversation.

"Just about finished, Sir. Would you like Robbins to take a look?"

Fits leaned closer to Rial, reached up toward the controls, found the communications program, and muted the line on their end. Then, he looked toward her helmet. "What do you know, Ensign?" he asked quietly. "Out with it."

Rial glanced toward him before looking back at the panels. "I know that he is from the outside, Sir."

Fits nodded. "I figured."

"Holding back, Ensign?" Jaan asked from behind them. He had wandered to the center of the cabin and was now standing near the orb.

"Just...being discreet, Sir," Rial answered.

"Not discreet enough," said Fits. "You've been close to much of what involved Robbins and his son. I'm not surprised at what you know, but let's not push too much. Very few others know anything at all. Do you know of any others in our division who do?"

"Besides you and the lieutenant?" she said. "No, Sir."

"And did the lieutenant tell you anything?"

"He only confirmed what I suspected, yesterday."

"Very well. If anything changes, you tell me. Until then, let Robbins contribute only when absolutely necessary."

She nodded. "Yes, Sir. Should I unmute now?"

"Go ahead."

As Rial re-opened their line to the rest of the squadron, Fits stood and looked back at Robbins. He was sitting again, with his hands on his knees, quiet. He looked calm, considering what was happening outside, and what had been said, and how close he was to the wretched places he had described two days before.

"Perhaps we should just..." Robbins started, looking at Jaan, and then at Fits.

Fits shook his head, held a finger up to his lips, and received a nod back from Robbins. "Just be patient?" he suggested.

"Yes," said Robbins.

"Scans complete," said Rial. "Sir?"

Fits turned back around and looked down at the glowing screens. On the right panel a map had been outlined. The storm's wall was at the top, depicted in heavy lines of white moving from right to left, east to west. Beneath it, in deep blue, was the ocean. On top of the ocean were the signals from all of the gulls in the squadron, all blinking green. Their gull was at the center, flanked by gulls Three and Four, with Gull Five behind them and Gull Two at the front. The ray's signal was right in front of Gull Five, blinking in white.

Speeds and gravity were displayed in the top right corner of the screen. Looking up at the windshield, Fits found the glowing, hovering crosshairs and saw the same readings beneath the icon. The wall of the storm was circulating at one hundred fifty miles per hour. The forces from the waters below were more than double what they would have observed near a coast. The only thing left unclear was the density, and depth, of the wall.

"All craft report," Fits ordered through the line.

The other pilots all reported back with the same data that Rial had obtained. Fits looked back at Jaan, who gave him a familiar, approving nod. Then, he turned and leaned closer to the controls. Looking at the data once more, he knew how to proceed.

"All craft," he said. "Push through at eighty miles per hour. Gull Two will lead. Recommend all craft roll to one hundred fifty degrees until engines adjust. If communication is interrupted, proceed to the other side as planned."

Murg, Hino, Laik and Yarl, along with the lone supporting watchers with each of them, all acknowledged. Then, following Gull Two, Rial accelerated. Fits knelt down again, and held tightly to the back of her seat. As they rolled to the left, he reached back for his helmet and quickly pulled it up and down over his head. Behind him, he heard Robbins and Jaan do the same.

Beneath them, the storm's forces rushed through the gull's engines, rumbling the floorboards. They broke through the barrier quickly, and a wall of water ran from the front end all the way back past their tail. Fits looked back and saw the glimmer of the ray's light, still close behind them. Looking ahead, and left and right, he saw hints of light from the other gulls. But, mostly, he saw fierce, constant rain.

The sounds from the outside, to his surprise, were not as overbearing as they had been outside the wall. They were more ambient than they were pressing. What had been roars were now steady, smooth grumblings. Their engines, however, were louder, working as hard as they could to pull in air and filter any debris. Looking up through the windshield, Fits saw more rain, and pale, cold winds.

"We're steady," said Rial. "The others look to be the same. Formation is not breaking."

"How are the engines?" Fits asked.

"Stable."

"Any sign of the other side?"

"No, Sir."

"Can we increase speed yet?"

"I believe so."

Fits projected his voice toward the controls. "Ensign Murg? What do you see?"

"Just the storm so far, Sir," Murg answered, through faint static.

"Can you scan?"

"I think…"

"Ensign?"

Looking out, Fits saw Gull Two pushed up and to the right by a sudden, barely visible gust. He held tighter to Rial's seat, as she adjusted their vector, quickly elevating and rolling right before bringing them back in line. He was about to speak again when she made another adjustment, pointing their nose to the sky for a split second and accelerating to reach a higher elevation before leveling off.

"All craft!" Fits called. "Report!"

"We're good," Murg answered.

Hino, Laik and Yarl had the same response. Checking the right panel, and looking around, Fits saw that all of the other gulls were also now flying at eighty feet.

"We can increase speed, Sir," said Murg.

"Very well," said Fits. "Proceed."

Following Gull Two, Rial pressed forward, steadily increasing their speed until they reached two hundred miles per hour. The gull began to cut much harder through the dense mist of winds and rain. Fits could see streaks of moisture shooting off of their sides, flowing straight and fast, along with the exhaust below.

"It was too strong near the water," said Rial. "We're steady now."

Fits nodded.

"Looks like the ray is still close behind."

"No surprise there," Fits replied. "Commander, Sir?" he called back.

"She's fine," said Jaan. "Unwavering."

"And our civilian friend? How are you, Robbins?"

"Queasy," Robbins answered. "But, I'll be fine."

They continued on, maintaining a steady forward vector. The map showed all of the craft in the squadron still in their original formation. The ocean behind them was now a thin, faded line of blue. The winds and rain of the wall were now shown as a hazy mix of dense, white lines, still seemingly unending.

"Scanning again, Sir," said Rial.

Robbins sniffed, and then loudly inhaled. Almost whispering, he asked "Does anyone else smell that?"

"Smell what?" Fits replied.

"Something terrible. Something…decaying."

Fits tried to concentrate. They had all added extra filters to their helmets the day before, based on knowledge from the civilian who was said to have studied the outside. Fits thought briefly about the ambiguous, but technically accurate things that had been shared about Robbins within all of the divisions. Then, he focused on his breathing. He could smell the recycled air of the cabin, and detected the faintest scent of water.

"No," Fits finally answered.

"Well, I do," said Robbins.

Fits looked back. "Even with your helmet on?"

Robbins nodded. "Yes. I…I think we're close."

"Alright. Understood."

Fits turned and looked back out through the windshield, and then at the control panels. They had been inside the wall for what seemed like much longer than the eighteen minutes indicated by the gull's system. Looking out again, he saw that the storm was much less dense. The droplets whipping off of the gull were farther apart than they had been. And he could see the light of Gull Two more clearly. Then, suddenly, they dropped.

"What happened, Ensign?" Fits asked, holding tighter to the seat back.

"Engine forces just decreased by twenty percent," Rial answered. She tapped away at the engine settings with one hand as she held firmly to the control handle with the other. "It wasn't me, Sir." She looked out, leaned forward in her seat, and looked left and right. "The other craft seem to be experiencing the same thing. It's the wind forces."

"We can't even see the other side yet," said Fits. "The storm's weakened that much? Already?"

"Yes, Sir. And still weakening. It's down to one hundred ten miles per hour. Now one hundred miles per hour, and...Everyone, hang on!"

The gull dropped again, and Fits felt his heart jump. The readout in his helmet panel indicated his elevated heart rate. As they leveled off, he took a deep breath. Looking down, past his boots, he saw the fading streaks of their white exhaust, and beneath them, an unfamiliar darkness. He was sure it was the ocean surface, but its color was nothing like what he was accustomed to, even on the most overcast days. He looked back at Jaan, who appeared calm, but ready. Then he looked at Robbins, who was holding tightly to the restraints over his shoulders, and staring at the floor.

"Robbins?" Fits called.

He looked up. "Yes?"

"Please, come and take a look."

The gull dropped another ten feet, and Fits felt their speed steadily decreasing. Looking down again, he saw the minimal detail of the ocean surface, just a few yards below. He stood, stepped back, and reached up to brace himself on the gull's frame. Robbins knelt down over the clear panels.

"What do you see?" Fits asked.

Robbins pressed his gloved hand into one of the clear boards, and lowered his head. Then, he pushed his helmet off, and as it settled over his right shoulder, looked up. "What I expected," he said. "We're here."

Fits looked out, beyond Gull Two and around it. The howl of the storm was still strong, but fading behind them, and the dense barrier had become only a faint mist, slowly floating from right to left. The outside was no longer pale, but dark, and shadowed in every direction. The gull had steadied, but he felt the lack of force beneath his boots, and the engines were getting quieter by the moment. As they floated forward, he looked down again and saw the gull's fin touch the short, slow waves of the ocean surface.

"Gull Two to Gull One," Murg called.

Fits moved over to Rial's left, and answered. "Go ahead, Ensign."

"I think we're here, Sir."

After a short pause, Fits answered. "I'd say so."

The watchers in the other three craft quietly agreed. Then, there was silence. Fits was sure that, like him, and the others with him, everyone in the rest of the squadron was taking it all in. For as far as he could see, there was darkness. Above, the clouds were dark, despite the time of day. The now audible sound of the gentler waves below indicated their position over the water, much more than the minimal light bouncing off of them. And then, suddenly, the smell hit him.

Robbins had been right. It was not unlike the smell of death. In his decades as a watcher, Fits had overseen only a handful of autopsies, and he had never forgotten the first body of a deceased, aged Lwoan that he had handled. The old woman had been close to one hundred forty years, and had lived alone for many of them. She had died days before, unbeknownst to her neighbors in the village. Stepping into her home, the wall of odor had hit him, and the ground watcher with him, with an insistence. It had been pungent, and nauseating, and seemed to be alive in the air, even in the midst of death.

Now outside the storm, the terrible mix of smells bore the same odors as the old woman's home. But, the gull's filters were keeping them from being overwhelming. There was also something unusual within them, something chemical.

"What is that?" Murg asked.

The other pilots posed the same question.

"The old world," Fits answered. "The results of the collapse, and the centuries of degradation that followed, and who knows what else."

"It's stronger than I expected," said Murg.

"It's like I said," said Robbins. "Like I expected." He stood from the floor, and took a step back.

"Indeed," said Jaan. "Good work, Robbins."

Fits looked back and saw his commander stand from the bench and step forward, stopping near the unmoved, twinkling orb. He turned back toward the controls to give direction to the squadron. "All craft," he started. "We will let the ray lead us, as planned. Track the ray's position, and hold until it is thirty yards ahead of us." He called back to Jaan. "Whenever you're ready, Sir."

A beep sounded from the right control panel, and the ray's signal showed it breaking formation. Fits listened, and heard the quiet splash behind them as it dropped into the water. It moved forward, beneath them, and its light shined up through the ocean's surface as it swam beneath Gull Two, and then dove further down and out of sight. Fits watched its signal on the panel as it moved forward, speeding through the water. The calmness of this ocean seemed to allow an ease to its movements that had not been possible on their previous expeditions. Within a few seconds it was thirty yards out and over one hundred feet down.

"All craft," Fits called. "Move out."

Rial sped ahead, behind Gull Two. Fits looked down at the map and saw the location target that Rial had placed within it. The estimated position of the broken container was twenty-five miles north and west. Looking down past her seat, he saw that they were now flying just a few feet over the water, and their fin, which would normally aid in maintaining speed over Lwo's wild ocean surface, was becoming a hindrance.

"Can you elevate any more?" Fits asked.

"No, Sir," said Rial. "This is the maximum without strong winds to feed the engines."

"Recommend dropping in, Sir," Murg called.

"We'll follow you, Ensign," Fits replied.

Ahead of them, Gull Two slowly dropped, a few inches at a time, until it had breached the ocean surface. Rial followed suit, slowly easing her foot from the pedal below until their fin was submerged. The bottoms of their engines entered next. And as their entire underbody was rocked, a heavy splash of dark water hit the windshield, and then slowly rolled off as they sped forward. Listening to the engines, Fits could hear a new smoothness, as if the water was easier to use than wind. Thus far, it seemed, Terre's group had done their job well.

"The ray's readings indicate heavy contamination," said Jaan. "And the water here is much more dense than our own. Pay close attention to your engine vanes and filters, Ensign."

"Yes, Sir," Rial answered.

"The same contamination we had near the mainland, Sir?" Fits asked.

"The same," said Jaan. "As well as others."

Fits spoke toward the controls again. "All craft. Be aware. The ray is reading heavier contamination, and various substances.

Increase monitoring of vanes and filters. And scan continuously."

The other pilots all acknowledged, and they all continued speeding forward, following Gull Two. For another few minutes, another ten miles, there were no changes. Smells continued to float into the cabin, just enough to remain bearable. Water continued to flow heavily through their engines. Fits periodically looked down through the clear floor panels, searching for the depths of the ocean below. Beneath their steady fin, which was barely illuminated by the light from the cabin, there remained only darkness. He looked up and out just in time to see Gull Two move sharply to the left. Rial followed the same path.

"Report, Gull Two," Fits called.

"Something bumped us, Sir," Murg answered. "Did anyone see anything?"

Rial shook her head. "I didn't."

Hino, Laik and Yarl said the same.

Robbins had been sitting safely and quietly on the bench, but Fits heard him stand at the sudden change in circumstances. He walked up and stood behind Rial.

"Bumps, sometimes, are just bumps," he said. "But, not always."

"What could it have been?" Rial asked.

"Could have been some sunken land, could have been a creature." He paused. "Was their gull damaged?"

"We've suffered no damage," Murg called. "Didn't even see

anything below."

"Good to know," said Robbins.

Fits looked at the map again. A dark, grayish-brown color filled the screen beneath their multiple signals. The ray's signal was still blinking strongly, and indicated a depth of four thousand feet. Ahead of it, the point showing their intended destination had become a radiating circle of light. Looking to the left panel, he saw the results of the gull's continuous scans. The speed of the winds over the water was barely ten miles per hour. The temperature was seventy-one degrees Fahrenheit. And, as expected, the air outside was full of contaminants, some of which Fits recognized. He felt a mild warmth, but nothing unbearable.

"All watchers," he called through the line. "Continue to monitor your body temperatures, and check your air for any toxins."

The other eight watchers in the flanking gulls responded affirmatively. Rial continued to guide them forward behind Gull Two, as she briefly held her right hand up near her helmet.

"My air is clear, Sir," she said. "It is warm, though. Given the decrease in wind speed, and the whirlwinds we passed through, I guess it's no surprise."

"Not at all," said Fits.

She looked at the map. "We're just a mile out."

"Coming up on our target," Murg called. "Prepare for full stop."

As Rial slowed their speed, Fits checked the map again and

saw that the ray had reached seven thousand feet, and had stopped descending. Another minute passed, and as they came to a halt, and hovered in place, the screen refreshed. The ray had not changed position. Looking out, Fits saw gulls Three and Four moving ahead of them. On their left, Gull Three's aft end swung around through the water, leaving its nose pointing toward the space behind Gull Two. Gull Four turned toward the same spot. Gull Five stayed in position behind them. Ahead of them, Gull Two spun in place, and its beams, along with those from the other craft, shone out onto the ocean surface.

"You might want to lower these lights," Robbins said.

Fits looked back at him. "Possible wild life?" he asked.

Robbins nodded.

Fits spoke to the squadron again. "All craft. Decrease beams to ten percent."

One by one, the lights of the gulls lowered, decreasing the visibility of the surrounding area. What had been a brightened surface of choppy water, full of mysterious clouds and with a defined mist lingering above it, became only shadows. Aside from the cabins visible behind their tinted windshields, the other gulls now only appeared to be outlines of smooth, faintly green metal. But, the heavy sounds coming from every one of their submerged engines seemed more evident. And with fewer distractions, so did the smells from the outside.

Fits shook his head and hesitantly took a breath. "Let's hope this goes quickly," he said. He looked back at Jaan, standing between the orb and the port side door, monitoring the tablet in his hands. "Sir, any images from below?"

Jaan nodded. "Some. It's mostly darkness, but she's found it, I'm sure. There's the shape of a large object. It's mostly square, but it has angled corners. And it's resting at an angle on…on what appears to be a…a mountainside."

"A mountainside?"

"Yes. It would seem the container never made it to the bottom of the ocean, just to what became a bottom. Hold on. The image is refreshing. There."

Fits walked back and looked at the tablet screen. He saw the container, in the midst of floating debris and cloudy flows, embedded at an odd angle in what was, in fact, the side of a mountain. The container's surface, barely visible even with the ray's light beaming out, appeared to be metal. There was clear damage, scratches and streaks likely inflicted during its descent along the submerged mountain. The ray's scans showed the container to be fifty feet long on each side. And atop its cube-like body, a crack ran from one end all the way to its center.

"The clouds must be our contamination," said Fits.

Jaan nodded. "Agreed. They're heaviest here, and flowing south, toward Lwo. The ray is scanning and retrieving samples. We can find out more later. Right now, let's get this done, and get back home."

CHAPTER 21
THE DEPTHS

Fits stood beside Rial and spoke once more to the squadron. "All craft. The ray has identified the container. It is as the Lords expected. Hold position, and continue to monitor the ray's signal, as well as the signal of the orb."

The other pilots all answered in the affirmative.

Fits looked down at Rial. "Ready, Ensign?"

"Ready, Sir," she replied, keeping her eyes forward and raising her right fist.

"Good."

He turned toward the orb. Jaan entered a command on his tablet, and the device's engines began to whisper below it. Then, swiftly, they began blowing. Fits moved to the port side door, and pressed and held the button to open it. With a low click, the door unlocked, slid inward, and then slowly slid back.

The darkness that had been evident through the door's translucent panel became clearer, and Fits leaned toward the opening. His tech engines began to hum, as softly as they ever had, as the low winds hit them. The smell from the outside strengthened, almost stinging his nostrils, but his helmet display indicated that his air was still safe. He stepped back toward the orb as he continued to look out into the darkness.

The minimal light coming from the squadron provided little comfort, or sense of position. The engines of their five craft were the noisiest thing in the immediate area. Besides them, and the low winds, and the shallow mist, there was only an endless expanse. Behind him, Robbins was moving. He turned to see the man leaning against the starboard side wall, tightly gripping a covered section of the frame, almost hunching over as he looked out the open door, at the dark place that was familiar only to him.

"Not the time for this, Robbins," Fits said. "Get yourself together. We have a mission to complete."

Robbins began to straighten up and nodded back. Across from him, standing next to the open door, Jaan looked ready. He held the tablet up in front of him and looked at Fits. Then, with a single tapped command, the orb bounced off of its small, metal mount. The light of its computer began to blink in a pattern, and it spun along its center axis, turning left and right as it triangulated its position. The sounds of sliding mechanisms emanated from its curved body. Then, with a blast of air, it shot out the door, and immediately dropped into the ocean. The splash sent dark water onto their cabin floor. Fits stepped back toward the door, and reached for the control again.

"Wait, Commander," Jaan said, holding up one hand to stop him.

Fits kept his hand over the button. "Sir?"

"Leave it open, for now. Let's make sure we don't have to bring it right back up."

"Understood, Sir."

Fits stayed near the door, holding on to the frame, listening to the sounds of a dead world. There were few. There were constant, weakly blowing winds. There was occasional splashing from the short waves. Looking out, and up, he wondered if the clouds lingering in the dark sky ever sent down any thunder. It would have been welcome, given the uncomfortable lack of heavy winds and nature's calls.

He looked back over his shoulder, past Rial and at the glowing map, where the orb's signal blinked. The device had descended just over one hundred feet. Its engines were not especially strong, and its design was hardly aerodynamic, but it was headed directly for the ray's position. He looked at Robbins and saw the man still standing firm. Jaan sat back down on the bench, his helmet aglow with the video and readings coming from the ray and the blinking signals coming from the orb.

"What do you see, Sir?" Fits asked.

"The ray is steady where she is," said Jaan. "I've angled the camera back upward. It'll see the orb when it gets close."

"Any time estimate?"

"It's slowly picking up speed. I'd say five, maybe seven…"

Jaan looked up, then jumped up from the bench, and quickly reached the open doorway. He leaned against the frame, bending one knee into it to keep himself stable. Fits followed suit, not knowing what his commander had seen or sensed, but preparing himself to act. Then, the gull bounced up and out of the water. The sounds of water spraying and falling from their engines filled the space. The same sounds came from the other four craft around them. The gull's alerts rang out, and Fits looked back to see every control panel radiating orange.

"Not again," uttered Rial. "Something alive below us, Sir."

"You sure?" Fits asked.

"Yes, Sir."

"It's big!" Murg yelled through the line. "I just saw it surface! Pulling back!"

Fits continued holding to the frame, and watched Rial's movements. She reversed the gull at high speed. Outside, the other craft were doing the same, giving space to whatever large threat lurked below. Robbins' steps were heavy as he left the starboard wall and went up behind Rial to look out. Fits looked down through the clear panels below her. The darkness of the ocean surface looked the same until something with a brighter hue began to rise toward them.

"Below us!" Fits called out.

"I see it!" Rial said. "Hang on!"

As she reversed the gull faster and swung the back end toward their port side, Fits looked out the windshield and saw a massive, sparkling appendage. It was as wide as the gull, and its curving shape flew upward, sending out water that crashed into their body. Large waves rolled beneath them. The radio filled with loud chatter from the rest of the squadron. Fits saw the other four craft curving away from the creature, as their pilots tried to maintain some formation.

"I see four limbs!" Murg called.

"I see five!" Yarl chimed in. "It's reaching for us!"

"Maintain distance!" Fits yelled past Rial.

"She's got the orb," Jaan said, not loudly, but strong and firm. "Distract her."

"Activate shields!" Fits ordered.

"Activating!" Rial yelled through the line.

"Activating shields!" Murg confirmed. "Keep clear of the surface!"

"Copy!" Rial answered.

As the other pilots followed the order, Fits looked around and saw the other gulls' roofs begin to reflect the new source of light. Their flat, round shield generators pulsed in bright blue, and the resulting fields of electromagnetic energy rolled down over their frames. He backed away from the doorway, and saw Jaan do the same, as their own shield floated down, humming and pulsing as it covered the opening.

"Firing!" Murg called. "Low yield!"

Fits looked out and saw the round shot of electric light shoot out from atop Gull Two, toward the largely-submerged body of the creature lingering at the ocean surface. The blast hit the visible part, whichever part it was, and a sense of static electricity filled the area.

Their shield was doing its job, protecting them from most of the resulting shock, but Fits could still feel it on his skin. His hair was standing all over his body. A loud, muffled groan came up from the water, filling the air, and weighing heavily on his ears.

"Anything!?" Fits called out.

"No effect, Sir," Rial answered. "It hasn't moved."

"It's still got the orb," said Jaan. "Again, Commander."

"Again!" Fits ordered. "All at once! In five, four, three, two…"

He looked out again as five simultaneous blasts of energy hit the creature. Once again, he felt the energy through his suit. He looked down at his arms and legs. He checked his status in his helmet display. His system had recognized the increased charges in the air, but everything else looked normal.

"It worked," Jaan said. "But…"

Fits turned to him. "But what, Sir?"

"It's off course. The orb is free, but it's directly under us, headed in the wrong direction."

"Can you redirect?"

He tapped away on the screen. "It's not responding."

"Maybe if you bring the ray back up," said Fits. "To push it back on course."

"She's not done yet!" Rial yelled.

Fits turned, and looked out through the windshield. More of the creature's body was emerging. Lit by their shields and low beams, its pinkish color was brilliant. Its shape was giant and curving, and now reaching over twenty feet out of the water. It was covered in tiny spots of various colors. And one large, dark circle, one of its eyes, flickered in their direction.

"A squid," Fits uttered, his voice low as he recalled historical images. "A giant one. It's as big as any ever recorded, if not bigger."

"Are you sure, Commander?" asked Jaan.

"Fairly."

The creature stopped reaching and splashing as much, and instead began to turn in place, sending out waves that were grazing their shields, seemingly taking stock of what the gulls were and how much of a threat they posed. Its other eye appeared and blinked in their direction.

"Any progress, Sir?" Fits asked, keeping his eyes on the creature.

"The orb's stuck in place," said Jaan. "And it's less than a hundred feet down. Two of the engines are jammed. And the hull is partially compacted."

"What about the contents?"

Jaan paused. "The canister is still intact. Navigation is functioning. It just needs a spin and a push. If we can get our friend here to leave, I can probably...Damn!"

"Sir?" Fits said, turning, surprised by Jaan's emotion.

"She's got it again."

"What's she think it is!?" Rial yelled.

"Right now it doesn't matter," said Jaan.

"Sir, we could turn back," said Rial. "We still have more of the compound. We can retreat, and reassess. We could better prepare, and-"

"No, Ensign," Jaan stopped her. "We are prepared. The contamination is still strong, and still moving toward the mainland. Now is the time."

Beneath the gull, more waves from the massive creature crested upward, and pressed against their shield, causing a clashing, shocking, upsetting sound. Fits looked out to see the creature's limbs, flailing again, almost in a pattern, as it tried to push them all away. His mind went to what he had done the night before. He had carefully removed the vent sections from every piece of his wind tech. And he had cleaned, polished, and added space between the precisely-formed vanes. Terre had, hesitantly, advised him on how to do it all. On the same call, she had done the same for Jaan. Only the other commanders had been made aware. Fits turned away from the windshield and looked over at Jaan, who had tossed the tablet back to the bench and was checking his tech by hand.

"Raise the shield, Ensign," Fits ordered.

"Sir?" Rial replied.

"Now, Ensign!"

"Yes, Sir."

Fits stepped toward the center of the cabin and shot a glance at Jaan, who shook his head.

"Please don't," Robbins said from behind.

"You got a better idea, civilian?" Fits asked, not looking back.

Robbins was quiet.

"Give me five minutes."

Jaan took a step toward the open doorway, but Fits raced by him, extending his left arm and pushing him back as he leapt up and out, and floated over the dark ocean. He whispered "seal," and his system responded, tightening the already-snug sections around his neck, forearms, and calves. It would not be completely water-tight, but he knew he could make it work. He felt his tech humming, pulling in as much air as it could, but he only reached a height of twelve feet before quickly falling. He saw the pointy, glistening end of one of the squid's tentacles, as he clasped his own hands together in front of him, pointed his helmet down, and crashed through.

The pressure from the water was heavy. Fits could feel it around his chest, squeezing. But, his tech was working. He had reached an initial depth of thirty feet before he began to slow down, and then drift. Around him, it was dark. There was a hint of light from the surface, but only a hint. He felt moisture near his wrists and his neck and knew that he had little time. He whispered more commands, and felt his tech adjust as he turned downward, toward the glint of what he suspected was the orb. A moment later, the faint signal in his helmet confirmed it.

An odd shadow, one of the squid's appendages, passed over the device's low light. As Fits straightened his body and began to descend faster, he whispered "record." His system chirped in confirmation.

The smells had diminished. The seal in his helmet was blocking almost everything. The aroma of the moisture now creeping up into his nose was more chemical than foul. He reached a depth of seventy feet and saw that he was level with the blinking light of the orb's computer. The surrounding waters were now darker, but he could see that he was within fifty feet of the device. Above him, a looming presence passed over his head, another tentacle. He knew the creature sensed something, but he was moving carefully, hiding his presence as much as possible. He got to within twenty feet. His display indicated a steadily-increasing, but still safe heart rate. He took a deep breath of his filtered air, and smelled more chemical.

A sudden force hit him from the left, a deep, heavy wall of water from the squid swinging at him. The light of the orb's computer was almost within reach, and Fits increased the power to his tech, pushing through the underwater wave. Then, there was a sudden stinging in his throat. He coughed out, and shook his head. The light was now getting further away. The creature wanted to keep its new possession. Fits swam toward it, until something surrounded him and began to squeeze.

The squid had grabbed him around the waist and much of the rest of his body. The strong, gripping tentacle covered him from his ribs all the way down past his knees. His arms were still free, and he pushed down on the hard, muscular, bumpy surface, trying to free himself. The creature only squeezed tighter. He looked out, and saw that he was once again getting close to the orb's light, because the creature was pulling him closer. His heart beat faster and stronger.

Barely able to move, Fits managed to form hand commands, and felt the surge within his gauntlets. In his panel, red warning language was displayed, but he already knew not to attempt a charged blast. He hoped that he would only need the exhaust. Pressing through the currents flowing around him, he brought his arms closer together. He managed to place his fists into the tight space between his chest and the tentacle. He pushed them down as hard as he could. The metal of his gauntlets rubbed against the squid's hard skin until he got both arms in, almost up to his elbows, and whispered the command.

His gauntlets thumped, and a blast of water shot between him and the squeezing appendage. A wall of tiny bubbles filled his darkened vision, and with the brief forces that now surrounded him, the creature had to let go. But, Fits felt his body starting to go numb. The squeezing had taken its toll without him knowing. He closed his eyes and breathed deeply. Moisture now filled his helmet. He could feel himself sinking. Opening his eyes, and looking at his display, he saw that his tech had lost most of its power. He had just enough for a boost. He whispered once more, with less breath than he had expected to feel, and each of his engines hummed with adjustments, as they raised him, tilted his body into a level position, and carried him forward.

As he neared the light of the orb, he regained some feeling in his arms and legs. He tried to clench his fists, and tried to move his shoulders, and tried to shake as hard as he could. His engines continued to hum with the pulling and expelling of dark water. He saw the light of the orb just before his helmet bumped it. He managed to shake his arms, and breathed deeply again.

The chemical odor had become stronger. There was even more wetness in his helmet. Dark droplets were rolling along the panel in every direction. He felt more water in his sleeves and near the tops of his boots. He reached out, and through his gloves felt the warmth of the orb's round, metallic body. With all the strength he had in his arms, he managed to nudge it, and heard a loud, bellowing groan. He looked around, searching for heavy, shadowed arms, before refocusing on the orb. Through the tips of his gloves he sensed the creeping heaviness of the squid's undulating flesh. He whispered more commands, and his engines carried him backward, and then sent him forward as fast as they could manage. He aimed his shoulder at the orb, and felt it move.

* * * * *

"Sir, it's been five minutes," said Rial. "The commander's signal is weakening."

"But, it's still blinking," Jaan said. "So, he's managing." He looked down at the tablet, as he had been doing repeatedly since Fits had pushed him aside and dove into the ocean.

371

Another loud groan filled the area, and through the windshield, Robbins saw two of the squid's massive arms flail about. The waves and splashing were strong, but the gull's engines had adjusted to the repeating forces. The craft barely moved.

"There!" Jaan said. "She's free. And redirected. He's done it."

"Great," said Rial, exhaling. She looked toward the controls. "All craft. The commander has succeeded. The orb is back on track."

"Confirmed," Murg answered. "We see the signal moving."

"But the commander's isn't," said Hino. "He's idle down there."

"And..." Laik called, her voice shaky. "And, we still can't radio to him. We need to..."

"Everyone," Jaan called, loudly, as he walked up behind Rial. "Remain calm. We still have a mission to complete." He paused, and glanced at the tablet. "The orb has just reached two hundred feet and still has to get to the container to release the compound. And we still have to be watchful of the creature. Gull Five? Drop back into the water and move up. See if you can get eyes on Commander Fits past your fin. The rest of you hold position, and distract the creature if necessary."

Laik confirmed, and the other pilots all answered in the affirmative. Robbins leaned back, stabilizing himself along the starboard wall once again. He turned and looked through their rear window, and saw Gull Five's shield retract. A few seconds later its dim light moved out of sight. Turning and looking out through the windshield, he saw the body of the creature, now slightly deeper than it had been. It was turning in place, and still sending waves out beneath and between all of them. He looked to Jaan, who had moved back to the open port doorway. He stood there, holding the frame with one hand as he watched the darkness. The tablet in his other hand was beeping and chirping in patterns, indicating the continued activity of the two devices they had sent down.

"Robbins, you look down too," Jaan said without looking. "The more eyes the better."

"Alright," Robbins answered.

He left the starboard wall, moved up behind Rial, and knelt down. As she lowered them back into the water, he felt the engines shifting beneath him. The dark water pressed up against their underbody. Through the heavy flows and viscous droplets, he saw more darkness.

"No chance there's a light on the fin, is there?" he asked.

"Not the fin," said Rial. "But just in front of it."

"Any change in the commander's position, Ensign?" Jaan asked.

"No, Sir," she answered. "He still hasn't moved. His signal's stuck at seventy-two feet, right below the squid's body."

"Then leave the underbody light off, unless the commander starts to ascend. We don't want the creature to feel threatened, or panic."

"Yes, Sir."

"We're seeing no sign of the commander," called Laik. "And no change in his position."

"Same here," Robbins said loudly.

"She's moving," called Yarl.

Robbins stood and looked out to see the squid turning and swimming east. Gull Four glided sideways, out of its way, and slowly, the massive creature pushed through the water, and then dove out of sight, leaving a trail of waves flowing in a line on the surface. The trail was another forty feet away when seemingly all of the creature's arms flew up, pointed upward, and then dropped out of sight as the creature swam away.

"The commander's signal is still in the same position," said Laik. "And it's faint."

"Confirmed," said Rial. "Sir, any orders?"

Jaan looked toward Rial, and then back at the tablet, hesitant. He looked out at the darkness again. "It's too risky for any of us to try to retrieve him," he said.

"Sir?" Rial pressed

"But, as soon as the orb is in place, I will send the ray back up."

Rial turned in her seat. "Sir, I will gladly go down."

"No, Ensign. Commander Fits is capable, and his suit and tech are durable. As long as his signal is live, then he's alive."

Rial looked hesitant, but spoke again. "Sir, he wouldn't leave any of us-"

"We are not leaving him, Ensign," Jaan stopped her. "Listen carefully. The water here may be weak, but clearly it is dense. And full of unknown toxins. Your tech cannot handle it. Your commander's, however, has been altered. He and I both made adjustments before we left, knowing that something like this might happen, that one of us might have to dive in. He beat me to it, and the fact that he hasn't sunk away proves that the adjustments worked. But, right now, we cannot risk another life. That is where we stand. Understood?"

Rial turned back toward the controls, and replied calmly. "Yes, Sir."

"Good. We are going to complete this mission. Hold your position."

"Yes, Sir."

Jaan raised his voice. "All craft. Did everyone else hear that?"

The other pilots, and their supporting watchers, all confirmed.

Robbins remained kneeling behind Rial, searching the darkness for a sign of Fits. Minutes passed. Following Murg's lead, the squadron came closer together, almost back to where they had been before the creatures' arrival. Only Gull Five maintained its position, off to their right, with its watchers' eyes surely on the depths, searching for movement from their division's leader. For another five minutes, they all waited, silent. Robbins' heart beat harder with each passing moment, as he considered Fits's predicament and the lack of movement from below.

"The orb has reached the container," Jaan finally said. "The ray's view is not perfectly clear, but I have eyes. Positioning."

Robbins remained kneeling, but watched Jaan as he worked on the tablet. He could not see much of the screen, but there were reflections in Jaan's helmet panel. A green light blinked, followed by softer, white lights. The only sounds were from the tablet's signals and confirmations. There was no sound from the depths.

"The orb's dispersing end is in place," said Jaan. "Extending the canister." He paused, watching the screen. "The canister has opened. The compound is penetrating the container…And…It is beginning to expand. Now, we wait."

"Compound deployed, and activating," Rial said through the line. "Sir, what about the ray?" she asked, tilting her head back.

"I've already called her back. She's moving up, heading directly for the commander's position. I'll have eyes on him soon. Is his signal still active?"

"Just barely, Sir."

"Is there any sign of more ocean life?"

Rial checked the gull's scans. "No, Sir."

"All craft," Jaan called. "Any sign of more threats?"

The other pilots replied quickly, confirming that their scans also showed nothing approaching.

"Still no visual on the commander," Laik added.

"Robbins?" Jaan said. "Do you see anything?"

Robbins looked back down, into the endless darkness, and

again saw nothing. "No, Sir."

"Shouldn't his tech have responded and raised him by now?" asked Hino.

"Not if he said otherwise," Jaan answered. "And, not if it's been compromised."

A silence filled the air, and though he suspected the worst, Robbins held his tongue. He had seen many people–and creatures, and objects–overtaken by unseen forces in the ocean. He had never seen anyone, or anything, retrieved. Not even remains. The fact that Fits's signal was still active was another miraculous sign of Lwoan technology. Five more minutes passed before Jaan spoke again.

"I have eyes on the commander," he said. "His helmet is blinking...barely. The ray is under him, and bringing him up."

Robbins stood and looked out through the windshield, and a moment later saw the ray surface. Fits's limp body was resting on top of it. The device lingered, holding him there between all of them, before floating toward their gull and heading for Jaan's position at the open doorway.

"Is he..." Rial started.

"Stay focused, Ensign," Jaan said, and tossed his tablet onto the bench. "We'll attend to him. Robbins? Come and help me."

Robbins quickly reached the port side of the gull. He braced one knee against the frame before leaning out the doorway and reaching for Fits's right arm. As Jaan reached for his left side and grasped him, and they slid him off the top of the ray, Robbins felt the limpness. Holding onto Fits's arm, he reached for his leg, and felt the heaviness. Fits was taller than most, but had never appeared to be as bulky and muscular as he clearly was. They pulled him all the way off of the ray, and the device, with its glowing front eye, drifted back, seemingly watching them as they lowered Fits onto the cabin floor. The door slowly slid closed. Dark water poured out of Fits's suit and began spreading across the floor.

Within the foggy helmet panel and behind dark droplets, Fits's face looked pale. Jaan tilted the helmet back, opening it, and then reached behind it, and found the connections for the assembly. As he carefully removed the assembly and set it aside, more water poured out from around Fits's neck, and Robbins could not help seeing the differences. Fits's hair had always been a brilliant shade of red, but now his beard looked almost black. The short, thick hair on his head was the same. Below it, his closed eyes bore dark circles. And there was a noticeable chemical odor.

Jaan found the hidden clasp near the neck of Fits's jacket and zipped it downward. It stopped just below the ribcage. Fit's chest was as pale as his face, and it was not moving. Holding his hand up to Fits's mouth, Robbins felt no breath. Jaan pressed on his neck with two fingers. Robbins saw no throbbing.

"Scan for life," Jaan whispered, aiming his helmet at Fits's body.

A red light blinked into his panel.

"Repeat," he whispered.

Another red light.

In one sweeping motion, Jaan clasped his hands together, raised them up near his chin, and then slammed them into Fits's chest. A small splash of water, almost black in color, flew up from Fits's mouth. Robbins felt for air again, but there was still no breath.

"Repeat," Jaan whispered again.

Another red light. Jaan repeated the slamming motion into Fits's chest. More dark water was expelled, and a sudden recollection flooded Robbins' mind. When Fits, over a year before, had pulled him and Devon from their makeshift boat onto the deck of the Hammer, they had also come out of dark water. In the salvage ship's cabin, Robbins had coughed up dark water, but he had been able to breathe, albeit with great difficulty. But, he did not remember a chemical smell, not even when they had first been overtaken by the ocean, and been dragged by undercurrents to unknown places, and eventually through, or beneath, Lwo's storm. He looked down at Fits again, and then up at Jaan, who had stopped slamming his chest.

"Get a mask," Jaan said, pointing toward the port bench without looking up.

Robbins stood, ran to the bench, and pulled open one of the compartments below the cushions. The large, curved, clear fronts of three masks shined back at him. He grabbed one, ran back to Fits's side, and knelt. Jaan took the mask from him and carefully placed it over Fits's head. The mask's frame and straps were black, as was the filtering device near the chin. It started working without the need for

379

activation. Robbins could hear, and see, the air being pumped in. Jaan tightened the straps behind Fits's head, making sure it was sealed.

"Why isn't his suit reviving him!?" Rial yelled back at them.

"It can't," Jaan calmly replied. "I gather that it could not. The power is almost gone."

As air continued to flow through the mask, they waited. Robbins watched Fits's face through the clear panel. It remained pale. His lips were drying out. His eyes were sinking. He looked at his chest and still saw no movement. Jaan slammed his clenched fists down into Fits again. He whispered to his system once more. Another red light appeared in his helmet panel. Then, hesitantly, he reached for the mask. He loosened the straps, and pulled it off of Fits's head, and tossed it to the back of the cabin. As the mask bounced off of a wall, and cracked against the floor, Jaan got to one knee, then stood and walked up behind Rial. He set his right hand on her shoulder before speaking.

"Watchers," he called, his voice steady. "We have lost Commander Fits." He paused. There was silence. "It appears to have been a combination of water, and the chemicals in the water from the container. And his body is beginning to bruise. There are also signs that he struggled with the creature. Whatever the case, it was too much for him, and his tech, as strong as it was."

A moment of shocked silence passed.

"Heard, Sir," Murg called.

"Heard," said Yarl.

"Heard," said Hino.

"Heard," said Laik.

"Squadron," Jaan continued. "Let it be known that Commanders Fits's last act was one of duty and service, to ensure that we, that the people, were more protected than he." He paused before continuing. "All craft. Stay in position. We will make sure that the compound works before we leave. And, continue to scan."

The other pilots all answered in the affirmative.

Robbins watched as Jaan squeezed Rial's shoulder. She leaned away from him and went back to monitoring the control panels. He stepped back, turned, and went to the port bench, where the tablet still lay. Robbins caught a glimpse of the screen, and saw an undulating curve situated above a fluctuating chart, before Jaan knelt down to open a compartment beneath the seats. He arose with a thick, gray blanket in his arms. He stepped toward Fits's body, held the blanket up with both hands, and gripped the rounded corners as he let it unfurl down to the wet floor. Robbins grabbed the bottom end by the corners, and felt the added weight within them before standing and moving toward Fits's boots. Jaan moved toward his head. Then, together, they knelt, and let the blanket cover his entire body.

CHAPTER 22
THE WAKE

Looking out, through the narrow gate and up at the night sky, Maia knew that the moon, though not yet full, was bright. The clouds had not parted in weeks, but they could not block all of its light. Its glow was steady, even if obstructed, and looking closer, she was sure that there were twinkles from the stars surrounding it. *Please*, she silently hoped, *help light their way*.

The cold winds from the north were whipping around and through her tech. Behind her, the observation area was quiet. She turned and looked down the shadowy corridor to see distant lighting, and Orve sitting in the same position he had been a half hour before, when she had left him to look, anticipating the squadron's return to the north station. They were now an hour behind schedule. As Orve continued to monitor from his workstation, she turned back around, and looked out at the sky again, and then down at the water.

In the late hour, the ocean was almost black. There was little to reflect. Only the tips of the waves gave off any amount of light. But, their heavy crashing indicated their strength, and the constant danger that lurked beneath the surface. She wondered what the orb had encountered beneath the waters outside the storm, if it had gotten there, if it had been successful. Her heart beat harder at the thought of a failed mission.

A faint beep sounded, and Maia turned to the wide display on her right. Gull Two's signal was blinking. It was ten miles from the coast.

"I see them," Orve called through the open line.

"Same here," Maia replied.

She continued to watch the display, and the signals of the other four gulls appeared. They were all approaching at high speed and low elevation, just as they had departed over fifteen hours before. She turned away from the lookout and walked swiftly toward the observation space. As she passed through the narrow doorway, and entered, Orve stood, and Gill took his place at the workstation. One of the screens there showed the same signals and data as the display at the lookout. Maia followed Orve, out through the arched doorway, and onto the platform.

The station's deck was empty, ready to receive the returning squadron. The winds coming through the high gate facing the north were heavy. Maia and Orve moved along the platform toward the gate, and looked out at the dark skies and seas in the distance. After five more minutes, the lead gull's light appeared.

"Sirs?" Gill called through the line.

"Go ahead, Ensign," Orve replied.

"There are only eleven life signs in the squadron."

Orve turned toward Maia, and she looked through his helmet panel, into his dark eyes. His subdued concern was the same that she suddenly felt.

"Can you identify the missing life sign, Ensign?" Orve asked.

"Yes, Sir. It's..."

"Go ahead."

"It's the commander, Sir. Commander Fits's signal is missing."

Maia looked out through the gate again. The lead gull's light was bright as it approached, as were the lights of the other four craft behind it. Glancing at Orve, she saw a stillness now resting over him. His stance had strengthened. He turned toward the deck, and she followed suit.

"Heard, Ensign," he finally replied. "Let us confirm before taking any further action."

"Yes, Sir," said Gill.

"We knew something like this could happen," Maia said quietly.

"Maybe it's a misread," said Orve.

"We can hope."

The lead gull entered with a rushing of wind, passing over the high gate, between the rock walls, and beneath the station's lights. Its exhaust blew out in cloudy white behind it, as it drifted down and passed by Maia and Orve, settling with its forward end toward the open entry that led inland. Three other gulls settled on the far side of the deck, all in a row, all beaming with light that brightened their green exteriors. The last gull descended in front of Maia and Orve. Behind it, the ray–battered, smudged, and lacking in shine–settled a few feet above the deck.

Maia looked through the last gull's windshield and saw Rial in the pilot's seat. The port side door unlocked and slid back into the cabin. Within the cabin, she saw Jaan standing, holding the tablet that controlled the ray in one hand, and holding on to the gull's frame with the other. She and Orve quickly raised their right fists up toward their helmet's in salute. Jaan saluted back, and stepped down onto the deck. His boot engines blew out white streaks as he stood near the open door. In her helmet, Maia watched his signal blink into view and listened as he spoke through the line.

"We have suffered a great loss," he said, his voice even heavier than usual. "But, it was not without purpose. Commander Fits single-handedly saved the mission, and in the process, gave his life."

Jaan turned and looked back into the cabin and downward. One end of a heavy, gray blanket was visible between the benches. Beneath it was the shape of a head, followed by shoulders and arms. Maia took a step forward and saw the rest of the long, covered body. Beyond it, Robbins was kneeling near the rear of the cabin, as if waiting for instruction. Maia tried to dismiss the sudden sense of relief at seeing him. Looking back at the covered body, a visible confirmation of a loss, she felt silenced. Following Orve's lead, she stepped down onto the deck.

"Commander, Sir," Orve started. "What happened?"

"We encountered nearly all of the trouble we anticipated," said Jaan. "And still, we were barely prepared. A creature, a giant squid, interfered. We were able to get the ray down to the container without much trouble, and sent the orb in behind it, but the creature appeared and took hold of the orb. When it was clear it would not let go, Commander Fits pushed me aside and jumped in. Somehow he managed to free the orb. But, in the process, his body suffered great pressures–likely from the water and the creature–and exposure to the chemicals being leaked into the ocean. We tried to revive him. It was all simply too much for him."

"Did he record?" asked Orve.

Jaan nodded. "Yes. But, when I checked his helmet, and tried to access the file, I found internal damage. I will leave it to you, Lieutenant, to find and decipher it. You are now acting lead watcher of the mountain division."

Orve saluted again. "Yes, Sir."

"Your watchers are ready to take care of the commander's body."

Jaan looked ahead, toward the gull idling in front of his. Maia followed his gaze and saw Murg and Hino standing there, helmets still on, holding a yellow gurney upright between them. Behind them, the six other mountain watchers who had also braved the old world all stood firm, in a single row, with their arms behind them and the winds in the station flowing around and through their boot engines, keeping them steady. Jaan motioned to Murg and Hino to approach.

Murg led out, holding one end of the gurney. Hino waited a moment and then followed, letting the body-length plank extend between them. Jaan stepped back as they approached the gull's open door. They slid the gurney in along the cabin floor. The slight scratching sound hit Maia's ears harder than it should have, and she felt a warmth rushing into her face.

Murg stepped up into the cabin, and moved toward the aft end, almost out of sight. Maia looked at Robbins again. He was still kneeling, focused on the covered body in front of him. Hino was about to step in, but Orve held up his hand.

"Let me, Ensign," he said.

Hino nodded and stepped back, and Maia watched as Orve entered the gull and knelt down near Fits's head. He slid the gurney into position, pushing one end toward Murg. Then he grasped the body below the shoulders. Together, he and Murg lifted the body up and over, onto the gurney. Maia almost shuddered at the sight of the limp arms dropping. Death on Lwo was infrequent. Watchers' deaths were even less frequent.

Orve and Murg took care to make sure every part of the body was on the gurney, then took hold of the straps on the gurney's sides, and carefully secured them over the legs and torso. Then, gripping the handles on either side of the gurney, Orve stood, as Murg did the same on his end. Robbins stood up after them, watching as they carefully moved toward the open doorway, turned, and stepped down, out of the gull and onto the cold, windy deck.

Maia took a step forward. Jaan set a gentle hand on her shoulder as Orve and Murg stopped in front of her. She wanted to be sure. She looked to Orve, who nodded, and then reached for the top of the blanket. Slowly, gently, she pulled back the heavy fabric. First, she saw darkened red hair, followed by pale skin and darkened eyebrows. Fits's familiar eyes were bruised and closed. His cheeks were a bluish white. His skin looked stiff, and bloated. There was no movement, and indeed no air whatsoever coming from his nostrils. But, somehow, his face conveyed a sense of peace. *He'd accepted it*, she thought. She took a breath, and smelling just a hint of decomposition in her helmet, brought the blanket back up, carefully covering the head and tucking the fabric firmly into place behind the neck.

As she stepped back, closer to Jaan, Orve turned. His back was to the body as he kept hold of the gurney and looked at the other, waiting watchers. All together, the six of them raised their right fists in salute, and then slowly lowered them back to their sides while lifting their left fists up onto their right shoulders, where they held them. As Orve and Murg carried the body forward, and turned in front of the gull and walked by the ensigns, Maia performed the same sequential salute, their salute of loss. She held it in place until Orve and Murg had entered the operations space on the station's west side and disappeared within. When she looked back toward the open gull, she saw Rial, now standing outside, near the craft's front end, completing the same salute. The young woman's signal stood out as it glowed in Maia's display.

"Are you alright, Ensign?" she called.

Rial turned toward her and nodded. "I'm fine, Lieutenant Sir," she replied. "Just shocked. Still shocked. He did not have to…I don't know why he didn't wait."

"He did his duty," Jaan said through the line. "He did what he knew had to be done."

Rial nodded. "Yes, Sir."

"What do we do now?" Robbins called, finally stepping out of the gull.

"Preparations will be made," said Jaan. "For a funeral, for a time of mourning. Then, there will be a promotion to commander. I will inform the Lords as soon as possible."

Robbins managed a quiet nod.

"Sir?" said Rial. "The rest of us need to…"

"Right," said Jaan. He turned toward the rest of the squadron, who were still standing in place, as if waiting for guidance, or approval. "Watchers! To your duties!"

A synchronous "Yes, Sir" from the array of voices came through the line, and Maia watched as the ensigns dispersed. Some of them reentered their craft. Others began examining the outsides, checking engine vents and hull sections for damage and debris. Robbins moved aside as Rial stepped back into her gull and went back to the pilot's seat. Through the windshield, Maia could see her working quickly, moving through unseen protocols on the glowing control panels. Then, she felt Robbins step closer to her. She turned to see him standing at arm's length, and looked through his panel to see a heaviness in his eyes that she had not seen before. But, she could not embrace him. Not yet.

"You two, follow me," said Jaan.

Jaan's dark red suit stood out in the cool, gray space, as Maia imagined hers did. She followed him, with Robbins closely behind her, up onto the platform and to the arched doorway. The door slid aside, and they stepped into the observation space. The watchers there, Gill and two others, were standing in the center of the room, away from the glowing screens of their workstations, speaking quietly to one another.

"Ensigns," Jaan said, as he tilted his helmet up and back.

The three of them turned, stood firmly, and saluted.

"Go," Jaan ordered. "Help your division on the deck. We will monitor things from here."

The three of them replied "Yes, Sir," and formed a line to the doorway, with Gill leading the way. Maia saw the same subtle thing in each of their demeanors, as they all passed by, donning their helmets as they marched. She had sensed it from the moment the missing life sign had been reported. It was a sadness, well-managed, but still evident.

As the door closed behind the ensigns, Jaan went to the workstation on the left, closest to the carved, rock wall between the room and the platform. As he tapped away on one of the screens, Maia felt Robbins' strong hands grasp her shoulders from behind. She touched his right hand with hers, and turned, pushed her helmet up and off, and as it settled behind her, looked into his now fully-visible eyes. Some of the weight in them left as he looked back at her.

"We are all on duty," Jaan said without looking up.

"Yes, Sir," Maia replied, and gently touched the side of Robbins' arm before turning away.

She moved to the center of the room, and looked to the workstations at the inner wall. Seeing no warnings, or unexpected signals, she turned again to Jaan, and stood firm, waiting. He stepped away from his workstation, leaving his tablet there, and turned to face them.

"I've just sent a message to the Isle," he said. "The Lords will soon be aware of our loss. I have also made them aware of our success."

"Then, everything worked?" Maia asked.

"Indeed, Lieutenant. After the commander managed to free the orb from the creature, it gradually made its way down to the container. Though it was clouded, and very dark, the ray was able to get an image of the device working."

He reached back to the workstation, took up the tablet, tapped in three places on the screen, and handed it over to Maia. Holding the small computer, she saw a few streaks and scratches on the housing and began to imagine the trouble that the squadron had encountered. Looking at the screen, she saw a recording playing. A time was displayed in the corner. The video had been taken seven hours after they had departed for the storm's edge.

The ancient, sunken container in the video was metallic, and light in color compared to its surroundings. Behind it there was a rocky, slanted surface, the side of a submerged mountain. The edges of the container were not sharp, but angled, softening the points of what would have been a near-perfect cube. There were hints of etched lines along the sides. And near the lengthy, jagged crack that had allowed the contents to escape, a dirt-covered panel revealed the end of what was likely a numerical designation. *There must be others*, she thought.

Jaan reached over the screen, and with one sliding finger, progressed the recording to the point when the orb became visible. Maia continued watching. The round device floated into view like a planet's shadow, covering the break in the container. Its small computer blinked from the barely-visible side facing the container. A bluish cloud began to emerge and spread. A few moments later the camera shifted, turning away from the orb and upward, to the near-blackness above. The shifting view of the fast ascent that followed revealed fleeting dark specks and shapes in the mysterious depths.

"That was when I called it back," Jaan said. "For the commander."

Maia looked up. "Why?" she asked.

"After he dove in, and after he freed the orb from the creature, he remained submerged, deep beneath the surface. We couldn't communicate with him, but his signal remained active, up until the point the ray lifted him out."

Maia nodded and looked back at the screen. The video seemed to be moving slowly. She thought, only briefly, of progressing it to the point Fits would come into view. Instead, she handed the tablet back to Jaan and took a step back. She looked at Robbins, standing calmly, with his arms crossed and his head down, and then back at her commander.

"It worked," Jaan said, setting the tablet down again. "The compound dispersed, and spread, just as it was designed to. Just as the Lords said it would. We stayed for another hour while it absorbed oil and debris. We even saw some of the blue foam reach the surface, where it continued to spread more. So, now, we only have to deal with what is here."

Maia wanted to feel relief, but it was not coming. Instead, she felt an uncomfortable sense of anticipation. She had lost fellow watchers before, most recently the lieutenant who had held her position. She knew the pain, the quiet anguish that would soon spread through the ranks. She had never truly doubted that the land would remain safe. The mission's success now seemed secondary.

"We will recover, Lieutenant," said Jaan. "As we always have."

Maia nodded. "Yes, Sir. I know. Sir, I…I didn't see the orb anywhere when the squadron returned."

"Right. After it had finished dispensing the compound, I was unable to call it back. I sent the ray back down and found that it was stuck in place. The engines were badly beaten from the creature's grip, and from its descent, and possibly clogged from the mix of the compound and the contents from the container. And with the power levels in our craft drifting below optimal levels, and hardly any winds to bring them back up, I decided to leave it. To stay any longer could have led to us being stranded."

"So, just how long were you outside the storm?"

"Nearly two hours."

"And what was it like?"

Jaan looked at Robbins. "I will let our newest watcher describe it for you."

Robbins shook his head and raised one open hand. "I am still no watcher," he said.

"But, you did take on the same burdens. And, you can better describe what we all saw."

Robbins shrugged and looked at Maia. "It was as I've always told you. The smells. The darkness. The…lurking death. But, I can say, I'd never been so close to one of the sea beasts."

"What did it look like?" Maia asked. "A squid, was it?"

"It had arms we could barely count, that were as long as five gulls in a row. Its body mostly remained submerged, but it was obviously giant, and powerful. And it was colorful. There was almost a…"

"A what?"

"A beauty to it."

"Beauty?"

"In the darkness, even with our lights low, it almost sparkled."

"It *did* sparkle," said Jaan. "Mother is still teeming with great life, just not human life."

Maia nodded. "Was that all the life that you encountered?"

"As far as we know."

Maia looked at Robbins again, and wondered, as she often did, how he had survived for so long, and how nature had carried him and Devon so far, all the way through the storm and into Lwo's seas. She had no words. As he looked back at her, it seemed he had none either.

"I will contact the other commanders," said Jaan. "Lieutenant, how is our division?"

Maia turned to Jaan and answered firmly. "Well, Sir. All is well."

"Good. You should return home. You *and* your husband. I will attend to things from here. Word will spread soon. Be prepared to speak with our airmen when the time comes."

"Yes, Sir."

Maia headed for the door, and motioned for Robbins to follow her. She quickly pulled her helmet back on, and heard him do the same as they stepped through the arched doorway and out onto the platform. To the right, Gill was speaking quietly with Rial, as they both examined the body of the gull that had last carried Fits. To the left, another mountain watcher was stepping out of the lead gull. On the far side of the deck, the other ensigns were completing return tasks for the other three craft. Still sensing Robbins close behind her, Maia opened a line to Dilah.

"This is Airman Dilah," she answered. "Go ahead, Sir."

"We're ready, Airman," said Maia. "Meet us at the end of the deck. The commander will be staying behind."

"Yes, Sir. On my way."

Maia walked left, heading for the wide opening that led inland. As she and Robbins passed the lead gull, the light from the nearby bird began to rise. They stepped down onto the deck and continued toward the opening. As the winds flowing throughout the station passed around her and through her tech, she looked back at her husband. He was just a yard back, and moving steadily, as if he had been traversing the winds for years. He raised his chin and looked out as the bird's light beamed into the station.

The sleek, red craft spun in place, with its front beams turning away from them as the aft end was eased back over the deck. The craft was just a few yards in as its ramp unlocked and began to lower. Maia gave Robbins one more glance before taking off. She jogged toward the ramp, and leapt up and on, just as it clanked against the station's deck. She walked up, set her right hand on the inside of the bird's frame, and turned around. Across from her, Robbins made his way up, gripped the wall on the port side, and turned to look back down the ramp.

The station remained full of activity. The three gulls on the left now radiated yellow light, and were hovering a yard higher than they had been. The last gull, far back and on the right, was still low and still idle, but Maia could see Rial moving around inside. Gill was still nearby on the outside. The lead gull, closest to their bird, was also idling. The ensign there was checking its front end. He turned toward the bird, looked out at them, and saluted. Maia returned the salute, and to her surprise, saw Robbins do the same. Then, she pressed the button to close their ramp. It arose steadily, and as they backed away, and it locked, she turned, looked out through the windshield, and felt the engines roar beneath them as they pulled away.

As Robbins sat down on the port bench and strapped in, Maia approached Dilah from behind. She held the back of the pilot's seat, knelt down, and looked out at the darkness of the land as their speed increased.

"Was it a success, Sir?" asked Dilah.

"It was, Airman," she replied. "The compound worked, and will likely continue to work, out there. Now, we have only to deal with the contaminants that still lurk around and within the land."

Dilah nodded. "That's good to hear, Sir…" She hesitated, as a gust pressed them from the east. She shifted both handles with ease and angled them through it. "Anything else?"

Maia thought for a moment, trying to find the right words. "Plenty," she said. "I'm sure there will be a full report soon."

"Understood, Sir."

"Take us home, then."

"Yes, Sir."

Maia took one more look at the night sky, and at the shadowy land below, as they continued inland. Then, she stood, walked back to the port bench, and strapped in next to her husband. As they began to settle, their gauntlets tapped gently against each other, and then slid apart. Silently, they agreed to not grasp each other's hands.

CHAPTER 23
A RETURN

The mountain division had chosen the southern coast for the burial ceremony. The watchers of the mountains all knew of their fallen commander's wishes before he had passed on. It was the coast from which he had most often watched the ocean, hoping that the rest of the world would reveal itself, that a restored old world would arise with a visible sun. He had told them all to hold on to his same hope.

Brun was steady, with one knee down and both boots embedded firmly in the hardened sands, as he looked out at the formation of the green-clad watchers. All but those deemed essential for the watching of the mountains and seas were present. Thirty-five tall, strong men and women were kneeling, still as stones, in five rows of seven, with two yards of space between each of them.

The raw winds at the coasts were the most dense, and the most dangerous, as rocks and icy droplets could accompany any rush of air. But the mountain division was the most accustomed to the dangers. Streaming lines of exhaust passed constantly and evenly through the boots and gauntlets of the ensigns, forming nearly-straight, stabilizing clouds between them, and dispersing at the ends of the rows and behind the last.

Ahead of their large formation, Orve was kneeling, facing the division. Behind him, a waiting, hovering gull radiated green light, as it gently shook from the constant forces of the storm. Its starboard door was open, facing the formation, and the metal casket, mounted lengthwise in the cabin, shined in the light that surrounded it. Through the side of the windshield, Brun could see a lone pilot, Ensign Rial, sitting with her back to the controls, facing the casket, waiting.

The intended time of silence had begun from the moment the formation was complete. Three minutes had passed. It would last for two more, as was the tradition. Brun continued watching, quiet. Shil was to his far right. Jaan was between them. Both of them were in the same kneeling, stabilizing position as he was. The three of them had also maintained two yards of distance, giving enough space for the winds to enter their tech and keep them in place.

Off to the left, another gull was hovering, with a lone pilot inside. Off to the right, there was another. Behind them, there were five more. All of the crafts' bright, white beams shined out, giving more light to what would have otherwise been a plain, gray morning. The clouds above were puffy and full. The ocean, beyond the foaming shoreline, was dark and wild.

A sudden, stronger gust of wind pushed in from the east, passing over and around all of them. A warning light blinked into Brun's helmet display. No one moved.

Through the open communication line, a single, heavy tone

sounded from the gull ahead of them, and then quickly faded, ending the time of silence. Brun raised his left fist, and then set it down firmly near his right shoulder. He heard the faint, simultaneous thumps as his fellow watchers all did the same. He breathed deeply, in and out, just once, as he bid a final farewell to his comrade of decades. Through the line, Orve spoke.

"As acting leader of the Watchers of the Mountains, it is my duty, and honor, to speak," he started. His voice was slightly distorted, but strong. "The time of mourning passes. Let our hearts no longer be heavy, as we have our continued task: to protect humanity, Lwo, and the world's future.

"Commander Fits served with great dedication, and courage, as a watcher of Lwo for over five decades. As he always said, and as we all know, he did not fear death. He feared the only thing that we all do: extinction. It was that fear that motivated his final actions, motivated him to take on both nature and another of Mother's creatures. And, as we all know now, he was more than prepared. Let us hope that, if and when the time comes, each one of us will be just as ready to sacrifice ourselves for the many.

"Now, as we send him to his final resting place, let us stand, and in his honor, further bear the burden of the storm."

Following Orve's lead, the watchers in the formation all stood. In the gull ahead of them, Rial did the same. Brun followed suit, carefully keeping his weight heavy in his boots, widening his stance as he arose, and holding his arms steady at his sides. He could feel Jaan and Shil doing the same.

"May Mother protect Commander Fits," said Orve.

"Mother protect him," the rest of them all said in unison.

"Watchers! Salute!"

Brun raised his right fist up next to his helmet, and held it there, and saw his fellow watchers do the same, as the storm's forces flowed more heavily around their raised arms. They all watched, as Orve turned away, marched swiftly to the open door of the gull, and leapt in. The craft bounced, and Orve turned within the doorway and continued saluting, as the door slowly closed in front of him until he was only a silhouette behind the translucent wall.

The gull's lights changed from green to yellow, and then to purple, a symbol of Fits taking on his final assignment. All around, the beams of the other gulls changed to purple, adding more color to the ceremony. Brun looked out, and watched as the gull carrying the casket slowly ascended and then turned away from the shore. It remained hovering, fifty feet above, as the gulls on the right and left flew up and out, and steadied right behind it. Then, the lead gull sped out. The other two followed closely behind, all of them heading to a point miles off shore, where Fits's casket would be dropped from high above, with a single tech engine affixed to it, and be carried down as far as the ocean would allow.

All of the ensigns stayed in formation, holding their salutes. Brun did the same, standing firm until the lights from the trio of craft were out of sight. The lights from the five remaining gulls changed again, to yellow, as the mountain watchers at the shore all turned away, and still in their five lines of seven, marched carefully toward their waiting craft. Brun turned toward Jaan, who had not moved. His salute remained firm, as Brun and Shil both watched him.

"Commander, Sir," Shil called, through a line that only included the three of them. "It is done."

"I know," Jaan replied. Slowly, he let his salute fall.

"Will you wait for their return?"

He nodded, still looking out at the ocean. "I will."

"Understood."

"Commander Brun," Jaan said, turning to look at him. "Until Lieutenant Orve and his group return, you are in charge of the mountain division. Hopefully they are kept safe, and it will not be long."

Brun nodded. "Yes, Sir."

"Lieutenant Orve is capable. It's why I did not hesitate to appoint him. But, he is still fairly young and may require some guidance. I want you to be his guide, as needed."

"I will, Sir. And, what about his promotion?"

"The Lords have acknowledged our loss. And they have asked that we wait two weeks. If the lieutenant is still fit, then we are to bring him to the Isle for the ceremony."

"Makes sense," added Shil, sounding almost dismissive. "They want to test him."

"And he will pass," said Jaan.

"I agree, Sir."

"So do I," said Brun.

"Commander Shil?" said Jaan, turning to her. "You have work to do, preparations to make. You are free to go, if you wish. Commander Brun and I will stay."

"Yes, Sir," said Shil.

She saluted, and turned toward the five lingering gulls. She moved cautiously, embedding each step into the sand, keeping herself on a steady line. Her exhaust flowed behind her as she neared the center gull. She saluted upward, to the watchers within, before passing between it and another gull. Thirty yards beyond the row of gulls, a lone, white puller from the city was hovering just above the ground, waiting. As Shil approached, it jumped up slightly and flew out to meet her. Its white lights beamed brighter, and as it stopped and turned, and its port door slid aside, Shil leapt up into the cabin. Then, the craft turned away and flew north, toward the Southern Range, which towered over them all from a mile away. Brun faced Jaan again.

"Hardly seems like a time for celebration," he said.

"Maybe not for us," said Jaan. "But, for the people, having endured this past year, it is the perfect time. We have to keep them…grounded." He looked up. "And whatever the watchers do, the moon will still grow full."

Brun followed his gaze and looked up at the dull light coming through the clouds. The day's moon, still hours away, would be nearly full, as would the next day's. But, the moon that followed would be completely full, and even if the clouds did not part this year, the night sky would still be bright.

* * * * *

Maia's day had begun like any other. She had arisen in the afternoon for a later shift. Robbins and Devon had already gone, taking with them the quiet tension that still lingered from the mission. She had bathed, and eaten, and tied her braids into a neat and proper set of overlapping rings, and donned her suit and her tech. Along with ten airmen, she had taken the ground lift up to the tower. And, as in year's past, with the month's full moon just hours away, there had been anticipation among them. But, it had been a quiet anticipation, with the excitement tempered by the recent loss.

In the tower, in the observation level, Maia had received a private communication meant only for commanders and lieutenants. Orve had been able to access Fits's final recording. The file had been distributed for all of the leaders to view, and to share with their divisions as they saw fit. Maia had accessed the file at one of the workstations and viewed it discreetly in a small window, taking care to patch the audio into her helmet.

Fits's struggle with the giant squid had been difficult and violent. The video was shaky, but in multiple frames, one or more of the tentacles could be seen pressing against Fits's helmet, with large suckers trying to grip him as he fought against the creature's power.

405

Fits's wet yells had been nearly muted due to damage to his microphone, but still discernible enough to hear his frustration. Subtle amounts of doubt and fear crept out through his intermittent panting. But, there had been no dread or terror or desperation. Fits had fought with the creature for several long minutes, dislodging the orb more with each passing moment, until with a lunging kick with both feet, aided by tech nearly drained of all its energy, he had freed it. Then, with the orb's light sinking quickly away, the creature had left. Fits's final, labored breaths, faint as they were, had lasted until he was taken up by the ray. The last moments of near silence, which came after he was clear of the water, had been the worst part of the recording.

Maia had managed not to shed a tear for the rest of the shift. With Jaan's approval she had told a number of airmen about the recording, but she had not shown it to any of them. After the report of the completed burial, acceptance had already passed through all of the divisions. She would leave anything further to Jaan. It was enough that a commander had been lost. Now, they could only learn from his sacrifice. What she had learned was that her husband had not underestimated the dangers outside the storm.

As the clouds grew darker, and night fell, Maia's shift in observation ended and Jaan took over. She felt heavy as she descended the lift to the tower's hangar, but the sight of her waiting bird brought a lightness to her heart. The sight of her husband and their son approaching and stopping at its front end brought joy. Dilah was nearby, having escorted them up from the village. With a salute, she left them, and headed for her own bird.

"I'm ready," Devon called through the newly-opened line, looking up at Maia through the panel of his gray helmet. "How long before we get to the city?"

Maia set a hand on his shoulder. It was late, and she could see the tiredness in his eyes. "Just a couple of hours," she said with a smile. "Maybe a little less. But, remember, we're not going into the city, just up to the forest."

"I know, I know," the boy said, nodding.

"But, we'll still be able to see it from there."

"Okay."

She touched Robbins' arm gently and motioned for them to follow her as she began preparations. They stayed close behind, quietly speaking as she examined the front vents, the side vents, the panels and connections, and the aft end. With her whispered command the ramp unlocked and lowered, tapping the metal floor with a clank as she stepped aside. The slightly diminished winds from the open entry behind them rolled around Robbins and Devon's boots, and through all of her tech.

Robbins nudged the boy up the ramp and followed closely behind him. Maia followed them up, and as she reached the cabin, pressed the button to close and lock the ramp. She watched as the two of them sat on the starboard bench, with Devon closer to the front end. Robbins strapped himself in, and then made sure the belts were secure around their son's shoulders and waist. Maia took her seat in the rear-facing pilot's chair and strapped herself in before turning it around.

Several airmen marched down the stairs from the mezzanine, saluting as they saw her readying the bird, and then departing in different directions, headed for other craft, or for the ground lift. Maia opened up the bird's engines, and felt the gentle bounce as flowing air was pulled through them and forced out below. She grasped the control handles at her sides, turned the bird about, and carefully guided them forward over the hangar floor, inching closer and closer to the wide entryway and the expansive darkness of the late evening sky.

"Ready?" she called back.

"Ready," Devon replied.

She pushed the bird out hard and was pressed back into her seat, as the engines roared and they left the tower. She increased their angle sharply, and in a matter of seconds, took them from one thousand feet to three thousand feet. The handles vibrated against her covered palms. The control panels blinked with yellow status lights and messages of stability. Though the outside was dark, visible streaks of cold, wet air began to pass over the windshield as they entered the clouds. Looking out at the front end, she saw sparkling crystals of freezing condensation. As she began to level them off, the engines gradually settled from an aggressive roar into a heavy hum.

"Everyone okay?" she called out.

"Yep!" Devon answered, sounding excited.

"And, my love?"

"I'm fine, Love," Robbins answered.

Devon sighed. She could almost see him frowning.

"Alright then," she said. "It's a straight shot from here."

"What do we do with all this time?" Devon asked.

"Well, I think we could all use a little down time. Don't you?"

"Maybe you and Dad. I'm fine."

"Well, *goody* for you," she said, smiling.

She let go of the right handle, and then disconnected her helmet and gently pushed it up and back. As it settled into the groove of the seatback, she heard Robbins and Devon remove their helmets, and then breathe out. She glanced back over her shoulder and saw that they were both still secure on the bench. As she turned back around, a heavy stream of wind blew directly at them from the west. She pressed down harder on the pedal and adjusted the front engine to take in the stronger forces. All of the engines blared for an instant before settling. Looking at the center panel and seeing the data from the storm's forces around them, she guided the bird slightly south before settling into an adjusted vector.

"What all is Auntie going to say?" asked Devon.

"Well..." Maia started. "The Day of Winter Moon, like the other holidays, will include some words about the first Lords' first declaration of the holiday."

"That sounds long."

"Don't worry. It won't be that long."

"Then what?"

"Then, I expect, the issues in the land will be addressed, briefly. This is a day of celebration, after all."

"So, when does the party start?"

"*Party?* What party? Where'd you hear that?"

"From another kid…or, student, in Elder Idha's class. I had to pretend I had been to one before and just couldn't remember the last one."

"Well, I don't want you to get your hopes up, Devon. There will be festivities throughout the land, in the villages and the shelters. But, I've agreed to be on watch. So, we can only celebrate here in the bird. But, like I said, we'll be able to see the city, and probably the shelters that are stationed nearby. And I'm sure something fun has been planned."

"How many shelters are coming?"

"I don't know yet. Most were invited."

"Okay. I hope it's enough."

"Me too."

"Okay. Um, Maia?"

"Yes, Devon?"

"How do you feel?"

"Just fine, Devon."

"Good. I'm, uh, sorry about Commander Fits. I liked him."

"Thank you, Devon. Me too."

The conversation among the three of them remained light for

another half hour. Gradually, it became just her and Robbins speaking, about the sounds from the engines, and the faint glows and flickers from the land below and from the sky above. Flying within the clouds, it was evident that they were not as dense as usual, and that the levels above them appeared to be ready to part. They were less than an hour from the forest when Maia heard the boy's heavy breathing, and looked back to see his head laying near one end of the bench, and his boots resting in his father's lap, with one restraining belt still secured over his waist.

"Saw that coming," she said, turning back to look out through the windshield. "How tired was he when you left home?"

"Very," said Robbins. "We uh…We heard a lot of chatter on the way. They found Fits's last recording?"

She nodded. "Lieutenant Orve was able to retrieve it from the helmet."

"Have you seen it?"

"Yes. I have."

Robbins quieted.

"Do you want to know what was there?" she asked.

Hesitantly, he answered. "No. It was enough being there. But, at least others will now know what lurks outside the storm. At least some of it."

"Agreed." She paused, looked out, and shifted the control handles to avoid a stream of icy crystals before returning to their vector. "You've been a little quiet since you got back. Are you alright?"

"Yes, Love. I'm fine. Still a bit in shock, maybe. But, I'm fine."

"I know you've said it before, but I have to ask again. You really had never seen one of those creatures that close up before?"

"No. Never."

"It looked terrifying, even without a really clear view."

"The whole world is terrifying."

She paused, thinking, pondering the unknown. "Well said. At least we still have Lwo, and the Lords' first hope."

"To see the world restored?"

"Right."

"Having seen what you've seen and heard what all we encountered, do you still believe in it?"

"I do. More than before you and Devon came into our lives. Into *my* life. Mother has kept us–kept Lwo–for a reason. You and I may not live to see it, but the earth cannot go on like this forever. It would be unnatural. A new cycle will come."

"I think you're right. And I hope we do live to see it."

"You, and everyone else." She let a silence settle between them, as she listened to the high winds outside the cabin and the bird's humming engines. She checked their status and their distance from the city before speaking again. "Did you want to go in after him?" she asked. "After the commander?"

Robbins hesitated. "It would have been certain death," he

said. "His tech barely worked in the water. I know mine wouldn't have."

"Did the commander? Did he want to go in?"

"I saw his eyes." He paused. "As it was all unfolding. As he was ordering everyone else to stay put. I could see the fear, but also the urge, to leap out, to brave nature. He just...He just knew better."

"Do you think he should have?"

"Should have what?"

"Leapt in after Commander Fits."

"That's a question for watchers, not civilians."

"You're not just a civilian. You never were."

He hesitated again. "I think he made a calculation. I think he knew that Fits's tech had faltered, and that his would too. He knew the other watchers' unaltered tech would fare much worse. And he knew any other loss would decrease the chances of a successful return, and possibly weaken your ranks. It was just...logic."

Maia could sense how much Robbins had accepted the watchers' ways. "I think you're right," she said. "It was a hard choice. But, it was one that commanders are expected to make. And one that others have made in the past."

"I've done some more reading in the past few days. I figured as much. How is Jaan handling it?"

Maia shrugged. "He hasn't made any obvious missteps since returning."

"But, how is he *handling* it?"

413

She shook her head. "I don't know."

Another hour passed quietly, and Maia checked the map. They were less than ten miles from the city. Carefully, she began to ease the pressure on the pedal, and shifted the handles to take them down out of the clouds. The cabin rocked and shook, back and forth, until they were free of the thicker air. She tilted the bird to the right, flew sideways into an adjusted vector, and then pressed down on the pedal again as she leveled them off. They descended steadily for another two miles until they reached an elevation of one thousand feet. The city was not yet in sight, but it was straight ahead.

"Where are we?" Devon asked. He yawned, loudly.

Maia heard him sit up in his seat, and looked back to see him reattaching the other two belts across his chest. "We're almost there," she said. She checked the map. They would reach the forest in less than five minutes.

"That was fast, Maia."

"You slept through most of it."

"And now I'm all rested up."

"Great."

The ground below them was mostly dark, but in the distance, and in multiple directions, Maia could see spots of light. Villages were not resting. Neither were shelters. It was nearly midnight, but all of Lwo would sacrifice time from the next day for the celebration. The year before, before Robbins and Devon had arrived, Maia had celebrated in their village. Jaan had spoken to the entire land, and

414

hours later, had come back to the village to celebrate with her and the few other airmen that were still awake. It had been one of the rare occasions when she had seen any real joy in her commander's face, joy from hope.

She took the bird down another five hundred feet, and as she did, saw the sparkle in the distance. The city was almost fully lit. And miles outside of it, around the eastern edge of the forest, she saw a row of lights forming a semi-circle. As they got closer, and the lights became brighter, she was able to make out a dozen shelter craft. Their green-hued silhouettes were steady in front of the forest's towering, swaying, shadowy trees. She descended another three hundred feet, decreased power to the engines, and gently pulled back on the control handles as she brought them to a slow stop. Now, with little more than a few miles of forest keeping them at bay, the city's brightness was more evident.

The shield was up. Its faint blue energy was constant. Maia tapped an icon on the right control panel, and then another, and found the feed from the city. A window filled the panel, revealing what Shil had told the division leaders to expect. There was a steady view from the city's southeast quarter, zoomed in to show a few still-damaged buildings. On the street level, four carefully-placed orange excavation vehicles sat, and between them, four hovering jumpers, with patrolmen waiting upon them. In the midst of them all was what had been a chasm. Now, where there had been only a dark, sinking hole, there was a calm surface of water, several yards below the street. The immediate area was full of light, and the reflection in the water revealed the heights of the buildings that surrounded it.

It was still a worksite. The high, metal fence still surrounded the wide circle. The patrolmen–with their jumpers turned outward and their lights blinking red–had clearly been tasked with keeping the area clear. The only civilians currently in the city were those working to repair the damage. Maia was sure that they had been ordered to stay away until needed. But, as she knew, they had not always been agreeable. And, it was the Day of Winter Moon. Unpredictable things could and likely would happen. She hoped that the workers were in their domiciles in the city's north, or at least at safe distance, celebrating out of the way of trouble.

From the feed, a song–a slow, calm arrangement of flutes supported by heavy strings, and backed by tempered, light percussion–arose. A line of text appeared at the bottom of the live image. It read 'Upcoming: Watcher Address, followed by Day of Winter Moon Events.'

"Look, Dad!" Devon exclaimed.

"I see it," said Robbins.

"Can we stand up?"

Maia nodded. "Sure, Devon. Just be careful. Come on up."

She heard restraints retracting behind her. Robbins and Devon's steps were slow and steady on the cabin floor as they approached and stopped a yard behind her.

"Can you see it well enough?" she asked, looking back at the boy.

"Well…" Devon started.

Maia raised her hand swiftly, interrupting his complaint, and then tapped a set of commands into the right panel. The feed left the panel and appeared within a larger box of light on the right side of the windshield. "How's that?"

Devon slapped his hands together. "Much better! Look at the water! It's…It's so clean looking. It's so blue."

"Compared to the ocean, I'd say so," said Robbins.

"And, I've never heard that song before," said Devon.

"Me either. It's very nice."

"We broadcast it every year on the holiday," said Maia.

"There was a different song in the summer," said Devon. "It was faster. And back on Founder's Day there were more drums."

"A song for every occasion," Maia replied. "And for every season. Look." She pointed at a corner in the displayed feed. "It's midnight."

The live video shifted to the right side of the feed, and a gray square was revealed, which then alighted with an emerging image. As the gray faded, Shil appeared. She was visible from her white chestplate to the top of her head. Her eyes were calm, and surprisingly kind. Her skin was smooth and shining. Her shoulders were steady. Behind her was the wall of the command office in the city's headquarters.

The camera pulled back slightly, revealing three other

watchers. They were all standing a few yards behind her, in front of the wall, with their helmets retracted. A watcher of the ground was on the left. Maia did not immediately recognize the young woman, but she had their characteristic heft and was clearly the tallest in the room. On the right stood a watcher of the mountains, a young man with deep black hair and dark eyes. And next to the ensign, as Maia had anticipated, stood Airman Malo.

Shil lifted an ungloved hand and gently nudged some of her dark, shining hair aside. The soft music got softer and quieter, until it was nearly inaudible. Then, Shil smiled, nodded, and looked firmly into the camera.

"People of Lwo," she started. "We are *still* here."

Shil paused and smiled. Maia smiled with her, and clapped softly, and just as she imagined the cheering that was happening in the shelters below, she saw the gleaming lights of the dozen craft begin to flicker, and shift between various colors. All of it reflected in the bird's windshield. She knew the same was happening with the other shelters still spread across the land, and in the many villages near them. A minute of reaction and applause always followed those words. Behind Maia, Robbins and Devon followed her lead, clapping softly. Outside, the winds continued to blow heavily around them.

"Now, before we celebrate another year..." Shil continued. "Before we look forward to another lifetime, we must face the reality of our existence. The storm is still strong and still unending. And, as she has many times before, this year Mother has given us more

418

challenges. But, I am pleased to report, the source of the contamination in the ocean was recently identified, with help from our Lords, and also with their help, has been neutralized. Details will follow, but let it be known that, just days ago, a squadron of brave watchers set out for the edge of the storm, and went through it, and contended with nature to address a pollution left outside of Lwo centuries ago.

"And, unfortunately, this mission was not completed without loss. As many of you have likely heard, Commander Fits, of the Watchers of the Mountains, gave his life on the mission. Even to complete the mission. So, a moment then, for Fits."

Shil lowered her eyes and quietly repeated his name, and then his age: seventy-six. As the moment lingered, Maia imagined all of Lwo speaking Fits's name. She whispered it, and heard Robbins and Devon do the same. Shil looked back into the camera.

"Lwo has also suffered the loss of a civilian," she continued. "Erul, who was set out to sea not long before the watchers' trek. He reached one hundred five years. A moment for Erul."

As Shil paused again, Maia whispered the man's name and age. Robbins and Devon did the same.

"Two losses just days apart is rare in our land," Shil continued. "But, it is a reminder that despite all of our potential, all of humanity's potential, nature remains, and remains dangerous. Lwoans, all of us, must always be cautious and vigilant. As you can see in the feed from the city's southeast quarter, nature has even found a way to make its presence known within heavily fortified spaces. The influx of water from below, all the way from the southern coast, has brought with it new life, and a need for us to adapt.

"The timeline for the city remains the same, as does the number of Lwoans who must now remain outside it. However, the new life, from the ocean itself, has provided an opportunity. Lwo's city will gain a new area of conservation in the form of a protected pond. Councilors and lead watchers have all agreed that it is the best that could come from this difficult circumstance."

As Shil paused, and the feed next to her became an empty, white block, Maia leaned back in her seat.

"What new life is there?" asked Devon.

"Some small fish," Maia replied. "Old species. When the city is open again, maybe even before, I can take you there to see them."

"Can we eat them?"

Maia chuckled and turned in her seat. "That's funny. You know hardly anyone here has ever eaten of a creature."

Devon laughed. "I know. Just joking, Maia."

"We haven't eaten any meat since we've been here," Robbins added. "There was a fair amount before, though."

Maia nodded, and turned back around to see a still image appear next to Shil. It was an old photograph, taken by one of the founders, of their approach to the various formations that would come to make up Lwo. There was a mountain in the distance, on the left side, surrounded by waters bluer than any Maia had seen in her lifetime. The Isle was off to the right, far beyond the mountain. Then another image appeared. It was of one of the first craft constructed, with the vanes of its wind engines mostly exposed and a group of older-looking, smiling people behind it. Further behind them, a few trees were being bent by what had been tolerable winds. Another image appeared, and Shil continued to speak.

"Here, you are seeing where Lwo came from," she said. "In these early years, our founders–all strong, all brilliant–were full of hope. Their hope remained, even as they faced new threats with each passing day. They still had some evidence of seasons, back then, in the beginning. And they chose this day, when they saw Lwo's weather turn coldest, as a marker, of their survival in the harshest conditions, and as a reminder, of the continuation of life that a full moon reveals. A full moon means that the sun still burns strong. It means that the earth still turns. So, let it be a reminder to us, that despite our troubles, life must go on.

"Lwo sees little snow in winter, unlike in ancient times. Lwo feels little heat in summer, unlike in ancient times. Our winds never get any weaker, unlike in ancient times. The storm does not allow frequent travel to see sights around the globe, as our founders' fathers did. But, we are here. *Lwo* is *here*."

Shil paused and looked steadily into the camera. Maia smiled, and clapped again, and the lights from the shelters below began to flicker and change colors once more. Then, the shelters' powerful engines started to roar, louder and louder. It seemed an excessive use of energy, but Maia could only smile again.

"And, Lwo will go on," said Shil. "So, people of Lwo, today, celebrate. Tomorrow, we continue our survival. To another Day of Winter Moon."

Shil tilted her chin upward and raised her right fist, saluting the camera, and all of Lwo. The watchers behind her did the same. Then, their image faded, and the rolling pictures from Lwo's past filled the entire feed, and continued from one to another. The music, the same song, arose again, to a volume higher than it had been before. Then, its pace increased, until it matched that of a heartbeat. Behind Maia, Devon clapped, and his boots began to thump against the floor. She pressed the button to turn her seat around. As it stopped, and she faced their aft end, she looked at the boy. He stopped mid-dance, almost embarrassed, and then continued, moving in a circle to the beat of the music.

"Never seen that dance," she said.

"I just made it up," Devon answered.

"It's just…It's just walking."

"Yeah. Walking with rhythm."

"It's strange. Move your arms a little at least."

She shook her head and smiled, as Devon did as she asked, staying in roughly the same spot, mindful of their place in the air, trying not to shift his weight too much as he celebrated. Robbins sat back down on the bench.

"No, no," Maia said, looking at her husband.

She unstrapped herself, stood, and took a quick look at the bird's status before walking over to him. She held out her open hands, and as he took them, pulled him up from the bench. He put his hands on her waist, and she grasped his shoulders, and guided him, rhythmically and fancifully, until his back was to the pilot's chair. Then she pushed him. He fell back into the seat, almost perfectly.

"Hey!" Robbins said with a laugh.

"You stay right there," she said, pointing down at him. "Just watch the bird, and let us dance."

"Fine with me," he said, and shrugged.

Robbins leaned back in the seat and watched the two of them. Maia shuffled toward Devon, bumped his shoulder with her hip, and then grabbed both of his hands. She turned them in place, until her back was to the starboard side, and his was to the port side. Then, she let go and followed his lead, as he added shoulder raises and fist pumps to his simple, rhythmic steps, and continued to match the pace of the song, even as it changed once again.

www.ingramcontent.com/pod-product-compliance
Lightning Source LLC
Chambersburg PA
CBHW050116030726
47505CB00011B/1979